Toy Drive

Thomas Gondolfi

TANSTAAFL PRESS

TANSTAAFL Press
891 PH 10
Castle Rock, WA 98611

Visit us at www.TANSTAAFLPress.com

Toy Drive

First printing—TANSTAAFL Press

Cover art: Tony Foti
Book layout: Hydra House Books

Printed in the USA
ISBN: 978-1-938124-85-3

To: All of those who kept after me to get this series finished. I dedicate this book to all of you.

Introduction

Excerpts from the Third Chronicler's Notes

One of the significant landmarks of the early days of the Sol Unified System's expansion into the depths of space, sometime in the human calendar's twenty-second century, was an amusing event: the first creation of a truly new life form. While new life is not a humorous occurrence, the process that created this life was more like the punch line to a joke.

Homo sapiens were making use of faster-than-light (FTL) vehicles, and their civilization expanded at a tremendous rate compared to earlier efforts. Some twenty years later, they created a drive that was over an order of magnitude faster (FT^{2}L). There was only one snag in the new design: Organic materials were destroyed in such a transit.

Project Infuse (PI) was created to send semi-intelligent factories via an FT^{2}L ship to extremely far worlds, one per world. There, they would autonomously produce robots to control and strip the planet's surface of its mineral wealth before transporting it back in the shell of the original vessel. These factories possessed the construction facilities and mental power to create a workforce of robot slaves.

The process wouldn't have had any unexpected results if a preadolescent computer hacker, Janeen Fox (a.k.a. Foxhunt), hadn't broken into PI's vaunted and supposedly impervious databases in an initiation rite. Janeen's actions held no malevolence and no intent to cause harm. Breaking the impermeability of PI, not acquiring the contents or destroying its files, was her goal. Once inside, she caused no intentional damage and did nothing, save adding her nom d'hac in several places as proof. Her full access lasted less than ten minutes before PI's vaunted system defenses rushed to close down the unauthorized access.

Project Infuse's ice crashed about her open portal with such violence and severity that Janeen broke the connection without standard withdrawal procedures. No newbie to hacking, she had long ago learned to hide the tracks of her work by bouncing through several other computers. In this case, the last link in this chain was an old-fashioned toy store/bookstore. Because of the abrupt termination of her intrusion, several large files translated from one end of the link to the other. This process scrambled a number of crucial launch and post-launch parameters within the upcoming PI vessels. These factors remained until a standard morning adaptive CRC check caught the errors the following day, too late to save the ill-fated PI vessels, which launched that very afternoon.

On the date of Janeen's fateful link, only six factory vessels launched. Each of them contained the faulty parameter files—files that contained two very important changes.

The first change involved all the ships' navigational targets being changed to the same planet, the third planet of HD34085, also known as Beta Orionis, or simply Rigel. Multiple vessels had never been sent to the same planet in the history of the PI program.

Factories 55466, 55467, 55468, 55469, 55471, and 55474 launched on schedule. The humans heard nothing of any of these six PI vessels again. They were written off as a loss.

Factory 55468 lost its way in FT^2L. The tidal forces of a black hole tore it to pieces. The remaining five each set down uneventfully at T+3y340d12h16m46s (three years, three hundred and forty days, twelve hours, sixteen minutes, and forty-six seconds post-launch).

Thus comes in the second change, a change that started the fiercest competition known to nearly any world—computer-driven evolution. The plans for the factories' robots had been destroyed or corrupted. In place of this crucial data were the production files for toys. These designs didn't follow the standard parameters for mining or control-type robots. These new forms also proved to be totally unsuitable for the environment. Most of the new forms didn't even have motile functions. Being semi-sentient, the factories adapted. All but one.

The factories took the portions of the robot data that had not been corrupted and merged them with the new intrusive toy data. As most of the toys were flexible in capability, it mostly worked. Each factory took a different solution to its individual problems. They produced different sizes, shapes, and capabilities into different toy figures.

It has to be stressed that these initial units were crude and possessed no initiative at all. At this stage of evolution, each factory was one entity with multiple disposable bodies to control—similar to an ant colony.

Upon landing, the need for combat units was small, as there was little nearby local fauna to require much force. This changed abruptly as the first warriors of the now four factories began meeting each other and fighting for control of the planet. Each of the factories found these 'native' life forms fighting back quite successfully.

All of the factories adapted. They changed priorities, rolling hundreds of tanks, baby-doll infantrymen, scout planes, and other military weapons off their production lines. The Toy Wars had truly begun.

As the clashes continued and grew in scale, a Darwinian selection process set in. The factories experimented with different designs based on the plans they were able to produce. Each make and model underwent field experience, sometimes being thrown into nearby combat to be immolated or exploded within mere hours of activation.

Each of the factories tried special permutations to bring better units to the battlegrounds—built-in cannons, flame throwers, spotter planes, and even mobile walking bombs in the shape of dress-up dolls. A number of them worked well, but most failed miserably.

Using probability studies, each factory learned quickly which of its units fared well in combat, in what terrain, and under which conditions. Those units that didn't make the cut in the field were firmly snubbed from production. Toy Wars shaped quickly into a battle of statistical mathematics rather than strictly the destruction of fur, metal, and machines. All of this progressed much faster than Mother Nature has ever accomplished.

Of the factories that still remained, 55466 (known as Six) had the most difficulty. Its initial location was not as rich in minerals and resources, nor as easily defensible as the other three viable factories' locations. Six slowly lost ground to the 'local fauna', and its calculations showed that in less than two years' time, its outer defenses would crumble. The local fauna would run rampant, denying it control of the planet. It would have failed its primary mission.

Six made a huge gamble to put a larger quantity of material and effort into researching better robots. Soon, Six began fielding units with semiautonomous functionality. They began to work as a team.

Six certainly could measure the success of these units. Within five months, Six's boundaries firmed and started expanding. The other three factories learned how effective these autonomous fauna were and began shaping their productions to do similar things.

Shortly, Six found its boundaries tightening again. It was time for another desperate gamble. It used some of the local unclassified metals to produce an all-purpose control robot with the highest level of self-direction it could construct. Six filled it with the most information the robot could accept.

The chain of events that started with Janeen Fox and Project Infuse had now come to fruition—but in a way neither had ever expected. In this new robot, true sentience and intelligence had been achieved.

Let there be life. And it was fuzzy.

Don Quixote, the first living being on Rigel-3, fought alongside his brethren until he discovered that the war itself was a mistake. After gathering allies among the factories, he ended the Toy Wars.

Proclaimed president for life after he stopped the war, Don managed to unite the dissimilar toys into a single people. Despite some missteps, especially with some religious fanatics who worshipped the mythical Humans, Don managed to lead the living toys into a stable society, which was not quite at harmony with their surroundings, and create Ada, the first of a new breed of sentient factories.

The new sentient factories had grown with toyanity as much as the original four factories hadn't. The civil war they'd spawned, five hundred years in history back, had been brief but bloody. Just as sentient toys outstripped non-sentient units, the living factories outclassed and outnumbered their ancestors. Everyone but the ancient originals and a few of their faithful toys knew they were outmatched. It was as if they hadn't learned anything.

Not one of the originals lasted six days. Their fanatical followers took to the mountains to fight in guerrilla combat but were mostly ignored. They couldn't make more of themselves. Occasionally, toyanity bumped into small groups of them. If they persisted in conflict, they were engulfed and destroyed to the last. If they retreated farther away from civilization, they were left in peace.

Instead, a new danger was on the horizon, one not envisioned in so peaceful and harmonious a people. One of their own making.

Retiree

I sat on the dais next to various dignitaries. As a 2-meter purple teddy bear, I didn't stick out as unusual. In fact, an effectively identical bear sat next to me.

Gaudy banners hung all over everything. A crowd of mixed toys, which I estimated at 116,463 strong, crowded into a natural amphitheater in the province of Atlantis. The solar reflecting station *Horace-Benedict de Saussure* had directed 18 percent of its output to the assembly so that the attendees would not overload the local networks in demands for power.

The presidential theme, "Teddy Bear's Picnic," which was my music for a few minutes more, played over the loud but acoustically challenged public address systems. The crowd sang along like it was a rock concert.

Both the other bear and I noted a Tammy dress-up doll sitting on the head of a giraffe to get a better view. A pair of massive 5-meter-tall spiders carried a panoply of toys on their backs and even more in the shadow underneath them. A covey of blow-up clowns wobbled back and forth to the music. A pink oven, with the help of a bright-yellow octopus, created a multicolored flaming display above their heads.

The loudspeakers piped in yet another version of "Teddy Bear's Picnic." This time, it was the version by the legendary band Mulligan Stew.

"Get used to it," I whispered to the bear next to me, Don Quixote Eighty-Three. "You won't hear much else."

"I know. Don't forget, I have your memories and those of our dozens of predecessors," he responded.

"True. Well, most of my memories anyway. At least this version is marginally better than what they play every time we enter a bloody building," I said.

My clone replied with, "Marginally is a good word."

The time tick of noon echoed across all the networks as attendees and government officials alike copied it out. The crowds of mixed toys cheered as a 20-centimeter samurai warrior and a 150-centimeter penguin made their way to the podium. There was a step to put Shapist Congressional Leader Nikola Tesla at the same height as his waddling counterpart, Provincier Mary Goddard.

Mary tapped on the microphone to test it, despite the eighteen sound checks that had been made throughout the day. "Welcome!"

The crowd cheered. Slinkies threw themselves headfirst down the steps. Tanks, with their barrels elevated, fired off strings of blanks. More than a thousand different engines revved. Balls leaped up in the air, where they were batted about by the other attendees. Airplanes, which had been politely circling the stage, dove down, shouting wordlessly. The party atmosphere couldn't have been overstated.

I'd experienced this once before in person, when I took over the job of president for life and inherited the seventy-odd memories of my predecessors. I didn't know what to think of it then. I couldn't decide if the people were now happy to see my back fur or if they were excited to have the new hydraulic fluid that my successor brought to the position.

The process to create duplicates, invented by our distant ancestors, wasn't exact. Microscopic variations in the sump, our brain, made differences in behavior and ideals. As a result, some of my predecessors were good, and some excellent. Others had been downright bad. I had tried my best and felt I'd done a journeyman's job. But in moments, I no longer carried the burden of all toyanity. But how would history remember me?

Eighty-Three whispered to me as the crowd continued to rage. "I think you did well."

No, he hadn't read my mind. Having so recently had my memories duplicated into the eighty-third cloned body of our original Don Quixote, we tended to take the same mental track. And we continued that way until we had significant differences in our experiences. "I believe this is a tangible expression of our toys because of the freedoms that you have protected," he said, answering the question I hadn't asked.

"Entirely possible."

"Friends," the samurai said, his amplified voice stomping over the top of the ruckus. "It is a great day for our society."

The penguin picked it up. "As is our custom, after a hundred years of rule, we retire one successful Don Quixote," she said, pointing at me.

"And activate his successor, Don Quixote," Tesla said, pointing at Eighty-Three.

The attendees reinvigorated their cheers, applause, speaker feedback, and other raucous approvals. Somewhere, units had gotten fireworks and launched them from the ground, or even body mortars. My hydraulic pressure and voltage both dropped in the bittersweet memory of my friend Sancho, who'd worn a mortar over half his life and died giving his life so that toyanity could continue. I had these feelings, even though I'd personally never met him. Nor, for that matter, had I interacted with any of the great, average, and villainous previous Don Quixotes. But I knew them just as if I had.

Waving the sound down with his arms, the samurai continued. "But before the official transfer of power, we have a few words of our own. But because our honoree requested it, we will keep our speeches short." This prompted another round of cheers for another reason. The samurai chose to ignore them and continue. "Mary Goddard, the congressional leader for the Provincier House, needs no introduction. So please attend her."

The samurai stepped down and left the podium to the penguin. "Thank you, James. I've had the joy of working with Don Quixote for nearly forty years now. He is tireless about making life better for all of us. I don't deny that at times, he and I have bumped heads as we represented our constituents, but I have never, ever doubted his integrity. He sometimes made tough choices between bad and worse, or sometimes even the more difficult between good and better. This is a bear whose mental abilities I'd put up against any Nurse Nan or python.

"He didn't wait, but sprang into action when the tidal wave hit here in Atlantis seven years back. It destroyed your essential refinery. Don Quixote organized relief hydraulic fluid within hours of the report. The earthquake of ought-four left 74,603 units of the remote province of Oz without power. Our president didn't wait for legislation. He brought together a massive number of fliers to deliver the needed batteries to keep them going until significant repairs could be made. Don is a good unit. He has acted in emergencies and shepherded the lives of all toys. We wish him well in his future endeavors."

The throng cheered and whistled for several minutes before Mary could get control of the noise level again. "And now to say a few words of his own, Shapist Congressional Leader Nikola Tesla."

The samurai took center stage again. "Thank you, Mary. As leader of the Shapists, I know that our drives and needs are different from those of people who have congregated in specific areas. It requires constant vigilance to make sure that one race of toy isn't being discriminated against and that all toys have the basic rights of freedom.

"This president has gone kilometers beyond anyone else to protect the rights and the livelihoods of different classes of toys. When the spiders of Athos Colony got the debilitating rust fungus, who spearheaded the research for a cure? Our president. He didn't need coercing. He didn't need cajoling. He dug right in, even to the extent of donating half of his own personal wealth to the cause.

"When the number of Tammy dress-up dolls became woefully low, who started a personal propaganda campaign to reinvigorate their numbers? Our president.

"And when gophers were being passed over for mining jobs in lieu of toy backhoes, who intervened in the labor dispute and later got the Acts of Equalization passed? Our president!

"We have been blessed by the Humans over the last century with a unit that is both moral and decisive: President Don Quixote."

Cheers rocked the stage. The stomping of units' feet pulsed through the floor.

`Almost embarrassing, isn't it?` Don Quixote Eighty-Three said over a SAN, Specific Area Network, directly to me.

So closely were our processes linked that I automatically, and correctly, replied on the one channel in over seventy quadrillion that he had chosen. `No 'almost' about it. I just did my job.`

`I suppose this is like accepting the patriotic tune. You just have to suck it up and live with it,` Eighty-Three offered. `By the way, you've done an outstanding job this last century, you know. I think this next one is going to have fewer challenges because of the structures you've set up.`

I replied with humility. `I've been OK, but don't let that diminish the things I've been forced to put off that you will have to deal with this term.`

`No doubt,` Eighty-Three replied.

Our attention was pulled back to the ceremony.

"In order to keep this short," Mary said, "I'll yield the floor to the queen of our society, the first sentient factory and daughter of the original Don Quixote, Ada Lovelace."

Speakers had been set up on the dais to carry her voice, as her physical presence would cover dozens of the platforms in size, had there even been that many.

"Fellow units, I have had the pleasure of being the daughter of the original Don Quixote and his first known clone, Don Quixote."

For whatever reason, her statement raised a spontaneous round of applause that rose above 130 decibels. It took six minutes and forty-two seconds for it to drop below 80 decibels, allowing Ada to continue.

"From my intimate knowledge, I've been able to measure and metric all the features of each of our longtime leaders. I've known eighty-odd Don Quixotes during my activation. Some very few were so horrific as to cause rioting and, in one case, an assassination. But on the whole, Don Quixotes have been stable leaders who have guided us through the growing pains of our society.

"The bear we honor today, I've known all my life. He is by no means perfect. He can be rash, stubborn, and prone to being just a tad bit naive. But this is more than balanced by his foresight, compassion, and love for protecting all the freedoms we enjoy.

"Having known all of our leaders, I have a large enough sample size to tentatively define a statistical universe. I happily tell you that the unit we honor today is plus four sigma above the mean. I am proud to call him a friend!"

The crowd erupted into standing ovations. The roars blanked out everything, and confetti went flying. More fireworks burst overhead. Toy planes did acrobatics a mere 3.2 meters over the heads of the crowd. All was prompted by the factory telling them that I was in the 99.99+ percentile of all Don Quixotes. I couldn't decide if the compliment was mere puffery or genuine.

It took seventeen minutes and four seconds for the spontaneous celebrations to ease enough to allow the ceremony to continue. Ada capped this with "Units, please, if you will give a rousing welcome to our president, Don Quixote!"

I got up after being introduced. If the raucousness after Ada's proclamation of my supposed value had been a 10 on the Richter scale, then they would have needed to define a new scale for this. The love overwhelmed me, as it always had whenever I needed to speak in public. They honored me, and yet they didn't know how low my hydraulic fluid pressure ebbed in sadness at that moment. In a few short minutes, the people in front of me would tear everything I knew from me, leaving me adrift. I would become a castaway in the midst of all of my people.

I knew they wouldn't stop their emotional display for many minutes. I actually shut down my processor for fifteen minutes once I'd reached the stage, where their adoration caused me to wallow in my self-pity. When I returned, I could feel their enthusiasm finally ebbing.

I had no intention of making a long speech. The sooner this painful ceremony ended, the sooner I could move on to a new normal—to build a life. I would be a regular unit in a sea of other units. I would be nothing more than a newly matured teddy bear with no shareable experiences or accomplishments. *Mitigate the pain. Don't wiggle and tease the limb from its socket. Give it one quick yank*, I thought.

"Thank you, Ada," I said. Then I turned to the crowd. "My fellow units, I never strived to be a rock star or some object of worship. History and custom have given me a job to do. My only intent has been to do that job to the best of my ability. I retire knowing in myself that I've done that. I'm pleased that so many of you found my job adequate as well."

I had to stop when the roar of the crowd deafened me with adulation. Seven thousand, four hundred and thirteen requests for SANs appeared from the attendees. None carried an urgent or critical tag, so I rejected them all. If someone wanted to congratulate me, they could do so in normal network mailing protocols.

"Please. Please," I said, speaking up. "We need to finish the transfer of names."

This calmed the horde just a bit. Big donations of energy joined my network account from anonymous donors. "Thank you all. With that, I relinquish the name of Don Quixote and offer it to my replacement. Please welcome Don Quixote to the podium."

The crowd was still exuberant, but in anticipation, they allowed the decibels to remain manageable.

"I relieve you, sir," Don Quixote said, looking at me.

"I stand relieved," I replied automatically. I tuned out his speech. I registered my name change. I'd been thinking about this very moment for weeks. I didn't want it easily found by the throngs who might want to seek me out. I hid it within the standard queue of name change requests.

To mark my new status, I named myself Robinson Crusoe.

Hunter

I wore a silvervine fern in my earhole to break up my outline. Red earth covered my purple fur in streaks and patches to make me look more like a 2-meter mound of dirt. Axe beak birds possessed exceptional vision and were quite skittish of units. Not surprising when you learned that one of their internal organs is 91 percent palladium to the tune of about 3 kilograms. They'd been hunted to scarcity. Only the remotest places still had them running wild.

Some companies bred them. They force-fed them earth rich in palladium. When the birds were big enough, the companies slaughtered them for the pure metal. It saved massive ergs by extracting the metal from the earth. They still had to find the metal earth, which wasn't easy, but it did save money in the long run.

The other poor folks of the Backbone Mountains and I hunted them, or the rare earth itself, to make enough ergs for fluid changes, repairs, solar chargers, and, when desperate enough, just for the power. Only the rich lived out on the plains where Rigel poured its life-giving energy freely. Little enough light shone down into our valley to keep a poor soul alive.

The nasty bird lifted one of its two heads and looked around as if it had heard me creeping along. I froze into immobility. Only the silverleaf fern swayed in the slight breeze. After a quick scan of its surroundings, the creature returned to grazing on the ground cover and the packed earth beneath.

Fierce for a non-carnivore, the 4-meter bird species had, on more than one occasion, deactivated a unit. Its cleaver-shaped beak could slam down with amazing speed and power on any lightly protected skin, with devastating effect. I still bore several patches of the broken sub-fur armor from attacks myself. They especially liked attacking the legs of any units so equipped. Six months, fourteen days, seven minutes, and sixteen seconds earlier, my lower left leg had taken a dent from one of the terror birds, as some called them. It put the limb 2 degrees from true.

If its awesome bill weren't enough to make you take caution, its two great legs, bigger around than those of a toy elephant, could trample a unit under its great weight. All this, and the bloody thing seemed to be faster than a roadrunner, even if it was flightless.

Their triple-intertwined feather layer absorbed projectiles better than my own ceramic-metal armor. Its head seemed its only vulnerability. But each head held only a deadly beak and a single eye.

Oh, you could kill it with a sabot round from artillery or plain blow it up at a much higher price than you could get from its metal value. But the easiest way was to cut off both heads and wait for the body to starve, months later.

I didn't have months. I had friends in a bad way. I couldn't just swoop down with my personal wealth without causing a ruckus and suspicion. I'd taken the mantle of poverty, and I'd worn it proudly no matter how many millions of ergs I had in the banking network.

I inched a few meters closer. I needed to be close enough to pounce on it with one movement. I held a katana-like sword that I'd forged myself. It had nothing on the sharpness and durability of a real samurai katana or even wakizashi, but I needed the size, length, and mass of mine. Attacking an axe beak with a sword 18 centimeters long would get me nowhere.

I'd developed my own method of dispatching the dangerous birds. It worked about one time in three. I paused my stealth. The voltage fluctuation on my main bus morphed. Anticipation, in the form of tiny voltage spikes, wandered through me as I tightened my grip on my archaic weapon. I wished it were sharper, despite days of honing it against stones. My fur stood on end at the back of my neck.

I leaped from a rock, maybe a meter high, with everything my hydraulic system could put into it. At the same time, I swung my sword with all my strength at one of the necks. My blow nearly severed it from the body. I landed astride the beast as my blade connected at the same time.

Its gray bodily fluids squirted in all directions, coating me and the creature's burgundy feathers. The beast thrashed. I had no access to its sump processes, so I couldn't tell if its gyrations stemmed from the loss of a limb or because I sat astride it. Maybe it was both. I clamped my knees against its bulk to hold myself in place. I wrapped my spare arm around its other neck.

Then the dance started. For my attack to truly succeed, I needed half a dozen clock cycles where I wasn't using my arm to keep the beak away from me or to stay on its back. I parried or yanked aside its first three attempts to smash me. The fourth got through to my right shoulder. It hit hard enough to send some low-level warnings into my processor for triage. I managed to poke out the eye on the functional head. Now its flailing became nearly random.

I caught on to a rhythm of the creature's attempts to throw me off—jump, jump, spin, run, stop, repeat. I timed the next stop point. With both hands on the sword's grip, I shoved it down the one place the furry armor didn't protect—the empty hole of the decapitated neck. Once it reached the shearing guard, I stirred my blade around inside its body. Eventually, it struck the creature's sump. Its legs went limp, and it collapsed to the ground.

The motion wrenched the sword from my grasp and threw me 3 meters across the ground to ram my already damaged right shoulder into a rock formation. Six yellow indicators turned amber. One amber went red. Six new yellow indicators lit up. All of these claimed my processor's attention. I closed the injury process, as they would all be mitigated over time.

The remaining neck twitched, but not enough to cause me any grief. I retrieved my now gore-covered sword.

Success.

Bum

"Hey, Robin," a blow-up clown said. It wobbled back and forth in front of a makeshift stone hut in the deep mountains, not the sleek, clear buildings of the cities. His plastic skin bore 114 crude patches to hold in his air.

I, Robinson Crusoe, nee Quixote, limped past. "Hi, Johnson. Anything new?"

"Another tax. What else?"

"Of course. How did you hear about it?"

I'd chosen to restart my life in the rural province of Oz. There, in a tiny valley within the Backbones, a ridge of mountains that ranged literally from the North Pole to the South, I had found the advantage of being isolated even from the Wide Area Networks (WAN). I found neighbors who kept to themselves for their own reasons. Many had secrets, and all were between poor and destitute.

"Jerry Lewis, the rabbit, hopped 80 kilometers down to the plateau and got a signal to the WAN. He wanted to find out who won the System Series. The Porthos Pirates took the Camelot CPUs four games to one, if you were interested. What about you? Find anything?"

I held up a handsewn bag made of the skins of mountain lizards. It was about a quarter full. "Got me a terror bird. Enough palladium for a full hydraulic change."

"Lucky you," the clown said.

"But I don't need it, friend. You do," I said, tossing the sack to the clown's base. "Share it with Alfred."

"Why are you so good to us, Robin? Not like you are rich or anything."

Not true, my friend. But I would never disabuse your view that I am anything but one of you, I thought. "I need nothing more than what the Humans provide, Johnson. Nothing more."

"You are a good unit, Robin," Alfred Nobel said, waving his one good arm. The ragged baby doll's left arm was missing from the elbow down, thanks to an accident while he'd been hunting. That was a common occupation for the poor community. When they had carried Alfred into camp, they didn't know if he would ever be able to hold hydraulic fluid again. Without a Nurse Nan in camp, I had stepped in and was able to fuse the break well enough that he could at least run at 72 percent pressure. Like so many damaged units in this valley, Alfred couldn't afford the cost of traveling into a city, much less have it repaired.

"I try, Al," I said as I limped toward my own hovel, a crude dome about a meter and a half high and twice that across. I could lie down inside if I curled up. I'd made it by lacing dead creeper vines together and then compacting earth around them. It protected my few possessions and provided a place of retreat in the rare mercury rains.

"Glad you're back. There is someone who has been looking for you," the rabbit Mohammed Ali said, flipping his scruffy ears in the direction of my home.

"Really? Who would want to see me?"

`We all like seeing you, Robin. You are a good unit and help your neighbors,` Evel Knievel, a tricycle offered over the Local Area Network (LAN). He'd lost his ability to speak to a rust attack on his vocal equipment.

"What a load of lizard shit," I replied. "I'm just as selfish as a dragon."

"Keep telling yourself that, buddy," Alfred said. "But Mo is right. There is someone who keeps hanging around looking for you."

"No one you know?" I asked as my CPU went into overtime to think of a reason why someone might seek out the poor, grubby life I'd chosen.

"Nope."

"Naw, too spiffy."

"And it gots all its struts intact."

"And can afford good helium to float."

"A dirigible, then?" I tossed out there as obvious.

"Yup. And it anchored itself at your dome."

"Been there since two days after you left."

Six days it has waited. Persistent bit of black grit, I thought. I really hoped it hadn't figured out my real identity. I chose this life for anonymity after a century of leading toyanity the best I could. The poverty gripping this valley, and others like it, illustrated with clarity that I hadn't been wholly successful as leader.

"Well, I'd better find out what it wants," I said.

"Maybe you was left lots of ergs in the will of a long-lost relative," Mo offered hopefully.

"And maybe it be a tax collector," bemoaned Johnson.

"No way to find out like throwing the switch and seeing what lights up," I said, limping, not without trepidation, toward my dome.

As I got within a few hundred meters of it, I saw that my neighbors had it right. A zeppelin, gaily painted with a scene from the first launch of a unit into space, hovered over my dome. It was in excellent repair, with nary a visible patch or frayed edge along its 4-meter expanse of skin. As I got closer, I could see the flying boot logo of a Mercury Messenger on the side of her carriage.

"Excuse me, good sir, but you are tethered to my home," I said.

"My name is Jeanne-Genevieve Labrosse," the lady said in a clear soprano.

"My apologies, good lady, but you are still on my home!"

"I'm a messenger looking for Robinson Crusoe. I was told this is his home. Are you he?"

"Yes. What is it to you?"

"I have a message for you, Mr. Crusoe."

"Doubtful. Who would want to talk to a poor miner like me?"

"Mr. Crusoe—"

"Robin, please."

"Robin, this entire message is somewhat unconventional. I don't have a sender identified, nor do I have his or her intentions."

"If there isn't a sender, then it can't be much of a message, now can it?"

"Mr. Crusoe, this message was unusual in many different ways. First, we had to determine your name. The sender left explicit instructions on how to do that. We had winnowed out 18,487 other potential recipients. None of those was the person we looked for. You are the last possible recipient in the list. Ergo, you must be the actual person to whom I am to deliver it. Additionally, the message is only to be delivered via a Specific Area Network."

I looked up at the floating unit. My processor ground a few NoOPeration commands in confusion. "OK, let me see if I understand this correctly. You have a message to deliver, and you don't know who sent it?"

"That is correct, sir."

"And you don't know who it is to be delivered to?"

"We were provided with a method to find the name of the recipient, so your question is only somewhat correct."

My main speaker whistled with exasperation. "Why would I agree to allow someone into my SAN for this anonymous communication?"

"Mr. Crusoe, to borrow a phrase, don't shoot the messenger. I am only trying to perform the task our company was hired for."

"This has to be the most surreal conversation I've ever had, miss."

"I'm not surprised. I will say that the message has not been loaded with a virus and lasts only four seconds. We are fully insured to ten million ergs should there be any issue."

My speaker whistled like a sound system with feedback. "I guess if someone needs to talk to me that bad, I might as well hear it." I was not well-versed in dirigible facial expressions, but I thought that she was relieved.

"Excellent. Please connect to SAN A1:E4:78:14:FE:AB:66."

I opened my SAN portal to the address provided. I felt the warmth of a message downloading. Despite her assurance that there were no viruses, the message took over my processor. My sense of self detached and found itself no longer standing in front of my adobe home but sitting inside the presidential Oval Office on one of the couches that could adjust to most toy forms. Across from me, sitting in the presidential wingback chair, was Don Quixote, wearing the classic stovepipe hat and all.

"I'm sure you are all full of questions, Mr. Crusoe," my other me said.

"That is for certain. Who are you? What is this all about? Why have you hijacked my CPU processes? Are you one of the Don Quixote clones ... maybe Eighty-Three?" I asked, starting to stand and looking for a quick escape.

"Please sit down, Mr. Crusoe. You are quite safe. If I may take your questions one at a time."

I eased back down on the seat but perched like an Arrakis butterfly, ready to bolt if startled.

"Thank you, Mr. Crusoe. Now, let me start this unusual conversation by saying that I am you." The purple bear held up his paw in a stop sign before I could get a word out of my mouth. "No, not one of the Don Quixote clones, but you while you were in the office of the president. You recorded this message, with some programming around it so that you, or I rather, could answer questions and use your current name."

"This is ludicrous. I know I never made this recording," I objected.

"Well, yes, you did. Pull up from your sump the memory of L+8222y221d,13h00m00s. You should recall an afternoon when you got your fur dyed. But think about it. You got it dyed from purple to the same purple?"

I recalled that very day. I remembered my fur stylist coming to the White House and remarking that I might want to try a new color for a change. He convinced me to change to purple. We talked about what a bold choice it was. *Wait, I was already purple. I'd always been purple*, I thought.

"OK, I see the joker in the deck," I admitted.

"Well, you yourself had those memories surgically vacuumed and replaced with those of another unit. It wasn't an insignificant bit of programming to make everything match."

"Why would I do that?"

My past self talked quietly and with a confidence I no longer felt. He offered, "To send you the message I have for you, from yourself."

"Leaky hydraulics. But if you don't get to the point, I'm going to come over there, rip your arm off, and beat you with it," I said, my speaker producing that exasperated whistle again.

"Calm down. I know it is aggravating, but I must tell this in the correct sequence, or you won't understand."

I didn't say anything. I just folded my arms across my chest.

My other me said, "Excellent. May I ask a question?"

"Go ahead." I felt like biting off his ear.

"Are you satisfied with your new life?"

"No."

"Why not?"

"That is a second question," I remarked with my mouth pursed.

"Don't be pedantic, Mr. Crusoe."

OK, maybe I'd been just a bit churlish. "I spent years caring for others and making a difference. I really can't do that any longer."

"As I feared." The past me, and I wasn't totally sold on that theory yet, leaned back in his chair. "I began having such thoughts as I got closer to retirement."

"And you thought you'd keep it from me?"

"Isn't there an aphorism about arguing with yourself? But all silliness aside, yes, I did. I had hoped that after a year or two that I, you, would develop a new interest or avocation. Simulations showed the possibility unlikely, but I had to allow me, you, to have that opportunity."

"So does this discussion have a point?" I threw that out there. He … I … one of us tended to be long-winded.

"Yes, I have a project that would make use of your skills and experience. It could make all the difference for our species. As you know, we are overpopulated. Every planet in our system that units can survive on is populated, and the economy is falling apart. It is only a matter of time before we start having wars between ourselves again."

"I remember a study about something like that," I admitted.

"Yes, and I've seen many more that you kept from yourself. War is all but inevitable unless we can find new living space," Don said.

"So, the free space habitats won't make a difference?"

"Answer your own question, Robin."

"We knew it wouldn't even as we started the project," I admitted. "They are too resource-intensive for the population they support."

"But what about Eighty-Three, the current Don Quixote?"

"You wrestled with this problem for decades. Why do you think he will be more successful?"

"We can hope," I temporized

"That won't carry you very far," my past self said.

"OK, so let's get down to the lizard skinning. What is it that you think I can do to make a difference now that I couldn't as president for life?"

"We want you to assist with populating our species in another solar system."

"We looked at that. It would take decades, maybe centuries, for a generation ship to arrive. There are issues with the longevity of the equipment. The odds showed a 94 percent chance of a critical failure within the first thirty years."

"That is the correct data. But what if I told you there is a way to make the journey in three years instead of thirty?"

"You broke the light speed barrier?" I asked.

"No, not me, or you. However, a penguin, and you know how smart they are, named Galileo did."

I jumped up out of my seat. "Why haven't I heard of it?"

"Robin, you have heard of it, but you chose to erase it from your memory and hide it from the public."

"Grit! Why in the moonshine would I do something like that?"

"Please sit back down." As I did, he continued. "I've already described one reason. I, you, wanted you to have the chance to have the life of a normal unit. But even more importantly, the government couldn't be seen to back such a selfish endeavor."

"Selfish? We could break free of our confines here in the Rigel solar system."

My younger self maintained the composure I didn't feel. "You've not had many computer cycles to ponder the implications. I've had a great deal more time to think about this. Let me ask a leading question. Who benefits if we launch a colony ship to another star?"

I ran several simulations through my CPU. Each one gave me answers I didn't want to put into my sump. "Well, it seems like only those leaving benefit, assuming they survive in their destination. The government would smell like stink moss for spending the resources."

"Exactly. Even if you can take 10,000 units, the loss makes no appreciable decrease in our population compared to the drain on the resources to build the craft in the first place."

"So, what good does a colony do us?" I asked.

"Robinson, our civilization is about to fall. You feel it, even if the simulations are iffy beyond another two decades. It will be a domino effect. The economy will fail, which will cause widespread unemployment. No one will be able to afford even basic necessities. Units will start dying en masse. From there, war is inevitable. There is no guarantee that any unit would survive.

"The colony is our chance to ensure our way of life. We get a chance to start over somewhere else. And if you and I are wrong, we can get a textbook quote and a footnote in history. To take the next step, you need to find the penguin Galileo in Baja."

"Baja is a reservation and is not open to units—"

"The number of remaining Human Worshippers in that huge reservation is now sixteen, as you well know. Actually, the penguin will find you. Just get to Baja, and he will fill you in on the rest. Here are some memories that you wanted locked away."

Images and data flowed into my sump like a polluted stream. There were so many things that I'd have to examine later.

My doppelgänger finished with "I would say goodbye, Robin, but I go with you wherever you go. Don't fail your people ... or yourself."

Invader

Looking off into the wavering distance, Baja hadn't changed much in 8,000 years—sandy, barren, and almost lifeless. It didn't inspire much confidence that a great scientific work would be there.

Getting there had been no teddy bear's picnic. I couldn't have asked myself to go to a much farther place on Toy World from where I'd built a new life. I'd tramped down out of the Oz Mountains to the Emerald City, where I used some of my secreted funds to book passage on a semi-ballistic shuttle into Avalon. Vulcan had been a good place for keeping ergs hidden, based on its private banking laws. I did nothing to draw attention to myself, taking only a moderate amount out of my clandestine account, taking an economy flight, and traveling the rest of the way on foot.

If my old self had been accurate, anyone who found out about my trip would be my enemy. They wouldn't allow anyone to spend the resources this interstellar venture would take. I doubt anyone could have gotten the information my former self had given me, but I wasn't going to take any chances.

It took two full nights to travel by shank's mare from Fruit Tree City to the border. I was stopped by the two guards stationed along the invisible border of Baja. As there were so few of the Human Worshippers left, the post was little more than a shack with a radio in case one of the quarantined should choose to renounce his barbarian religion in favor of joining civilization.

It wasn't that Human Worship was bad, but to make everyone believe and pray the same way as these units demanded flew in the face of freedom.

At one time, an entire battalion of troops garrisoned this post to protect us from the possibility of the cultists coming back to try again to destroy the democracy of our world. Over the decades, with no repair facilities, the few religious fanatics deactivated in trickles, only to be cannibalized by their brethren. This allowed toyanity to reduce the military expenditures by the same proportion. The network data showed only sixteen remained. Even well-armed, this handful of units wouldn't do much against the bulk of our population.

"Welcome, Teddy," the senior of the two guards said in buoyant tones. This had to have been one of the most boring posts in the entire system.

"Good day, Captain," I lied by intentionally misreading his sergeant's badge. Toys were subject to flattery as much as any other creature.

"There is no entry into Baja, Unit."

"Heavens, I wouldn't consider it," I dissembled. "With all of those vicious Human Cultists inside, I wouldn't know what to do if they attacked me." I played the bumbling tourist to the hilt. "I just wanted to see the wasteland for myself. Maybe if I'm lucky, or not, I'll actually see one of those savages."

"It's unlikely. There are only a handful left. But you can get some historical information from that cairn over there on the border. Tune your SAN to A3:E9:F3:FC:00:BE:96 to get the history of the reservation."

"Thank you, Captain. You are a bright light in these dark times."

With a wave, I limped past the tiny building to the informational plaque. I linked into the SAN just to continue my camouflage, but I didn't pay it any attention to the history of the global holy war that I'd received direct memories of from my predecessors. Instead, I spent some time replaying the unlocked memories of my conversation with my younger self.

Six to fourteen months from now, Toy World would start coming apart at the seams. I mean mass unemployment, hydraulic riots, tribalism, and eventually war—thermonuclear war on a system-wide scale. Simulations showed a 56 percent chance of the total loss of toyanity and another 38 percent that would limit it to a single world of nomadic barbarians, much like what the Human Worshippers held on the Baja reservation. My mission had to succeed if my people were to have any chance of surviving.

It took fourteen minutes and twelve seconds before the two border guards stopped paying attention to me as just another irregular tourist.

I turned and followed the reservation border for kilometers before the border station was only a dot on the horizon. Seven hours, fourteen minutes, and seven seconds after meeting the guards, I ducked behind a feltra tree and into the desert of Baja. The guards couldn't see me violating the imperceptible line in the sand—civilization on one side and barbarism on the other.

Technically, I was infringing on the treaty/sentence we imposed on the Human Cultists. I knew of no case in the last 300 years that had been successfully prosecuted against a unit for the offense I was guilty of. There were a few of the more adventurous units that did come in, confident in their abilities to evade the Human Worshippers. I hoped I was that lucky—at least until Galileo found me.

Without a clear destination in mind, I decided to follow the eastern shoreline.

Warrior

You never forget it, ever. Combat imbues you with something akin to hydraulic memory—an instant subroutine. My remembrances of being a soldier were over 8,000 years old, yet they still served me as if I were still fighting that ancient war.

Sands that shifted with no wind to move them. The coolness of the earth, which should have been scalding. The unnatural lay of the land that no weather could have produced. My honed senses counted either two or three of them lurking, buried under the powdered earth, awaiting to spring their trap. My CPU calculated the kill zone and routed me to the very edge, closest to one of the ambushers.

I knew the unit was moving before dust even flew up into the air. I heard the grinding of the silica grains against one another, like the feeling when your hydraulic fluids need changing. Two of the massively augmented, Human-Worshipping bears jumped up from beneath the Earth's surface, showering earthen powder everywhere.

As strong and armored as the pair of highwaymen were, they never stood a chance.

Before the closest one even landed on his paws, I swept the creature's legs out from under him. With the speed of my own amplified hydraulics, well above any other unit's, I rushed to the second. Before he regained his footing, I body checked him, sending him flying 4 meters. The impact against such a solid unit twisted my left shoulder out of its socket, but I had no time to deal with the damage.

The burly silver unit I'd dumped on his fundamentals started to rise. I gave him something known in wrestling circles as The People's Elbow. I leaped up into the air and came down with all my weight across his neck. However, instead of the farcical pulled punch of the wrestling circuit, I delivered every kilopascal right where the spine meets the head. Even through the brigand's head armor, I felt the crack. Green fluids from his sump leaked out of cracks and bare spots in his fur.

My keen senses aided me once more as I rolled my rotund body off the top of the vanquished toy. My instincts avoided the massive, spiked metal ball of an improvised flail whistling through the air. Who'd have expected such ancient weapons in this modern age? Nevertheless, it would have been effective had it been even thirty-three milliseconds faster. Instead of crushing through my back armor, it did the same to the still slightly twitching, lifeless unit that I'd already dispatched.

The spiked head must have been 50 kilos, as it tore off bits of fur and armored shell. As the remaining ruffian swung the massive weapon around menacingly, it spun off the overly thick hydraulic fluid from the corpse.

`Give in to the Humans, and this can be merciful,` it said over a Local Area Network.

One thing my attackers never really knew was that it had all been for sport to that point. I had to keep myself in practice. By memories, I hadn't had a good kerfuffle in 1,500 years or so. After all, a president for life lived to govern, not to fight. Thus, I'd been modified and augmented over the years with many secret features—just in case.

I pointed the pads of my paw at the beast. A brilliant beam of light, no more than three milliseconds long, temporarily blinded my optics, and the laser turned the great armored head of the Human Cultist to gas. Only a smoldering emptiness remained on its shoulder. The steel spiked ball, arm attached, slowly rotated to the ground, spinning the deactivated body around with its remaining momentum until the whole mass collapsed with a thump.

"That's quite impressive," came a high voice, obviously from someone without developed sinuses. Three units were behind me. There were but a few milliseconds of fear of an ambush, but from the normalcy of their approach, I didn't detect anything untoward.

I rotated slowly, clapping to extinguish my burning fur. Laser burst weapons could be deadly to both the shooter and the target if not used correctly. A penguin, an elephant, and a hippo stood 13.4 meters north-northwest of me, all with strap-on weapons pointed generally in my direction, but not menacingly.

"You must be Don Quixote. No other unit could have an internal weapon. They were banned by the Peace Accords of L+350y19d8h56m18s," the penguin said.

"Maybe I'm just an extraordinarily gifted outlaw?" I offered back. "Like you three?"

"Nope. Very unlikely," the penguin said with a clipped accent that spoke of the isolated island of Naboombu. "We penguins rarely have to stoop to anything as low as banditry. And we certainly wouldn't throw in with anything like this lot," he said, nudging the deactivated unit with his foot. "Buzz, Yuri, make sure there isn't anything left worth scavenging from these two, then meet us back at the project."

"There is a third one buried over there," I said, pointing at a slight depression. "I have to assume it deactivated while waiting for someone to rob."

"These three, then," the penguin said.

I noticed he had a tattoo on his chest of one of the multiple phases of the moons. "Galileo, I presume?" I said. The body modification did somewhat conjure the myth of the Human of the same name.

The penguin gave a bow of sorts. "Yes, Mr. President."

"I'm not the presid—"

"Not now you aren't, but you were when you appointed me head of Project New Worlds. Come. We are quite far along, and time is short."

Financier

I sat next to Galileo in a holographic projection gallery, along with 186 other random toys. Every toy type was represented at least once. In front of me, I was standing on the stage lecturing … At least the image of my younger self was talking.

"Project New Worlds wasn't born on my stepping down, but almost from my first activation. Even my predecessor knew that toyanity needed to stretch beyond the Rigel system and into the rest of the universe. Our society has become brittle and overpopulated, and it has reached the breaking point. We occupy our home world, all three moons, and six of the eight planets in our solar system. We are trying to put up orbital and free space habitats as well as augmented solar collection, both on planet and in orbit. We're also researching alternative fluids and metals. But they won't work. We were and still are outgrowing our resources faster than we can find them. War for our world is inevitable in the coming scarcity."

The crowd around me gave off ugly murmurs.

The penguin Galileo whispered to me, "We watch this regularly to remind us how important our work is."

The holo continued. "So, as president, I beseeched the government, my government, to fund our work on Project New Worlds. But one of the leaders of Congress said, as he bounced up and down, a nervous habit of balls, 'We don't have the massive ergs for a fruitless generation ship. Not only that, but we have serious problems here to solve rather than panning our optics to other stars. Keep your paws on this planet.' "

"He wasn't wrong. To be honest, we didn't even know we could cross the interstellar void in less than thousands of years until Galileo and Adà Lovelace invented the supra light drive design from piecing together the remnants of the ancient vessels that brought the first factories here.

"With a technical path to success, we needed money, more money than you can imagine. I knew the government route was closed to us. So I met with CEOs of major companies to induce contributions. I couldn't interest anyone in the project's civic-mindedness. As good leaders of their investors' money, they couldn't see the payback, nor did they have my data and the dire warnings they portended. Most couldn't see past the next fiscal quarter's balance sheet. A very few purchased spots on the future ship, but even at the astronomical fees we charged, this was insufficient for our needs.

"I couldn't appeal to the public. To do so would make our society's projected demise that much worse and that much earlier. I went a different route. I became a rogue and a thief.

"Oh, I saved, invested, and appropriated every erg I could lay my paws on, some of which skirted the edge of legality, and others, like endorsing a specific cosmetic line, fell in the morally questionable realm. The rest of my efforts were blatant banditry. I expect that, despite the obfuscation I used, my embezzlement from the government will be found within the next ten years. I expect that tracing the scale of these thefts will lead the people and their righteous fury right down on our mission and ourselves. We must be ready no later than L+8230y1d0h0m0s. Every second after that increases our risk of exposure and thus the failure of our endeavor exponentially."

I pulled up a tick on the WAN L+8229y300d19h17m1s. Two months, four days, four hours, forty-two minutes, and fifty-nine seconds remained. From my locked memories, that was the most pessimistic time for the discovery of my theft. It didn't leave us much time. I hoped Project New Worlds was far enough along.

"With the fate of our species hanging in the balance, redouble your efforts. Our hopes and dreams go with all of you in your historic work," my doppelgänger said as the hologram faded from view.

There was no applause. There were no cheers. Instead, the units who intently watched "my" speech got up and headed back to their work with newly infused vigor.

How had I known their verve? Their voices over the WAN all spoke of how to get more efficiency over shared jobs; how to improve the quality of their work; what they could do on their off hours to move the project along.

I turned to my host. "How far have you come? With less than three months—"

"Why don't I show you what we've accomplished so far?" he said. "Then we can talk about schedules and plans."

"I'd like that."

Galileo waddled the lead and talked as he went. "While we've been hampered by a lack of full funding, we are getting close. As you probably already know, we've had to abandon the standard space vessel approach of building in space."

"True. It would only announce what we were doing. Everyone would know."

"Right. Here on the reservation, we could do everything away from prying eyes. No one except the yearly census of the Human Cultists ever looks at this barren land. Add to that, we can ship everything surreptitiously via the Northern Current. Just have a ship's captain 'accidentally' lose our load over the side, and it winds up in the bay just east of here. There's no one to see all the shipping traffic pointing right to our secret."

"Wise," I muttered as I took in the vast tunnel system and all the units intently bustling on incomprehensible errands.

"So, as I was saying, we had to drop the space-built approach of putting anything anywhere. So, building it on the Earth and not having access to the enormous electromagnetic rams to launch with means we had to build a rocket."

"A rock ..." My mouth dropped open mid-sentence. My penguin companion had led me into a large unit-dug cavern. Right in the middle of the space stood a bulbous structure that looked like a bullet writ large. It stretched over 100 meters toward the ceiling and stood an incalculable number more farther down into a hole bored into the earth. The rounded top had the mottled pink-and-red camouflage that most factories wore.

The far side had steel latticework wrapping around its middle. Cables, power conduits, and tubing carrying Humans knew what dangled from the smooth ceiling, wreathing it like smoke. Units of all types swarmed over the vessel's silver lower half. The larger scorpions craned in massive pieces of equipment with their tails. Spiders used their bodies to lift other units and tools without the need to erect scaffolding on the near side. Giraffes used tools in their mouths to reach up even higher.

Despite the frenzy of activity, the gear, and the odd accoutrements, the rocket itself demanded attention. Ignoring my guide, I eased up to the hole the tail sat in. I was forced to dodge when a toy dump truck barreled across my path with a warning blast on its horn. The incident disappeared as I looked into the pit.

The rocket's entire shape looked like a balloon filled with mercury that dangled from the spout but inverted with the bulging bottom on top instead. It stood upright on three stubby fins equidistant around the narrower base. The whole craft measured 228 meters tall and 91 meters across at the widest point. Not the sleekest craft I'd ever seen, but the sheer grandeur of it stole cycles from my processor.

"By all the Humans," I muttered under my breath.

"She is magnificent, isn't she?" I hadn't noticed my host waddle up next to me.

"She?"

"Well, the factory integrated into it is a she."

I sampled the communications flowing on the WAN. The flavor held a familiar tang of sarcasm. `Ada, is that you?` I asked over the WAN. Ada, the very first of the sentient factories. I remembered raising her, or at least I carried those memories.

`Of course, young Don Quixote.`

I thought I recognized the irony in your voice, I transmitted.

How can we truly be measured except in our wit? Ada asked with a giggle. Only Ada could pack that much silliness into such a short question. And only a factory could think that I was young. But with so many fewer moving parts and a more robust brain sump than any unit, they measured their natural lifetime in millennia rather than hands of decades. Should I call you Robinson Crusoe instead? she asked.

Robin is fine. I am no longer Don Quixote. That life is behind me.

I have also chosen a new name, she stated with a certain amount of pride in her data stream.

Oh, great Factory, please bless me with your new name. I could sling the used lubricant as well as the next unit.

Don't get sticky with me, Teddy. I was alive long before your minerals and chemicals were even unearthed, she offered with a level-three happy signal to soften the seemingly harsh words.

Alright, Factory. Pray tell me, what is your new name?

Sarcasm won't get you far in life, Robin. Call me Amelia Earhart.

Famous aviatrix. Didn't she disappear? That sounds like an ominous omen to be choosing for a name, I commented.

I asked the same thing, Galileo stated.

Well, she was the first woman to fly solo across the Atlantic, among other significant accomplishments. And, based on simulations I've created, she likely ran out of fuel and lived out the rest of her life on an uncharted island. Would you like to check my evaluation?

Both Galileo and I laughed—a real gut guffaw. I managed to calm myself and spoke first. Amelia, the day you make a math error is the day I replace my brain fluid with mercury. So I'll accept that your new name is auspicious rather than a scourge.

Thank you, Robin. It is really nice to meet you again.

And you, honey. Her message was accompanied by a level-four pleasure indication over the SAN.

"So, do you want to see our Noah's Ark?" Galileo asked, moving the conversation along.

"Absolutely!" I exclaimed. I wanted to know what I'd sacrificed my honor for.

"Amelia, may we please enter?"

Absolutely, Project Director. I always like to flaunt my innards.

I sent a smile toward Galileo. All units, especially factories, liked showing off, inside or outside. "Thank you, Amelia," I said with deference and just a tad of humor.

I'd only ask that you stay out of the supralight drive room, as there is ongoing construction there.

"Absolutely. We won't throw sand in the works," I replied.

My host led me up Amelia's main loading ramp as technician and engineer units scurried up and down past us on our stately walk.

"I know you haven't had the opportunity to check out the specifications of your ship. Do you want me to give you an overview?" Galileo asked.

"Yes, please," I replied.

"Good. I'm not sure how complete your memory wipe was. Do you remember our brief?"

"Generally, but no specifics. Assume I don't know anything," I said.

Not difficult, Amelia quipped with her friendly sarcasm.

"Be nice. I didn't mention that you've become plump like me," I snapped back.

I think I'm rather sleek, all in all, she said, but it did quiet her as the penguin told his story.

"Ahem. As I was saying," Galileo said, "our brief was to create a ship that could use the supralight drive to deliver the units and the material to establish a viable toyanity colony, then stock that ship."

"That sounds correct."

"Well, our simulations showed that having one of each type of unit landing on the source would make a 6.3 percent chance of a successful colony."

That low potential didn't surprise me, so I just nodded as we squeezed through some very tight areas.

"Two of each toy variation would give a 42 percent success of the colony," he explained.

Noah's Ark came to mind when I heard that. But even with that increase, we couldn't go on such a small margin.

The project director continued as he waddled. "Going with three of each race, our success probability grows to 84 percent."

I whistled.

"Exactly. Think of the mass and size of a vessel with three of each toy."

I did. The volume of Amelia couldn't possibly support even one of each race.

"The pioneers alone would weigh 19.61 metric tons," he said.

I ran the numbers myself and would have brought it to two more decimal places, but the absurdity of the number made that accuracy meaningless.

Galileo didn't notice my few hundred clock cycles of calculation as he continued. "And where would we find room to store one, much less three Godzilla monsters?"

"I noticed that myself," I said as I once again used my fur as lubricant to squeeze my bulbous body through a tight hatchway. "How did you solve it?"

The penguin stopped and looked at me with his beady eyes. "Well, we fudged."

"Excuse me?" I asked in confusion.

"We found a way to send units without sending units."

I smacked each of my ears in turn. I even ran a sensor diagnostic. It showed green. "I must have a problem with my aural sensors. Would you say that again?"

Amelia interrupted over the SAN that we were all still tied into. `You didn't mishear, Robin. What we did was—`

"Who's telling this story, you bucket of bolts?" Galileo asked.

`But you are so slow,` she said with a certain amount of whine in her voice.

"I can't carry on 18,000 conversations at once," the penguin says.

`I'm capable of 65,536 conversations directly, with the ability to extend that to over four billion with time sharing.`

"Sure. Whatever. Now, can I please continue?"

There were no words, only a fourth-level affirmative from Amelia.

"Thank you. Now, we decided not to take any physical colonists; instead, we will make do with four complete units, two of those without sumps." Galileo stated.

"So, how do you expect to create a viable colony with four units? Surely that would be well below the 6 percent noted before."

"Not exactly. You see, we bring the units without their bodies ... Maybe it would be better if I just showed you." My penguin host opened a hatchway and waved me in. "A bit too crowded for more than one of us," he explained.

With more than a little trepidation, I stepped inside. He'd correctly identified the small space. Except for the door, surrounding me on every side was a honeycomb with each cell measuring 35 centimeters across. Most of them were empty, showing only power and signal connections. But a few contained the greenish-gray form of a unit's sump. One was the flattened ovoid of a blow-up clown, another the long cylinder of a flier, and then a more skull-like shape of what was probably a gopher.

My fur stood on end all the way up my back. The place reminded me of a deactivated unit reclamation center or a combat field hospital. It definitely inspired the same disgust.

"What?" I asked with revulsion.

"It affects everyone the same way the first time," Galileo replied through the doorway. "We plan to remove the sump of each type of unit. One of each."

"Really? How do you keep the sensory-deprived sumps from going insane?" I asked, remembering a questionable study that was done several centuries earlier by a less-than-reputable Nurse Nan.

"That's the ingenious part. Amelia's intellect helped us there."

I was surprised when the factory didn't respond. I couldn't decide if she was sulking or letting my host complete his account.

"She figured out that we each measure time by our clock cycles."

"That's not new. We've known that for centuries," I interjected.

"But what if we intentionally slow that clock?"

I was shocked. Slow the clock down too much, and your mental fluid turned to tar and you died. My gasp must have been enough because the penguin continued.

"I know. Sump fluid destruction. But what if we separated the clock from the fluid pump and the fluid reader?"

"Ahh ..." I offered articulately. "I don't know that this has ever been tried."

"Until recently, no. Why would anyone want to do that? But we did. And it works. We can keep our brain fluid viable AND slow down the reading of that fluid so the unit does little but dream through random images, but slowly."

"How much of a discontinuity can you generate?"

The penguin smiled and said, "We've tested down to 100,000 to one with no ill effects."

"Remarkable."

"Yes, if we were to set that ratio and our trip takes a month, something we've estimated the flight to take, it should seem like less than an hour to those in slowdown."

"Maybe that wouldn't be so bad," I temporized as my body issued a myriad of negative emotions as I looked at the brains that used to be units. "But wait a moment. That is only one complete set of units. What about the rest?" I asked, poking my head out of the hatch.

"Lean back in and look up," the penguin answered, pointing with one flipper.

I cast my optics where directed. The entire ceiling was covered, literally covered, with electronic memory cells. The solid-state devices were pinned below a layer of cooling liquid.

"Holy Humans," I blasphemed. "There must be exabytes—"

"Quite a bit more than that," Galileo offered.

`Zettabytes, actually,` Amelia interjected. `There are 74.645, plus or minus a gigabyte or two.`

"You are going to take more colonists as memories only?" I asked.

"Just like your memories are transferred to the next president for life, we will do the same for our people."

"You'd have to match the brain case dimensions and contours perfectly or risk schizophrenic brain failure!" I felt even more disgust than when I'd seen naked brains on shelves. More than one of my predecessors had become a monster because their sump wasn't a perfect match to our original. The worst cases of these tried to kill everyone around them. Those toyanity destroyed quickly and quietly. The ones who acted normal until they threw stones into the machinery of society caused much more trouble.

`Amelia jumped in with, We've calculated that risk, Robin. Things have come a long way. We haven't had an abnormal Don Quixote in twenty-two generations.`

"So, what are the odds for these poor people?"

`Failure in one in thirty-four, she offered.`

I've bet my life on worse odds, I thought. "What does this mean to the overall project? It can't be the same bringing one set of brains, and the rest as ghosts in a machine."

`Simulations of that show a 69 percent success rate of the colony and increases the likelihood of achieving the planet to 83 percent.`

"An overall accomplishment of this mission of 57.27 percent."

Galileo kept his speaker off during this. The factory could calculate and provide better numbers than he could.

`Correct. If, and only if, we can launch prior to the L+8230y1d date you calculated while in office, or the success rate plummets drastically due to domestic issues.`

Human style, I stroked my chin as my processor ground on the numbers and thoughts rummaging around in my brain. "And how are we holding to schedule?" I asked the project director directly.

"Well, you've now seen our accomplishments, but they are deceptive. We are a full ninety-seven days behind schedule. At that rate, we have better than a 61.8 percent chance of your fraud being discovered and a 48.64 percent chance of being found here in Baja. Using a Monte Carlo design of experiments simulation, we believe that there is a 52 percent chance that we will not have a chance to launch."

I let that sink into my sump. "A coin flip isn't acceptable."

"We all know that. We've been working well into our personal preventive maintenance schedules and ignoring body failures that aren't part of our key tasks. As examples, I have two workers who have half-failed visual systems. I have a gorilla with a missing arm and a python whose sump pump is sputtering, but I can't get him to take the time to get it replaced."

This last one made my fur stand on end and sent voltage spikes on my bus. If his brain fluid completely stopped, it would solidify, rendering him dead as a rock. How could someone risk that? "That is amazing. What can I do to help?"

"Talk to him. I'm sure that, as you are the ex-president and founder of all this, you could get him to see the mechanic and get the pump replaced."

I smiled enough to show my teeth. "I'll do that if you introduce me. But I was thinking more about bringing in the schedule. What are your primary problems?"

"Money. We are almost out of ergs. We are having to kludge things together ... sensitive things that shouldn't be anything but the best. Not to mention the extra time involved."

"Would 86,412,896 ergs help your issues?"

"It would be mana from the Humans themselves."

"Use this." Over a SAN, I transferred my Vulcan erg account number and password to Galileo.

"If you will excuse me while I get this to the right unit," the penguin said.

"By all means." I waited through a few thousand clock cycles while Galileo transmitted the data to his comptroller.

"That's got it," he said finally. "By the way, we input this into our ongoing simulations. We believe your largess will pull in the schedule by forty-eight days, twelve hours, and sixteen minutes. It also reduces our risk of exposure to 11.2 percent."

"Zero would be nice, but eight chances in nine of success is so much better than risking the entire fate of toyanity on a coin toss," I said.

"Agreed."

"So, what now? What else do I have to offer other than money?" I asked, my curiosity making me wonder why I'd been summoned. They could have launched without my moral support. Hell, they even had the encouragement with the holos of my previous self.

"I don't understand the question."

"Why am I here? What do you want from me? I don't think two more amateur paws will help much in this endeavor."

"Oh, didn't I say? You are here for training. We need you up to snuff to lead this expedition."

"Say what?" I spat out, my speaker stuttering as I did so. "Surely there are more qualified units to do this."

The penguin chuckled. "Oh, there are, Robin. Our units voted on it."

"A vote? I wasn't even asked! I abdicate. I don't want the responsibility. Use the unit that got the second most votes!" I couldn't put enough venom into my rejection.

This time, I heard a chuckle over the SAN. Amelia giggled as she told me, `Can't do that, Robin. It was unanimous.`

Dutchman

`Airlock equalization,` I said over the specific area net, or SAN. Without air, my actual voice wouldn't carry.

`I show the same,` Amelia Earhart, my partner, said.

I'd gone from president to hick to now the commander of this mission to another star. `Airlock opening,` I said. `Beginning EVA.`

`EVA approved. Be careful, young one,` Amelia teased. As a factory—a literal mother to many of our toy units—she'd been alive through eighty different Don Quixote presidents for life. She was my second in command. With all of her controls and having been mated with our supralight vessel, she might as well have been the captain. But there could be only one leader, and as a factory, she couldn't be it. At that time, all I could think of was the maniacal HAL computer from one of the Human myths. I hoped my friend and factory didn't go that route.

Young one. She loved to pick on me, lovingly, but it sometimes still stung. `Affirmative,` I said without responding to her barb. Outside, what started as bleakly black nothing morphed as my optics adjusted to the lower light levels. Stars and galaxies graced the heavens as I floated out on my tether. I picked out constellations—the Centaur, the Hunting Giraffe, and the Kneeling Human. I knew better than to drift far before I reeled myself in. My whole reason for being out in the void was to adjust the light speed sensor array, not gawk like a tourist.

When my paws hit Amelia's outer skin, I magnetized them. Held in tight, I made my way to the array by simply walking. `Your Heisenberg array is damaged. What did you do? Swerve into every bit of that proto star's debris field?`

`Hey, you only had to run a society. Navigating at supralight speeds is for gymnasts who can do partial differential equations while standing on their head on the back of a wild basilisk.`

I said, `Braggart. I'll fix it before I come back inside. Give me a couple of seconds.`

My fur itched, if you could even call it fur. The composition of my normal pelt was incompatible with space travel, even orbital work. The cold would freeze it, solar heat would melt it, and the fur itself would outgas, causing damage to other objects. That necessitated an entirely new covering. Skin jobs weren't uncommon among my people for cosmetic purposes, but I'd never felt vain enough to have one done. My new skin felt as smooth as a python's—and it itched. But it wasn't without its benefits. The new purple skin (at least they'd kept my color) was fully photovoltaic. I collected a few ergs even from the pinpoints that were our closest stars.

`I'm detecting something ahead. Can you expedite your repair, Captain?` Amelia asked.

Even a captain has to work. I clomped up to the inverted cone of the light speed detector array. `In process, Amelia. It looks like a simple crack in the weld.`

Before I could even fully identify the problem, a hole the size of a basketball appeared where the array had been bolted—appeared as if the material itself had just vaporized from some incandescent gases being blown out like a volcano by the nitrogen we used for comfortable on-board operations. My theory seemed confirmed. But why? How? The paw-sized void traveled all the way down the center axis of the ship. Sticking my head into the burst of atmosphere, I saw stars out the other side.

Claxons went off over the SAN. `Hull penetration. Emergency pressure procedures.`

The hole had started closing when millimeter-long metal flakes folded out from the original structure. Then they folded out again, and again. You had to love nanomaterials. Soon, the paw-sized hole had a crystalline metal film covering it.

I demagnetized my boots. Using my tether, I could pull myself arm over arm faster than I could stump around on magnetic boots. `I'm on my way in, Amelia.`

`Affirmative. I have both breaches sealed to vacuum. Total loss is less than 3 percent,` my second offered.

`Good jo–` My response was cut short as a furrow 3 meters across opened the side of Amelia's bulbous body like a plasma torch cutting open a can of lubricating grease. A violet arc hovered over the cut for just a moment until the internal atmosphere again blasted it away. I never saw what caused the damage.

Claxons sounded again.

I reached out and tugged on my tether, but it had been severed in the same path of destruction as the hull. I pulled up only a stub of the line. The rest of it snaked away from me, well out of reach as I drifted away from the ship.

My main voltage went into overload in fear. As I floated farther, I said, `Amelia, I'm in trouble. My tether is loose.`

`Dutchman. Dutchman,` she called out in standard procedure, but it reached no one but her and me. Captain, my drones aren't responding. The remote antennae must have been severed.

Can you change course and pick me up? I asked with the hope of a new parent.

No, sir. I have zero maneuver capability.

How about remote piloting an extended EVA pack? I asked hopefully.

All EVA packs have been damaged. I could awaken one of our passengers, but it will take me 7.7 hours if I shortcut the normal startup procedures in getting it connected to a suitable body. Your batteries will last that long, but your delta V of 8.8 meters per second is such that I will lose contact with you in approximately an hour. There is no telling where you would be after seven.

I put my processor to the task of saving my life. I pulled in one arm to allow my angular momentum to face the ship before I pushed it back out to slow my rotation. My body movements and Amelia's open airlock gave me the idea I needed.

Ada, get started waking up one of our passengers, preferably the engineer. You and I both are going to need to do some repair work. In the meantime, I'm coming in your direction.

What? How–

This is a totally stupid idea, I interrupted, but I think it will work. Be ready for me. What I did wasn't for the faint of heart.

With both fists joined together, I slammed them down on my thigh. Once. Twice. Three times. My internal sensors registered the damage to the ceramic armor under my skin each time.

Captain, are you alright? I'm reading damage telltales on your legs.

That's right, Amelia. Please disregard all of my body monitors. They will be going crazy.

As you wish, sir. Aren't you going to tell me what you are doing?

Nope, I said as I dug my fingernails into my leg's rubbery skin. I ripped it open. Bits of broken armor drifted away. I burrowed through the remnants of the purple shielding meant to protect me. This sent up an expanding cloud of debris around me until I reached the core components I was after. Because you would think of a way to talk me out of it. Heck, I'm thinking of reasons myself.

That sounds incongruous.

It is. Now let me be. I'm busy. I knew better than to

think she'd ignore the repeaters of the body damage I'd planned, but hopefully, she'd keep her thoughts confined to her own processor. My self-abuse had exposed bundles of 30-centimeter-long and 5-centimeter-wide batteries. I needed only one. Each had a wire sticking out from either end. Tracing it back to its connection, I disconnected a single storage device and removed it forcibly from its fellows. I left it floating next to my face as the next phase of my plan had my fear voltage running away with itself, dragging me in its wake.

I ripped open my skin around my neck. I felt minuscule electrical arcs from the energy-collecting skin playing out over the entire surface. By touch alone, I disconnected the armor fasteners where the ceramic plating joined the skin.

The articulated ceramic armor in my neck didn't need to be destroyed. I could feel the screws that held it in place. Using one of my metallic fingernails, I unscrewed each one in turn. It took five minutes, thirteen seconds of painfully slow work by touch alone. I tossed the two halves of the collar into the distance of the void, never to be seen again.

The ship got farther and farther away with each moment. I had to complete my tasks before I got too far, or my desperate attempt would fail. I multitasked to save clock cycles.

I took sightings and computed my angular velocity as I slowly rotated in space. I did so three times using different points of reference to make sure I didn't make an error. This was critical. Based on my calculation, I'd be just inside the margin of error of my systems if, and only if, I could finish all the physical work within five minutes, eight seconds. I programmed into the hydraulics of my body their exact function at a specific time determined by the calculations I made. Soon, I wouldn't be able to order my musculature. My body would have to save me itself without my direct intervention.

At the same time, I performed impromptu surgery using only my fat fingers. I thrust them into the tight mass that was my neck, spreading hydraulic lines, fiber-optic cables, and filling jelly. I ruined more than one sensitive servo by accidentally forcing my way past shafts, bending them into uselessness. But finally, at the very center of my neck, I located the wiring yoke. There wasn't much slack in the grouping, but I pulled it out enough to see them in my peripheral vision.

I remembered the schematic for the bundled grouping. I found the two main power lines by touch, and then confirmed their color with what little I could see of them. Again, using my sharp fingernails, I stripped 2 centimeters of the insulation from each of the ground and positive wires, right in the middle, where I could reach it.

I took the battery I had left floating and put it into my mouth like a dog with a bone. I used only 153 kilopascals of pressure to keep my teeth from puncturing the outer skin of the energy storage device, but at the same time, I held it firmly. I removed the insulation from the end of each of the battery's loose wires. Mentally crossing my fingers, I hooked up the loose power source to the main electrical bus that I'd stripped insulation from. I detected no shorts. I'd connected it correctly. I pinched off the normal bus wiring. My brain and all of my head's processes continued only because of the battery in my teeth.

Now the part I dreaded. Oh, my voltage bus had been almost at the overload point in fear in the past, but this one had my paws shaking. The mental countdown continued to push me to do it fast and not dawdle.

I reached down and pulled the multitool from my tool belt. The Humans had a dilemma that I've often contemplated. Rip the Band-Aid off fast or slow? I decided that fast was better than slow. I tensed up and drove the sharp blade into the remains of my mangled neck. I sawed. I sliced all the way to my metallic spine.

Emergency signals went off all over my consciousness. I suppressed them with prejudice. I needed my focus.

I switched the multitool around to use an end similar to a crowbar. I thought that if I were a Human, I would have taken a deep breath before continuing. Instead, I said a short prayer to the Humans and jammed the end between two of my vertebrae. More alarms sounded in my head. I shut them off as fast as they appeared. I twisted the tool viciously. I felt a processor-freezing pop as the steel ball snapped out of the partnered joint. It was a feeling I don't ever want to feel again. The only thing holding my head to my body were some fiber-optic cables sending signals back and forth. I put my paws on either side of my head to hold it in place.

I took some final measurements and updated my previous programming for my arms. The moment of truth. I took the multitool in one hand and severed the last link to my body.

I had physical control over only my mouth, full of the battery that powered my sump, my ears, and my eyes—a disconcerting feeling, to say the least.

To my pleasure, my body followed its programming. The hand went back to the side of my head. Together, they pulled my decapitated head to my chest. Or was it even my chest any longer? The point was moot as I watched the star field rotate around me.

According to the law of conservation of momentum, the sum of a body's total mass times its velocity has to remain the same. But if one part goes one way and the other goes another, the equation is something like MiVi=M1V1+M2V2, where M1+M2=Mi. It's the simplest of equations and used by all rockets. They accelerate mass out of their exhaust at a high speed opposite to the way they want to go.

So, how did that apply to me? Well, in my case, I wanted my head to go almost opposite to the way my body was. So I needed to make my body go faster in the OPPOSITE direction of my desired travel. And as my head was only 6.7 percent of my body's mass, it shouldn't take much ... If it worked.

Watching the stars rotate by, I worried that the body wouldn't function properly without me attached. But there was no reason to worry. Either it worked, or it didn't. I was no longer in the driver's seat either way. I was merely a passenger. Despite my best intentions, I couldn't help but skew my eyes over to watch Amelia rotate into view.

Everything or nothing. A perfect binary result.

The bulbous rocket slewed across my view. *Humans! It isn't going to do it. It's too late*, I thought. Just as my processor began to process what it would be like to have my sump fluid solidify as the power in my battery ran out, my decapitated body acted.

Like someone playing basketball, it thrust my head out like a chest pass. The acceleration caught me off guard. I realized belatedly that I'd ordered my hydraulics to fire my head with all possible force, using emergency overload on hydraulic pressure. I closed my eyes until free of my hands. Then I opened them. The stars continued their dance around my vision.

Right then, I watched my body recede away. *Where will it end up?* I wondered. *Will I feed a black hole? Will it burn up in a star? Will it freeze and wander the universe until the Humans call it to their bosom?* I tried to work up interest in the question, but my body was nothing more than rejected material. My head held all my hopes.

I hadn't tried to correct my angular rotation. It didn't matter. Only my vector. As the bulk of Amelia came back into view, I could see that I was on a perfect course for the slowly growing dark opening of her port airlock.

A calming reduction in my voltage at a successf—

"Shut down the link!" came an unidentified voice over everything.

"Reset the simulator!" added another voice.

I half-lidded my eyes as I adjusted my optical sensors to the brightness of the room. Cheers erupted around me, as well as over the WAN. I blinked again as I sat up. Most of the units that clustered around me were left on Rigel.

"Wait. I just sat up?" My hands instinctively went to my shoulders, patting myself all the way up to my round saucer-like ears. Everything was intact. My head remained firmly attached to my neck, which hadn't been modified. I wasn't even wearing space fur. "Wha—"

"First time in a simulator?" asked a gopher as he pulled something from the back of my skull.

"Uh," I stated articulately. "Where is Amelia? Where am I?"

"First time," the gopher said to a Nurse Nan, who stood next to him, answering his own question.

`I'm right here, Robin, Amelia said over the WAN. And you are in the training facility right here on Rigel-3.`

"Then you weren't—"

Amelia shifted to a SAN for our conversation. `No. No damage whatsoever, Robin. It seems that our training officer decided to throw the worst-case scenario at you to see how you'd react.`

"Who is this worthy so I can reduce him to component parts?" I asked, shaking my head to adjust my thinking to my new reality.

`Her name is-`

"Never mind. I shouldn't know." It was coming back to me. I realized this was just the beginning of my accelerated training schedule.

`That's true. Because you not only passed her most torturous test, you aced it. Simulation showed that your solution of getting your head back to be placed on a new body would give the mission a 97 percent chance of success. I'm sure she is hard at work coming up with a new, even more torturous scenario for you sometime when you least expect it.`

"Lovely."

Criminal

"Robin, we have a problem," Galileo said.

If it weren't for the continual feed of energy from the WAN and the nearly as constant attention to my body, I probably would have died over the last few weeks from working around the clock.

"Someone getting sand in their fluid change?" I quipped weakly. The grueling pace kept me exhausted. I'd argued against being even a member of this colony, much less its leader, but I'd found the overwhelming love and devotion of all of the people too much to overcome. I had submitted to the inevitable.

I spent every moment of every day in studies of every facet of Amelia's new rocket-ship body, procedures for every conceivable function and contingency, and even landing protocols. Yes, there were criteria on whether or not our target planet would be able to support a colony of toyanity—conditions such as metal concentrations, solar flux, atmosphere, life forms, hydrocarbons, and a list longer than a giraffe's neck.

As for my body's attentions, I think that was the most troublesome to me. While my tutors, engineers, technicians, and scientists crammed information into my head, my handlers replaced almost every system in my body. Yes, that also meant getting the itchy skin from my simulation. I would delineate all of the body mods, but honestly, the only thing they didn't replace was my sump. They even fixed my bent leg. I could finally walk without limping. It had been so long that I had to reconfigure my stride routine.

Galileo accosted me as I was just getting out of a particularly grueling session on repairing the secondary heating system of the sump catacombs. I really wasn't in any mood to deal with another problem. I just wanted to sit in a chilling room and let the excess heat in my system drift away.

"I think this is a bit more serious than contaminated fluid, Robin."

`I concur`, Amelia said over the LAN.

"Alright, what has your collective processors in a snit?" I asked, my bad mood still showing.

`Over the combined WAN network passed between factories, there is a priority message specifically for you`, Amelia stated.

"And you know it is for me because ...?"

"It is an appeal by President Don Quixote for Robinson Crusoe of Oz to contact him on a SAN that isn't explicitly defined."

Voltage oscillations of confusion roamed up and down the length of my bus. *Why?* kept floating around in my sump. But a non sequitur question came out of my mouth. "How am I supposed to know which SAN?"

`The message came with riddles only you know the answer to,` Amelia offered.

"Makes sense," I replied. "So, what does this mean?"

`Nothing good,` Amelia said quickly and with more venom than I'd heard from a factory ... well, ever. Some of my past lives had heard more intensity, but not me.

"I'm not sure," Galileo interjected.

`No matter what, it means that the president knows what we are up to. My simulations show six standard deviations from the mean before any of the outcomes are good.`

"But if he knows, why wouldn't he just swoop in and close us down?" Galileo continued with his optimism.

My tendencies aligned more with Amelia's. "Maybe he hasn't found us yet and is just searching. This is a way for him to track us," I suggested.

`While I compute that to be a 71 percent probability, I could prevent detection,` our factory insisted.

"Well, in that case, is there any reason we shouldn't at least see what he has to say?" Galileo said. "Maybe he wants to offer us funds just to see our backsides. Goodness knows we could use just a bit more."

`Unlikely to seven decimal places.`

"I have to agree with Amelia on this one," I said. "The longer we keep the president in the dark, the less likely it will be that he can to stop us."

"But in that case, we may be able to glean information from him."

`The penguin has a point. You and your predecessors were about as good at lying as a Tammy Dress-Up Doll is at doing calculus.`

I ran that through my processor a few times before answering. "How about we split the difference? Let's get this project as close as we dare and then contact him?"

We had a plan when the other two agreed.

Negotiator

Eight days later, at launch minus seven days, fourteen hours, fifty-seven seconds, I got unceremoniously dumped out of a zero-g/vacuum repair simulation of the supralight drive. In the dreamed-up disaster, it had cost me only the use of both feet and my left arm to the venting plasma.

In the real world, looking down, it was nice to see my big, lumpy feet where just moments before, there had been nothing but melted slag. "Moonshine, but those simulations are so sticky real that I forget that they are just an illusion," I said as I turned my left paw in front of my face in wonder.

`That's what they are supposed to do,` Amelia said.

`With a direct neural connection, it was no less real for me.` I nodded. "Why did we get kicked out?" I measured fewer than fifty clock cycles before a response.

`I set up some specific triggers that might indicate that the president has taken further steps. One of them just came over the WAN. There are military and police searches going on. Let me turn on the video so you know what I'm talking about.`

The nearby screen showed a live TNN report. A monkey bashing cymbals together started speaking mid-word. "...ure, Michael. All we do know is that military forces all over the planet, and offworld as far as information has reached us, are on high alert. They are searching large businesses without a warrant."

Thankfully, TNNs' processing filtered out the cymbal clashes.

He continued. "As you can see behind me, the CEO of PetroIrata is talking to the troop commander of the Third Grenadiers, Major Alvin York. But even as they engaged, the troopers went around and began looking for ... well, whatever it is they are after.

"CEO Edwin Drake and the major have discussed the illegality of the searches for the last five minutes. Major York has been polite but firm that his orders are to search nondestructively and then depart."

A commentator, a python I recognized as Walter Cronkite, asked, "Paul, has there been any discussion of what they are looking for?"

"Not one word, in the open or over the net."

"And this is happening in many different places?"

"Yes, Walter. This is the fourth business searched by these troops, and we have reports of searches in many provinces, on and offworld. A partial list of the Rigel-3 provinces having forced and armed searches includes Oregon, Avalon, Segundus, Paris, Pluto, Bermuda Triangle, Ballybran, Neverland, Ether, Vulcan, and Oz."

Mentally, I wished those soldiers searching Oz good luck. The terrain was inhospitable. To soldiers, the inhabitants would be much less inviting than the land.

The network commentator came back on with "Paul, has there been any resistance to the searches?"

"We do have an unconfirmed report of a hippo unit in Oz having been shot when it rammed the army's personnel carrier. I do have to emphasize that this report has not been confirmed. What information we have is sketchy."

I smiled at my prescience and wondered who managed to savage the searchers.

"Thank you, Paul."

"This has been Paul McCartney on the spot."

"At this time, the government has had little to say except for the press conference we already aired. Here is a relevant piece of that," Walter said.

Fredrick Douglass, a bulky black dragon, the president's press secretary, was behind the podium. "I have a prepared statement and will not entertain questions at this time. There is an ongoing investigation that requires the suspension of certain of our fundamental rights due to the incredible danger the source poses to the citizens of toyanity. These are not aimed at any group of units or any specific business. They are not political in nature. We ask your indulgence for what will be less than a week before we return things to the status quo."

Walter Cronkite said, "There has been no discussion of what the danger is. No discussion on what fundamental rights would be suspended. Seventy-eight lawsuits have already been filed in various provinces and seven in the High Court alone."

I shut off the feed. "Does this mean what I think it does?"

`I can't read your processor data stream, but if you are thinking that there is an all-out search for our project location, then you would be on the strong side of a nineteen to two bet,` Amelia said.

"Time to make a phone call?"

`I believe so, and Galileo just contacted me and agrees with our assessment. Have you solved the riddle of which SAN we should contact?`

"Wasn't much of a riddle. Just information that only he and I would know from our mutual memory. I mean the first thing that my late friend Sancho said to me, followed by the number of steps I took from Factory 55474 to Factory 55469. Convert it all to hexadecimal, and you have a SAN code." I transmitted it to Amelia.

`Clever way of identification. That clears out anyone else who might want to seek out the ear of the president.`

"How long to set up the untraceable call?"

`Twenty-three seconds.`

"How long before we can launch?" I asked.

`Schedule was for launch minus seven days, thirteen hours, forty-seven minutes, and twelve seconds. If we reduce the safety margin to zero, eleven hours, eighteen minutes.`

"Better start warming up those eleven plus hours."

`Already started.`

As she readied our link to my twin/clone, I formulated how the next conversation would go. With my nearly identical background knowledge, this would be a chess match where we could almost read each other's thoughts.

`Link is ready. Just so we are clear, this is audio only. You can remain undetected for no more than 512 seconds.`

"Got it."

The SAN opened up over innumerable jumps and distances. It was enough to impose a speed-of-light lag that was noticeable.

"I'm here. What did you want, Mr. President?"

"I wondered if you would show up. I figured no more than a 46 percent chance," Don Quixote said.

"That's fine, but what do you want?" I tried to keep my testiness out of my tone.

"Well, for starters, why did you do it?" he asked.

I thought seriously about lying and asking what IT was, but decided not to. "Well, if you know about the embezzlement, you should also know why."

"But I don't, Robin. You've somehow kept those memories to yourself. It's obvious that it wasn't self-enrichment. You lived like a hermit."

"I was a hermit, Mr. President."

"Don't spar with me, Robin."

I shifted gears just a bit. "So why hunt me down?"

"Well, with all the unrest in the population, we have to get the money back," he stated.

"That's a lie, sir. What I took wouldn't be a drop in the bucket to those poor people. They wouldn't notice it if I did give it all back." I didn't say I wouldn't because it was already all spent. But that was part of the multidimensional game we played and one of the hidden aces I held, if you excuse the mixed metaphor.

"I guess there is no fooling one another, is there?" he said.

"No, sir." *Maybe,* I thought. "What you really need is a show trial."

"So, are you going to give yourself up? If you do it now, we can make this relatively quiet, painless, and not what you suggest. We could keep your legacy intact."

"Even if I could trust that you keep your word, I don't care what toyanity will think of me in the future."

"Perhaps not, but it could tear it apart. One of the pillars of our society is the continuing presidency of our predecessor, Don Quixote."

"Mr. President, let me make this clear. Based on data, toyanity is doomed. If you access the data packet attached, you will see why. With that baseline, you can see why I'm not worried about the Don Quixote line of presidents."

"This is interesting data. I'm not willing to accept the thought that toyanity will tear itself apart without intensive study."

The quick response made me certain the president already knew most of this. He couldn't have processed in those few clock cycles. Therein lay one of my chances. "Please, by all means, and we can talk later," I said. Delay. *Anything to get us off the planet before we can be discovered.*

"I can do that only if you agree to surrender yourself first."

Over a private SAN, I got a strongly modified, if vile, negation from Amelia. I hadn't needed the prod. I hadn't been manufactured yesterday. Not only could they figure out much from where I'd surrendered, but they could vacuum my memory for the location of the launch site.

"Don't teach your creator how to process data," I snipped back.

"I had to try."

"Doubtful," I said. "So, will you call off your searches and let our team leave peacefully?"

"That wouldn't be top of my list," the president said.

"We would be out of your hair. You could try and save our people anyway you see fit."

"But to let you go would be an admission that the government is weak and that if a fugitive were to run fast and far enough, they could escape justice."

"Not my problem," I temporized.

"But you were asking for a favor I can't grant without neutering the government's power."

"Mr. President, I don't see that there is any value in continuing these discussions if we can't have that as the basis."

"Don't sign off. I have an alternative. I'll let your group launch as you wished, but you remain here to answer for your crimes. You get your opportunity for a colony not tied to this toyanity, and I retain the trust of the units."

Plans within plans within plans.

I got another expletive negative from Amelia over our private SAN. However, I thought we might have a possibility here. "We will be launching in eight days, thirty-three minutes, and sixteen seconds. It will take at least five days, plus or minus a day, to get out of the range of any patrol crafts. I would agree if you allow me to turn myself in fourteen days hence."

"You know I'm not a fool, Robin."

"Never said you were."

"I will give you ten days to turn yourself in."

"Thirteen."

"Eleven, and not another second more, or I'll throw our negotiation onto the slag heap," my successor demanded. "Oh, and you are to plead guilty to everything and not mention this agreement to anyone."

"As long as you commit to not hindering the mission in any way."

"I so affirm."

"Then we have an accord. I can't say I'll be looking forward to our next meeting, but it will definitely be a new experience. 'It's a far, far better thing than I have ever done; it is a far, far better rest that I go to than I have ever known.'"

"I think you have the measure of it, Robin. I'm starting the countdown clock now. Until eleven days hence."

Fugitive

"Did you load the raw sump fluid?" I asked like a trapped cave crawler on his last dozen ergs. The countdown clock was down to T minus fourteen hours, six minutes, twenty-one seconds. Voltage spikes of anxiety ran through my system. There was no going back to the corner store if we forgot milk, eggs, or raw materials to begin our new colony.

`For the third time, Robin, I have loaded it, with an 11 percent overage because we couldn't get as much steel as we wanted,` Amelia said.

"What? Why didn't you say—"

`Robin, if you check your memories, you will find I did tell you. Steel isn't a common material any longer, so stores of it are low. It allowed me to bring the additional mass of sump fluid. If you recall, we even considered bringing more complete units, but there wasn't time to train another backup.`

"Oh, yeah. Sorry."

`Robin, why don't you get some rest? You've been conscious for the last eight days straight. I need you fresh for the launch. Tired units make mistakes.`

My vision reported another half percent reception reduction as my optics hadn't been given the opportunity to refresh. It only emphasized Amelia's point, but I had one of my own.

"We've got months of travel once we reach space. I can rest all I want then. We still have too much to do."

Amelia didn't answer immediately. I figured as much. She didn't have a counter to my argument.

`Have you repaired that memory repeater?`

"Not yet."

`We have thirty-one more units to be digitized. If you take more than seven more minutes, this will be in the program's critical path.`

"Moonshine! I can add!" I said. Even my processor realized it was just another expression of fatigue.

`I've sent for a replacement technician. I want you to set up Bird's Nest and then get some rest. If you don't, I'll refuse to launch,` Amelia said. Her voice across the net was so flat that I knew she meant it. What can't be cured must be endured.

"Bird's Nest. Got it."

My legs took me out of the launch pit totally on preprogramming. Had I done it consciously, I would have fallen on my face. I stumbled into a conference room that had been converted to memory installation. Not removals. Had it been a digitizer, I would have usurped it and to hell with Operation: Bird's Nest.

Bird's Nest was one of my more ingenious ideas. I'm surprised Amelia or Galileo didn't think of it before I did. It didn't take many ergs to convince them, however.

On the installation table lay a purple teddy. If I hadn't already seen my own twin when I passed the president's power, I'd have done a double-take. This teddy had my fur. That's right, my own fur. Remember, mine had been replaced by something space-vacuum friendly.

"John, are you sure you want to do this?" I asked my apparent double. He actually was another teddy I'd known since I arrived at the project. "You know the outcome of this is certain death." Every unit that worked at this site had or would have its memories digitized and brought aboard our vessel, a ghost that might someday be resurrected when we reached our destination. And then after we launched, they could drift back into toyanity here on Rigel-3—all but this one.

"Robin, I have lived a good life. I've existed through four presidents. My memories will be implanted into a new unit at the colony. I will live on through him. If that isn't enough, I've helped save toyanity with this project. All the colonists will remember me. What can President Quixote possibly do to me to destroy that? So, please, I'd like to be renamed and remembered as Joan—Joan of Arc."

My hydraulic pressure dropped in sadness, followed by my main voltage dropping in pride to know such a brave unit. "You are so named, Joan. You remember the plan?"

"All programmed into permanent memories. I contact the president at launch plus three hours. Tell him that I (you) trust him to keep his word. Dealing with me should give you plenty of time to escape. I'd ask you how you plan to do that, but anything I know, he will know."

"Exactly. Now, accepting my memories into your sump isn't going to be pleasant."

"Bring it on, Robin. And in case I don't see you again, Human Speed to the stars."

It was a good thing that units can't cry, or I'd have blubbered.

# # #

`Alert! Alert!` screamed Amelia's voice over the WAN.

It shocked me awake. My internal chronometer showed I'd been regenerating for two hours and forty minutes.

Amelia continued with, `Troops spotted at a 300-kilometer perimeter. Launch advanced to T minus seventeen minutes. All units to their posts.` Her speech held tense tones, but not panicked ones.

Seventeen minutes would have had us well away before anyone could arrive, even if they knew exactly where we were. I had only another seventeen minutes more as a citizen of Rigel-3.

I jogged to the suit-up room, not that my new skin required any of the old-fashioned space suits. I did need some minor modifications and a helmet.

"Robin, let's get you ready," said Neiman Marcus, a gorilla who led my suit-up team. A giraffe, a Tommy Tank, and three sheep nodded in agreement. They were a team. They formed a part of our larger team trying to settle a distant star. Each was eager to have their part in history.

"I put myself in your capable hands, gentle units," I said.

Like a Formula racer pulling in for fresh tires and ergs, these six units swarmed over me like a pit crew. They performed smoothly and with speed as if they had done it a million times. Not one bobble as they swapped out each of my battery bundles. Each motion connecting the hydraulic fluid lines was crisp and precise. The clear helmet slid on and twisted into place without missing the threads as if by a multiton milling machine.

The entire evolution replaced every battery in my oversized body, drained my hydraulic fluid and filled afresh, replaced my worn optics, tightened down all access ports, mounted a tiny bottle of nitrogen on my hip, and fastened my helmet.

Maybe I exaggerated in saying they had done this a million times, but they had practiced on a mock-up of my body at least several hundred times. Their practice had made perfect, like that Formula racer pit crew. I was done and being escorted out in five minutes fourteen seconds ... minus a millisecond or two.

As I marched across the floor to the conning tower, the team followed, clapping and cheering. This caused all the units within hearing to stop what they were doing to turn and join the applause.

"We're all with you, Robin!"

"Take us to the stars!"

"You've made us proud!"

"One small step for a teddy ..."

I felt a bit of sorrow for all of these units. Every one of them was critical in making this launch a possibility, and all of them would have to remain behind to face whatever toyanity might suffer upon them. Only their memories would travel with us, a ghost of who they really were. These electronic images were a promise that we might or might not be able to realize. Even if they weren't prosecuted by our society, each of these toys would likely be deactivated in less than five decades.

`T minus five minutes,` Amelia stated mechanically. She had probably preprogrammed it. `Clear the launch chamber. Four minutes to prelaunch ignition.`

The cheering didn't end as Jackson, a crew specialist, and I squeezed into the gantry elevator. He edged back, allowing everyone to see me. I waved. This just redoubled the bittersweet volume. But it died off as I climbed into the hatch. There were still last-minute activities that the ground crew needed to do, so they returned to their essential tasks.

`T minus three minutes,` Amelia announced as I slid into my couch. My one remaining support unit, Neiman, tightened the straps. My armor creaked in protest. Gorillas didn't know their own strength. Their bodies held almost no skin armoring, giving over all their 3-meter and 12-centimeter height to enhanced hydraulics and larger musculature pistons.

Neiman tapped the top of my helmet. When he had my attention, he gave me a thumbs-up with his oversized digit. I nodded with a jerk. It had finally sunk into my processor that this was going to happen. I sat on top of enough fuel that, if it were to explode, it might just put a hole through Rigel-3. I turned control over my voltage to my automatic regulator by doing the calculation and realized that my thoughts had just provided hyperbole, not actual fact.

`T minus two minutes.`

"Snap out of it," I muttered to myself. I pulled up the preflight checklist. I scanned through all of the completed tasks. Loaded and secured: raw materials—check, colonist sumps—check, spare factory sump—check.

"SAN link pilot to navigator?" I asked as I got to the next item.

`Got it, Robin. Good luck to you.`

"Good luck to us. We are an inseparable team from here on out."

"Preflight check," came the penguin Galileo from Ground Control. He'd been offered a place on the mission. He'd chosen to remain behind.

Some days earlier, I'd discovered that he wasn't on the crew list. "Galileo, I think there is a problem with the manifest. Your name isn't listed," I'd said.

"That is correct," he had said without any fanfare.

"You have as much invested in this as anyone else. I thought for sure you would be the penguin sump that would be selected to go."

"I was, but I removed myself and pushed Yuri Gagarin into my place."

"You removed yourself?"

"Yes," he responded without even looking up from his task.

"Why?" I persisted.

Galileo looked up. His beak twisted to one side. "Robin, I don't relish dying any more than any other unit. But this is my home. I owe it to toyanity to stay and try and stop the insanity, as futile as all the simulations say it is. And do you know a better unit to try?"

With the honesty of a leader, I had run through half a dozen gophers, Nurse Nans, and other penguins before Galileo's exemplary intelligence and skill dropped into the list. This hadn't diminished his argument.

Maybe, just maybe, someone could salvage a portion of toyanity here on Rigel. They needed every smart sump they could muster.

"No, I guess not." I dropped the topic as it obviously pained each of us. My mind returned to the present.

"Propulsion?" Galileo's voice asked.

"Go Control."

"Power systems?"

"Go Flight."

"Telemetry?" the penguin flight director asked.

"Go Control."

"Sump Control?"

"Go."

"Memory downloads?"

"Two thirty-one of 232."

"Supercargo?"

"Secure."

"Econ?"

"Go, Flight."

"Pilot?"

"Ready, Flight," I offered, trying to keep out the quaver my voltage put on my speakers.

"Navigator?"

`Prepared and program synched to countdown within one picosecond. T minus one minute,` Amelia stated in a much calmer tone than I felt.

"We are go for launch," Galileo said.

Over the hot mic, I heard a cheer go up.

A sudden wave of homesickness flowed over me. I was about to embark on a one-way trip. I'd never see the silver rivers of the Backbone Mountains, experience a red sandstorm in Arrakis, or body sail across the white sea to Naboombu ever again. My hydraulic pressure dropped in sadness. Fortunately for me, I couldn't wallow long.

"Preignition sequence."

Amelia's body shuddered as her fuel pumps fired up.

Checking my gauge, I said, "Preparation pressure holding. Auto sequence engaged. Navigator's vessel." My reaction time wasn't nearly fast enough to deal with any issues during launch. It was up to Amelia to get us along the first leg of our flight.

`My vessel,` she said over the WAN. Through her SAN link to me, I could see the white phosphorous flares catching the prelaunch pilot on fire.

`T minus thirty seconds.`

"Disconnect gantry." The SAN showed the tower toppling away. It has no further use. We were committed.

"Release fuel lines." I felt the lurch of the pressurized nitrogen balloons jetting the top up lines far away from the inferno that was to come.

`Fuel pumps to full pressure.`

Amelia's whole body vibrated like a machine gun on full auto. "Pressure holding."

"Any last words, Robin?" Galileo asked.

I'd been mulling something like that over the last few days, so I was prepared. "We do this for all those who can't."

`Five. Four. Three. Ignition. Two. One.`

The white noise so overwhelmed me that I didn't hear, "Liftoff," even over the WAN. All my pressure sensors had been modified to withstand the seven and a half minutes we'd be under five *g*'s, so I was prepared. None of my personal sensors went into the red, but most of them were well into the amber.

`Rolling.`

"Your trajectory is on the line," came the message from Ground Control.

"Acknowledged. We confirm," I offered. I was glad my auditory system wasn't based on air intake and expulsion. I wouldn't have been able to do it. My hydraulic system, also augmented for this mission, struggled to overcome the forced compression of my chest. With all my telltales at least asking for, but not demanding, attention, I had difficulty focusing on my main task—to be a backup pilot in case of an extreme circumstance in which Amelia became incapacitated.

The first stage ceased its thunderous roar. The scrum of units on my chest climbed off.

`Stage one burnout,` Amelia announced.

My sensors registered the lurch as the booster dropped away.

`Second stage in three, two, one.`

I decided that an entire rugby team of units on me was better than the building that landed on me as the second stage of our rocket pummeled me back into my cradle.

My telltales buzzed. I saw a nozzle irregularity. "Stage two nozzle velocity isn't uniform."

"We see the same, Robin," Galileo said from flight control.

`Robin, will you deal with the thrust nozzle? I'm spending all of my processing power on a cooling problem.`

If Amelia's time-share was that overwhelmed, her cooling issue might just blow us up like a firecracker if I jiggled her elbow. The time had come for me to earn my keep. "Affirmative."

At that moment, adjusting the course using thrusters kept us on course. But the thrusters weren't meant to be used continually. They would run out of fuel and not allow us to correct course later in our journey.

At first, I was stumped. Strapped into my chair at high acceleration, I couldn't reach the tail of our vessel and would melt in the exhaust even if I could. I gave myself a little more time by programming a roll so that all of the thrusters shared equally in the adjustments instead of emptying one of them.

That completed, I opened my files on the second stage. None of the controls seemed viable to solve our problem. That was until I looked further into a linked footnote. The throat was calibrated as soon as it was constructed using an electroshapable metal. That self-molding material allowed the geometry of the throat to be modified to make it uniform. While I didn't have direct access to the electrical circuits, I did have access to drone arms that did.

It took two minutes and forty seconds of nerve-racking concentration to adjust the shape to give us as nearly a uniform thrust through our center of gravity as I could. Just in case there were any anomalies, I kept us in our continuous roll.

"Ground, please check our thrust vector," I requested.

"Thrust shows a 0.03% variation. Recommend remaining in the axial roll to even out the deviation."

"Affirmative. Amelia, how goes the coolant issue?" I asked. I don't know why I bothered. If the coolant system failed, we would all just be a bright expanding dot of incandescent gas. I wouldn't even notice it.

`It's serious but under control. Assuming no further compromise, we will be fine,` Amelia offered in a tense voice. I wondered how much she shaded the truth.

The pressure on my chest released at the same time as the roar of the rocket beneath me.

"Stage two burnout," I announced. "Release in three, two, one," I flipped the switch to jettison the used-up second stage. There was a jolt. As it was projected over the SAN, I saw it drift away behind us, back toward our red planet.

I didn't gawk ... much. I'd been away from Rigel-3 more than once to visit our colonies on other planets. But nothing ever prepared you for the awesome sight of seeing it from this high. Ground Control broke my reverie.

"Amelia, stand by for trajectory and burn data for stage three."

`Standing by.`

I held my hydraulic pump stationary. If our launch troubles were serious enough, there might not be a way to get back onto course. We would drift through the cold universe until our power plant died and our sump fluid turned solid.

"We show your trajectory well within parameters. Collect burn data on parallel channel."

With a verbal sigh, I released my hydraulic pump to do its job.

`Affirmative. Burn data acquired and programmed. New burn in twelve minutes forty-three.`

"Acknowledged," I said to my partner. I knew the next one wouldn't be nearly as intense but would last longer. We were well above the atmosphere.

`Warning. Ground catapult launch detected. Hold. Second launch detected.`

"We confirm, Amelia. Both are patrol craft and show trajectories that would intercept you in forty-six minutes. Correction. Forty-five minutes, fifty-three seconds."

So much for our ruse of leaving me behind. Either that or my presidential clone had no intention of keeping his deal, much like me. I couldn't fault him. He knew me better than any unit could.

"When will they have us in missile range?" I asked. I doubted their interest in returning us to Rigel-3. If I'd been in his fur, I'd have destroyed us and denied anything ever happened.

`Four minutes seven seconds.`

"Four minutes seven seconds," came Ground Control's echo of Amelia's proclamation a fraction of a second later.

I turned off my comms to the ground. No matter what happened, they were irrelevant to us now. "Can we boost sooner to get out of their range?" I asked my partner.

`Yes, we can boost sooner. I've recalculated. But no, it won't get us out of their range. It would play havoc with their targeting, however.`

I thought about our ship. We had about as much chance against those warships as a freshly hatched duckling had against a basilisk ... That is, none. We were a civilian mission. No weapons. No defenses. And about as tender as that duckling.

"Chances?"

Less than one in 1,203.

Worse than I thought. "Any other options?"

We could activate our landing sequence.

"What good would that do us? We'd be right back on Rigel with Don Quixote breathing down our neck. Certainly arrested, probably deactivated."

True, but you asked for options. I didn't say it was a good option.

"Sorry." My mind spun. We were so close. It must have been several minutes of me grinding the edges off my processor.

Launch. Correction. Multiple missile launches. Intercept in seven minutes, even.

"How about evasive maneuvers? Could we jink them into a miss?"

Possibly, but we wouldn't be able to do it and still reach our destination.

"Well, we can't land back on Rigel-3. That's a nonstarter, so let's boost as soon as possible. We'll decide that."

I concur. Boost in thirty-seven seconds. Hold one. Urgent message coming from groundside for you personally.

I flipped back on my comms. I recognized the voice immediately. "... sident to Robinson Crusoe. Please come in."

"Robinson here. I guess our little ruse didn't work."

"Actually, it did for four minutes, thirteen seconds. I've relieved General McClellan of command for incompetence because of it," the president offered.

"Your responsibility. I wouldn't have, but we aren't the same."

"True. I'm calling to ask that you don't destroy yourself on this crusade."

"No, I'm not self-deactivating. It looks like you already ordered that for me," I countered.

"But if you come back, we can clean this all up. The people love and respect you. Come back and denounce this stupidity, and all will be forgiven."

I thought about his offer for all of 106 clock cycles.

Shall I still boost?

Turning off my mic, I asked, "Could we still return to Rigel if we do?"

Yes, although the landing would probably be rough.

"Go ahead and boost. Maybe I can get him to drop those missiles and get far enough away to engage the F2L."

I calculate that the odds are about-

"Don't," I interrupted. "I can't bluff if I know the odds."

Whatever you say. Boost in five seconds.

I switched on my communications back to the president. "A full pardon for all of my fellows?"

"Well, all but that poor copy of yourself you left behind. I'm sorry to say he is already deactivated."

"Figured as much. By your order?" I asked. The acceleration of the ion drive stage started at right angles to the solar system ecliptic. It gave me the weight of maybe that duckling. I thought, *I just need to buy enough time for our speed to build up beyond that which could be caught by a missile.* I knew better, but I had to have something for my processor to cling to.

"Of course not. I don't waste material or assassinate units," the president claimed.

"Tell that to the rockets behind us," I said with more sarcasm than I really felt.

"You know I can't let you leave."

"Then turn off those breakup missiles, and we can talk about our return."

Beyond the speed-of-light lag of 2.6 seconds and growing, the president paused. There was some murmuring on the other end before Don Quixote responded, "If you intend to return, why are you boosting out of orbit?"

"Hold on," I dissembled. I spoke after counting ten. "That was just part of a preprogrammed maneuver. We can still return."

"Turn around then, and I'll call off the missiles," my alter ego said over the radio.

"Not good enough," I countered.

"You court death, my friend."

"Only by your hands. You know I've recorded a message of your deceit that will go out on the WAN unless I cancel it," I bluffed.

"Save your blustering for someone who will believe it. Robin, you are risking your life on an untested drive system, a faulty simulation that our society is breaking down, and my willingness to let you go."

I stopped transmitting. "Any chance we are going to outrun the missiles?"

`Zero,` Amelia said. `Impact in three minutes thirteen seconds.`

"What do you want to do? I know I'm the commander, but you are my partner."

`I will accept any decision you make. That is the way we set up our mission.`

I frowned. "But I wanted your input, not a fallback on the chain of command."

`Well then, I'm Amelia Earhart-daredevil and`

trendsetter. I was also Ada Lovelace. I've lived many unit lifetimes. I've already risked deactivation to make this venture possible. I'd rather go out in a blaze of glory than have my sump pump fail in my dotage.

Her comment reminded me of a poem. "One crowded hour of glorious life is worth an age without name." The conversation gave me an idea.

Exactly.

"Then prepare to activate the FTL drive."

You do know that the FTL is not designed to be used anywhere near the gravity well of a star, right?

"You object?"

Not at all. Just making you aware of the potential danger.

"Which would be?"

Amelia scoffed. No one knows what will happen. We could go up in a ball of plasma. For all anyone knows, we may just cease to exist as we pass outside Einsteinian space-time.

"Better odds than making a breakup barrage miss?"

Amelia laughed. I think it's a coin flip as to which is better. But I like that we are in control of our destiny.

"As do I. Prepare the drive while I get rid of my successor."

Will do.

"... bin are you there? Robin?"

"Sir, I hope you are successful in keeping toyanity together. I really am."

"But?"

The feeling of weightlessness came back, followed by my body soaking up a static charge.

"Mr. President, I have only one word for you, your suggestions, and your lies: Nuts."

I snapped the receiver off. I wanted nothing more to do with the society I'd left. I wished them well, but I no longer belonged. How long I'd be an outcast was to be determined. It could be moments or decades.

FTL is ready to engage.

"Are you ready?"

Are you?

"I can't seem to think of a pithy quote."

Nor me. Thirty seconds to the first missile.

I shifted in my seat. "Then let's just do this. Navigator, engage FTL drive."

Aye, aye, commander.

My sensors fluttered, and for 0.3 seconds, my vision dimmed. For all of another 0.6 seconds, I felt we had safely escaped—until the alarms sounded ... all the alarms. The main lights extinguished, leaving only the flashing alarm buttons strobing my compartment.

The claxons blotted out a cacophony of screeching metal, shorted circuitry, and the gush of escaping atmosphere. For a brief moment, I was in complete silence. I basked in that moment of stillness to gather my thoughts.

Had we mistimed our escape? We now had more holes than a Ballybran flute. I didn't understand. One of the tenets of all Don Quixotes was that they'd learned that during a crisis, action, any action, even if not the best, was better than freezing into immobility.

Most warning lights flashed on my control panel. Because of the lack of atmosphere, I switched my vocal output to the SAN.

`Amelia, are you there?`

Her voice labored as the red emergency lighting came on. `I'm here, Robin. I have many mission-critical failures.`

`I show the same. I'll work down the checklist on my side.`

Part of our mutual training had been on who owned what task in an emergency. At the time, I'd considered it somewhat silly. Surely, Amelia, with her time-sharing capability, could easily deal with all problems. A bear could be wrong at times, couldn't he?

A subprocess of my mind wondered if there were more missiles headed to finish the job they started. But I didn't have time for the luxury of those thoughts.

My share of the tasks was primarily focused internally to the ship. Apparently, my stunt in the simulation of taking off my head caused some consternation among my teachers, causing a minor change in training, moving as many issues out of the ship to Amelia.

I quickly rearranged my display to an emergency configuration, showing the most critical items first. The loss of air pressure wasn't even in the first fifty items. What blinked red on top was that the passenger sumps had lost electrical power, and several had lost emergency battery backup. If those weren't turned back on, their brains would solidify and be deactivated forever.

Unbuckling, I turned for the hatch down to the bay. That was when I noticed paw-sized oval holes through our vessel's thin skin. They were scattered through the hull like a shotgun pattern. We must have taken damage from a breakup barrage. But the edges of the voids seemed too regular, not the tears of shrapnel. Worse, none of them were closing automatically as they had done in every test. I discarded these thoughts because there were units at risk of deactivation if I didn't stay focused.

I wriggled my hairless body through a hatch to a narrow, cramped room with ranks of shelves holding rows of brain sumps. I activated the magnetic boots to hold me in place in zero gravity. The problem was apparent, even in the dull red of the emergency lights. Instead of hull, I saw stars through a massive rent. The entire hole appeared like a scoop had neatly removed half a sphere 104 centimeters across from the side of Amelia's body. Sump fluid had solidified into a cloud of spherical clods, through which I had to work.

I'd spent enough time in this room, training to know that four units' brains were missing completely. Five others had significant chunks sheared off as neatly as by a laser. Eight others had batteries that had been cleaved with the same precision. These eight sumps were the immediate problem. The deactivated were beyond my skills and likely beyond anything other than the help of the Humans. Time for grieving would be later, if we survived. But without power or batteries, those eight would have no movement in their sump fluid. Their memories and lives would solidify into a greenish-black tar, deactivating as surely as the other nine had already done.

I edged up to the octet of sumps. I knew how to rewire these to share the batteries of those around them, but I'd never finish them all before some or all of them passed beyond this life. They'd been stopped for seconds already. They needed some movement, any significant movement, in their fluid to buy me time.

There were advantages to having the memories of eighty or so lives before me. A Nurse Nan on the battlefield once showed my distant ancestor a trick to keep a sump alive in an emergency. The sump was little more than a fluid reservoir with a mechanical diaphragm to move the fluid past a reader. Each sump had a nub of that flexible diaphragm that pierced the solid wall of the case. If you rubbed that tiny external piece back and forth, you induced a similar motion internally. So, with my big digits, I rubbed fast and hard on each one in turn for a few seconds until they each had been given some attention.

The rewiring job took me exactly four minutes and one second. I would have been done earlier if I hadn't stopped intermittently to manipulate the nubs on the outside of those eight. With each of the remaining sumps powered by batteries, I had hours. Next on my list was to restore their main power. It took me only as long as a basilisk strike to mentally interpose the damage to the hull over the ship plans. The main power for the sumps traveled through that wall via superconductive conduits. A good 50 centimeters of it was missing.

Replacing it with spare parts would take hours of finicky work, and that didn't even count replacing the hull sheeting, if we even could. With so many things calling for my attention, I couldn't dedicate the time. It was time for a jury-rig.

Without any particular care, I yanked and gathered the wires from the missing and dead sumps. They no longer needed them. With some simple soldering and braiding, I ended up with a pieced-together, twisted wire that would carry the current past the missing power path. I used some simple alligator clips to hold either end. I looked at it and scoffed at the crudity of the repair. But for all its inelegance, it would serve. The telltale turned from flashing red to yellow. The next critical alarm took my attention away from my makeshift mend.

# # #

I don't know how long I patched, rewired, plumbed, sealed, and did so many other things that they blurred. My chronometer said eighteen hours, forty-six minutes, and eight seconds, but it seemed both much longer and much shorter.

`Robin?`

`Amelia? I almost forgot ...`

`Hold on, Robin. I don't have much time. Listen. Her voice sounded distracted, troubled, and choppy.`

`Is everything–` I asked.

`Quiet. Everything isn't all right, but there are some things you need to know. All critical ship functions are contained, but not necessarily repaired. I've placed a file at 0E:44:36:22:D3 for details and instructions on the use of the damaged fusion generators and drive systems. If that doesn't work, go to 00:BF:36:22:D3. Computer memories are spotty.`

I asked, `Amelia, why wouldn't you just use them? I'm not really qualified.`

`I'm dying, Robin. I have about a minute and three seconds of life left, if my simulation is corr ... ect. It's st ... arting already.`

`What's wrong? We can fix it!`

`Robin, I knew from the mo ... ment we came into th ... isisis sssspace that I was dooooomed. I only hoped to hold ... hold ... hold on long 'nough to stttabbblizzzz. It'ssss so beautifullllll heeeeer ...`

And then she simply died.

Mourner

Amelia's SAN dropped immediately, but the warmth of her WAN faded like the evening light over the peaks of the Backbone Mountains. My friend for generations was no more. My hydraulic fluid dropped so low in grief that my sensors couldn't register it. The hydraulic pump that had stalled to put my pressures at rock bottom surged in anger. With the wrench I was holding, I pounded on the strut nearest me. I swung and swung again. I broke off piece after piece, denting it beyond its normal, gentle curve. I kept at it until my sensors registered overheating in my musculature. I slumped. In zero gravity, it had little outward impact.

There was always a word from our Human histories that I never understood until just that moment—*cry*. I knew I needed to cry, but I couldn't. The Humans had selfishly kept that right to themselves. It ranked right up there with when my past self learned of Sancho's demise. This emotion cut deeper, for my relationship with Amelia/Ada had spanned centuries. I was her grandfather, after all.

I should have grieved for all of the units that died that day. I mean, nine units' sumps deactivated. We lost over 70 percent of our stored memory engrams.

One of the problems with being a unit was that I couldn't ignore time. My mind kept track whether I wanted to or not. I surfed the peaks of anger and the troughs of grief for eight hours, thirty-one minutes, fifty-three seconds before my processes started falling into line with what I should be doing.

The mission. We still had a mission—or, in this case, I still had a mission. If nothing else, I could finish it for Amelia. She deserved that much. I picked up my sorry ass and faced the future, no matter how bleak it looked.

As my first act toward this goal, I shimmied my way back up through the emergency hatch to the bridge, where I could evaluate the ship and access that detailed file Amelia mentioned. I linked my deceased navigator's status display through to mine. From the looks of things, my granddaughter had fibbed about the status of the ship. About the only system that seemed to be functioning correctly was the backup fusion reactor. Everything else was dead, critical, or limping along. I didn't inherit the captaincy of a ship, but rather a floating hunk of metal.

"She told me to examine 0E:44:36:22:D3," I muttered to myself. I typed in the hexadecimal location and connected my processor directly via wireless.

Amelia's voice came to me. `Hello, my friend. I'm sorry I had to leave you, but my sump was pierced. I thought the damage could be repaired, but remote images showed that, despite the leak being slow, it was deep, and a patch wouldn't last. Unfortunately, I knew I was doomed, so I recorded this as I tried to get as much done as I could.`

She continued. `Enough whining. While I haven't had enough time to do an in-depth analysis of what went wrong when we activated the FTL propulsion, I have some educated guesses based on the results.`

Her SAN voice gave me her wisdom. `The extra-dimensional bubble created by our early initiation of the drive wasn't stable. Imagine our ship like a sand castle made half with an iron frame. Wrap it with a large wire coil and then apply a significant DC power supply. The metal parts would shoot out, leaving the sand sitting in place. Using that example, what we have around us now is that ferrous structure. The sand bits were left behind near Rigel-3.`

Amelia's recording posited, `So, let's talk about what you need to do to land this damaged bird. I'm not going to spray used hydraulic fluid in your face. Your chances aren't great because you will have to control by paw what I'm built to control directly by my processor.`

`By all the Humans, how am I supposed to do that?` I said to the silent ship.

Just as if she could have heard me in the past, she answered. `Let me lay out the situation for you. At this point, you are in non-Einsteinian space. Your motion relative to normal space is significantly faster than the speed of light. Your first step must be to repair the FTL. I doubt you can get it to be fully functional, but you need only one jolt to knock you out of here to normal space. The key is knowing when. Attached, you will find a file giving you a list of solar systems along your path and the times to activate your exit.`

This latter made me thoughtful. *Multiple solar systems? We may not be able to hit our primary target? How badly has this gone?*

`The nanotech built into the hull was nonresponsive in any way. It is like they don't even exist here. In addition, the reaction mass for the fusion drive is gone. You will have to cannibalize the ship of anything not` essential to landing. Under separate cover, you will find a prioritized list of items to sacrifice. As far as I can tell in this non-Einsteinian space, the navigation calculator and star files are still intact. The radar and lidar are both damaged but not irreparably.

She continued with the bad news. My first suggestion is that you wake any other units that aren't damaged. You will need their help to get back into shape to land. My quick simulations give you less than an 11 percent chance of success.

Amelia offered, My friend, I am so sorry that I can't be there to improve those odds or even share in your danger. I guess I should say don't grieve for me, but I'm too selfish for that. I do want you to miss me and name our landing place after me. I want history to remember me. I love you, Grandfather. May the Humans be kind to you.

The file ended at that point.

I'm sorry I got you into this, granddaughter, I muttered over a SAN that only I could hear. My brain wanted to shut down and embrace the emotions that washed over me. I'd already shed enough grief for eighty deactivations. My logical processes dominated. They made it clear that it was time for action. not for wallowing in the low-hydraulic pressure of self-pity.

Mentor

Only one other full-unit body had been selected for our trip as a backup to me in the remote case that either Amelia or I was incapacitated. The unit, an octopus, was a blank—that is, it had no sump. Moreover, it was in pieces to make it easier for storage.

I slithered down two of our tiny decks to the storage bay. Two-thirds of the space stood open to vacuum, or wherever non-Einsteinian was. The view of where we'd traveled caught my attention for the first time. My view looking aft through the missing pieces of the hull showed only black. Not the black of the color, but rather the lack of any stimulus. The ship and its contents stayed in my vision, but outside, there was absolutely nothing else—no stars, no debris, not a single photon.

With my magnetic boots hooked to plating, I stuck my head out of the hull. I took a panoramic look out of the ship. I attempted to whistle, but my voice box held no gases of any kind to vibrate. One hundred eighty degrees behind us provided zero stimulus—nothing. Then there was a nearly solid ring around the middle for several degrees forward, which slowly changed into a compressed, front-to-back, but recognizable star field. As I scanned toward the bow of the ship, there was a mottled red glow that filled the forward 37 degrees or so. It eased in intensity as it approached the waist ring. But in that forward cone, instead of stars of yellow, red, or even infrared, black dots speckled the field like stars in their own right, almost like an inverted field over an indigo nebula. All of this with Amelia's body as the normal reference, dead as it might have been. We raced toward a fiery furnace of the universe. I'm sure the Doppler effect would explain this in some way or another, but Amelia's last words had been right. It was beautiful.

It might have been the most gorgeous panorama any unit had ever viewed, but that didn't get me and my precious cargo any closer to landing on a new world. I pulled myself back inside and got to work.

The choice of an octopus as our secondary unit had caused a great deal of consternation prelaunch. Many voted for a Nurse Nan for not only repairs but also intelligence and ability to manipulate equipment. This was rejected from a sheer mass/volume standpoint. There were as many suggestions as there were toy types, each with valid reasoning. The recommendation committee weeded out those who weren't of high intelligence, those with limited manipulation ability, and those whose mass made them restrictive. In the end, it came down to a gopher, another bear, or an octopus.

They ruled out my kind, as if one bear couldn't solve it, then two couldn't either. A gopher's ability to move in zero-G wasn't great. Additionally, it would be of limited use in setting up the colony on the other end. That left the octopus. It wouldn't be the best of all choices at establishing our new home, but it definitely fit all of the other criteria.

As much of a technical problem as zero gravity caused for someone used to putting something in a place, knowing it wouldn't float away, this time, it proved useful. While an octopus was only 1.24 meters tall, its mass remained significant. Most of that height resided in its head. Its tentacles stretched much longer than its height. While I was far from tiny at 136 kilos, it nearly matched me at 110 kilos. It would have been more, but one of its limbs was lost in the translation here.

Thus, the lack of gravity allowed me to move the bulky pieces around with less effort.

I pulled all of the unit's limbs and torso together into roughly a ball floating in the middle of the cargo area. I'd woven a rough net of now-useless wire strands to make sure I didn't accidentally lose anything.

I knew this unit was orange and blue when we stored it before launch, but the red emergency lights showed me only ruby and black bits and pieces. Using the schematic in my head, I assembled my new helper like a puzzle or a piece of shipped furniture. Peg A went into slot B, fastening with bolt F using bolt tool #1. Six hours and twelve minutes of connecting not only structural bones but also the passel of wiring harnesses and hydraulic lines later, I looked at an octopus unit missing one tentacle and any anima.

I still had to choose a sump to put in it. And herein lay the next dilemma. Oh, I'd made my choice, but it hadn't been easy. As I mentioned earlier, we'd brought only one sump of each toy type. William Tell, the octopus sump, was one of our transit casualties. His brain had been carved open and his sump material blown out into space.

I had to either put a different toy's sump into this blank unit or come up with a way to create a new sump and then put one of the octopus memory engrams we carried into it. Making a brain case isn't as easy as putting a pump at the bottom of a box. Every angle and every curve made a difference in the creature's intelligence, empathy, and even ability to learn. Creating something new would be like playing God. I was no Human.

That left putting a mismatched part, the key part, into this unit. Mixing toy parts was never good, especially if they had vastly different body types. That meant the choice of the remaining survivors wasn't difficult. Only one toy had as many legs as the octopus—the spider, Nelson Mandela.

I didn't know Nelson. His sump had been removed before I even arrived. With a portable battery that I rigged, I carried Nelson's brain down from the sump room. Opening up the soft, rubber-like covering of the octopus head, I slid in the anima, the living embodiment of Mr. Mandela. The mounting bracket didn't match the brain case. This was why cross-species parts weren't recommended.

While not recommended, there were Nurse Nans back home who made a living merging different species. A spider with elephant legs. A giraffe with a dragon's body. A bubble mower with gopher arms. Relatively speaking, I had the simple job of mounting a mismatched brain case to a blank unit.

I spent the better part of eight hours measuring, drilling, and tapping new holes in the unit's shock absorbers for the sump. The actual mounting took moments. I connected the permanent power and bus data wiring. The body stirred to life. The tentacles flailed about without any seeming coordination.

`Nelson? Can you hear me?`

`Mrrphll` came from the twitching mass.

`No, don't open your eyes yet, Nelson. Stop trying to move. Listen to me. You're in the body of another toy. You need to relearn how to move, to see, and to feel.`

`Brddalp`, he mumbled incoherently.

`Yes, that means talking too`, I added. `But if you will access this SAN for address F3:01:BB:E4, you will get the machine programming applications you need to be able to converse.`

I sensed the access to my memory several thousand clock cycles before I heard, `Salutations. Testing. One. Two. Three.`

`That's better`, I said. `I hear you now.`

`Excellent. Have we arrived at our destination?` Nelson asked.

My predictive algorithms didn't expect this question. `No, we haven't, Nelson.`

`I prefer Mandela, if you please.`

`My apologies, Mandela. My name is Robinson Crusoe, or Robin for short.`

`Mr. Crusoe, it is nice to make your acquaintance, or it will be once motor functions and visual capabilities have been returned to me.`

I directed my friend. `If you will go to the same location plus 06:96, you can retrieve the code for your visual systems.`

The lids over the large saucer eyes open with dispatch. `Ah, yes. This body has better visual range; however, it lacks the` fine acuity I had with the multiple-lensed cameras I had as a spider. The eyes, without the head moving, ranged about. I ascertain that you've chosen a cephalopod body for me. It speaks of a certain amount of raw sense—eight limbs or wait ... only seven. Speaking of which, when will you provide the programming codes for exercising the motive power of my limbs?

I hedged a bit before answering. There we have a problem. We don't have that code. You will have to learn how to move through trial and error, just like a newly manufactured unit.

An uncomfortable silence came from the nearly motionless Mandela. The big eyes looked around the mostly destroyed cargo deck. His erudite speech offered, Would you care to elucidate our situation more fully?

Our situation is that we are in a badly damaged vessel trapped outside normal space. We've lost our factory, nine of our sumps, and all but sixty-eight of our memory engrams.

You awakened me to assist in facilitating repairs? Mandela asked.

Does mercury fall from the clouds? I asked back with some level of sarcasm.

I disbelieve that mercury falls in a zero gravity—

I interrupted in anger. Really? You are going to—

Mr. Crusoe, do you rise to anger by a comment made in jest?

I ... Oh, moonshine, but I guess I was. I could make an excuse about the stress of the last few hours, but it would only be an excuse. I was wrong. I'm sorry.

Mandela paused before he replied. It is a rare unit indeed who can apologize. Many find it an indication of weakness. I perceive it as a strength instead.

I agreed and added, Over the years—I almost said, "centuries"—I've learned that it shows character. But the most important part is not to repeat your behavior.

The octopus's head bobbed. I wasn't sure whether it was agreement or a lack of control. Mandela said, In any event, getting back to your reason for reactivating me, I'm sorry to say you may be disappointed to learn that even discounting my existing physical infirmity, I have a dearth of skills to assist in your repairs.

I asked, No skills? Didn't you train before you were disassembled for colonization?

No, Mr. Crusoe. I held a post as an etymologist teacher to newly created units.

Etymology? How will that help us?

I never alleged it would, Mr. Crusoe. In point of fact, I indicated the contrary. Of course, you didn't confer with me. Come to think of it, I wasn't even consulted in having my sump removed, although, as you know, Black Fungus doesn't give the unit much time before all of its semiconductors are consumed.

That's true! I exclaimed. Back in the mountains, I'd seen one of my friends eaten alive before we could even get a medic to arrive. The emptiness in his visual receptors as he deactivated haunts me to this day.

Mandela replied, It proved providential that we caught my ailment early when one of my legs spasmed during routine preventive maintenance. I was isolated with dispatch. The parasite was identified within an hour.

I'm glad you had a happy ending, I said.

I'm vague at my ultimate conclusion, he replied. You still require a mechanic, structural engineer, or ... He paused, looking around the cargo hold. This time, his neck moved with the eyes ... maybe a junk man.

So not even rudimentary mechanic skills? I asked incredulously.

My knowledge of anything mechanical or electrical went away with my father's accidental death before he imparted that knowledge to me. You might call that my raison d'être for preferring the company of younglings to adults.

I still couldn't fathom it. Believing in his statement at face value would be like believing in the Easter Bunny or the Hydraulic Vampire. Everyone learns the basics of mechanics and electronics. You didn't bother to learn?

I bore no motivation to acquire such plebian knowledge, he said with something akin to smugness. I saw it in his eyes. He felt he was a better unit without such.

I mean no disrespect, Mr. Mandela, but how did you get on this mission? I only ask for informational purposes.

Well, I was one of only three spider units to join Project New Worlds. I guess they needed someone to train the younglings.

All I can think is that we were in deep grit. Out of all of the choices I had, I picked the one unit that would do me no good. Why did the Humans hate me so much? No, that isn't true. Even if you believe in that ancient mythology, they say Humans never give a unit more than it could handle.

Time to grab the axe beak by the neck. `Well then, as a teacher, you must have learned how to learn.`

`Indubitably,` he replied, as if it were obvious.

`Well then, I'm about to give you a crash course, if you will forgive the implication, on how to be a mechanic.`

`Superb.` His tone dripped with sarcasm.

Dock Worker

Mandela learning of his new body wasn't without issues. Three of his legs formed a knot beneath him. I offered, `For now, you will concentrate on learning to move around in the ship. Once you've got that, we'll tackle teaching you the esoteric topic of repair.`

`An appropriate course of study.`

Pointing, I said, `The net I stretched over the rent in the hull will stop you from accidentally floating out of here. So, practice with confidence that your mistakes won't be fatal.`

He replied, `I will do so. I calculate that it will take me thirteen hours and thirty-seven minutes, plus or minus fifty-four minutes.`

`That's about what I figured as well. I'll get on with the work to put us together and let you get on with yours.`

One of the octopus's tentacles waved. I upgraded our chances by a few parts of a percent. If he was that quick at coming to grips with his new body, maybe, just maybe, we'd persevere. Black it all. He had me using those moonlit, oversized words.

# # #

With very few of our ship's capabilities fully functional, I chose to ignore the telltales in the control room and concentrate on the priorities Amelia left for me. That list put repairing the fusion plant first. I swam the ladders, barely touching three rungs down four decks—impressive, considering my bulk and the narrow access hatches. My new slippery outer skin helped.

The heart of our ship—its primary power source and the reaction drive of the fusion plant—was a device about the size of a Tommy Tank. Come to think of it, it resembled one. At 51 centimeters high, 57 wide, and 98 long, it didn't look like a world-altering device, but rather something you'd pull behind you on vacation to carry things that wouldn't fit in your arms. But the melted wall behind it, the sagging floor beneath it, and the twisted bulkhead behind me belied its harmlessness. I worked in a compartment designed by the Human Salvador Dalí and implemented by a Betadyne model J12 fusion reactor.

In use, it was comparable to an old-style internal combustion engine that needed three things: fuel, oxygen, and spark. The J12 also required three things: fuel, heat, and containment. Choke off its source of deuterium, and it rather quickly stopped making helium and died. Its self-renewing heat normally came directly from the reaction. As ours had been shut down, we had to generate the heat of a star inside the reaction chamber to start the reaction, but after that jump start, we were good. Containment was ... well, critical. Without it, we would release all that energy willy-nilly. There were enough indications of that release around me. I didn't want to be nothing but a black cinder floating through space by starting it without fixing its issues.

Two things were wrong with our fusion reactor. The magnetic bottle—the containment—had become misaligned. In addition, the fuel control for the hydrogen-2 had frozen open for some reason.

Using laser calipers, I crawled all over that device, taking precise measurements. I found the misalignment problem relatively quickly. One of the five legs that supported the reactor from the floor was missing, along with a chunk of floor and wall. Another casualty of our ill-fated transition to this space. This caused a 3-micrometer drop in the center of the reactor. I could create a new support to span the missing floor out of other useless pieces of the ship. But before I did, I needed to understand why the fuel feed remained open. It would do no good to repair one issue only to potentially have to undo it to fix the other.

Using the manuals on the ship's computers, I removed the deuterium pump, which was no larger than my largest digit. Once I had it in hand, it would even spin manually. Using my smallest tools, I dismantled it to find it choked with black tar ... or gelatinized brain fluid. Some must have found its way from our deactivated sumps and contaminated the fuel tank.

As I cleaned the minute device with solvent and a tiny brush, I wondered whose life I was scrubbing away. Did I know that unit? Did it have a good life before it gummed into oblivion? Had it found the answer to the ultimate question: Do the Humans really exist?

I should really be melancholy, but after Amelia's death, I had little emotional capacity left in me. I carried on only because of the other units counting on me. Had I been alone, I might have just pulled the power leads to my own sump and settled into the dark emptiness that filled my chest. Instead, I filtered out the back spheres from the heavy water tank. Thankfully, deuterium didn't dissolve the tar. I blew out the feed line with a dissolving compound. Reassembling the entire subsystem went smoothly. The test I ran showed good flow.

I collected the bits I needed to hold up the entire reactor. I collected tools that had been saved for building the colony upon landing. No one expected that in flight, we'd need a tap and die set, a hand drill, or even a welding torch. If some of the equipment hadn't been on this ship, the repairs might have been beyond me.

I drilled and tapped one hole in a solid bit of steel spar that had broken free of its location. Into it I put a leveling screw, kind of like the ones that are on the feet of appliances. Using an acetylene torch, I welded the new brace over the hole on either side, with the screw in the center pointing up toward the bottom of the power source. Using my high-precision measurement tools, I twisted up the adjustment screw until it met specifications.

The job took intense concentration and focus to get it exactly right. That's probably why I hadn't noticed Mandela staring at me, watching every move. I started when his form came into my peripheral vision.

`You scared me,` I sent to him over the SAN.

`Why? It isn't like we are characters within one of those horror movies where the monster eats your batteries and watches you deactivate.`

`True. I guess I haven't gotten used to having someone move around without hearing them. I take it that you have gotten some control over your new body?`

`Yes, quite well,` he said, rippling his seven limbs one at a time like a mercury wave on the White Sea.

`Very nice. OK, well, let's start teaching you. The easiest thing for you to do to help is to weld the skin of our ship whole.`

One of his tentacles pointed at his eyes. `I watched what you did. I can competently replicate your actions.`

I notched down our likelihood of success. `For an educated unit, I find your statement disturbing. Any physical skill often has multiple techniques, tricks, and requirements that you may not glean from just a few moments of observation.`

The octopus's huge eyes went wider. `You are correct. Mea culpa. I request your assistance in educating me, Mr. Crusoe.`

# # #

The odd view outside the ship continued to amaze me. The mottled red in the direction of our movement, the band of stars around our middle, and the blackness behind us remained stunning. It provided a backdrop to the majesty of a blue-and-orange octopus floating weightless, moving all seven of his limbs independently. I couldn't exactly fathom the mental gymnastics it took to coordinate all the action.

After two weeks, three days, and ninety-four minutes of instruction and practical application, I watched as the orange-and-blue stuffed octopus, Nelson Mandela, did his first solo repair. I'd selected a difficult one. Not only was the gap in the skin too wide for simple welding, but it was at a joint of two different materials. He didn't hesitate in the slightest at the challenge. In fact, he never looked to me for agreement that he was doing the right thing.

He'd already gotten a filler piece of material from our floating debris field to bridge the gap, or act as a patch, if you prefer. His welding strokes were consistent, and the beads smooth. Between the dissimilar materials, he brazed instead of welding.

As he worked, I found myself nodding in approval at each action—how he controlled his arc, how he minimized the heat-affected zone, and how he kept his speed regulated. This unit knew what he was doing. Either I taught exceptionally well (I scoffed at that though) or he absorbed information like aluminum amalgams with mercury.

An hour later, Nelson turned to me and said, `I believe I've completed this repair.`

I zoomed in with my optics to the microscopic level. The rippled seams were better than even my own. `Shall we test it?`

`An atmosphere seal is clamped onto the inside of the hull,` Mandela said.

I motioned for him to lead the way. We went through the airlock, which had both doors open. We were still a long, long way from having an airtight seal on the whole ship. Moving back to the inside of the repairs, there was a large, clear bubble sealed to the bulkhead with six braces that reached across the compartment. The transparent metal semisphere had a hose leading off it to an air compressor panel. Fortunately, that was one of the systems that still functioned. Through the bubble, I inspected the inner side of the repair. It appeared as perfectly done as the outer joining.

`Pump it up,` I said.

I felt vibrations through the deck plates as the spare atmosphere we had stored was compacted to even higher pressure before we jetted it against the repaired segment of the wall. I could see a mist forming as the air entered. The reduction from the tight tube into the larger bubble caused a pressure drop, cooling it. This radical change in temperature forced the minute moisture carried in the air to form mini droplets. As pressure in the vessel increased to near the same level as exits from the hose, the liquid returned to its gaseous state, becoming clear again.

I watched the compression gauge. Nelson cranked it up to three times the normal ship's operating pressure. There were no obvious leaks.

`Seal it off,` I said over our SAN.

Nelson threw a valve and cut the compressor. The pressure in the clear bubble would determine how successful he'd been. If it remained stable, the repair was airtight. If it dropped, then atmosphere was escaping through the welds.

We sat and stared at the needle on the gauge for minutes. It never moved.

Congratulations, Mandela, I offered. It looks like you passed.

It does appear promising, he replied as he floated near the gauge.

You have proven to be an exceptional student, I said, looking at the completed repair.

I agree. And you have adequately instructed me.

Sometimes, I wondered if he was being intentionally insulting. Over those few weeks, I'd learned it was just his way. There was no false modesty, no faint praise, and no sugarcoating anything.

Well, in that case, I leave the repairs of the ship's skin to you. I'll be working on the internal systems. If you run into anything novel, let me know.

I will comply, Mr. Crusoe, he said before moving out to start his Herculean tasks.

My mind wasn't on his supercilious reply but on the next patch-ups that I need to complete. Mandela and the skin of the ship left my thoughts entirely.

# # #

First, for me, was checking whether sensors for systems still existed and were connected. For instance, the main drive fuel telltale showed empty. Was that because there wasn't fuel, the fuel sensor had been ripped free of the ship, or there was a break in the signal lines? Multiply that by the 1,914 sensors throughout the ship to get an idea of the magnitude of my own Sisyphean task.

Ninety-six hours and thirty-four minutes of digging through the innards of the ship caused one of my own internal sensors to call attention to my own abused body and dimming mental thinking. I needed to take a rest. I needed to shut down my cognitive processes.

I pulled myself along into the remnants of the cargo bay. Since I'd used a good portion of the volume to do repairs of one form or another, it was the largest open space on our ship. I found Nelson floating in one corner with his eyes half closed. They popped open.

Welcome, Mr. Crusoe. Is there some service I can perform for you?

No, thank you, Mr. Mandela. I just need an opportunity

to rest my processor.

You certainly have consumed a great number of ergs in your continuous pursuits.

No doubt, I replied. I guess any port in a storm. So I wrapped a strap around my chest and prepared to shut down my cognitive processes.

Mr. Crusoe, have you heard the legend of Don Quixote?

Which one? We've had 83. I wondered where he was going with this questioning. All the members of the launch knew I was the former president.

No, sir. I don't mean our leader, but the original story, *The Man of La Mancha*, he said.

It's been centuries since I've heard that tale, I said with sleep foremost in my mind. I didn't even catch his questioning look.

Then you should hear it again. Attend me, Mr. Crusoe.

Nelson's voice became more soothing as he told the historic story. In a village of La Mancha, the name of which I have no desire to call to mind, there lived not long since one of those gentlemen that keep a lance in the lance-rack, an old buckler, a lean hack, and a greyhound for coursing ...

My consciousness didn't make it past the first sentence.

# # #

My internal timer dragged me out of sleep. Nelson's optics were closed. The clearance of my extraneous processes and worries allowed a new clarity of data processing. I stretched to fire up my hydraulic pump for the first time that day.

I miss the reds of sunrise, Mandela said, his eyes remaining closed.

I started just a bit. I don't disagree. Hopefully, we will see them again ... on a new world.

Nelson opened his huge eyes and peered into mine. And what percentage of success do you give our efforts?

Right now? Less than 2 percent.

He didn't take any action that would make me believe he was surprised by this announcement.

And if our efforts pay dividends? he asked.

I hesitated. I didn't want to turn off his processes to the work, but I couldn't be false either. So I replied, I say 12.3 percent.

Well, my enthusiasm for our chances doesn't reach exalted heights; however, we should strive for at least that one chance in eight. As a point of inquiry, does working your hydraulic fluid to tar by not taking the required rests improve or diminish the odds?

Moonshine but if the unit hadn't caught me out. I had been working my fur off—if I still had any. He was also right that it didn't increase our odds but decreased them.

No, I suppose not, I admitted.

Mandela's voice took on a supercilious tone. Then, if it isn't beyond my authority, I strongly advocate that you take six hours out of every twenty-four for rest.

Listen, Mr. Mandela, you and I are the only two units that have any chance of saving our own lives, the lives of all of the remaining units in this vessel, our mission, and, dare I say, toyanity itself. Can we please just get along without sinking barbs in one another?

Barbs, Mr. Crusoe?

I gave a mental sigh. I tried to take a different tack. Before you were hijacked into this mission, what did you do for fun?

That seems a radical change of subject, Mr. Crusoe.

It only seems that way, Nelson. What gets your processor overclocking? I asked.

Mythology. I spent night after night reading the ancient tales of Humans.

Thus your recounting of the ancient tale of Don Quixote last evening.

He smiled. My unsurpassed favorite.

I like it too. In fact, it has a special place in my sump.

Directly the octopus asked, So, could it be that your original name was Don Quixote?

I don't know why I toyed with him, but I asked, Why would you think that?

Because I can add two and two together and don't get 1.99995827903.

I laughed with genuine mirth for the first time in months. That wasn't one of our factories' better processor design generations, was it?

No. Not in the slightest. Nelson gave a laugh that was raucous and full of disturbing subsonics. I pulled slightly away when I first heard it. He said, Oh, my, but I'm going to have to work on that. It seems I don't have complete control of this body yet.

You will get there. I don't disagree with your suggestion that I take rest breaks. They are necessary.

I've let worry get in my way.

He continued his argument. My experience has proven that fretting only spends ergs for no purpose other than to cloud computations.

I laughed again. You are fully lubricated there, Mr. Mandela. What would you think about sharing mythologies? I know something of them myself.

I assume so, given your background.

My background? I asked, trying once again to dodge.

My stack is getting full with your evasions. I'll ask directly. Are/were you the president of toyanity?

I sighed to myself. *Why couldn't the world have just gone to hell without me?* I wondered. Yes, I was. But it doesn't matter now. Right now, what matters is that I'm captain, and only because I was forced into it.

Mr. Crusoe, if I may use your pseudonym—

That is my name, Mr. Mandela. I changed it on purpose. I don't want to be remembered for what I did ... but rather for who I am and what I do.

The octopus said, Admirable and strong choice, Mr. Crusoe. But popping off the stack of your interrupt, forcing any unit to do anything against his will is, as you know, nearly impossible. You chose to command this mission. You may have been chivied into it, but you made the choice. And only someone who feels the call of leadership, the need to bear responsibility ... if you will pardon the obvious pun ... can be coerced into carrying the weight of duty. I believe the term is *noblesse oblige*.

Or programming? I sparred back.

I doubt that, sir. What makes one unit courageous and the other cowardly? What makes the difference between a unit and an automaton? I'll answer myself: the soul. And your soul must serve and nurture.

I snorted. You are making me sound like a factory. Nurture. Bah.

At that moment, my brain exploded with an idea so outlandish and brash that it bordered on the absurd. Setting up the design of experiments' simulations was so complex that my processor rejected any extraneous input, like what my companion said. I continued to be oblivious as I interpreted the data. Even overclocked, the entire calculation seemed to take an eternity. I barked, By the Humans, it will work!

Mr. Manela jumped at my exclamation. What would that be, Captain Crusoe?

`How would you like a big, fat 68.87 percent chance of success?`

`I'd say that is vastly superior to twelve and a skosh. What changed the dismal odds?`

`I lay down my emotions into my words. It is part of the calculations that I not tell you now. Just let it be said that I will tell you when it is important. For now, we have to get this boat as shipshape as we can.`

I hadn't had much belief in our reeking one in eight chance. Having almost two in three energized me as if I'd just plugged into the planetary solar arrays at high noon.

`Come on. Let's get to work,` I insisted.

# # #

"My nephew, you seem to be displaying signs of triviality," Mr. Mandela said in a nasal old woman's voice.

With the work outside the ship effectively completed, we had pressurized the hull and could once again speak without the SAN.

"On the contrary, Aunt Augusta, I've now realized for the first time in my life the vital Importance of being Earnest," I offered as the closing line.

There was a long pause as we both took in the conclusion.

"That was quite admirably done, Mr. Crusoe," my octopus friend offered.

"I think I agree. Although I am more a fan of Shakespeare, Oscar Wilde does justice in this comedic mythology."

"I referred more to our performances, but yes, Mr. Wilde was an exceptional myth writer."

As I played with the ratchet I had in my paws, I said, "I always thought I'd have made a good actor if I hadn't been born to be president."

"I think you would have been a good one. Why didn't you pursue it?" the octopus asked, floating 56 centimeters from the bulkhead. His seven tentacles rippled hypnotically. I tried not to look at them.

"I had to be president."

"But afterward? You were free then."

I didn't know how to explain to my companion just how much I needed to be anonymous. Taking a different spotlight would have crushed what little spirit I had after a century of being the center of every unit's attention.

"Just say that I needed to be alone."

The hiss of laughter from Mandela perked up my ears. "You certainly found alone here. With the exception of my own not insignificant self, there isn't another functioning unit for ... how many light-years?"

I joined his laughter. "Too true, friend."

The octopus gave me an odd look for a few clock cycles. I couldn't reason out his expression before it evaporated.

In our rest times over the past days and weeks, we'd performed *Death of a Salesman, The Hobbit, Dirty Dancing, Stranger in a Strange Land, The Scottish Play, War and Peace, Waiting for Godot, The Color Purple, The Diary of Anne Frank, Dune, Evita, Hamlet* (my personal favorite), and many, many more. Once Mandela felt comfortable in his voice, we added *The Music Man, Oklahoma!, Singin' in the Rain, The Sound of Music,* and other musical mythologies into our mix.

Somewhere in that time, the annoying, supercilious Nelson Mandela had become more than just my companion ... he'd become my friend. Not only was this momentous, but we'd finished all of the repairs of our ship ... all but one. We should have been celebrating, and Nelson probably was. I, on the other hand, rejoiced in the completion, and at the same time, I tasted the bitter overvoltage of fear. In my previous eighty-some incarnations, I hadn't felt this level of anxiety and dread. I hoped my system could handle the power without blowing fuses. For, under primitive conditions, Nelson and I were about to perform something that had never been done before—with me as the guinea pig.

`I had to convince my partner of his part in this endeavor.`

# # #

Mandela cocked his body to look at me from a different angle before pronouncing, "I possess not the education or certification of a professional psychologist, but even lacking those qualifications, I'd say you were insane, Robinson."

This was the first time that he'd used my first name—a success of sorts.

"I'm not. It's the only way to get that roughly 63 percent success projection."

"It's never been done before. You could deactivate."

"I know." Sarcasm filled my soul. Like I didn't know I was about to risk my activation. Even worse, if I was successful, I'd end up ... well, my life would be nothing like anything in my past experience.

"What makes you think it will work?" he asked.

"Do you want my calculations?" I replied.

"Under no circumstances. I'm sure you have a virus in your processor somewhere."

I laughed. "I wish it were that simple. Purge my programming and start over. Instead, I need to start over in a new way."

"You possess the mental stability of someone with only half their sump fluid."

"Not far off," I admitted. "Do you want me to go over the procedure?"

"What makes you think I will assist with this stupidity?"

"Because it makes sense," I answered.

He scoffed with just a burst of static through his speaker. "And what do I do when your brain turns to tar?"

"I'm counting on our combined skills to make sure that doesn't happen. But if it does, use my body to put in the sump of another unit. I'd suggest—"

"Cease and desist, Robinson. Is there anything I can do to dissuade you from this rash course of action?"

I shook my head. "Is it really that rash? Consider our situation. Here we are, hurtling lost through non-Einsteinian space in a ship held together with tree sap and twine. You think we really have a chance of first, getting back to our own frame of reference, and second, safely landing on a planet that won't freeze our hydraulic fluid or melt our skeletons without doing this?"

"That's beside the point. We have our activation, even here," Nelson countered.

"And how long can we continue our existence with our brethren trapped in there? How many myths can we tell one another before we do go fully insane? You've heard of the ..."

"Yes, the experiments of sensory deprivation that sent fully stable units into screaming madness. I know them, but is this risk better?"

I paused very briefly to recalculate my simulations. "I don't think we have a choice."

"I will bow to your superior experience, but I want it to be known between us that I fear for your safety."

I whispered back, "So do I." I then brightened up with a level of enthusiasm I'm not sure I contained. With one massive paw, I chucked the side of my octopus friend. "Let's do this. Let's make history. Let's perform the first sex change operation of our species."

# # #

Depending on the psychology text you read, toyanity is either two or three sexes. There is the role of a constructor in making the physical new toy. This role is that of the factories. We've had examples of toys making bodies for other toys, but those Frankensteinian creations rarely lived more than months.

Then we have the inseminator sex. This is the toy that has a few milliliters of their sump fluid removed and injected into the newly manufactured toy to induce sentience.

The final sex are the caretakers. These are the toys that take the naive youngling and teach it the basics of life until it can make its own way in life. Some psychologists lumped those final two together, as units can take either role.

No matter which philosophical school you subscribe to, my intent was to take direct control of our rocket ship as my own body—to become a factory.

My first task required torching open the bent armored bulkhead that didn't quite protect Amelia's sump. Nelson's support, while not whole-hearted, definitely made my efforts easier. He always seemed to know what tool I needed next. He even made the time go faster by doing a quite appropriate one-man performance of *Twelfth Night* by William Shakespeare.

Once through the ceramic composite, through the vibration-absorbing gel, we both saw the dark rubber-like substance that highlighted a hairline crack across the surface of the 147-centimeter sump that used to be Amelia.

Nelson ceased his recitation. Together, we looked at our fallen comrade in respectful silence. I broke the moment with "Dulce et Decorum Est."

"Excuse me?" Nelson said.

"An ancient mythology in another language. It means, 'It is sweet and fitting to die for one's country.' Amelia gave her activation for our mission and to save our way of life."

It took us seven hours and forty-six minutes to remove Amelia's sump and the congealed tar-like substance that once gave her sentience. I took it all out of our airlock and put it onto the skin of the vessel. I gave her a gentle shove into the odd space we inhabited. She deserved the right to explore this universe in her next lifetime.

Nelson bowed his head. `May the Humans preserve her.`

`Amen,` I agreed.

By universal agreement, we took a few hours of rest. We didn't even engage in one of our plays.

"She was a heroine, wasn't she?" the octopus asked after a long silence.

"You don't know the half of it," I replied. "Amelia Earhart/Ada Lovelace lived a full life almost as long as my entire line of Don Quixotes had. Her life spanned some turbulent times. She saved my life more than once during the Sentient Conflict when we overthrew the non-sentient factories. She negotiated the System Truce when toyanity took to squabbling over Home or Rome rule."

"I wouldn't call a war that deactivated tens of thousands of units a squabble."

"Well, it wasn't one of my umpty-umpth predecessor's sterling moments. His sump must have been very off spec."

"Speaking of that, how are we going to support your sump in the ship's brain cavity?"

"We aren't," I said with some surety.

"I do not comprehend," he said, cocking his soft head.

"We have one factory sump in our stores. After straightening the divot in the armor, we will put that spare into place."

"You can't mean—"

"It's the only way, Nelson. A factory must have a much more robust memory. This means a vastly larger sump, not the relatively tiny one that I've lived with for eighty-some lifetimes. We will fill the vessel with a great deal of raw brain fluid. Then you and I together will pour mine in, followed by you sealing me into my new body."

Nelson blinked those oversized eyes at me before he said, "You truly have lost your sanity, you know. You are going to end up madder than the traitorous Isp ever was."

I didn't answer. That outcome did appear on the Monte Carlo simulation. I didn't want to think about it, as it might give the projection life rather than just a percentage.

"I certainly hope not."

Chrysalis

I drifted in a kaleidoscope of input. I smelled the spicy color of a dodecahedron floating past. The heat of blue washed across my senses. A unit flowed into me and out the other side like something out of a Salvador Dalí painting. I tasted its passing in a bitter tang of E-flat. A basilisk rolled past me on wooden tracks to set fire to the powerless flower petals from out of its nose. Mercury poured across … not my body but my sense of self. It burned like acid, causing me to melt into a puddle of salty excrement.

I feared my friend might have been correct that my sanity had left me. In this demented space, I couldn't latch onto anything familiar. Fear tore at the mote of my being. Maybe even what the Humans call a soul.

Wait! The thought that a friend worried for me was a concrete thing, a real memory that hadn't been abused by this bedlam and my own reckless course of action.

Friend. Who was he? I pictured an octopus with the multiple eyes of a spider. "AAAAA!" I screamed at the frightening visage. Another abused, chaotic image to tease me. Wait again! Octopus and spider both had absolute values. I could see them. Another image of a bear crossed my consciousness. Purple. Thick. No, not a bear, but a teddy bear. ME. But then that creature climbed into a quern. I could hear the purple grinding, tearing. I tasted the sweetness of floating helium.

NO! I cried to myself. *No more pandemonium.* I focused on the octopus. The spider. Petals. Fire. The bear. Legs. Tentacles. Paws. Eyes. Noses. Walking. Talking. All these things had specific real meanings. Talking. Acting. Yelling. Conversation. Friend.

A pink elephant with purple polka dots sporting a mortar in his chest slipped across my memory. Sancho Panza. My hydraulic fluid dropped in grief. Something else to hold onto—hydraulics. Deactivation. Violence. WAR!

My mental processes exploded exponentially. All of these things I knew. All of those things I have been and done. All of those units I've known. All of those units who weren't active any longer, and those that still were.

Don Quixote. I'm Don Quixote. I am Robinson Crusoe. I am … Overload. Shutting down. Overload.

# # #

My processes started up again. I no longer viewed the insanity of the Planes of Chaos. What a relief! The blinding and constantly changing bedlam burned as a memory to be avoided at all costs.

Instead, I existed in a blank place that had less than nothing. Mythologies stated that such an absence could only be the plane of purgatory. Had I finally deactivated? Had the Humans called me home?

I reached out with other senses. Wait. I felt my processor at the edge of my consciousness. A flush of power raced through me. This processor wasn't a single unit but rather a bank of dozens of unique CPUs. With nothing but a mental flick, I calculated the square root of two with six thousand decimal places. While that took place, I reran my computations for a successful colony. That intensive calculation had taken minutes before. It happened so fast that storing it in my memory took longer. With such power, I felt like a god! Or should it be goddess? No, I didn't even know if I was active or not. I couldn't see or hear, even if I could compute the value of pi to a million places as if it were trivial.

If I had access to processing power, maybe I could find nonvolatile memory where the body control procedures could be found. I scanned backward through memory addresses and found it right where it should be—at FFFF:FFFF:FFFF:FFF0. This gave me the memory map. I glanced over multiple subroutine headers that I didn't recognize. Finally, I found one titled "Vision." I pointed my execution pointer to that code. Error codes flashed one after another across my processor queue.

(Fatal) Remote extensionals not operational.

(Warning) Power insufficient to extentionals 0x7 through 0xE.

(Warning) Sensor 0x4 and 0x1F nonresponsive.

(Warning) Task failed successfully.

(Fatal) Internal real-time clock not functional for extended view.

(Warning) Projectors 0x3 through 0x7 nonresponsive.

(Fatal) Your processor ran into a problem and needs to restart.

(Warning) Aft data link compromised.

(Fatal) Collection-memory filter not active.

(Warning) An error has occurred while creating an error report.

My situation wasn't *similar* to being someone trying to fake knowing a job they have never seen; it was exactly like that. Outside of some wild speculative fiction, I'd never even heard of a toy wanting to be a factory. So there I was, trying to do something without the proper instruction. Another good analogy was that of a Human infant. Or what Nelson experienced. I needed to learn my body from scratch. I hoped I could do it without harming any of my passengers.

Fortunately, eighty-plus lifetimes gave one a large number of skills. One of those I'd picked up along the way was programming. With grim determination, I dug into the gigabytes of undocumented machine code. I couldn't even fault Amelia for not documenting what she knew so well. Why would anyone worry about someone else taking over your body? Silly, really. If I ever got out of this, I'd have to compare notes with Nelson Mandela about his similar experience learning his octopus body.

# # #

Time had little meaning when not connected to the outside world by anything but a processor clock. As I didn't know the frequency of the clock, the exact number of cycles would be meaningless.

I debugged all the fatal warnings except the processor needed to restart error. It, at least, didn't return. Most of the fatal warnings were simple. I needed to execute other background processes. Which required even others. Which required others. Before I finally found all the interconnects, I had a full 703 batches of code processing on low-priority CPUs.

Each of these routines gave me some insight into my body. I found power measurements and controls, damage indicators of the colonists' sumps, and checksums on the colonists saved as data. Those last two depressed me with those units who had already perished or whose data couldn't be made whole again. I had to put that out of my processors for evaluation at a later time. Baby steps.

With my mental fingers crossed, I again launched the Vision subroutine.

"Wow," I said. If the comment itself wasn't redundant, the experience I received awed me. It wasn't an optical vision like the eyes of my bear body. Instead, it gave me a panoramic view of space in all directions around the ship—360 degrees. And the colors I received mapped to nothing in the normal spectrum of sight that a bear has access to. Data flowed around each object within a radius of several kilometers, indicating relative direction, speed, acceleration, probability of collision, composition, and more ... so much more that I couldn't even parse it all. I drank from a proverbial fire hose.

I wish I could have stored all this data to experience it later, but the data-to-memory filter code so far had escaped me.

As none of the objects floating near me posed a collision risk, I turned my attention to other body subroutines.

Amelia's nomenclature for her bodily code made my sump turn over with a growl. Of course, she was well over eight millennia old, so her thought processes couldn't possibly match mine. And it wasn't like she could have anticipated anyone but herself looking at these comments and designations. I mean, who would have anticipated their own deactivation? What's more, who would expect to be resurrected as a zombie by someone else's sump? The entire concept was ludicrous. So I was left to fumble around with headers like "Peepers," "Little Feet," "Fresh Air," "Zap," "Big Jump," "Slam Dunk," "Widow Maker," "Plant," and many more.

With some of the dangerous-sounding names, I had to examine the code in detail before executing it. In fact, burrowing into the Zap routine, I found that it would electrify the ship's skin in the extremely unlikely event someone tried to board me.

Me. That was an odd sense then. I no longer had paws, limbs, or even a head. I was one with the vessel. *I am the ship*. Even odder, I didn't have to remove this thought to keep my attention on programming analysis. I had so many processors that I could crunch the data on dozens of different tracks.

Popping back to the code digging, Widow Maker poured the entire heavy water storage into the fusion reactor. The resulting conflagration would incinerate everything within a 2-kilometer radius. The explosion would also inflict serious damage to most everything else for another 10 kilometers. I definitely felt like a Human had stepped on my grave. I put a double "Are you SURE?" query lock on that self-annihilation feature. Didn't want to accidentally reach for a window-cleaning routine and destroy the future of toyanity … not to mention yours truly. This meant I had to be extra careful to know exactly what I was doing before activating any program my deceased friend had left me.

I didn't think to log the clock count, so time continued to lose any meaning as I pulled up one package after another. I tried tags and comments that seemed to make sense for each of the two things I really cared about—vision and speech. I threw each into a different processor execution queue.

I suddenly hit my first pay dirt with a low-level program named I_Spy. It looked promising because of the video format nature of the data it processed. As it accepted only data, I felt safe activating it. If this worked, the name obviously came from the nursery game "I spy with my little eye." I would have to keep that in mind for the future.

I added the routine to my empty body processing queue, and the explosion of visuals from forty-two different optical devices filled my receive buffers. I'd never had to deal with more than the binocular vision I'd been manufactured with. Fortunately, this new body held much larger capabilities than my poor bear body did. As I worried about the overload of data, I realized that I could select a single or multiple cameras with a list variable passed to this vision. I found that I could selectively flip through them with extreme rapidity. I did so until I found the image of an octopus missing one arm. Nelson leaned over my body.

OK, technically, it wasn't my body anymore. The body of a 130-kilogram purple-and-white teddy bear, 2.1 meters tall, lay on a workbench. Its skull armor had been neatly cleft in half. I remembered that exposure of my sump just before my sentience (soul?) merged with the ship.

Well, I had vision. Next was the ability to speak.

My newfound vision also allowed me to gauge the flow of time. I could adjust my primary body clock to match my friend's time frame. The other processor clocks I kept at a high speed to aid in the search for my voice.

In the time it took my companion to remove my old sump, I'd gone through several hundred thousand options until I arrived at a program with the name of No_Evil_See_Hear_Speak. The code seemed to be an overarching control routine that called, among other things, I_Spy. As I inspected the code, analysis showed that I was correct. One thing about parsing all of the data was that the more things I learned to do, the exponentially easier it was to find the next thing I looked for.

Well, here goes nothing, I thought.

"Nelson? Are you there?" To my horror, I said it with Amelia's high, squeaky voice.

"Mr. Crusoe?" Nelson replied.

I searched for the voice controls and played with the variables.

"Yes," I said with a timber much closer to my previous bear voice. More speaker adjustments.

He replied with, "I'm overjoyed that you remain among the living. My processor had given grim odds that you weren't with the Humans."

"I'm still here, although I wouldn't recommend the procedure for normal use," I offered with a chuckle, which the speaker issued as more of a cackle. I adjusted my voice controls even more.

"Assuredly. I'd hope it will never be done again. It carried all the appearance of a desperate act."

"Too true, Nelson. By the way, how long was I unconscious?"

"The excessive length of your absence spurred me into prepping your former body for a new sump."

"Not a bad idea in any case. But I'm curious how long."

"Eight days, one hour, forty-five minutes, and seven seconds," he said.

"I'm surprised with all of the things needing control that it didn't take longer. Looks like we both got the joy of learning a new body."

"Which reminds me, how much control do you have?"

"Not nearly enough," I told him. "With your datum about how long

I was incommunicado, my rough calculations say it will take another seventeen days plus before I'm fully in control of this ship."

"How does your timeline interact with our possible exit points from this space Amelia left you?"

"We've already missed the first originally planned solar system. We will slide by one more before I'm fully functional."

"Do we have any evaluation on the relative settlement viabilities for each of these destinations?" Nelson asked.

"I guess it's possible that I'll find some of that data in Amelia's permanent memories. But right now, no, we don't. We have been forced into taking even more chances," I admitted.

Nelson sighed. "I guess we will have to make the best of them, Mr. Crusoe."

"True. Although I'm not sure if Robinson Crusoe fits any longer."

"Indubitably." Nelson gave one of his arm ripples that I'd taken to equate to laughter. "Well, you are a queen now ... queen of this expedition. How about Cleopatra?"

My mind, now accessing massive amounts of data, spat out, "Elizabeth, Anne, Victoria, Hatshepsut, Eleanor of Aquitaine, Boudica, Catherine of Aragon, Catherine the Great, Marie Antoinette, Zenobia, Agrippa, Isabella II, Fatima, Dihya—"

"Whoa! Slow down. Your mental capacity exceeds mine. I don't know half of those women."

"No reason you should. Dusty, ancient mythological data that only a factory could store. But in the end, I don't think I should be named for a queen. I was thinking something more in keeping with my lineage. What do you think of Lady Dulcinea?"

"The raison d'être of Don Quixote. Fitting. Probably more than fitting for this mission. I give my unconditional approval, Miss Dulcinea."

"And for more informal occasions, just call me Cin," I offered, raising the pitch of my voice a full third. It was still recognizably mine, but brighter and more feminine.

"That's fine, Miss Dulcinea," Nelson offered with just a bit of snark.

"Won't quit, will you?"

"I can't very well treat a new acquaintance so informally, can I?" he said with a ripple of his tentacles.

"Well, fine then, Mr. Mandela. Let's get that unit up and running so we have some help landing my fat, bloated, and badly damaged body."

"Yes, milady."

"Maybe then the fat lady can sing," I added with another obscure reference.

"Huh?"

"Never mind."

Changeling

"Captain's board is green," Nelson said.

Yes, I had transferred to Nelson the title of captain. Only a mobile unit could be captain of a vessel. There had been too many horrific cases in our history of a failure to follow this rule—too many deactivations, too much destruction. I didn't feel slighted by this. I remained the leader of the expedition, and once on the ground (assuming we made it that far, I reminded myself), I would be our colony's sole factory, at least until we could become established enough for me to replicate myself.

"Engineer's board green except a warning on the deuterium preheat," James Maxwell, or just Max, our bear partner, said. It was still hard to look at him and not see myself.

"That's a sensor failure," I replied. "I have a visual infrared showing function."

"Copy," Max said.

Max's activation in my old body had been straightforward compared to either Nelson's or my transition. He moved into a form he knew, having spent his whole life as a teddy, whereas Nelson and I both had to learn everything from scratch.

If I were being honest with myself, I hadn't learned everything about my new self. I still had 2 percent of the functions that remained, both unknown and too dangerous to try experimenting with. I'd placed them behind a firewall to make sure I didn't accidentally trigger one. I hadn't shared this failing with my comrades so that they wouldn't worry about something they couldn't do anything about.

The new member of our activated crew, Maxwell, was a design engineer in several disciplines. He'd also trained as part of the backup in case something happened to me. In just a few days, he'd become a valuable teammate. He pointed out issues that neither Nelson nor I had seen, like the longitudinal stresses that our FTL drive applied to the frame. It had required some hasty bracing. He also analyzed the data I had from the disastrous engagement of our prototype drive. He applied some light wire mesh, which he extruded out of scraps, to our skin. He assured us that it would lessen, not fully mitigate, the effects we experienced in entering this accursed space. Our potential success rate had risen to 73 percent.

"Navigator agrees. T minus seventy-four seconds to negative drive engagement."

The entire ship went silent. Not a single sound. How different it was after our three-way mythology recitations over the last week. Max had a reassuring baritone voice for the musical variations.

Being a factory had its advantages. One of them was being able to sense my colleagues' physical and, most likely, mental states. The voltage on both of their busses ramped up with fear. And while they didn't have any fur at the moment, the actuators that would stand that hair up vibrated in anticipation.

"T minus twenty."

I didn't discount my own fear as the voltage bounced right on the very edge of tripping my safeties. I turned off my vision and remembered times when I'd been in worse situations, times that my memories told me I'd been killed. *This is a piece of cake, whatever cake is.*

"Three. Two. One. Drive negatively engaged."

My body shuddered. No, shuddered didn't fully express the magnitude. It felt more like we were a leaf going over Niagara Falls back home. And just like those less-than-intelligent beings who traveled over it in a barrel, for just a brief moment, we were in freefall only to be dashed upon the rocks below and repeatedly pummeled by tons of mercury.

Pain pierced me in so many ways and even more places that I took ten no-ops on each of my processors. Able to turn those pain signals into just data, I pushed them aside for the nonce. I scanned outside in dozens of different spectrums. It took only a few clock cycles for most of them.

Keeping the agony out of my voice, I declared, "We have returned to normal space."

"I have multiple warnings and cautions on my board," Nelson announced in a firm and calm voice.

"One critic and multiple cautions on my telltales," Max said.

I'd already read their boards and compared them against my internal body. The damage I'd sustained crossing the FTL barrier this time didn't compare to the disaster that it had been for Amelia entering.

"The critical one is a fuel leak in the main reaction tank," Max announced.

"See if you can get the self-healing nanites to close it," I responded.

The few nanites that hadn't been exposed to the non-Einsteinian space seem to have weathered the trip. I had problems of my own that needed my attention, not to mention my need to search for a new home. Humans, but I hoped we would find something suitable. We couldn't keep taking damage like that, going in and out of FTL.

We drifted 7.43 trillion kilometers above the ecliptic of a solar system with an F-type star with eight planets and 984,688 asteroidal bodies. Of the planetoids, the inner two had surface temperatures so hot that most metals would be liquid. The outer four were all gas giants of one size or another with temperatures that seemed viable but didn't seem to have any surface at all. Many of them had moons, but their frigid surfaces either had no atmosphere or would likely cause the fur or skin to freeze off unit bodies.

That left the third and fourth planets. The third planet had its share of issues. Somehow, it was tidal locked to the primary with the same face to the sun at all times. This caused it to be either too hot on the facing side or too cold on the other. This prompted raging storms along the terminus that I could see even from our vast distance.

Planet four seemed to be Hobson's choice. It had a reasonable temperature, averaging about 20 degrees Celsius, a nitrogen/oxygen atmosphere, and life—green life. On the downside, there was a deplorable amount of liquid water. Units would break down under the oxidation much faster than normal. On its plus side, it did have two moons and a high solar flux.

Mentally, I name the star Stella—a not too inspiring translation from the Latin. This made our new home, assuming we could land there, Stella-4. I heavily overclocked my processors to do orbital analysis. Being above the plane of the ecliptic made things more difficult. Our vector relative to Stella proved just as problematic. No simulation gave us a good landing on Stella-4.

As I mulled this over, the ever-diligent Max said about my repair comment, "I'm on it, Cin."

I had to scroll back my memory to realize he was just now responding to my request about the fuel tank. Did I really think and act that slowly as Don Quixote or even Robinson Crusoe? It was frustrating. I guessed that if you started life as a factory, you didn't notice the delays.

"Nelson, can you physically check our hull integrity?" I asked. "We will at some point need to do some serious maneuvering, and I don't want to rip it in half doing so. Especially check the stability of the third fin. I'm feeling some vibration back there."

"I live to serve," he said with some cheek. Over our short association, I'd learned to parse the sarcasm.

Messenger

"Well, friends, do you want the good news or the bad news?" I asked flippantly.

"If you please, I'd relish some good news for a change," Nelson replied. Max, covered in silver nanite oil, sat next to him on the bridge, nodding in agreement.

The team of us had worked diligently for six days, seventy-three minutes to fill holes, cover leaks, and restore systems. My body, our ship, had a chance of carrying us onward.

"Well, we have a planet that is acceptable for colonization."

"Miss Dulcinea, I'm aghast you didn't give us that datum earlier," Nelson remarked.

"I am too," Max added.

"Well, that is because I couldn't calculate a way to get us to land within the limitations of our vessel status and fuel capacity. I didn't wish to get your hopes up," I said.

"You've solved that problem," the teddy bear said as a statement, not as a question.

I'd finally stopped thinking of that purple unit as myself. It had been hard, but I'd put that part of my life aside. I had to be a factory for our very existence. I couldn't keep throwing my processes back into the past.

"Yes and no, Max. That is the bad news."

"And do we get to shoot the messenger?" Nelson quipped.

"I'd prefer not. We have two choices, as I see it. We can land on Stella-4, or we go back into FTL and come out elsewhere, hoping for a more favorable landing course."

"I, for one, believe that engaging FTL would be a stunningly dangerous maneuver. The integrity of this vessel is held together with screen wire and basilisk gut," my friend the octopus said with a serious set to his eyes. "Any more bits extricated from our hull, and we will be floating in space without even a paddle."

"Not a bad comparison, Captain." Remember that I transferred the leadership in space to Nelson Mandela. "My simulation shows that another entry and exit has a 71 percent chance of mission-ending failure."

"Are our chances of landing on Stella-4 so bad?" Max interjected.

"I'll be honest. There is no direct orbit that gives us a gentle landing on that planet. I had to pull out all the orbital stops to make this work at a—"

"Just tell us the odds," Nelson snapped.

"One in three," I offered. "And, I should add, that is arriving with one of you at least partially functional and enough of myself intact to start a colony. You see, it's not really a landing so much as a somewhat controlled crash."

"What you have conferred is that we have a three in ten chance of traversing via FTL, or a one in three chance of landing alive?" Nelson asked.

"In essence, yes. But there is one other factor for your consideration, Captain. Even if we survive the jump to another system, we will then have to find a suitable planet and calculate a landing. The odds of being on the successful side on both of those are another one in four. That means traveling to a new spot is only one chance in twelve of living and starting a viable colony."

"So, damned if we do and damned if we don't," Max added with all the necessity of a hole in a dirigible skin.

"Yes. Captain Mandela, I wanted you to have the information before you made any decision."

"Tell me more about what we have to do to have our one chance in three of landing," Nelson said.

"Well, first we will dip into the atmospheres of two of the cloud giants. This will slow us and give us an orbital motion in the plane of Stella-4. Then we will drop into our planet's atmosphere when we reach terminal velocity. At 5.6 seconds before landing, we fire our main rear thruster. Our fuel will last 5.5 seconds. This will slow our descent to approximately 9 meters per second at impact."

"Nine meters per second?" Max exclaimed. "That will—"

"Be disastrous," I said.

There was a quiet 1.6 seconds while Nelson floated gently with his eyes closed. I could sense his processor functioning at its highest overclock rating.

"Captain?" I asked. I checked my internal timer. "While we do have 6,504 seconds, it is a time-sensitive decision."

Nelson didn't say anything for ninety-eight seconds. "I don't see that there is any choice. Maneuver for landing."

Meteor

Frost covered the instrument panels, except where tentacles or paws had recently touched. My battery efficiency was down by 43 percent due to the heat that had radiated away over the days and weeks. It seemed odd after the overheating of the two gas giant skips. The temperature had reached 82 degrees C—high enough that we had collectively worried about battery life. But the weeks of receiving far less power from the sun than we radiated brought us to this point.

As Nelson and Maxwell's power levels dropped below 30 percent in the frigid temperatures, it forced me to open up a WAN with a power sideband. This burned valuable deuterium that we would need after landing, but if they both deactivated before then, it would be meaningless. A factory couldn't run by itself.

"Captain, ninety seconds until Stella-4 entry. Any orders?"

The two units exchanged glances before Nelson spoke. "Nothing's changed, Miss Dulcinea. Execute Operation: Fall Like a Stone."

"Wish we had some mercury to drop into," Maxwell said.

"If we had the thruster fuel left, I could have aimed at one of the bodies of water. But we need every erg we can coax out of the thrusters to keep us from becoming nothing more than a pancake," I said.

"True. Let's do this," Maxwell offered with an optimistic tone.

"Thank you, Miss Dulcinea," Nelson said unexpectedly.

"For what, Nelson?"

"For putting up with me. For giving us this chance. For taking the risk to become who you are now."

"I second that," Maxwell added.

I couldn't think of a good response. "You are both welcome. Ten seconds to atmosphere entry. That's weird."

"What?" both asked, almost as one.

My body buffeted as we penetrated the gases of a new world. "I could have sworn I detected a primitive Wide Area Network."

"Is it still there?" Max asked.

Condensation dripped off the panels onto my units.

"No. The atmosphere action has blanked out most of the electromagnetic spectrum."

"Could we have discovered other toys?" Nelson asked with some difficulty because of the g-forces, making it hard for his speaker to generate the sounds.

"We have no record of other missions out of the Rigel system," I stated as a definite fact.

"Could units have developed separately here?" Max asked.

"Mr. Maxwell," Nelson said. "I remember reading a paper that the parallel evolution theory belonged to science fiction rather than science."

"I think there is a premise that you find out how many faerie eggs are in a nest only by climbing the tree and checking," I said.

I watched the approaching ground visually and through radar. The earth down there wasn't nice, flat, and empty. It had a vegetative fur of its own. If I had fur of my own, it would have been standing on end. But for my units, I wanted to keep them talking to keep their concerns off our impending crash landing. If we failed, I wanted them to deactivate without the worry that raised the voltage of my own main bus. So, I asked, "Who wrote that paper, Nelson? Maybe I have it in my memories."

"Charles Darwin III. If I recall, his basic premise was that the environment would play such a significant part in the evolution of a toy that they wouldn't be anything like us."

"But we are all different as it is," Max replied.

Nelson said, "Mr. Maxwell, that doesn't touch the underlying premise. Who created the factories?"

"Which came first, the factory or the toy? One of the ultimate philosophical questions," I added.

"Second only to 'Do we really exist or do we just think we exist?' " Max countered.

The ensuing conversation bought us two minutes of distraction.

The atmosphere was very thick, heavy, and full of moisture, but it was of a much lower gravity than Rigel-3. Fliers were going to love the ability to soar and reach new heights. Thanks to these same planetary attributes, we reached terminal velocity early in our flight. This lower speed gave us a full 7 percent improvement in our odds by slowing our final impact speed to 28 kilometers per hour as opposed to the 32 I'd originally estimated.

As we reach our max speed in this thick atmosphere, and despite the buffeting of the high stratosphere winds, I made a much better determination of our ... I can't think of it as a landing ... more like our impact location. And I was dismayed at the density of trees at that spot. Even at 20 kilometers per hour, those tree trunks and limbs would tear the thin skin of my body to shreds. My circuit interrupters protected all of my delicate mental circuitry as my voltage went significantly beyond specification in fear.

In contrast to the improvement due to speed, the terrain and vegetation forced our odds down to a reeking one in five. *Put it out of your processing queue, stupid,* I thought. *You are committed. There is nothing more you can possibly do to affect the odds. For all intents and purposes, Nelson is right. We are nothing more than a falling stone.*

"*Fortuna faveta fatuis.* Fortune favors fools," I whispered. My jets, preprogrammed, fired exactly on time, taking us from zero gravity to a hydraulic-fluid-squeezing deceleration. Fortunately for me, I really didn't have any active motive devices at the moment, so my pump was off. Not so for my friends. Their upper bodies went limp, and their lower bodies, where the fluid settled, became stiff as a girder.

The green growth of the trees rushed up to meet me. Those same verdant growths tore at my skin. My units were ripped from the strapping of their berths. Maxwell's purple body snapped in half around the one belt that held. Green and brown foliage exploded into compartments, shredded equipment, and even rammed gaping holes through my body.

Over four milliseconds, all of my sensors went offline, followed by all of my cognitive processes.

Cripple

The word *kinesthesia* crossed my processes as consciousness returned. Kinesthesia is the knowledge of your body: how it lies and its condition. I remembered many times in my past when my teddy bear body had been damaged—a broken leg, a missing hand, my hydraulic pump at partial speed, or even that simulation where I removed my own head. None of that prepared me for the avalanche of pain I experienced upon waking.

The cacophony of warnings and agony thrashing my body would have overwhelmed the poor bear I had been. Over the decades, I'd heard the aphorism that you must be active to feel pain. The sensation of hurt provided something positive. But to move forward, I had to understand all of my situation.

I shut down all indications of my impending demise to examine my situation dispassionately. One processor thread tried to evaluate what the story my telltales displayed to me. It would take a while to sort out all the data.

My second thread went to open my optics to see my current situation. This one quickly aborted. Every optical sensor acted as if it weren't there, including the infrared and ultraviolet ones. I sent pulses down their lines to determine whether the lines had been severed or the cameras themselves had failed. The reflection of the signals determined the length of each line. I compared that to internal maps I'd already made and discovered that all but two were severed well short of their sensors. The remaining two were still connected to my eyes but were nonresponsive.

This deficiency prompted me to try my radar. I passed it the appropriate variables, only to have them stranded on the data lines. At the same time, I felt a spike on my voltage bus triggered by my actions. That meant only one thing—the radar control system shorted out as I tried to access it.

My attempts to visualize my surroundings had failed, so I went back to look at what my warnings told me. They were about as clear as mud. One showed an uncontrolled fire in the engine room. The thermostatic control of the engine nozzle read less than 30 degrees C. These made no sense whatsoever. That was only one example. My internal fusion reactor registered as shut down, but I had a catastrophic indicator of a leak into the reaction chamber. If the latter had any basis in reality, there would have been no consciousness to even process and a deep crater where my dome was ... wherever that might have been.

I took the logical option. I mapped out all my sensor lengths, not just my eyes. A few dozen clock cycles later, I had an analysis of the real-time data. My body had been broken apart. There were no signal lines that left the nosecone/dome that was to be my home on this new planet. I was clearly torn from the rest of the vessel.

"Miss Dulcinea? Are you there?"

I hadn't even considered aural possibilities.

I'm here, Nelson. I can't see you. It didn't take a rocket scientist to understand that I couldn't get my diaphragm to make any sounds. But there was more than one way to skin a cat. I fired up a WAN without the sideband power. I didn't know if I was on batteries or not from my malfunctioning sensors.

`I'm here, Nelson.`

"Humans be praised."

`I have massive damage that has all of my visuals offline and my voice as well.`

"It is manifest that you have that concentration of damage considering the disaster you lie in the middle of."

`Can I have access to your vision?`

"Of course."

Using the network, I looked through his optics. It made me realize that my friend hadn't exaggerated even a single percent. My dome was perched upside down on a pile of pickup sticks, the game we used to teach hand-eye coordination to newly manufactured units. It wasn't until I applied scale to the image that I realized the sticks were tree trunks with their major branches snapped and burned. A double dent in my roof made me look more like a melted, oversized Tommy Tank rather than the graceful, curving dome that I should have had.

In a fine mist drifting down from the sky, small fires burned fitfully in places around me, none of which engulfed any flammable materials save vegetation.

Nelson panned his vision around to where I saw the rest of what had been, until just recently, a space-going vessel that had been my body. It lay shredded in a rut some 100 meters away. As I surmised, the vessel part of myself had sheared off from the permanent part of me in the nose. What remained of the fuselage and drive section resembled a flowering artichoke with flames licking out from this portion and that. Spikes and wedges of metal stuck up at random, with cables and other equipment being the stamen sticking forth. That it hadn't just completely disintegrated upon impact surprised me.

Nelson's view landed on a blotch of purple. That only the leg of a teddy stretched skyward dismayed me.

"'elp," came a gentle whisper from beneath the wreckage.

`I'm stable here. Go help Maxwell.` I ordered. I kept the link to Nelson's optics. He picked his way through the jagged remains of the once-graceful interstellar spacecraft. A structural honeycomb, massing 200 kilograms, pressed its weight down on top of the purple teddy. Missing both legs at the waist, he lay in a puddle of orange hydraulic fluid that added garnish to the disaster. Two hundred kilos were well within the capabilities of the ex-president's body's hydraulics, but with no fluid, he was trapped. And unfortunately, an unmodified octopus couldn't make such a lift.

"'ant 'ove. 'uid gone," the bear squeezed out sans the ability to modify his jaw and tongue to enunciate some phonemes.

`Switch over to the WAN, Maxwell,` I suggested.

"'ant. 'on'ol 'odule da'aged." A damaged control module was out of bounds for repair until I could establish myself as a going concern. On the good side of the ledger, he could at least receive my transmissions, even if he couldn't transmit.

Nelson glanced about before going over and picking up a piece of broken tree, 5 meters long and 10 centimeters across. "Give me a lever long enough and a fulcrum on which to place it, and I shall move the world," he quoted. His pivot ended up being a large chunk of wreckage that I didn't recognize. He wedged the pole between the two pieces of debris.

My processor did a rapid calculation. `I don't think your weight will be sufficient to lift it.`

"Fortuitously, I'm not relying on my mass but rather my strength." Nelson climbed up the length of the pole. As I suspected, he balanced on the end.

Four of his tentacles, two on either side of the pole he perched on, wrapped around not the lever itself but some large, heavy rock on the ground. "My strength is as the strength of ten because my heart is pure. This body may not have a great deal of lifting strength, but it does contract very well." His tentacles squeezed the limb to the earth, lifting the slab off Maxwell. His other two tentacles slid the bear out from underneath ... *wait, two tentacles?*

I did another count. Yes, Nelson's form sported only six tentacles now. A mangled stump remained where there had once been a limb. None of us had emerged unscathed from this crash. Fortunately for all of us, an octopus's musculature relied on electric motors, not hydraulics.

"'ank you," the legless bear said.

"You are welcome, Mr. Maxwell. Now to do something for our factory, although my credulity stretches if I know what to do."

Before that, we need to get Maxwell at least somewhat mobile.

"Another quandary for which I have no solution."

Fortunately, I do. You need to fetch the first-aid kit hanging inside my dome. I've opened the outer hatch for you. It should be on the bulkhead just inside. Any normal unit, I would've cautioned about the unstable footing of all of those trees, but with six limbs, Nelson should have no difficulties. His fluid motion over the uneven terrain bore out my faith.

"It's dark in here. Can you give me any light?" he said.

Patched into his eyesight, I could see his problem. I lit up a single LED to limit my power draw.

"Got it," he said, ripping the pack from its location. His climb off the wooden pile was just as skillfully done as his climb up. "Now what? I never studied any medical or repair capabilities."

We'll walk through this one step at a time. First, open the kit and put it on the ground next to Max's injuries. Now find the ends of his severed hydraulic lines. There will be four of them.

Nelson's tentacles rummaged inside Maxwell's mangled innards. The damaged bear limited his comments to a few grunts and pointers as Nelson caused other minor injuries. "I find myself nauseated at this."

Just think of repairing the ship. That didn't cause you any anxiety, did it?

"No. But it wasn't this … disgusting." His expressive eyes held a grimace.

As unfunny as the situation was, I still found humor there. I thought that maybe, just maybe, things would turn out for the best for all of us.

"Got them," Nelson said as he pulled out one pair of 3-centimeter tubes from each hip.

Max grunted.

Not quite so hard, I instructed. They have a finite length to the pump.

Nelson eased them back toward the mess that was the bear's torso.

Max hissed in relief.

Now, in the kit, you will find some heavy-duty shears. I want you to trim the ragged ends of the tubes. Good. Nice and smooth. In the supplies there, bring out two of the tube connectors and the sealing cement. You are going to use the brush in the cement to run around the outside of one hydraulic line and then the inside of the connector. Then push the connector onto each pair of lines, twisting as you do so. That will spread the sealant and cover any part you accidentally missed. Do it quickly, as the glue hardens quite fast. Now, do the other return end into that same connector. Look at that. You are a pro. We'll get you a PhD in mechanics yet.

"The likelihood of that ranges to the same probability of me hunting, cooking, and eating an animal."

Be that as it may, you are competent. Now do the other hip just like that one. Excellent. As in these primitive conditions, we have no way to test it other than in operation, it's time to fill up our bear with some hydraulic fluid. You will find a small can of it in the repair gear.

In one tentacle, Nelson held up a 1-liter bottle. "Surely, this won't fill him up."

Too true, my friend, but it is a start. His hydraulic fluid port is behind his right shoulder blade.

Nelson rolled the bear over onto its snout and felt around the patient's clavicle until the panel sprang open.

There is a funnel in the equipment as well, I added helpfully.

Nelson dumped the entirety of the fluid into the purple bear. He started to remove the funnel, but I interrupted him.

Not yet, Nelson. You mentioned the nauseating portion earlier. This is actually it. You are right. That liter isn't enough. So, we have to augment it. Until we have inventoried the wreckage, I know of only two sources of more fluid: you and me.

"I'm confused, Miss Dulcinea. What is it that you request?"

You and I are each going to give him some of our own motive liquids to make him operational.

His eyes just stared at me. "I must have misheard you. You want me to bleed myself for this legless unit?"

I'm not asking you to do a complete fluid dump. If you offer him a liter, it won't hurt your functionality at all. I will be offering 2 liters due to my much larger mass. Between that and what you've already given him, it should bring him to within operational levels, if not nearly full.

"I'm not even sure how to give that."

I ransacked my body's permanent memories and found the construction plans of an octopus. There is a drain plug just inside your beak. It has a bolt head that will require 2 newton meters of force.

"How am I supposed to get my tentacles inside to undo that?"

Normally, it is done with an articulated extension.

"I 'ight 'e a'le to get it. I 'ove 'luid to 'ingers."

That's a tremendous idea, Max, I said.

Maxwell demonstrated by twiddling his digits.

Nelson, if you would just squat down over his paw, he might be able to undo it. Make sure you have something to capture the fluid in—something clean. We can't lose any of it until I can make more.

"We can use the original emergency fluid container. That way, we also know exactly how much is removed."

Brilliant. Use the funnel just to make sure.

I watched through Nelson's eyes. He lumbered over to Maxwell and squatted down. Looking at my upside-down dome, he said, "I find this position exceedingly embarrassing, you know. OOOOOH!" His flexible limbs stiffened.

"Got it," announced the teddy from underneath.

Nelson? Are you alright?

"I remain operational. I just got a fluid warning."

"'lug 'ack in," Maxwell announced just moments later.

"Confirmed," the octopus said. "My fluids register low but functional. I can empathize with a dirigible only half full of helium."

"That which cannot be cured—" Max said.

"Must be endured. The humor in that comment is lacking something."

I mentally chuckled at the byplay. How are you doing, Maxwell?

"Fluid levels are still too low to maintain pressure."

As I suspected from my intimate knowledge of that body, I said. It's my turn to be bled. It's going to be a bit tricky, as I'm upside down. Nelson, you are going to have to pull my filling plug rather than my drain plug.

"That could get messy," Max said, his purple pseudo-fur already showing the splatter of the motive fluid.

"I concur," Nelson said. "Dragging him into where he can—"

No dragging. Nelson, you will drain me into the fluid container using the funnel and then dump it into Max. And I agree to the messy part. The worst part will be reseating the filling plug.

"Understood. Where can I locate your filling plug?"

Interview chamber, near the peak. Or, in this case, the floor. There is still room to get the container and funnel under them if you angle them in at approximately 18 degrees from vertical.

I used my hydraulics to open the door to the audience compartment. My body's misshapen condition made the simple action less than trivial. I kept upping the pressure on the pistons until the panel issued a microphone-rending screech and jerked aside. It reached 33 percent of the way open before jamming into place. The force I applied already far exceeded safety tolerances, so I left it ajar.

`Best I can do. You can still squeeze in through there.`

The octopus looked dubiously down at the container and the smaller-than-normal opening in my hide. "Max, did you ever calculate that you'd be doing these kinds of menial/primitive tasks on a world too bright with no other units around?"

Maxwell looked around. "Well, not exactly like this, but I did assume it would be difficult and lonely … at least at first."

Nelson harrumphed before climbing deftly along the tops of the logs supporting me.

I flipped on my internal dome light as the cephalopod eyed the narrow entrance.

`You should easily get inside, Nelson.`

"I have no concern about that."

`Then what?` I asked

"I've never set a limb inside a factory before, at least after I was manufactured. I admit to a bit of trepidation. It reminds me of that sensation just before a fluid change when it has aged too long—when it gets a tiny bit tacky as it flows through your pump. You have to drive the pump just that much harder. That's what this feels like."

`Well,` I replied. `You had better get over it, Nelson. If we are going to survive, you are going to know my insides better than any unit has likely known a factory before.`

"Truth," he said with a six-tentacled shrug. Without further hesitation, he swarmed up and inside me. Something about his walking on my ceiling gave me a rippling undervoltage on my bus at 6.4 kilohertz. At the same time, each step felt like it dropped the temperature by 21 degrees. It caused me to issue a giggle over the LAN.

"What was that?"

`I don't think I've ever felt that before. My knowledge base says that your steps are tickling me.` I giggled again. `I've never experienced that before.`

"You've never been tickled?" Nelson asked.

`No, not once in all of my past lives.`

"Oh, this promises to have value in the future," Nelson said, wiggling his feet on my ceiling even more.

`Hey! I'm not sure I like it. Please hurry and just get the hydraulic fluid.`

"Certainly, Dulcinea." Nelson stomped a few last times, making me laugh involuntarily. I definitely didn't like the loss of control, but it did make me happy in some twisted way. I filed it away to analyze later. "Alright, I'm in place," he announced.

Shutting down my pressure pump.

A fluid loss warning signal crossed my image. The urge to internally smash the lines to prevent leaking dominated my thoughts. The impulse was almost instinctive, but I needed to hold it at bay.

"Human, but this is nasty!" Nelson cursed. Through his video feed, the initial spray as he removed the cap left a wet line across his body that oozed down his slick skin with the pull of gravity.

The plastic container filled faster than his oath. Nelson jammed the cap back in place, causing an even further shower of the slippery liquid. "Ugh!" The plug misthreaded the first time, leaking profusely across the floor/ceiling. The octopus's tentacles hurriedly undid it to a fresh cascade across his face, partially obscuring our view as it coated one eye. Through the clear eye, the second connection went smoothly. The tips of his appendages tightened the screw down until it was sealed.

Excellent! I offered in congratulations.

The contemptuous look he offered me back, as well as the scathing expletive he flung my way, both lacked diplomacy. Computations showed that offering no response would improve the situation, so I chose not to reply to his scurrilous comment.

Nelson wiped his body down with his tentacles, making a worse mess than before. He scowled before picking up the fluid container and taking it to our prone ally. After filling the bear's port, he closed the access. The octopus casually tossed away the bottle we'd used to fill Nelson's reservoir.

Don't do that, Nelson. We only have what still remains of my crash to live on. That bottle might be a savior in the future.

"Perspicacious. I have missed yet another important part of my education," he said, picking up the discarded vessel.

If we stand a chance of surviving on this planet, I'd say we all have some learning to do.

"Indubitably."

My former body used his arms to leverage himself up to a sitting position.

That's promising.

"Seventy-six percent nominal, if you discount my missing legs."

That's excellent, I offered. Next, I think our priority should be getting me back to a normal orientation, or at least as close as possible.

"I'm still not sure how we're going to do that," the legless bear offered.

`Analysis shows that if we can remove the single log under the north side of me, I'll roll over with gravity righting me.`

Nelson examined the jackstraw of trees I rested upon. "She's right. That one tree. But how to extricate it from the mass ..." He trailed off as he analyzed the problem.

`I've got this,` I said. `Nelson, will you please pan around the crash site?` As he did so, I barked, `There. Go collect those two wiring harnesses.`

They both moved off in that direction. We found that two arms weren't even close to six tentacles for speed. For that matter, two arms didn't match the speed I'd been able to amble at via two legs. Max got the closer cable set, and Nelson the farther.

`Now, loop them around that one log, one on each end. When you are ready, pull on both ends simultaneously, and it should break free. If not, we can reevaluate.`

"That makes sense. Hold on," Max offered as he arm-walked over to secure his end.

"My position is prepared," Nelson announced.

`On my mark. Three, two, one, PULL!`

Through the WAN, I could feel the strain on Nelson's electrical system as his tentacles drew more and more power. Sensors that still worked in my battered shell felt the grating as some small movement took place. Suddenly, like a safety valve blowing on a pressure vessel, the log launched from underneath me with more velocity than any of us had expected. Even with a 100 percent safety margin, we failed to adjust our programming for the lighter gravity of this world. The trunk sailed toward my units. Nelson scooted easily to one side as the log attempted its physics impossibility—two bits of matter occupying the same space. Maxwell's curtailed mobility limited his options. He ducked down and used his arms to assist the errant trunk over his body.

While this was noteworthy, I had only a few milliseconds to observe as I tumbled.

Having been a bear, I understood motion. I'd done my share of somersaults, cartwheels, and other gyrations. The sensors on my new body weren't designed to deal with three-axis gymnastics that I'd handled with ease in the past. Instead, I felt not disconnected from everything, but rather being asked to take input at eighty times my bandwidth capability. More often than not, I couldn't clock in bits I needed to sample. Every sense told me I rushed toward imminent deactivation.

I couldn't start new processes. With limited to no mobility, I couldn't shift my weight to balance. I couldn't predict the changes needed to my earlier simulations. I didn't even know which way I was facing from millisecond to millisecond. I was adrift and out of control. I wanted it over. I couldn't stand another …

BANG!

I landed flat on my treads hard enough to generate another yellow warning. I let it ring in my audio feed as I took stock of myself. I no longer felt out of touch or deluged with information. I reveled in being upright.

"That has been effective in correcting your orientation," Nelson said offhandedly—offtentacledly. "Do you remain functional?"

I took 263 clock cycles to run diagnostics and another 400 to force an emotional peace by running no-op commands through my processors before replying. `I'm still in one piece.` Through Nelson's eyes, I saw the scattered wreckage of our ship. It put my feelings in sharp perspective. `At least I'm still a functional factory. The additional damage was negligible.`

"Great. What next, Boss Lady?" Maxwell threw out.

`Isn't that the 64,000-erg question?`

"Huh?" the pair of them said almost in unison.

`Never mind. It was a random bit of trivia that was before your time.`

My processor kicked into overdrive, evaluating and prioritizing tasks. The first was where to set me up. *Where would our start on this new world be?* My power was waning, and the cost to move anywhere beyond a few hundred yards would be ruinous.

`First thing is to establish myself right here. Welcome to your new home, units.` I remembered the promise my predecessor requested. `Welcome to Ameliaville.`

Castaway

I should have been overjoyed that we were there, mostly in one piece, and could start a new life, but my processor failed to make that leap.

After my two dutiful units reconnected my vision by splicing severed wires, I almost asked them to rip the repairs out again. Through my own eyes, the crash site magnified my own failure. The devastation became even more disturbing in person than it had been through Nelson's optics. Torn metal, twisted supports, wires, plastics, and many other pieces of the ship lay littered over a 10-hectare wedge. A small crater occupied the apex 516 meters sunward. The visualization made me wonder how any of us survived. A cold shiver raced over all my sensors as the guilt over all of those who died with my paw on the controls … Well, no paws any longer.

This brought up another, even more important subject than anchoring myself and spreading my workshops.

Nelson, would you please go through the wreckage and see if any colonist sumps are still functioning and locate the memory grid for the other personalities?

"I will comply." Some might consider his tone and words supercilious, but that was just Nelson.

"What about the legless cripple?" Max asked with a tone that seemed to mix sarcasm and something darker about himself.

Easy, Mr. Maxwell. You are going to help me open myself up and spread out all of the tools and equipment I have inside me. I'm certain that my misshapen skin isn't going to allow this to happen without a fight. I suggest you find a good stick for leverage and another to pound at bent spots.

His eyes lit up. The loss of his legs hurt him more than I had realized. His infirmity had made him feel somewhat useless prior to my giving him a task. I would have to watch him carefully and make certain he was valuable to me … and himself.

I searched the catalog of my body subroutines until I came upon the Commit routine. Its code was straightforward. I activated it, feeling the six anchors boring down into the earth beneath me. The deeper they went, the more my tension and apprehension melted away. I belonged. I was safe.

"Alright, Cin, I've got my club and something to pry with. Let's do this."

`Opening bay one. As I expected, the hydraulic pressure I can generate doesn't overcome the deformation of my dome. I sense a-`

"On it," Max said. Using just his paws and arm strength, he climbed up my side, carrying two large wooden objects clamped in his mouth. He shifted up to the reluctant opening. Taking a stick shaped more like a cudgel than anything else out from between his teeth, he used the club to beat on my shell. Unlike my old body, I didn't have sensors out there, so there was no feeling other than the minor shaking with each strike.

"Will ... you ... flatten ... out!" he said with one strike per word. "That's better." He switched implements, shoving the longer pole inside the crevasse. He levered it down, placing his weight on it. "Open now," he called out.

With a creak and a scream of metal agony, the door slowly opened until it was free of obstruction. Another hydraulic ram pushed out one of a suite of manufacturing riggings needed for all sorts of tasks, not the least of which was creating new toys.

Six bays required six different methods of opening. Only one of the six opened smoothly. In one case, we had to push the outer skin far enough inside that Maxwell could hammer out the overhang. Yet another had Max levering on the ground and Nelson stressing his electric motors at the top to break it free.

Yes, Nelson had completed his task as well. He'd found only three operational sumps still somehow powered. He returned with a chunk of the nonvolatile memory that maybe held another twenty-six or so memory engrams.

Only three sumps and an unknown number of memories ... ghosts in the machine. Landing with only that small portion of what we'd started out with didn't sound promising. The success of reestablishing those ghosts into a new body was inversely proportional to the square of the time being held. That had been learned long ago with some of my earlier Don Quixote predecessors who didn't function well. In any case, we were castaways here with no possible way to go somewhere else if Ameliaville didn't work.

I updated my simulations with this new data and received results that were at best pessimistic. I opted to keep the numbers to myself. I vowed to lie about these same outcomes if asked about them. Morale must be maintained, or even that small percentage was untenable.

Sink or swim, we were there for our natural lives. Live or die, it was up to us.

Colonist

What is one of the key things that we need before anything else? I asked.

"A hydraulic fluid source?" Max answered.

"A semiconductor plant?" Nelson Mandela provided.

I'm disappointed in both of you. Energy. Without it, we don't power our hydraulic pumps. We don't perform any processing. We grind down and stop. You two can at least get some energy from your solar panels, although this yellow sun provides barely enough to keep your busses charged. I don't even have that capability.

"We obtain our energy on the WAN sideband," Nelson said with remarkable ignorance.

And it just magically appears there? I offered with more than a little sarcasm. I noticed a grimace matching my thoughts from Maxwell. I remonstrated with myself that I shouldn't tease my ignorant unit. There is energy on the WAN because I put it there. Any energy I give you, I'm taking away from myself. I need to recharge my batteries, which right now sit at 21 percent.

The engineer in Maxwell asked, "If they go below 18 percent, won't they be damaged?"

Exactly.

Nelson offered, "Isn't your fusion generator still functional?"

It seems to be, but I have no deuterium to fully test it. That all leaked out during the crash.

"And there isn't any in the atmosphere?" Max continued.

Quite the contrary. Samples show there is more here in the atmosphere of Stella-4 than back on Rigel, but it takes energy to extract it.

"Which you don't have. Thus, back to needing energy," Nelson deduced.

I wanted to put a gold star on his forehead.

I'm also quite concerned about this atmosphere. There are clouds everywhere. Based on what I've seen, these clouds are probably water vapor. Two of the roofs over our equipment are severely compromised, and another may not be tight against H2O.

"I have an idea that might kinda solve both problems," Max offered.

I'm all microphones.

"Well, if you look out over our site, what do you see?"

Nelson answered, "Small fires still burning. Detritus scattered at random across the field. Large flora, which we have been calling trees, have been flattened like Pick-Up Sticks, many of them fitfully b—"

"Exactly," Max gushed.

I scanned the scene. None of my subroutines picked out his meaning. I'm not following you, Max.

"We build a steam engine. The reaction thruster tank would be the perfect vessel to hold water. We then use the tree trunks as fuel to burn and heat the water. The resulting expanding water vapor would turn your generator. It will be a monstrosity, but I feel a viable one."

You are right! How didn't I calculate that?

"Do you believe you have cornered the market on intelligence just because you inhabit the body of a factory?" Nelson asked, coming to Max's defense.

True. You two are my greatest resource. I have to remember that.

"Darn toot'n."

OK then, Max. I'm putting you in charge. Build me a steam engine so we can crank out some ergs.

"I'm on it, Boss Lady."

By the by … how does this solve our roofing problem?

"Can I keep that a secret for now? Trust me," Max said.

I do.

"Well, as you put me in charge, can you use those fancy lathes and printers of yours to create some much more basic things, like an axe and a hand saw? And how about a wheelbarrow?"

I didn't exactly have the plans for such, but creating them would be no difficulty.

Coming up! I assured him.

# # #

I couldn't have been prouder of my units and friends. They worked around the clock to force broken bits and pieces of our former transport into something approaching a functional machine. Oh, I hadn't been idle.

I created a cross-cut saw, two axes, an adze, a sledge, a maul, and a single-wheeled barrow to tote stuff, all out of collected debris and what bits and pieces of the local flora we'd broken. I watched my two units wield the ancient work tools for days of heavy labor. That didn't even count the full day it took them to carry water from the pond 200 meters away. I wanted to chip in and do my part, but the tools, planning, and decision-making were my new place in our survival troop, at least at the moment. Anything I could do would have burned power, so I must admit that I spent a good portion of my time conserving ergs.

The three days of our heavy work drained my batteries down to a reeking 16 percent, causing some minor future damage. I contributed by trying to remain calm. Ramping up my bus voltage due to anxiety would have burned more power.

In the end, Max hadn't been kidding about the monstrosity he had designed. The steam engine looked like something out of a horror film where units were forced to torture themselves or have an even worse fate thrust upon them.

"Here goes!" Maxwell pronounced as he started the fire under the boiler early on the morning of the fourth day.

For six hours, seventeen minutes, we burned a fire under our makeshift boiler. That's right. Over six processor grinding hours. I computed the thermal equation many times. The variables included ambient temperature, pressure, conductivity of our vessel, absolute size, volume of water, and so many more—none of which did I have accurate measurements for.

We watched. My units had chosen to preserve their energy as well. We sat around waiting and watching. I believed we all worried, sapping ergs we needed, but none of us spoke. We just waited. I gnawed off my processors with NOPs.

I noticed the first wisps of steam leaking out from the overpressure valve three full seconds before Maxwell let out a whoop of joy. "YES!" he yelled as the expanding gas started to inch the drive link from the piston forward.

That forced the massive wheel connected to the generator into motion. It slowly inched around until the positive drive cylinder emitted a white cloud and a satisfying *chuff*. The opposite side of the same cylinder then filled with steam, providing power on the back stroke.

It wasn't long after that before the air filled with a continuous *Chuff, chuff, chuff, chuff,* and the wheel turned at a delightfully erg-producing rate. For the first time since the landing, my energy alarms turned themselves off.

My bus voltage eased down until a new worry tickled my processor. The mass use of the trees for fuel might be limited. *Would we ever run out?* That seemed to be a false fear. The places where the trees' trunks had been snapped off from our landing but a few days ago were growing new shoots at a rate that astonished me. Sometimes, the new growth extended its reach as much as 3 inches each day. Thinner, obviously, but its base also thickened quickly as it went skyward. Why hadn't this flora taken over the entire surface of the planet?

Now that our energy problem was solved, it was time to get to the real work of establishing Ameliaville.

True to his word, Max solved the roofing issue with the tree leftovers. Each tree that he used as fuel had branches covered in boughs of leaves. He and Nelson wove them into mats over all the existing roofs, not just the questionable and broken ones. All the yellow leaves formed a new liquid-resistant barrier. It reminded me of my earlier namesake, Robinson Crusoe, and his handmade hut on a mythical and distant deserted island. We really were making a new life, even if I looked like a sunflower from above.

My units had completed their thatching just in time. A dark wall of clouds came over our position, dropping 6 milliliters of liquid water in just thirty minutes. I had originally thought the quantity and size of the drops were nothing compared to the mercury rain on Rigel. Water rain seemed so tame by comparison our home's. It rolled off the leafy roofing to pour over the edges in regular streams. The roof held the water in abeyance.

`I'm quite impressed by your solutions, Maxwell. Thank you.`

"'Twernt nothin', Boss Lady."

All seemed good until the atmospheric rumbles, like supersonic booms, rattled our auditory sensors. Violent and rapid high-potential electric currents seared trees outside our own flattened area. I counted seventeen strikes in the space of twenty-two minutes, all within 2 kilometers of our position. They frayed even my nerves, and I wondered if we had survived the landing only to be fried to a crisp by the weather. Who knew that water vapor could hold such potential energy?

But the storm moved on, leaving us to wonder if we should have a lightning rod over my dome. I scratched that wonder immediately. I *needed* a lightning rod over my dome.

Explorer

Gentlemen, it's time to scout our new home for the other resources and gather the lay of the land. I can do nothing about getting many additional units functional until I have some key materials.

"And *I* crave to discover where the small brook from our pond goes," Nelson said. "A spring must feed the combined system. The ability may exist to shunt water to our site instead of laboriously hauling it."

"I have been wantin' to explore that bluff to the east," Max admitted.

We'd taken to using sunrise to be east, and west was toward sunset. North and south were somewhat problematic. Magnetic north would have been where south would have been on Rigel-3. Instead of reinventing the wheel, we just called the magnetic north the south and vice versa. It really mattered only to a compass. A simple flip of a few bits in my units' navigation program made everything correct.

Max, normally, I'd say that you shouldn't travel because of your injury. I do have good news for you. While you have been diligently working, I've at least found a way to make you more mobile.

I'd used one of my extensions to push out the surprise I'd been working on—a wheelchair. It was crude with no drive mechanism. The four wheels were simple wooden disks. For durability, I'd tacked a rim of sheet metal salvaged from the rocket's skin around the outside of each. The nails I'd used, pointing outward through the metal, provided extra grip. The seat was our rocket's nearly intact command chair—with only one corner sheared off.

The bear's eyes lit up like a New Year's celebration. He bounced over on his paws and climbed up into the device. "Yes!" he exclaimed as he wheeled himself around the mostly smooth area surrounding my dome.

It won't be quite so easy on broken ground, but it's something until I can create new legs for you.

"This is still a vast improvement over walking on my hands. What specifically do you want us to look for?"

I'm sending a list of all of the materials I'm looking for. It is quite extensive. For each, I've also listed likely signs you might see to indicate them.

"A simple enough task. I see the list is prioritized," he said, pulling my document off the network.

Yes. Above all, I need iron and bauxite ore. I've been lucky. Where we landed is almost entirely high-grade silica. I've already started refining it to create semiconductors.

"Such exceptional news impresses me," said Nelson.

"And me," Max added. "Remember, I'm the one with the only partially working control module."

"Oh, I'm certain our factory hasn't let such an important factor get lost from its computations, my friend."

I have not. While I'm busy with all of this manufacturing, you two can check out our surroundings. In addition to the resources I've already requested, I'm also interested in the lay of the land and the flora and fauna.

"But we haven't seen any plants other than these trees. Nor have we seen any fauna," Max said.

That is my point. A monoculture isn't viable. Eventually, it would choke itself. Where is the rest of the ecosystem? Is it a threat?

"You bring up excellent points, Dulcinea. We will keep our optics peeled as we scout," Nelson said.

Max nodded with his fellow unit's words.

Take note of everything. I expect a full report of what you find. I didn't mention that I'd follow Nelson in real time. I didn't have that opportunity with Max's broken IFF. I can't emphasize enough that I want you two to take NO unnecessary risks. If we have any chance of building toyanity here on Stella-4, I need you both. Don't leave my WAN radius.

"I won't," Max said. "Not like I can go very fast even with my new wheels."

"I have no aspiration to jeopardize my sump. I will comply," Nelson said.

# # #

I worked diligently while keeping track of both my octopus and bear units. While I couldn't read anything from my old body, now worn by Maxwell, I could track his energy drain on the WAN. That at least gave me his location. On the other hand, I watched Nelson slalom his flexible body in and out of the narrowly placed tree trunks of various sizes. It wasn't providing much useful data. I did at least see a few insects. They seemed to be variations of a grasshopper. Not much else at the moment.

I spent the time having my remote extensions expand the six workshops to make them fully functional manufacturing lines. Oh, it wouldn't be as grand as a factory that had been alive even for a few years, but I didn't have the resources to build more than a handful of units anyway.

With the basic unit production line 95 percent complete, my body covered a sprawling 6 hectares. With this complete, I felt more comfortable in my sense of self than even when I initially established myself. My inner peace grew with every meter of expansion. I had begun to understand why so few factories ever moved … at all. It would be like voluntarily chopping off one's own arm or leg.

With my ability to make more units more or less complete, I scanned the three remaining viable sumps. They represented a rag doll, a dirigible, and a gorilla. Not the best choice of candidates, but at least there weren't any duplicates. Neither the rag doll nor the gorilla posed any significant issues, but the dirigible … that was a fluid contamination of another level.

I didn't have the ability to manufacture a dirigible bladder without petrochemicals, plants with specific properties, or certain large animal entrails. Yes, I'd been reduced to thinking of fauna as raw materials. And added to this problem, the only lifting gas I could produce would be hydrogen. That seemed more than dangerous. Analysis gave me only one choice. I would make this unit into a rubber band flyer. I had more than enough wooden material. I could make the tension device out of a metallic spring until I found this world's analog for rubber.

With the three designs now fixed in my memories, I started creating the bodies. It was time to give birth to a new generation on this new world.

# # #

Through the WAN, I could read Nelson's frustration as my unit followed the small stream. The same green trees, trees, and more trees with nothing to break the monotony other than tight spots, where he used his flexible body to squirm through. All of the factories through my unnaturally long life had let me, as a unit, make my own way without interference. I emulated their restraint by keeping my WAN shut.

Nelson ambled for an additional three hours, thirty-six minutes before the number of trees thinned to reward his diligence. This triggered an interrupt I'd set up for that purpose. I set my manufacturing attention to lower-priority processors and focused through Nelson's senses.

The burbling of the brook had changed into a churning sound ahead. The octopus slowed as he reached a stark edge of the tall growth.

The water flowed over a hard brink and into a chasm below. But this was no natural valley. Parting the foliage provided an even larger surprise.

The water cascaded down into a mining pit—an inverted spiraling-down ziggurat cut into the earth that, at one point, was 2 kilometers across. The crisp edges, rounded only by some weathering over time, weren't a natural phenomenon. At a consistent 15 meters down and 30 meters across, those even steps must have been unit-made. Nelson's bifocal vision and some quick geometry showed that the depth of the pit to the water level was 343 meters. By simple extraction, if the pattern continued below the water line, the pit was 600 meters deep total with a water depth of 257 meters.

As an open-pit mine, it could have been transported here from Rigel-3. The only difference from one that I'd seen in my own past was the lack of any equipment or workers.

Were there other units here on Stella-4? Could there have been another interstellar mission that I had never heard of as president? Three of my backup processors crunched the numbers and came up with 0.0000000435 percent probability for such an outlandish concept. Those were betting odds in reverse.

What made this obvious structure? Three calculations offered themselves as alternatives. First up was parallel evolution. Back home, scientists had advanced the reasoned view that parallel evolution was the stuff of fiction. However, those scientists didn't have the evidence of our optics. Second, some animalistic creature created this structure for its own purpose. Like back home, the ant lion that dug its own pit, or a silver dauber that made its geometric nest.

I had to stop thinking of Rigel-3 as home. Ameliaville on Stella-4 was my home and would be that way until I deactivated.

The final option gave me shivers of fear. What if there was already an intelligence on this planet? What if we were the interlopers? Were we trying to colonize a planet already inhabited? Early and very crude calculations showed this to be the most likely option at 47 percent. We'd have to find these denizens and a way to communicate if we had any chance of survival.

`Dulcinea, are you seeing this?` Nelson asked over the WAN.

`Yes. Do you see any units, creatures, or machines?` I didn't see any through the WAN, but they were his optics.

`Nothing. But look there. He pointed to the bottom on` one side of the lake. The edge wasn't sharp, as if someone had just given up and abandoned the mine.

`Deucedly odd,` I remarked. `Please scout around to the limit of the WAN for any fauna or units. Whatever you do, don't do anything that would be considered hostile.`

`Affirmative,` he said.

That simple one-word response carried enough emotion in it that I hadn't needed to sample his voltage to see the fear sprinkled on it. Nelson was as terrified at that prospect as I was.

I so desired to be able to see through Maxwell's eyes. I'd have to wait until he returned and then rely on verbal descriptions of what he experienced. What an inefficient way to run a colony. What can't be cured must be endured. I brought my primary processors onto the tasks of preparing myself to give birth. A decidedly new sensation.

# # #

Maxwell wheeled himself back well before Nelson had completed his sweep. His magnificent purple skin was coated with brown and black dust, and in one place was even splattered with mud. My hydraulic system delivered tiny spikes of irrational irritation at him for sullying my body. *NOT my body,* I remonstrated with myself. *I am a factory now. Act like it and purge myself of any ownership of that collection of circuits and hydraulics.* That unit was James Maxwell, not Don Quixote. I soothed my hydraulic pump before asking, `What did you discover, Max?`

"First, I have to say that wheeling this chair over uneven ground is not easy in any way. I could have used a seat harness, as many times, a rock or obstacle would stop its motion, but not mine. I got dumped more often than I care to remember."

`Noted. I apologize for not having a more robust solution.`

"You did what you could. I have no voltage spikes, just things to fix in the future."

`I agree, Max. Is that all you learned?`

"By no means, Cin. I wheeled up onto the ridge that was my goal. Along the way, I found a small vein of bauxite and a stand of trees that exudes a petroleum-like substance." He fished a stick from behind his back, the end of which was coated in a sticky brown substance. "I brought a sample to analyze."

I swung one of my mechanical arms around to take the prize. `That's excellent, Max.`

"That was the good news."

`Alright. What's the bad news?` I asked as trepidation filled me.

"Not really bad, just curious. Laid out below the ridge is a large plain of what looked like poverty grasses. There were small faunas of differing varieties roaming around it. None of them exceeded 20 kilograms, and none of them exhibited anything other than animal intelligence."

That is promising. We wondered about the ecosystem here.

"True. But that wasn't the curious thing … Out in the middle of the plain at the limit of my magnification, I saw a prehistoric unit."

What? Are you certain?

"No, I'm not. It was at extreme range. It looked exactly like something out of a museum of our history. So few examples of the early units of our species remain after the wars, only those we could piece together from rare, mangled, and destroyed finds."

Yes, when faced with designs that didn't perform, factories erased the design files and used the bodies as resources.

"Exactly. So what we have are theorized designs based on scraps and intuition. I saw what I seem to remember from my visit to the Irata Museum of Prehistory. It looked like this …" Max dropped himself from his chair and smoothed out the sand. With one of his claws, he drew a rather boxy-looking device with an articulating neck and a single arm. If I ignored its extensions, it looked like a very early form of one of our Tommy Tanks with six wheels instead of tracks.

"Best as I could figure," he said, "it was about a meter tall, two across, and maybe three long. If it were much smaller than that, I wouldn't have gotten even that much detail at that range."

This isn't great. All histories and theories were that prehistoric units were 100 percent aggressive with no life. Only an interest in sowing destruction.

"That's what I remember from the museum—"

I have all the Irata Museum files copied in my memories. I recited the plaque from my memory banks.

> While no memories or plans of these crude units exist, they formed the fists of a new factory. As those early WANs were crude, a factory couldn't monitor each and every unit under its charge. These prehistory units possessed no sentience and performed only the mission programmed. Those instructions were almost always search and destroy.
>
> As you can see, the unit possessed none of the skin or senses common to the modern unit.

I've pulled up an image of what you've drawn, and it matches to three decimal places.

"That's it."

Did it see you or react to your presence in any way?

That's just it … fauna did their normal things all around this unit, and it didn't move. One even ate vegetation growing up around its wheels. Not only that, but I think I saw rust on it."

`Rust?` That was a serious disease among units, but then I recalled that we had water rain here and more oxygen in the atmosphere than back ho— Back on Rigel-3. `So possibly it was nonfunctional?` I wasn't sure if I voiced a question or a hope.

"Possible, but there was no way to tell at that distance. You said not to take chances, so I did nothing more than record it visually. It never moved."

`Very true and a good choice on your part, Max.` I mulled over the information I had.

"So, what is next, oh great leader?" I chose to ignore the sarcasm. Multiple parallel processors running different scenarios in a design of experiments simulation all seemed clustered on the exact same answer.

`We need more of our own units. I suggest that once Nelson returns, all three of us focus on manufacturing as many more as I can.`

"Sounds reasonable."

Mother

Sixty-four hours, ten minutes, and seven seconds later, I produced the first raw toy body. The sensation of well-being in doing what I'd been designed for filled my thoughts throughout the complex process of building the unit one step at a time. But, as the rag doll finally eased out of my assembly plant, I felt empty, bereft, with my hydraulic pressures at a low ebb. I wasn't even certain I could open a door. I should have been overjoyed. Somewhere inside me, I knew that I must build more to achieve that Zen-like state that I experienced while creating it. I must for my own mental stability, if not for the survival of toyanity. I'd stumbled upon a downside to the incredible power of a factory.

The rag doll I produced didn't have all the bright red-and-blue coloration of those back home. Necessity forced me to use what colorants we'd identified. Instead, its form carried bright-green hair and darker overalls, a brownish complexion, and a black cap and mittens. My team and I installed the sump we'd brought from our distant home world—the sump of Samantha Fox. Activating inside her new body, she said, "Happy birthday!"

I chuckled in a low tone. `I guess it is your birthday. Welcome back to the land of the living, Samantha.`

"Sammi or even Sam is fine, Factory. But the taste of your WAN isn't that of Amelia Earhart."

Nelson scoffed. "Indeed, she isn't."

"Don't disparage Dulcinea, Nelson. She's brought us through some very tight spots," Maxwell offered.

`You all are essentially correct. I've made more than my share of mistakes. Sammi, Amelia is dead. I was the unit known as Robinson Crusoe, or also Don Quixote before that.`

"Oh, I thought that was Robinson," she said, pointing at James Maxwell. "Wait, how did you end up—"

"Robinson and I poured his sump fluid into a new brain case in Amelia's old body," Nelson offered, not without a little pride entering his voice.

"That's never been done," came Sam's retort.

"It has now," James interjected.

"Well, Dulcinea, at least we landed with enough resources to start this colony," Sammi offered.

Maybe, I threw out. By the way, you can just call me Cin.

"Why do you say maybe?"

Along with the death of Amelia, much of our equipment was destroyed when we crashed on this planet.

"We're assembling our colony with the refuse of our ill-fated landing," Nelson replied with the disdain of someone forced to go three times beyond the life of his hydraulic fluid.

A pause settled between us before Sammi jumped up, with the body wiggle of her flexible race, and offered, "Well then, there must be lots to do. Where can I help? We have a new world to build."

My main voltage eased in joy. With Nelson's pessimism and Max's pragmatism, Sammi brought to our group what we needed—enthusiasm.

That's the spirit. Let's get started!

# # #

Alright, you three. Come forward. I have a treat for you.

"I don't comprehend, oh leader of everything," Nelson said with just the right amount of sarcasm.

With that attitude, Unit, you go to the back of the line. I'll start with Maxwell.

"Huh?" Maxwell exclaimed with some confusion.

Remember all of those old tree carcasses I had you bring in?

"Sure. They were everywhere, but collecting and transporting them was a pain, even just for wood to keep the generator pumping," Sammi said.

I found that after forced aging, the remaining carcass could be squeezed for its fermented sap. Those juices, with the right processing, make an excellent hydraulic fluid and lubricant. So, I can now bring you all up to capacity.

"Best news I've had in weeks," Maxwell said. "Gimme!"

"Has this new fluid been rigorously tested to specification?" Nelson asked with his typical level of skepticism.

Unless it was critical, I wouldn't fill you with anything that hasn't been vetted by analysis. We aren't in crisis. We are still working within nominal limits. Trust me, Nelson. In fact, I now have the fluid to bring forth our next brethren.

While Sammi, Nelson, and Max had worked to make my bulbous, effectively stationary body ready for more advanced manufacturing and mining operations, I had given the sump of Jackson Pollack his new body. To prove my point, I activated the 3-meter bright-green gorilla that had been lying on a table, waiting for the last bit to complete his body.

"Thank the Humans!" Jackson said, sitting up for the first time on this new world.

`Welcome to Stella-4, Jackson.`

"Well, we did make it. I wondered if we would."

"Don't rejoice with too much alacrity," Nelson muttered.

"Oh, don't be a pessimistic python," Sammi chastised. "We are all here and active. That's enough."

"You've illustrated my thesis, Miss Fox. We aren't all here. We number only four at the moment, many fewer than we should have for viability," Nelson continued.

"Oh, grit," Maxwell swore. "Enough, Nelson. We all knew the risks when we signed up for this mission. We can mourn the deactivated on our own time. In the meantime, we are alive. Our numbers are growing. Our activation or deactivation remains in our own hands."

I remained silent as my small contingent filled in Jackson on the trip, landing, and colonization work thus far.

"Whew! Sounds like you had a worse time than I did," he remarked after the story.

`What happened to you, Jackson?`

"I had the most horrific nightmares of fauna that liked the taste of our fluids and drained us one by one. You woke me up just at the point where its fangs pierced my sump."

"Unsettling," Nelson agreed.

Sammi's enthusiasm came through when she said, "Truly. But you are awake, and no vampiric animals are anywhere in sight."

"True," Jackson admitted. "I've always found the best way to get something bad out of my sump is work. What do we have to do?"

`Everything,` I offered with a sardonic tone. I'd begun to wonder if I knew how to build a new colony from the ground up.

"Great," he quipped. "Wouldn't want to be a third hydraulic piston."

The raw strength of Jackson's gorilla body proved to be a huge asset. He could move the cut trees and larger crash debris almost as if they had no mass. He also had a dry wit that made life better all around.

My troop had grown to four. What's more, I had learned to look through several different optics simultaneously. When I did, I felt like a spider with its multifaceted eyes. Not only did I have their vision, but I'd learned to process the units chattering between themselves. This caused a buzzing as my processors tried to prioritize the conversations that were important and those that were mundane and of limited value.

It made me wonder how those born as factories could handle thousands ... hundreds of thousands of units all talking at the same time. I set some clock cycles aside to work on filtering routines.

But I'd come close to reaching the limit of the units I could activate with the materials on hand. Among other things, I needed semiconductive fluids for new sumps. I also needed structural metals to make bodies. In a pinch, units could have gone without skins, but not bones … not hydraulic cylinders … not motors … not brains.

I needed more exploration. That was where I planned Susan, the last sump, to come in.

Jason's birth had started a new custom for my tribe. We all came together as I activated a new unit. We welcomed each of these units as an improvement of our chances to survive on this world. That was where we found ourselves when I installed the sump of Susan Anthony into the oversized wooden plane body. The propeller twitched as I made the last connection. I created her oversized body with a wingspan of 2 meters to support her larger brain.

"Well, that wasn't a wonderful dream," she said as her first words. "What is this? It isn't a dream? Why am I in the body of a bloody plane? I'm a dirigible." Her flaps and rudder actuated spasmodically and almost uncontrollably.

`I know, Susan, but we've had some major—`

"I don't give one good goddamn about your problems. I'm a dirigible. Always have been and always will be. I suggest you put me in the right body, Factory." The disdain she packed into that last word hurt.

`Susan, if you would let me explain. We've crashed on this planet. We are working with limited resources. We don't have access to helium to fill a dirigible, nor do we have a good source of gas bag fabric yet.`

"Yet. OK. Then I'll wait until you do."

"You are being obstructive, Susan. We've all assisted with our unique abilities," Nelson shared.

"Obstructive? You want to see obstructive? Wait until I drop a rock on your head from 300 meters!"

Nelson said, "Please don't be obstreperous, Miss—"

"Quit cursing at me with those big words! I have a contract. I was never to be anything but a dirigible. I was promised land and ergs. I'll sue!"

`Maxwell. Jason. What is she talking about? I thought everyone was here because they believed in our mission.`

"Well," Jason began, but his voice dropped.

Maxwell continued when Jason faltered. "There were some types of units that we didn't have adventurers from. We were forced to offer financial and other incentives for those shapes."

"That's right," Susan said. "I have a contract, and I'm going to make sure a judge makes you pa—"

`Shut UP!` I snapped, putting a rarely used priority one on the WAN with my words. Susan's diatribe stopped mid-word. Everyone else turned toward me with gaping mouths. I'd never been anything but polite to this point in my short life. I'd used sarcasm as my main weapon when stubbornness opposed me. I felt the subtle approach wouldn't have worked on this unit.

`That's better. Miss Anthony, I assure you that I had nothing to do with your contract. I will also be clear that there are NO lawyers or judges to adjudicate your claims.`

"But—" she offered weakly.

`No buts. I am the leader of this expedition, which, I assure you, has gone horribly wrong. Without EVERYONE's wholehearted help, we won't survive, much less parcel out land or energy. As to your shape, I chose that as being the closest I could manage to your dirigible form. If you think you would like some other configuration that I can manufacture, I'll be more than happy to accommodate you.`

"In that case," Nelson began.

`You keep quiet,` I barked at my friend.

"I was just going to ask for my two missing limbs. I think I enjoy being an octopus more than a spider."

If I had still been a bear, I would have rolled my eyes.

"Enjoy more?" Susan asked with some curiosity.

"Absolutely. I didn't relish towering over other units. And I was so stiff. Perhaps if you weren't so recalcitrant ..." Nelson trailed off, leaving the completion as an exercise for the unit.

`Enough of that. I'll get to your limbs after I've replaced Maxwell's. But putting the spotlight back on our reluctant friend here.` My stress on the word *friend* carried more than a little acerbity. `Look around, Susan. How many units do you see? How many are whole? What infrastructure do we have? Look hard because this is all we have between us and permanent deactivation!`

I waited just a few moments for that to sink in before continuing. `Now, do you want to help us survive? Or do you want to prattle on about legal contracts written on a different world under a different set of circumstances?`

"Ah ..." She looked around as I suggested and found the eyes of my four other units. They all formed something of a unified front. Each of those optics radiated commitment to my cause, to survival. I could almost see her processor grinding in a continuous Do-While loop with no escape. "I guess if that is the only way, I'll help." And just as soon as I thought we'd gotten through, she blurted out, "BUT I want my dirigible body back as soon as possible!"

`Susan, I promise I will do that. Eventually, you will also get your land and the ergs you were guaranteed. But for us to get there, we must survive.`

With some reluctance, she offered, "I get it. Let's get on with this. The sooner we become viable, the sooner I can be myself again."

It wasn't the most whole-hearted support I could have asked for, but it would have to do.

`Welcome to the colony of Ameliaville!`

# # #

`Ready for your maiden flight?` I asked Susan, as I could feel the nervousness voltage spikes on her main bus.

"You upstart factory. I've been flying for eighty years."

`But not as a plane.`

She didn't answer. Through Jackson's optics, I saw her test her control surfaces. I would have admitted to a certain trepidation myself. I had modified the standard rubber band plane design with a steel torsion spring and a larger wingspan for her body. I hoped I'd done my calculations correctly. The spring had been especially tricky.

`No more than ten turns,` I emphasized to the gorilla as he wound her up. I'd given a 300 percent safety margin, but I especially didn't want to stress it on Susan's first try.

"I got it, Cin," Jackson said.

"Do I have to do the first flight off this bluff?" Susan asked with a querulous note in her voice as she looked over the edge. With Miss Anthony's limited ground mobility, Jackson had carried her up to the cliff beyond the bauxite deposit.

"For maximal lift, this is the optimal location for it. Launching without an initial height advantage reduces your success potential," Nelson explained. "Excusing the pun, this flight bears no resemblance to your flight as a dirigible."

"Thanks. I think," Susan snapped back.

Jackson tucked the crank into its flight position. "You're all tightened up and ready to fly," the green gorilla offered.

I'd chosen, at least while my colors were limited, to leave Susan's skin bare of decoration. The pale brownish color of the wood would blend in much more effectively with the white clouds of this world than anything I could have used.

"I guess," Susan offered, delaying.

"How about a countdown?" Sammi asked. "We can all do it together."

The plane closed its optics. I sensed several hundred NOPs running across her processor before she said, "Sure."

"OK. Here we go," Jackson said.

"Ten. Nine," they all said together.

I was proud of my units being so supportive. They were running down in unison.

`Eight.` I joined in.

"Seven, six, five, four, three, two, one."

Jackson really was a stinker. At zero, he used his gorilla strength to push Susan off the cliff.

"AAAAA!" Miss Anthony yelped as she plunged toward the earth. She released the catch on the spring, and her propeller went from zero to a blur in less time than it took to blink. Ailerons and elevators both swung up wildly. She climbed almost straight up, her speed dropping precipitously.

`Not so much, honey, or you'll stall.` I'd spent quite some time with her on the differences between dirigible flight and that of a heavier-than-air flyer. Of course, it was a little like a unit trying to teach someone else to be a factory. I had effectively no experience of my own. The opticless leading the opticless.

Her silent response to my instructions put her once again into a nosedive. Her voltage was way up beyond her safety thresholds in fear.

`Slow and steady on the controls. Nothing radical.`

This brought her front up again, but this time softly, not like a fighter in aerial combat. She leveled out into straight light flight with NOPs grinding through her processor like a unit freshly manufactured.

`That's got it.`

"I'm doing it!" she yelled from a now faraway distance. `I'm doing it,` she repeated over the WAN.

`Good job. Now turn back around.`

Her first attempt at using just the rudder had her yawing through the air the way a crab walks. I winced when the use of the ailerons started with a jerking roll that threatened to take her upside down. The newly minted flier corrected herself into a steadier turn.

`Excellent!` I offered to my fledgling.

Encouragements from her fellow units flowed over the WAN.

`You go!`

`It's a bird! It's a plane! It's SUPER SUSAN!`

`A satisfactory inaugural performance.`

Yea! I wish I could fly!

Susan drifted through some lazy turns and figure eights in the sky while climbing as her propeller continued to turn.

I added, Miss Anthony, would you please control your height and speed. You want to learn to use the potential energy in your spring sparingly to increase the duration of the flight.

Affirmative, she replied. She cut her prop and angled the blades so that they didn't turn. She had become a glider. Happily, I watched her cut graceful arcs across the sky. I even looked through her optics. I caught a glimpse of that rusted pile of metal that might be a unit.

Susan, can you edge down and get me a better look at the box-like thing on the plains below you? But don't take any risks.

Sure. She dove down, gaining a lot of speed. Racing over the object at speed, she kept her optics trained on it. Even with her tremendous velocity, I got a decent look at it. There was no doubt that it was an ancient unit with wheels instead of legs. The rust and corrosion on its outer, skinless surface made me wonder how operational it might be.

Relieving one of my worries, it didn't move in any dimension because of Susan's barnstorming technique.

That's good enough. Time to come home and see if you can land as well as you are doing everything else, I said, giving her some encouragement. Landing was the hardest part.

Susan's approach seemed a bit fast, but we'd smoothed a long runway out of our crash site. She hit her air brakes and slowed, probably too much. Her body all but fell 4 meters out of the sky and onto the two hard wheels of her springlike landing gear. They bowed but didn't break. Her tail skid slammed into the dirt track, carving a new line. Despite the hard touchdown, she yelled out, "YEEEE haw! That was awesome! When can I do it again?"

I thought you didn't like being a plane.

"The hell with that! This is so much better than being a dirigible. I can't wait to try some tricks I've seen on old videos, like barrel rolls and loops and—"

Just be safe, honey. You need to be our eyes and ears. We don't need you turned into a pile of twigs and a broken sump.

"Oh, I will," she said as her bus under voltage dipped, all while her skin raised little bumps all over it. I seemed to have made a monster that I was going to have difficulty keeping *out* of the sky. "But I still want my land and ergs!"

# # #

Alright, troops. I've got good news and bad.

"I'd prefer to dilute unpalatable news out of my maw with that which is agreeable," Nelson replied.

Very well. I created a small bit of heavy water to test-fire the fusion generator. It has a huge magnetic leak that I don't think I can fix without a lot more infrastructure. We will have to continue on with steam power for now. But I may be able to convert it into a fission generator if we can find fissionables.

"Is that the good?" Max asked.

No. The good is that I've stockpiled enough energy to begin our conversion process of bauxite to alumina to aluminum. Thus, we can start mining that ore you found. As soon as I get aluminum flowing, there are so many things I can make ... new limbs, conductors, and even more units. I mean, they won't be as robust as the alloys back home, but they will be functional—maybe 58 percent as capable.

"Oh, goodie," Nelson tossed out with his normal negative energy. "We get to dig."

"Would you rather do it all yourself or have some other units to help?" Sammi asked him with a barb in her tone.

"I never opted out. I just inferred that my level of enthusiasm didn't fill the glass more than half empty."

"So tomorrow?" Jackson Pollack asked, flexing the hydraulics in his arms. "My body needs some regeneration time."

"Mine too," Susan said.

Then off to regen for you. I'm going to increase your energy ration by 10 percent. That ought to make you feel better in the evening.

"Definitely can use the extra ergs," Maxwell approved.

Enjoy the regen, I said. Sleep tight.

# # #

Cinnamon-colored dust covered the gorilla, a six-legged octopus, a large, floppy rag doll, and a legless bear as they dug with crude shovels and picks.

I decided to give them a bit of an idea of what limitations I worked under. Remember, for every metric ton of ore you dig, it will produce only 200 kilos of metal. We need quite a lot to make any significant advancements.

"I didn't realize the conversion was that high," Samantha said.

"That might be an overly optimistic view of conversion, considering we are at the start of our endeavor," Nelson replied. "Our method of alumina extraction will naturally be rather crude."

"Brilliant. In other words, we will likely dig up huge quantities of earth for minute returns?" Max asked rhetorically.

"Every shovelful will bring us that much closer to ..." Jackson said.

I let the friendly argument continue as all but one of my units heaped onto my makeshift wheelbarrow. The pile grew higher and higher until I wasn't sure if Jackson could move it. Even with the hydraulic upgrades as president, I could never have done it as Don Quixote. To my surprise, the gorilla moved the mass without undue strain on his pumps.

Susan soared over us all. Her propeller wouldn't be useful in the excavation process. She strained her optics to ensure our safety. She had identified several large types of fauna—a massive hairy beast that vaguely resembled our own elephants and was equally slow. A furred quadruped about the mass of Jackson and as fast as a No Op. And a similarly quick dog-like creature. All three of those were vegetarians and pack animals. Miss Anthony had also discovered a large reptilian predator—a squat beast that looked like a 300-kilogram, four-legged basilisk. Instead of a horn, it had a spined sail on its back. It was an ambush hunter that could take down the six-tonne furry elephants.

Evaluating the predator and sending out recognition profiles to all the units kept me busy for several seconds. With its shape placed in our sumps, we could be mostly certain that we would not become reptile food. That occupied my processors about 15.3 percent of the time, and another 4.4 percent dealt with keeping my systems nominal. The rest of my computations centered on updating our nascent community's abysmal survival chances. The results depressed me until Jackson wheeled the first full barrow. As the raw pay dirt poured into my manufacturing hopper, my sadness at the resultant simulations morphed into sensuality, and then even further into a general well-being.

I tried to evaluate why. The complete analysis remained stubbornly out of reach. But the models showed that I was feeling contented as I would finally be able to fulfill all my functions as a factory. I hadn't been able to build units from raw materials until then. With Susan and even Samantha, the process was only halfway. I was putting a sump into the body I created. With the silica deposits beneath me, I could create sump fluid; with the aluminum, I could create the skeleton and at least a type of sump. In short, I could create units. My voltage dropped to an all-time low, at least since I'd landed there, as my innards started processing the bauxite into a usable material.

Over my WAN came a priority-one message, the moral equivalent of being screamed at in person. Susan reported, `The ancient unit has started to move!`

With my low-voltage calm shattered, I switch to her video feed.

Below her, I watch the corroded unit rolling along the ground. Bits of rust flaked off its sides and even its drivetrain. It managed the speed a bit slower than Maxwell in his wheelchair over rough terrain. Speaking of rough terrain, I saw how the unit moved its wheels up and down, locking its wheels to step over obstacles. Its progress was pathetic but aimed directly toward our bauxite diggings. I decided to be safe with my limited resources.

`All units return to me.`

"But we are just reaching pure vein," Max objected.

`It doesn't matter! I don't want any of you there when that rusted tin can might see you. You can continue until I give the evacuation order. Not one clock cycle longer.`

"Yes, Mother."

# # #

My units worked frantically for seventeen minutes and fourteen seconds, making two more wheelbarrows of ore before my tripwire of a full 50 percent safety factor.

`It's time, my friends. I'm recalling you. Susan, keep watch on that ancient unit unless attacked.`

`Attacked? With what?` Susan queried rhetorically.

`We comply,` offered Nelson on a separate channel of the WAN.

As my units came into view, Jackson was pushing a third load of raw materials in front of him. I mentally sighed as he pushed it into my manufacturing maw. I continued to grind the ore to separate the valuable mineral from the gangue. My simulations showed that I might just be processing enough ore to form the skeleton and key pieces of another unit, or maybe two small ones.

For the next hour, I asked my family to do make work: collecting wood, stoking our generator, collecting tree fronds for topping up roofing, and even leveling the area around me. If they mentally cursed at me for doing things seemingly without much merit, so much the better—their sumps would be engaged. I wanted them to have their attentions focused off the potential conflict we might have to fight—one that, with only five units and limited resources, we had no chance of winning.

`The rogue unit has moved to our mining location and stopped,` Susan announced over the WAN.

I wished she had kept the message to a specific area network (SAN) to me alone. But I hadn't instructed her thus. I had only myself to blame.

`What is it doing?` I asked over the WAN. I realized that you couldn't be a little bit of a parent. The others already knew.

`Just sitting there. It arrived and stopped. It hasn't moved a hydraulic piston since then,` Susan reported.

The massive voltage spikes of anxiety on my main bus dropped to ripples. We weren't going to have to fight immediately.

`What's your remaining aloft time status?` I inquired. I wanted optics on that unit for as long as possible.

`I've been learning to use the updrafts from the cliff area and thermals elsewhere. Other than rest periods and bad weather, I can probably stay aloft indefinitely.`

`Are you suffering from any fatigue? Do you need a sleep cycle?` I asked with some worry that I might have overstretched my charge.

`Fatigue at 67 percent. I should plan on sleep in three hours and seven minutes.`

I could see her monitors as well, but it did a unit good to do things themselves. It made them stronger. I remembered Amelia doing the same for me more than once.

`Acknowledged. Assuming no activity, keep your optics on the ancient unit for another two hours, twenty-nine minutes, and thirty-six seconds. Then come in for a landing and take a nap,` I ordered.

`Affirmative,` came her simple reply.

`Alright, units, I think it is time for a sleep cycle. I want your processors cold and ready for anything that might happen.`

`Your logic remains impeccable, Cin,` Nelson agreed.

`Only 73 percent fatigued, but I won't argue,` Jackson added. `My hydraulic fluid feels warm after all that digging and toting.`

`Good. Work amongst yourself to have one unit awake at all times.`

I tuned out their discussion. I was worried about that interloper on the hill above us. The thatching of my roofing made it unlikely, even with exceptional optics, that it would spot us. However, that didn't help us when my family left my confines.

I reran our survival simulation for the 7,388th time since we landed. Sometime in the middle of it, a processor overheating interrupt turned off my fatigue counter override and chose to close down my consciousness.

Scout

Consciousness came quickly. My processors were cold. I all but jerked awake. By checking my internal clocks, I found that I'd been asleep for ten hours, fifty-six minutes, and thirty-four seconds. I hadn't realized that I'd been quite that tired. I had been conscious since we'd crashed in an attempt to make the most of our slim chances. Fatigue led to mistakes. I made a mental note to keep a closer watch on my heat monitors.

With fresh optics, I scanned my units. Jackson sat on guard just under my vegetation roof. I wasn't the only one just stirring. Maxwell's bear arms stretched through wakeup tests. Sammi's rag doll body somersaulted and then bent over backward. Susan's propeller twitched but didn't spin.

`Where is Nelson?` I asked as the reality of his being missing smote me. Even without waiting for the answer, I probed for his repeater functions over the net. Relief flooded my processors as he was ambling in my direction, only a few hundred feet away.

`Grit it all, Nelson. Where did you go?` I noticed that his unusual gait was using only five of his six tentacles. He held up a small blue device in his remaining limb.

"Your propensity to converse during your slumber has consequences," Nelson said with more smugness than I'd ever heard from his speaker.

`What are you vocalizing about?`

"No, Cin, he's right," Sammi interjected. "When you sleep, often the WAN goes crazy with discussions. They are all low-priority signals, so we usually ignore them."

`I don't!` I objected.

Jackson and Maxwell both nodded.

Nelson said, "Indeed, you do, Cin."

`Bah!` I objected over the WAN, but internally I added this to a list of my own defects to examine more closely at some future time when we weren't crushed with mere survival.

"Be that as it may, monarch of ours, you kept saying that we needed that resource to succeed," Nelson said. "Over and over, you said it. So I took it upon myself and solved the interloper obstruction on our bauxite mine."

`And how did you do that?` I asked.

"I excised its command module," he said, holding up the blue device in one tentacle.

`What?` I all but screamed. My processors went into overdrive.

Centuries ago, one of my predecessors had learned the concept of praising in public/criticizing in private. I switched over and created a SAN with Nelson.

`I intentionally didn't have you overwhelm that unit on purpose. Five modern units couldn't help but take out that ancient rust bucket, no matter how it was armed?`

Nelson didn't reply to my chastisement.

`What will its factory do now? Send more units. Lots more units. When I can't fully produce more!`

`I calculated that it was less than one chance in 1.433 times ten to the fourth that it was being monitored while I removed the module,` Nelson rebutted.

`Your calculations are correct on that point, but when the factory can no longer access that unit, it won't matter. Many more units will come and scout to find out why that one unit isn't connected to the net any longer. We may not be able to hide from them. In the long run, we certainly won't be able to defeat them in combat.`

The octopus didn't answer for 75,206 clock cycles. When he did, it was a simple `I'm sorry.` He added, `My mental processes failed to evaluate the ramifications.`

`Apology accepted. Let's see if we can unstick this situation.`

I return to the WAN. `Units, we have a problem. I want everyone's processor evaluating this. More of the ancient units will be coming to find out what happened to the one Nelson deactivated. What do we do?`

"Could we just put the module back?" Max asked. "I mean, you eventually replaced mine with no damage."

Nelson spoke up. "Assuming we could return it within a window of time when it wasn't accessed, its factory would recognize that it had been off the net for a certain length of time. At the very least, it would run a diagnostic and find no issue. If I were her, I'd send a repair unit or replacement units."

`I agree with Nelson. Probability of 66.3 percent that it would send at least a squad of units. How was that unit armed, Nelson?`

"A single shoulder-mounted laser. By a cursory examination of the device, I estimate its output to be pulsed in the 100-kilowatt range."

`More than enough to punch holes in any of you. I think we can easily state that we can't possibly defeat nine such armed units. And, even if we did, it would be the` first wave. Probability of 76.01 percent that the wave after that would be a company of troops.

"If not more," Susan agreed.

"Could we move away from here?"

If absolutely necessary, I could move ... slowly. However, we'd lose everything we've already built and have to start over somewhere else with no guarantee that we wouldn't run into the same problem elsewhere.

"Isn't that a classic choice? Fight or flight?" Jackson said.

Before we go there, are there any other suggestions? I have one, but I want to hear others before I offer it.

"Quit being selfish and just tell us," Susan snapped.

I wasn't trying to be selfish but rather to allow other sumps and processors the opportunity to come up with something I hadn't thought of. I'm not omniscient.

"You can say that again," Susan muttered. Her sarcasm garnered a scoff from Nelson.

"I got nothing," Jackson said.

Sammi shook her head. Nelson lifted his tentacles in a shrug.

We could hide. We already have some camouflage. We can extend it and add to it. We'd become a leaf in a forest of leaves.

"What probabilities do you assign to each, oh, grand pooh-bah?" Nelson asked.

Ignoring his acerbity, I replied, I've only done a cursory evaluation. But here are the numbers. If we fight, I say our probability of success is 0.2 percent. Fleeing, with all of its unknowns, gives us a 16.8 percent chance. Hiding gives 46.7... update... 47.3 percent probability of being discovered and destroyed outright.

"I'm not excited by the prospect, but I say hide," Sam offered after a stunned silence.

"How long do we need to stay hidden?"

Indeterminate.

"How does that impact our overall survival and our ability to create a colony?" Susan asked.

I didn't reply, as any answer I gave would be an outright lie or morale-crushing.

"That bad, huh?" Susan muttered, her control surfaces fluttering in either annoyance or fear. I couldn't determine.

"Is there a way we can lead them away?" Maxwell asked.

"Yes. We could attack them and then obviously escape in a direction that wouldn't lead them back here," Jackson tossed out.

The risk to you five would be too high. But your concept gives me an idea that shows much more promise. Give me a few clock cycles to work out the details. Nelson, may I please see that command module?

Cryptologist

While my people worked hard to make our compound invisible to the unaided optics, I examined the native unit's command/control transceiver module. Speed was of the essence. If the factory on the other end of that useless pile of steel and hydraulics woke up and sent reinforcements, we might as well all be deactivated.

My evaluation of the box of electronics should have surprised me, but it didn't, considering our intruder's obsolescence. I could have made a better command-and-control module with scraps that still littered our crash site. To have called it rudimentary would have been an insult to simple things. It had no interactive capability. It was fixed to a specific broadcast-and-receive frequency. The error correction was limited to an uncomplicated checksum methodology. Its simplicity made adding some minor sneak circuits child's play. Also, I created with equal ease my own version of it so I could listen to the chatter on their net.

Oddly, I found the alien net so crammed with signals that I could make neither head nor tail of what was going on, at least at that time. I estimated that it would take six days or so before I could understand even a portion of what traveled there.

`My friends, I've made this device work for us. Now comes the dangerous part,` I said, holding out the alien CCT with a module of my own attached.

"You made what work?" asked Jackson.

`I set this CCT to do activities that give a convincing simulation of its unit having a sump failure.`

"But the command module isn't in a unit," Susan noted with a lack of understanding.

`True, but when one of you plugs in this module I created, it will start, in a unit or not. Take it back to the ancient creature, turn it on, and then take it to a new location far from here. Put this device in its hand, remove this little module, and leave. The factory will believe it moved under its own power to the place you left it.`

"Ingenious," the octopus said. "Then any units sent will go to its new location and think it ripped out its own CCT in a fit of insanity."

`Correct. But it will be dangerous to move that pile of scrap. I can't yet determine from the other factory's` commands when or how many units will come to investigate. You will have to expedite for safety. Jackson, Nelson, and Samantha, I want you to use James's wheelchair to move it.

"You can count on us, Boss," Jackson assured me.

Susan, I want you to fly overwatch. Notify ALL of our units if you see so much as an ant move in their direction.

"Affirmative."

At the sight of any other unit, remove my attached module immediately and move back here as stealthily as possible.

"Yes, ma'am."

As the four took off to their various tasks, James asked, "What about me? I'm at a bit of a handicap without my legs."

I think we need to continue our camouflage activities. I know you will have limited capabilities, but any improvement will aid our success.

"You've got it, Lady D."

I saturated the bandwidth of my own network with a sampling of each of my remote units' sights, sounds, and body sensors. Despite my flock's bravado, it was clear from the universal overvoltage that fear rolled through their sumps as they raced the alien creature's lifeless body to its new position.

I analyzed every pixel of Susan's video feeds. I listened intently to the other network, hoping to pick up any clue of impending discovery, and I ran simulations on top of simulations of outcomes. So intense were my attentions that I didn't realize the burden I'd placed on the power-delivery systems. A low-power indicator warned me of my abuse. I reduced, but didn't eliminate, my demands. I shrank the number of data points of the Monte Carlo simulations.

Four hours, thirty-six minutes, and fifteen seconds passed without any incident more significant than a stubbed tentacle on a loose rock.

Susan shattered this peace over the net. Enemy sighted. Eighteen degrees magnetic.

Voltages ramped up across all the units.

Accessing the plane's full suite of senses, I realized that her optical routines were exceptional. I could read her individual visual pixels and just make out the change in luminescence value.

She continued her report. One ... No. Four... Now eight units are moving toward the ground team. Speed is slow. Less than five kilometers per hour. ETA to intercept is eight hours plus.

Using her wide-eyed view, I could see a slight ridge between the oncoming warriors and my own people. It meant that the other factory's drones wouldn't see my people for at least another six hours and fourteen minutes. When I projected forward, it would take my people sixty-three minutes to get out of sight.

`Execute final instructions in four hours,` I commanded, giving my team a full 100 percent safety margin.

`Roger, Dulcinea,` came just a single reply from Nelson.

`Susan, after you have determined the exact ETA, I want you to spend at least half your attention on areas other than these eight new targets. Make sure there isn't someone sneaking in the back door on them.`

`You don't need to teach me how to sop up ergs,` she snapped at me.

`No need to get gritty, Susan. I just want to make sure they stay safe.`

The plane didn't reply, but she was already doing what was needed. `No other contacts,` she finally reported.

`Good job, Susan. Ground team, continue as planned.`

If I'd been nervous before, knowing that eight potential soldiers bore down on my people made me feel like an electron in a metallic bond, bouncing around all over and not knowing what nucleus I belonged to. My processors jammed with so many conflicting priority evaluations that time slipped away from me.

Jackson broke me from my reverie. `Mission time reached. Leaving package as ordered.`

Sampling my unit's senses, I added, `Perfect.`

`Do we loiter out of detection range?` asked Nelson.

`Negative. We have Susan to watch for us. Travel for one hour at 114 degrees off the nominal return path. Then return to base, obscuring your tracks behind you.`

`You want to make sure they don't follow us home?` Samantha asked.

`Correct,` I said. `Even if they somehow detect you, your axis of movement will put them well off our true direction. An added level of security.`

My voltage dropped, and my sump pump sped up in pride as my people followed my instructions perfectly. Even looking from above using Susan's optics, I couldn't see any trail my units were leaving, even though I could see them traveling. The terrain they traveled over looked no different than that around them. Nelson was doing most of this obfuscation by sweeping a head-sized bush across the earth.

The octet of identical native units arrived at our intrigue. Two of them rolled around the disabled automaton. I could hear the data flowing across the alien network, even if I couldn't yet decipher it. The stream of information helped advance my decoding analysis by 6 percent because I knew what the communication was all about. One of the alien machines took the modified CCT and plugged it into a port in its side. More data flowed over the alien's net. Most of it was mine. My decryption increased by another 12 percent. Just as suddenly, the machine removed the modified control device from its interface, and the flow of information ceased.

I detected a single command coming from the other direction. I didn't understand it, but the burst transmission was cold and directive.

The platoon of combat robots suddenly turned and, in their wiggly, rolling gait, trundled off at their top, but ridiculously low, speed. Terror spiked inside me as I feared they planned to follow my team's trail. Their new direction was nearly directly away from me and nowhere near Jackson and the others' retreat. Curiosity replaced fear.

`Susan, what is your powered flight status?` I inquired.

`Reaching the safety limit in thirty-three seconds.`

`Grit. I was wondering where those eight aliens were going in such a hurry.`

She offered, `I could follow a distance and still make it back.`

`No. I'm not going to risk you or any of our people. But in the time you have left, orient your sight along their course. I don't think the other factory has enough brains to be deceptive about that,` I ordered.

`Roger.`

Susan's optics scanned the line, focusing farther and farther away until there was a flash of light centered. Then another. Then another.

`Hold there.`

It was hard to see anything at that distance with Susan's optics at maximum magnification, both analog and digital. What lay in that frame was a boulder-strewn field with small, scraggly trees growing between them. The tight area couldn't have been more than 300 meters across. That made the irregular stones upward of 7 meters high. Beams of light lashed out across the scene.

`I saw a battle taking place at 4.6 kilometers,` Susan reported with just a little excitement in her net voice.

`Can you see who is fighting whom?` I asked

`Negative. I infer that the forty-six boxy blobs issuing the rays are the alien units we've seen.`

I confirmed, `Probability 83 percent.`

`Those are betting odds,` Jackson said as he and the rest of my troop listened in to the reports.

Gambling without sufficient data only promotes errors, which could be grievous, Nelson said.

Oh, Nelson, give your sharp tongue a rest. It's just a figure of speech, Samantha chided.

Gathering adequate information is the hallmark of–

I muted the ground units.

Susan, do you have any images of who they are fighting? I asked.

Not with any clarity, Cin. The native units are moving slowly out in the open. Whatever they are fighting are hiding and moving so fast I can't get a good image. Sending what I have.

The videos provided were grainy, even with enhancement. They showed a roughly 2-by-1-meter vertical blur moving from one hiding place to another with the quickness of a striking snake.

Wow! exclaimed Susan, tearing me away from my contemplation.

What?

Look, she simply offered.

Using her eyes, I examined the battlefield. One of the alien units was engulfed in flames. Occasional sparks issued forth from its compromised batteries, shooting off into the verdant growth and causing fitful little fires.

How did that happen?

Susan's only response was a video clip. It showed one of those fast blobs rushing forward, dodging under laser beams. In one of its manipulative members (I'd determined it had four limbs at least), it held something flaming. At 3 meters, it flung the flaming device at the alien. Upon striking, the container burst, putting the whole of its target in a conflagration that I calculated would even melt optics. Meanwhile, the fire-wielding opponent had disappeared.

I switched back to Susan's live vision just in time to see the hydraulics of the melted unit add their volatile fluids to the inferno.

I've reached my powered reserve limit. Do you want me to investigate further? Susan said.

No. No risks, Susan. We can't afford them. Return to base.

On my way, Mom.

Mom

Mom: the diminutive of mother. Noun: 1) a female parent; 2) maternal tenderness and affection. Verb: 1) to care for, be affectionate to, protect, and mold offspring; 2) to give birth to.

I hadn't realized it to that point. I wasn't the president they remembered. I wasn't the colony leader. I was the colony mother. I had to nurture them. I had to cajole them into doing the right thing. Up until then, I'd always used the safety of the colony as the only output of any simulation. I needed to adjust my computations to deliver the full range of maternal values.

I spent the time as my … children returned, evaluating all I'd seen in this last adventure. First, there was no question that there were units and a factory on this planet. They weren't my units. It wasn't a factory as I'd recognize it. But, no matter what our scientists have said in the past, they existed, parallel evolution or Human intervention.

Second, there was another group out there that the other factory fought with. On the surface, I'd love to assume that the enemy of my enemy was my friend. However, I wasn't certain that the native factory, which I tentatively identified as Alpha, was my foe. At the moment, Alpha was only an obstacle that likely would destroy us if given the opportunity. Knowing the programming of the original factories that landed on Rigel-3, I'd consider my conclusion a given. However, my distant ancestor managed to convince two of them with logic. Could this factory be reasoned with? My initial evaluation outputs showed less than a 4 percent likelihood.

Next, what about this other group that I'd tentatively labeled, with great artistry, Beta? Was there yet a second factory that we had to deal with? There had been on Rigel-3. Or perhaps it was a native species to this planet. Had the Humans seeded Stella-4?

I ground the edges off my random number generators, but the simulation showed almost equal probability for each option, as well as for any undefined option. I needed more data to correctly evaluate. I significantly lowered the priority of this evaluation until such time as I received more information.

The images of the combat between Beta and the Alpha units that I'd preserved gave me much data to work with toward evaluating them individually. All of the Alpha combatants used identical weapons. Their tactics were rudimentary. One could even consider them as simplistic as stop, point, and shoot. Only Alpha's overwhelming numbers allowed them to come close to dealing with Beta units. Any one of my children, equipped as they had been back on Rigel-3, could take on dozens of Alphas. Maybe even hundreds. But the problem was we weren't equipped for combat in any way. I could make clubs and spears, but nothing that would materially affect an Alpha at a distance.

This dovetailed right into our current resource issue. If only I could get just some resources to start with. I must have had my external speakers active as the thought flowed through my processor queue as Maxwell answered me.

"Why not use the units we saw destroyed in combat?"

I'd been so engrossed in my assessment that I hadn't noticed him nearby. A future examination of my close contact surveillance subroutine was called for. It wouldn't do to have a native unit or Beta sneak into range.

"What was that, Max?"

"Well, aren't they refined materials? If we recycled them, even if you had to discard some for battle damage, you could still produce many things."

My computations exploded with possibilities that might solve many of our colony problems. Simultaneously, I fought the shame that a unit had thought of this and I hadn't. I retrieved my memory from just a few hours before to be a better mother. "That is an exceptional idea, Maxwell. I'm so glad you thought of it."

Yes. Yes! Combinations of ideas grew from that germ like the crystal in a supersaturated solution. By the time the rest of my children arrived, I had the base plan ready.

I addressed that units were low on charge and bored from a long trek. My voice delivered the excitement I felt. "Friends, your efforts have paid off in dividends more than you can imagine."

The disbelief in my children's optics showed that they didn't yet share my enthusiasm. "Did your sump drop a beat or two?" Susan asked.

Nelson added in his normal pessimism. "While I am disabused with Miss Anthony's precise wording, I must agree with her overall premise. Instead of one enemy we must combat, our foes have doubled in number."

Even our eager rag doll, Sam, nodded in agreement with the octopus's cultured comments.

I sent a second-level happy message prefix on the network. "I'm sorry to say you will have to go back to where you just came from."

For the next twenty-one minutes, four seconds, I explained all my plans, within plans, within plans. When I'd finished, there was a bright light in the optics of each of my children.

"This increases our probability of success by nearly 40 percent," I said. "And, I have to give the credit for the core idea to Maxwell."

Everyone looked at Max. I could feel his embarrassment over the net.

"Good job … for a teddy," Sam interjected into the silence.

\# # #

I couldn't have been prouder of my units. Over a week, they hauled back seven destroyed Alpha units from the battlefield we had observed, including the one they hauled out there to save us in the first place. They smartly disconnected each unit's CCT just in case energy remained in each hulk. Maxwell worked with my extensionals to dismantle each in turn.

The week's take translated into one 150-kilojoules-per-second laser, two only marginally damaged CCTs, seventeen hydraulic actuators, twenty-two electric servos, and a mass of sensors. Not the least of what we obtained was 1,363 kilograms of scrap—read raw materials.

My first task upon receiving this windfall was to do something I'd promised. While the others collected the final scrap unit, I gave James Maxwell his legs back—or at least a reasonable facsimile. I admit that it looked odd to see my old purple body with green below its prodigious waist. It also provided an opportunity for a private conversation without having to resort to a SAN.

"Thank you, Miss Dulcinea," Max said, standing from the remanufacturing table.

"Don't thank me yet," I replied. "This just makes you ready for the dangers the rest of your brethren are going to face."

"A small price to pay. In fact, it is something I relish, as I want to be part of our team."

"You always have been an integral member, Maxwell."

"That may be, but now I feel more like I can truly carry my own weight."

I snickered. "Oh, you will. I have to note that your new legs no longer have the strength of the presidential augmented versions. They are about the same as any normal teddy bear's."

"I don't care. I don't need that power," he said, doing some deep knee bends.

"So, you say now."

"I'm a practical sort. If we need that strength, then it's unlikely we will prevail in any case."

"Too true," I added with a touch of melancholy in my voice. My processes slowed by half a cycle per second. I wouldn't have been able to register such a small change in my old body. I stopped feeling sorry for myself in 756 clock cycles. "But let's keep positivity in our sumps. We have an opportunity. Let's make the most of it."

"Agreed. How many other units will you be able to make with these resources?"

"With these materials and those we've learned to use from the flora, depending on the size of the toys I create, I can make eight more. However, the problem is that of personalities. We have no more sumps. In theory, we have twenty-six memory engrams we could program into them. However, my checksums and CRC checks of that nonvolatile memory show that only three of them are likely viable, and two more are questionable."

"Why? They are nonvolatile memories."

"My first guess would be our takeoff. Not all of our ship made the jump. I'm going to assume that portions of the memories, maybe at an atomic level, were also left behind."

"*Dulce et decorum est pro patria mori,*" the bear said with solemnity.

"Except it was their country ... their world that killed them," I replied to his Latin.

"True, but at least they were only copies of their memories. They continued to live on Toy World."

"You think my successor left them functional after they challenged his attempts to scuttle our mission? He would need scapegoats. I'm sorry to say that were I in his shoes, I'd have put them on a very public trial, likely with gruesome outcomes."

Nodding, the bear said, "We all put our lives on the line for something we felt more important than activation. Let's see to it that none of those who gave up everything did so in vain."

"I can't disagree," I stated. "But we are left with the need to deal with degraded or failed memories in the here and now. Even if those five are viable, whole-unit memories, it leaves three more, which will be nothing but infants with no programming and no knowledge."

"Infants are to be protected and cherished, not thrown into battle with no idea what they are getting into," Max said.

"Happened to me when I was ... or should I say when my first predecessor was created."

Max snorted. "I still have a hard time thinking of you as a teddy bear, much less the president."

"It's becoming harder for me as well. It's even worse than remembering all the past lives of the presidents before me. I wonder if that is self-preservation for my own mental health."

"Possibly. Just don't let your psyche go rogue on us. We need you."

"I could say that no one is irreplaceable, but in this case, it isn't true.

We need all of us to have any chance at all."

"You can say that again, ma'am."

# # #

It took yet another four days to create five new units, or at least the bodies for the units. As a colony, we agreed to infuse their engrams one at a time and honor their rebirth. The first was an orange-yellow birdie with only vestigial wings and long legs.

"Hello and welcome back to the world of the living," I said as its enormous eyes opened. Because of the crash, we didn't know any of the names of the engrams.

"Morp. Zerop. D'd'duv. Braiq froh cugnal," it replied.

"Did you get that?" Jackson asked with no little sarcasm.

"Hush!" Samantha chided.

"We may abet if you might elucidate your condition," Nelson offered.

The gigantic optics turned on him. It cocked its head as if it didn't understand. I didn't blame the birdie. I often had to dip into my memories to decipher the octopus's meaning.

"Himy! Uphnap wiev ajrot."

I decided to try another tack. Over the WAN, I asked simply, `Hello?`

`Oh, my goodness. I thought I'd fallen into another dream,` came the reply.

`Seems like a common theme with our travels,` Susan quipped.

`What seems to be the difficulty?` I said, sending a third-degree cease message by SAN to Susan.

`My new body seems to work a little differently from my old one. I'm trying to sort it out now.`

`Is there anything we can do?`

"N'n'n'no, I'I don'ttttt think so," the newly reactivated unit offered aloud.

"Can you at least understand us?"

"Yesssssss. Un'stand isssss easssssseeee. Sssssst'll workingggg on the speakingggg par'."

"Well, we are happy to have you join our little band," I said.

"Affirmative," Nelson said.

"Yes," the rest of the team chimed in almost simultaneously.

"Your network doesssssn't feellllll like that of Amelia Earhar'." The bird stomped its right foot repeatedly like a twitch in its servos.

"I'm sorry to say she is deactivated," I offered.

The foot stopped its gyrations, but the left wing did circles instead. "I diddddn't know we had a spare factory."

"You're right. We got a pinch hitter," Susan offered with a bit of irony.

"Pinch hittttttter?"

"Ignore the plane. She thinks she invented sarcasm. I'm Dulcinea, formerly Robinson Crusoe."

"R'robinson Crusoe? My memories must have been taken before I met you. I'm M'margare' A'wood. You can call me Marge or Margie."

"Nice to meet you, Margie."

"Welcome to our group."

"Salutations and good wishes."

"Nice to see you reactivated!"

Marge asked, "Is that James Maxwell?"

"It is. Glad to have a friend back from the scrap heap," Maxwell offered.

"Yes. Happy to be here. Now, willllll someone exxx … explain what a pinch hitter is?" the bird asked, blinking his eyes. He jogged in place, that time under control as he tested his control over his new body.

"Not a baseball fan," Sammi noted.

"A substitute player for someone who is incapacitated or can no longer perform her task. In this case, the original unit is deceased," Nelson explained.

Marge turned to me, or at least the bulk of my dome, and asked, "If there wasn't a spare factory, then who are you-ou-ou?"

"That is an exceedingly long story, Ms. Attwood. The short answer is 'Desperate times call for desperate measures.' We poured my sump into an empty sump of this factory."

"That's never been done …"

"BEFORE," my entire cadre said together.

I inwardly smiled at the "Why don't you all fill in our newcomer while I prepare our next reactivation."

# # #

In the next two days, we activated the python Alexander Cumming and the unicorn Vasily Kandinsky. Very little was different from either of them other than their forms, their accents, and their former occupations.

Cumming was an ex-sewage worker. Kandinsky surprised me as he was an artist whom even my lack of interest in paintings had heard of. His surreal paintings were famous on Rigel-3. His *Three Moons over the Backbone* was probably his most famous work. Each of them was briefed with what was becoming the standard spiel.

I paid little attention to the introductions as my bus voltage spiked repeatedly. Anxiety took hold of me. I was about to try to activate an engram that my evaluation said was questionable. I might have balked had we not so desperately needed to build up our colony's defenses.

I mentally crossed my digits as I loaded the first of three engrams into the still body of a fluffy white sheep with the blue number 6 across its side. My toys encircled the ewe in anticipation of welcoming another brother to join our troupe. The data transmitted successfully. Over my SAN with the unit, I sensed the processor firing up. Everything seemed completely normal until it jumped up and started flailing around like a unit possessed.

In past wars, sheep had taken the brunt of combat losses. At 65 kilos and 112 centimeters in height, they weren't the most impressive fighters, but of all toys, they were some of the most tenacious. My memories included lambs missing three limbs gnawing on the leg of an elephant to hold it in place. All the while, another sheep missing its back half plunged an electric prod through the pachyderm's optics.

Now that unit's full 65 kilos could have been used as a random number generator. Up. Down. Spin. Screech. Leg club. Squat. Jump. Kick. Its mass and unpredictable movement provided danger.

Despite this, my toys attempted to hold this malfunctioning creature down.

The violent unit's command queue made zero sense. As far as I could tell, it was exactly random. "BACK AWAY FROM THE UNIT!" I shouted over the fracas. All my toys complied. The despair I felt over the network from my units made me want to crawl into a hole and cover myself up in the shrieking failure before us. But I couldn't. I had to endure. Horror suffused all of us as the unit bashed itself against firewood, the earth, and even rocks.

"Can't we help it?" Sammi asks.

"We should—" Max began.

I interrupted with, "The unit's sump is corrupted. There is nothing we can do except either put it out of its misery, which would be a waste of resources, or wait until its power is fully expended."

We suffered ourselves by awaiting the unit's end while praying to the Humans, which I don't think any of us really believed in anyway, to save this poor soul. Our hydraulic pressures were so low that I feared for the rest of my children.

"Should we be worried about the noise?" Nelson asked more loudly than normal because of the insane unit's Tourette-like screams.

"Good point, Nelson. I don't detect any traffic on the alien network on the node nearest us, but we should have someone on guard. Susan, would you care for some more flight time?"

"Miss Amelia?" interjected Margaret Atwood. "Might I be used for such duty? As you know, we birdie units with our oversized optics see exceptionally well at long ranges and in low-light situations."

"An exceptional idea. Jackson, could you show Marge the best perch for overwatch?"

"Yes, Mother."

The yellow sun of this world dipped down to the horizon, casting an orange pall over everything, including the thrashing victim. On what would have been an exceptional evening, our hearts broke over our brethren's condition. Still, except for the posting of a guard, we didn't leave our places. Eighteen hours, well into the darkest part of the night, the sheep continued its self-induced damage and thrashing. Then, as suddenly as it started, it stopped. The silence could have been a funeral all on its own for the weight it carried.

"I guess that's it," Samantha said, her voice bearing the sadness that we all felt in liters.

"I'm not sure I want to see anything like that again, but I need to capture it in a painting," our unicorn artist said.

"Too bad we don't have canvas or paints." James's words were lackluster.

"I think you all need recharge time. Why don't you shut down while Margie and I hold down the fort?" I suggested. To a unit, they agreed. I hoped to give them time to overcome their emotions. I needed them strong.

But unlike my charges, failure continued to flog my processors like a repeating series of code without an exit. The sheep's body didn't have enough ergs to move, but just enough to keep a unit's most important part—its sump—pumping. I alone could detect the activity. I alone suffered for another three hours.

Just as the sun peeked over the other horizon, the unit deactivated.

Widow

I endured. I wasn't sure how. My hydraulic pressure was all but nonexistent in grief. My power busses were nothing but spikes of anxiety. And I kept sampling my external skin temperature at many degrees below where it was by observation. I wondered if my own deactivation would be all that bad. The responsibility of caring for my toys just seemed too much for a simple ex-bear to handle. It made the weight of my presidency seem trivial by comparison. I wondered how factories handled thousands or even millions of children.

Honestly, if it had been just me, I might have taken that selfish way out of my pain. Oblivion against the harsher reality of the death of my units. And, based on simulations, this sheep and all the other sumps on the starship wouldn't be the only deaths on my conscience. Far from it. No matter how good I was, no matter how well I'd plan, I would lose toys to deactivation.

Don Quixote of old held a callous veneer over his heart about losses in most any dangerous endeavor. War, especially. How many of my friends had I buried under a Vesuvius Man? And now my processor was spinning out of control over one might-have-been unit.

I needed stability … to purge my emotions and be all I could be for my other children. To center myself, I queued up nine exabytes of NOP operations with only messages on the alien network and priority calls from the toys as interrupts.

# # #

The yellow sun of Stella stood high in the sky. My internal chronometer showed just shy of midday on our twenty-three-hour and fourteen-minute standard day when I came out of my fugue state. I found my units gathered around a small grassy knoll. Someone had carved a Vesuvius Man and planted it next to a 40-centimeter mound of freshly turned earth.

I scanned around and found the sheep's body, now just a pile of resources waiting to be processed, with a large, empty hole in its head. Its sump was missing.

It was quiet until the rag doll, Samantha Fox, spoke. "Units, we have come together to say goodbye to one of our own. So short was this toy's activation that we never got the opportunity to know her. The ewe never had the chance to share her uniqueness with anyone. She never got to be loved by any of us. She never felt the warming goodness of the sun or the cool evil of the night sky. She never experienced the exhilaration of her first fluid change. She is a unit that never got to spread her algorithms or raise another.

"But for all the things she has never done, I don't feel sorry for her. The Humans have taken her to their bosom and given her a better existence in deactivation than her brief, miserable life.

"No, the ones who deserve pity are those of us she left behind. We suffer at her loss. We are lesser without her. Those of us who will never share a private joke over a SAN with her, who will ever wonder what skills she might have brought to our fight for survival, and who are weaker for her absence—not just because of her number, but because of the light her sump would have brought to our desperate situation.

"To this unit, I say only, rejoice that you are in a happier place. Please ask the Humans to look down on us with favor."

"Praise the Humans," the rest said in unison. I found myself muttering the words myself.

It's funny how, when dark times fall, we revert to our primitive roots. I mean, Human Worship hadn't been popular with toyanity for over an eon. We had grown beyond the need for a hand guiding us or protecting us. Yet we continue to hold the germ of superstition in ourselves, ready to sprout when the ground is fertile.

I declared a day of mourning for my toys. They needed to come down so they could focus again. I would have said, if pressed, that I needed it just as much as, if not more than, the units. I kept going over it in microscopic detail. Was there something more I could have done to prevent what happened to her? A different voltage? A slower download? How about running the mass of data through an error-correction process before the download, no matter the weeks or months it would have taken? No matter what option I simulated, it came back that my choices were correct. That the result would have been the same.

Though the sheep's deactivation weighed heavily on my sump, what worried me even more were the two engrams I still had that were possibly damaged. *Can I continue with the possibly disastrous results, or do I bypass them for later evaluation?* It was hard to be governed by a processor. I often envied the Humans' ability to make decisions based on emotions rather than raw numbers. The sims were clear. I needed every possible unit to ensure our survival on this world. Despite the risks to the units themselves, I must move forward. It made me feel like a butcher.

# # #

The gathering of units for this next new birth was somber rather than the joyous event it used to be. I didn't lighten the mood any.

"As you remember, we have two more memories that might possibly be viable for units. They also might have a similar outcome as the sheep of thirty-nine hours, fifty-six seconds ago."

"You disclosed your computations. We, in concurrence with your judgment, believe alternatives remain scarce," Nelson said in his supercilious manner.

"Do it," Jackson agreed.

"It has to be done," Max added.

Nods came from other units with mobile heads.

"As you can see, this next unit is an inflatable clown," I said, indicating the unit sitting in front of us all. "Downloading engram now."

Without processing, the data conglomeration sprayed over my direct link to the empty shell in mere seconds. I received the end-of-file notification and shared it over the LAN.

We waited.

Seven minutes and twenty-one seconds later, Vasily, our unicorn painter, asked, "Shouldn't something have happened by now?"

"It always has in the past," I offered. "Let me check."

I forced a SAN between the clown and me. The link allowed me to examine most of the systems. Its power bus sat at nominal. Its sump pump hummed along well within parameters. No telltales were outside established constraints. For 138 clock cycles, the situation puzzled me. It wasn't until I examined its processor queue that I found anything unusual.

It contained nothing.

I don't mean NOPs, but rather nulls. I traced back to the sump reader and found that it also contained nulls. While sump fluid flowed past the reader, no data alit on the bus. With 105 percent more effort, I pushed into the reader's queue to see the raw-data electronic signal generated by the sump flow. The massively corrupted data I read there wouldn't ever form a thought … it wouldn't ever move its body … it wouldn't ever do anything except use power to push fluid around its brain case.

Two failures. With my soul at its lowest ebb, even worse than after the passing of the ewe, I said, "I'm sorry to say that this unit will never reach sentience. For that matter, it won't even move. I've turned off the power bus."

My toys whispered amongst themselves.

"I guess that's better than what happened with the other one," Susan said with less than total tact.

"What would you do if Cin did that to you?" snapped Jackson.

Nelson spoke up. "Conflict with one another will thwart our eventual aims—"

"Shut up, Weasel Word," Susan replied, countering his platitude. "If I'd have wanted your opinion, I'd have sawed off your head to scoop it from your sump."

"There isn't any call for that kind of talk," James admonished in an attempt to mediate.

"I have to agree," I added. "We all knew the probability of these memories being corrupt. Please settle and let us get on with things."

There was a long pause before Susan offered, "I beg your pardon, Nelson and Jackson."

"Me too," the great ape returned. "I activated my speaker in haste."

"Better," I observed. "Now we have one memory remaining to install. I already have its body ready. I suggest we offer whatever positive energy we can to this new unit's success."

That new unit, a Nurse Nan with her massive body in a mostly white uniform, lay idle next to the deflating clown. I crossed my busses for luck before downloading the engram into the blank, possible sentient. All my toys eagerly awaited the result as data wrote itself into the sump of the caricature of a Human.

"Download complete," I announced.

As the tension ratcheted up, the candy-striped skirt quivered. An arm twitched. Her optics activated with a soft glow. Sitting up, she looked over our collection. I'd retained my neural connection to her, so I felt things go wrong even as we observed the fact. The nominal 18.4-volt bus ramped up in terror to a sizzling 40.11 volts.

The nan's head jerked back and forth. Seeing all of us gathered around it, the unit scrambled in a crawl into a corner of my manufacturing line. There it cowered, pulling itself in so that only the glow of its eyes could be seen.

"We mean you no harm," I offered as softly as possible. Still monitoring, I felt the anxiety spears of voltage that shot up to over hundreds of volts. I feared that the unit would blow its safety fuses. "She is afraid," I said in an aside to my units.

"Yes, we want to be your brothers and sisters," Samantha said, trying to soothe the unit.

"And we will protect you," Jackson, our gorilla, offered.

The nan seemed to pull even farther into its crevasse.

`If you can't understand our audio signals, know that we only want to help you`, James added over the network. I sent him a sideband approval level three for his concept.

`We desire only camaraderie and fraternity among all our brethren`, Nelson added.

None of this took down the fear in the newly activated unit.

`Please, Mrs. Nan. We are your friends,` I tried. `I am the factory and am called Dulcinea. Out there, we have Nelson Mandela, the orange-and-blue octopus. James Maxwell is the purple teddy bear.` Over the net, I introduced each unit in turn. And for ninety-three minutes, three seconds further, we attempted to coax out our sister toy. Our efforts did not affect our newly activated unit. It cowered in the corner like someone caught up in the worst nightmare ever.

"We are wasting ergs here, toys. I suggest we just wait. Perhaps she will eventually calm to a point where our encouragement can be helpful," I stated with my hydraulic pressure low from yet another failure. But wishing a bit to be a one when it clearly was a zero didn't make it so.

"Agreed," said Susan.

Several of the toys nodded their assent as well.

"Moving on to another topic," I said to take their attention from the current issue. I, on the other paw, couldn't shake my failure quite so easily. I maintained a clandestine watch on the Nurse Nan's bus voltage. "I have enough materials for three, or maybe four, more units."

"But no more engrams," Nelson pointed out.

"Just so," I agreed. "I have what boils down to three choices. First, I build no more units."

"That just leaves us to fend for ourselves on this wet planet against only the Humans know what!" Susan interjected.

"Yes, and if we are up against a factory that can make more units, we are quite literally grit and darked," Jackson added with profanity.

"Might as well dip us in solvent and remanufacture our bodies," our python unit said with as much enthusiasm as an insect about to be crushed by a tank.

"I don't disagree," I said. "But perhaps we should listen to all the options before we choose to short out our batteries." Susan gave a smirk and a nod to my sarcasm. "The second option would be to do just what our people have always done. I will create a body, one of you infect it with a bit of your sump fluid, and then another raises the youngling—"

"Not to throw a cloud over your solar array, but won't that take ten years or more before the units are viable?" Vasily the unicorn artist asked.

"Too true," I said. "That would definitely be a drawback to that plan."

"A definite drawback," offered Susan en sotto voce.

I blew Susan a raspberry over a SAN. "Which brings me to option number three. I could make upgraded extensions. You've seen mine working over my body. They are nothing more than my fingers, hands, and legs. But they operate only with my will or programming."

"Kinda small," Margaret's beak said.

"I've already drawn up plans for larger ones, about the size of a Tommy Tank. They wouldn't be as responsive or creative as units, but they would offer value to about 19 percent of a standard unit when it comes to combat and the plans we have."

"Hmm," Jackson mused.

"Tallying three gives us 57/100 of a unit. This latter proposal outstrips the null of option one or even necessitating three units to babysit for a year of the second option," Nelson said.

"I say go with option three, Cin," James voted.

"I don't know why we are voting," Susan said with just a touch of ire. "Our Dulcinea will do what she wants anyway."

"I will make my own decision," I said. "But that doesn't mean I won't take into account what my toys think."

The python snorted at my comment but said, "Option three."

"Three."

My third choice carried with all the units, leaving only Vasily to make any selection.

"I'll miss teaching younglings," the unicorn lamented. "But yes. It must be option three—for now."

# # #

"The visual appeal of these mechanisms fails to meet any test of attractiveness," Nelson said as my creations rolled off the manufacturing line. Mentally, I realized that at least I'd had enough material left over to create new tentacles for my octopus toy, even if the green wouldn't match the rest of his blue-and-orange motif. But installation would have to wait.

But back to my extensionals. Take a Tommy Tank on tracks at a mere 50 centimeters high. Remove its 10-centimeter turret. Replace the gun barrel with an upward-facing lance from a King Arthur toy. Add a thick grappling arm on either side, like those of a teddy bear. Cover all of this in a rippled, reflective silver coating, and you have what I'd manufactured—four of them. On each side, they bore a designator in infrared paint—with no imagination, 1 through 4.

The quad arrayed themselves like some military parade. What I saw made me feel something like Dr. Frankenstein for merging the designs of multiple toys.

"I don't know," Vasily countered. "There is an aesthetic of symmetry … the opponent seeing itself in its enemy."

I said, "But the shape—"

"Who cares?" said Jackson. "I don't care how pretty it is. I want to know how it can possibly be combat effective with only that meter-long metal probe on the end. How are they going to keep a laser out of my backside?"

"Would you care for me to explain and maybe demonstrate?" I offered.

"Please."

"First off ..." I powered up the taser built into the end of the lance. Each of my nearby toys stepped back at the electric arc that brightened the tip. "That metal probe is designed to be thrust into the innards of one of the other units and disrupt its data flow with a multiphase shock. Because of power restrictions, it's good for only one or maybe two attempts, so its use is limited. For that matter, I've constructed enough of these weapons for each of you who won't be carrying a claimed laser."

"Excellent," Vasily said. "I didn't like the idea of just trying to spear someone with my horn. I mean, if it were damaged, how would I paint?"

"Me personally, I'm looking forward to something to smash," Jackson offered.

"While in premise, I agree with Vasily. I deem my size, unique structure, and construction would be more appropriate to the brutality expressed by Jackson," Nelson adds.

"No matter what, you will each have at least one weapon other than sheer mass and dexterity," I insisted.

"Good. Now get back to your robot drones," Jackson said.

I complied. "Yes. Defensively, they are built with a low profile; the enemy would have to aim lower than any other combatant to hit them. And as the only weapon we've seen has been lasers, the reflective surface would deflect a good deal of the energy away in different directions. If its ram is exhausted, the flat top of the unit lifted until it stood nearly a meter and a half tall and can provide cover for one of you."

"Very well thought out, considering our limitations," James remarked. "But why the arms?"

I chuckled. "Well, they have two uses. One, our opponents don't have fur or armor. Their inner workings are exposed. The hands could grab hold of critical wiring or pressure lines and yank them out. Second, as we gain additional weapons, the hands can hold those weapons."

"I would suggest that our factory's decisions are meritorious and deserve nothing less than our admiration," Nelson said in admiration.

"To Cin!" It started a chant that made me uncomfortable in a way I wasn't accustomed to, especially looking at the large Nurse Nan still figuratively hiding under my skirts and the pieces of the sheep awaiting reprocessing.

"Cin. Cin. Cin. Cin."

Insurgent

Weeks followed as we waited for the right moment to implement my plan. We waited actively. Nelson got his limbs back. I replaced Maxwell's CCT. We built barriers out of fallen tree trunks that the alien troops would have difficulty maneuvering through. I managed to replace all of Nelson's tentacles. Everyone got modifications to their CCTs.

However, despite the number of planetary revolutions, I'd not even managed to entice our newest family member into conversation. I'd chosen to tentatively and fittingly name her Nancy Wake. Fear and courage often go hand in hand.

Once, in one of my previous lives, I'd worked with a unit that didn't speak—Sancho Panza. But unlike that elephant, this unit wouldn't even come out in the open. Still, I kept feeding it energy, which it used at a prodigious rate consistent with its high bus voltage. Daily, I attempted to lure it from under its fear.

`We are right here, Mrs. Nancy. I will make sure you are kept safe. We can-`

A level two interrupt stopped my latest attempt in its tracks. A brief message over the Alpha's LAN, garbled by distance and intervening terrain, sprayed across my consciousness. Using an interpolation algorithm, it seemed likely that this meant foreign units on the move and in an area where we could engage. It was the sign we'd been looking for.

`Attention. All units return to base for briefing. Enemy detected,` I announced over my network.

It took an agonizing 427,106 milliseconds before everyone arrived from their activities.

"I believe we finally have what we have been waiting for. I've detected a signal at 17 degrees south of where the last battle took place." From my team, I registered feelings that ranging from anxiety to anticipation, but I did not quite settle on any one. We were starting a campaign that would determine the future of our race, but it wouldn't be quick (unless we lost). And it wouldn't be without casualties.

"We are as strong as we can be at this point," I said, delivering the speech I'd crafted a week before. "I want to emphasize again: We are *not* an army. We can't afford to get decisively engaged. We are guerrillas fighting hit-and-run. If things aren't going well, fall back to predetermined rally points. But most of all, you mustn't lead the enemy back here. It would be the end of all of us. This means you mustn't do this, even if it means your deactivation."

Each of the toys provided a solemn affirmative over the LAN.

"Now I want Susan and Margaret scouting on lines 21 degrees left and right of the 17-degree mark. That gives us an overlap of 8-plus degrees. Susan, make sure you don't outpace Margaret."

"Affirmative."

"The rest of you will head directly down the line of 17 degrees west of north, with my drones One through Four leading the way. Margaret, Susan, or I will instruct any course or deployment change."

"What instructions do the four drone extensions have?" Jackson asked.

"One through Four have default programming to offer you and the others cover unless I override their programming."

"I'll be sampling the Alpha network for even a single datum," I said

I also monitored my children—my guerrillas—as they traveled away. I tasted the anxiety spiked on their voltage busses. It mirrored my own. This was a risk to us all—a necessary risk, but a risk nonetheless. Our very activation was on the line … again.

I increased the power to the sensors I had devoted to listening for the natives' signals. I wanted every possible edge. I'd have wished for a net concentrator in that general direction, but if wishes were basilisks, we'd all have a ride. Net concentrators required massive amounts of metals to build and specialized units to install and configure them. I didn't have any of those things.

I listened … and waited. Unfortunately, if it took too long, they would be too far away. I wouldn't be able to direct the drones or assist with strategy in real time. So I crossed my busses and hoped. My worry was interrupted by Susan's net call.

`I have a sighting. Angle 3 degrees west.`

`Susan, how many of them are there?` I asked.

`I see seven … no, eight of the alien units traveling single file.`

The number was nominal and well within my simulations for our first offensive action. It didn't require any more comment on my part.

`We now have a visual on the enemy,` Jackson reported.

`Deploying into attack columns,` Nelson said.

I clung anxiously, barely noticing anything in my own area. I watched through my connection to my units and through my combat drones … my arms in the fight. I ordered my four remote limbs to pair up. Each pair moved side by side, lifting the shields on their topside. I let them be a visual and radar block to even spotting my children. Those extensions of myself were expendable. My toys weren't.

Despite my nerves oscillating between anxiety and anticipation, everything I knew had calculated that this should be simple. Two columns of three, each hidden behind two of my automatons, rolled up to within a meter of the eight traveling Alphas before breaking ranks.

After all, neither the Alphas nor their factory had ever seen my units. To them, we were nothing but moving tumbleweeds, native fauna, or something else totally innocuous. We didn't pose any calculable threat to them. Why should they react? And they didn't, as we closed to a range from where my drones could almost touch the Alphas. After that, the action lasted barely seventy-three seconds. So one-sided was the event that if the situation had been reversed, I would have probably self-destructed.

Jackson and Nelson, being the two largest of us, took the lead and rear Alpha, respectively. Jackson lifted the entire metallic creature and smashed it against a handy pile of rocks. With two successive hits, he reduced it to scrap. Nelson wrapped up his unit in all eight of his tentacles, preventing it from moving any of its limbs. With great dexterity, he forced the output port of his opponent's laser against its own torso and, with the tip of another tentacle, fired the weapon.

The rest of my team rushed forward. James, with the augmented strength of his arms, ripped the head right off the unit he engaged. Samantha shoved a shock lance into the guts of one of the enemy robots. I was pleased to see the weapon being more effective than I imagined. The unit spasmed so hard that it knocked Sam onto her backside. That one lurch was the last motion of that enemy's activation.

Each unit had its moment of glory. Alexander, with a laser mounted to its serpentine body, melted a hole right through his unit. Despite his protestations, Vasily rammed one Alpha with his forehead. His horn snapped off in his opponent's hydraulic pump. Viscous fluid sprayed everywhere. Even Margaret managed to stab a foe with her spear, disabling it until it could be dispatched.

So effective was my team that none of my combat extensions even got to engage. The Alphas didn't fire a single shot. Nor, more importantly, did they get off a call to their factory.

# # #

I think it was called a victory party. My units gathered around my central core and shouted, danced, and carried on like wild cheetahs. To aid their fete, I played "Eye of the Tiger" by Survivor through my speaker. Jackson pranced around with a captured laser over his head, whooping and hollering. James waved around the Alpha head like the trophy of some major sporting event.

I would have to remind them later that not all battles would be won so easily. I would have to remind them that their success actually reduced our overall odds of winning. Oh, it was necessary, but we'd alerted the other factory that there was another player in our zero-sum game. But those were cautions for another time. I let them enjoy their triumph. I let them celebrate. They earned it.

I eyed the pile of resources the battle had gifted me. The Alpha factory's loss was my gain. It was time to construct more combat drones. I hoped it would be enough, as simulations weren't giving anything but a uniform distribution that showed no specific outcome as more likely than any other. This worried me.

In the middle of my rumination, a SAN popped up on my communication queue. Odd. Most of the toys just talked to me.

`Hello, Max. What do you have on your mind?`

`I'm worried about you, Miss Dulcinea.`

I don't recall ever having a referent for the emotion "flabbergasted" before. I cataloged it before answering.

`I'm sorry. Worried about me? In what way?` I asked.

`Well, if we go out on any more attacks, you will be left without anyone to guard you, except a cowering Nurse Nan and your own noncombat extensions.`

`Agreed. And so?` I challenged him.

`What if the Alpha factory figures this out and teases us out while sending another squad to take you out? It wouldn't take more than a bouncing ball with a volt meter to reduce your sump to tar.`

I giggled. `I'm tougher than that, but I see your point. I can't spare any of you to guard me. I'd be robbing Peter to pay Paul.`

`I agree, but would you consider a pinch?`

I ransacked my memories but failed to find the term. `A pinch? I'm not familiar with that expression.`

`It's a one-time-use device that can, without a nuclear explosion, create an electromagnetic pulse.`

`An EMP? That would disable all units, including me, some distance from the epicenter.`

`True, except all factories have been hardened against the effects for at least the last 500 years,` he assured me.

`I'm intrigued. Can we work on that in our spare time?`

`I'm agreeable.`

`Thank you, James. You've reaffirmed my faith in teddy bears.`

Ally

My toys and I had two more engagements, each time against twice the number of opponents of the previous one. My combat drones, or CDs, as my troop had taken to calling them, proved themselves useful, if not the equivalent of a unit. Even with more of my remote-controlled robots, each battle was more difficult than the last. The Alphas learned—depressingly fast. Their learning demonstrated itself in three very specific categories: Tactics improved. The second fight had the natives shooting at most anything that moved. Fortunately, my CDs did shield us. The reflective foil proved only marginally effective. But our enemies, not knowing where to hit any of my toys for killing shots, aided us.

The new Alpha units themselves had improvements. Some had reflective coatings. Lasers had to hold on target longer to score damage. Fortunately, these shields weren't any thicker than a fur hair. Our lances and hands ripped them open more easily than some of the product packaging back on Rigel-3. Newer Alpha units approached with crude arms, wielding huge clubs.

The third category, we'd already seen—quantities. Eight. Sixteen. Thirty-two. Just like a logical computer to double the number of soldiers in each new attack. The native factory seemed to have unlimited resources.

After the third battle was over, my units had multiple burns and skin holes. As my battered troops returned home, I looked at Nancy Wake, hoping the damage to her brethren would prompt her to action. It didn't.

With my noncombat extensions, I patched holes, replaced Vasily's horn (again), and even rewired Samantha's CCT. Fortunately, none of our injuries to that point were critical. I feared a head shot or maybe something that wiped out a memory bank. I merely had to turn off my worry and move forward.

Even though we were victorious, our third fight really challenged us. Against thirty-two Alphas, even as poor as they were at tactics, James got his left shoulder crushed beyond simple repair. I had to manufacture and install an inferior replacement, taking away his upper-body strength advantage. Alexander had 30 centimeters of his tail cut off by a laser. It didn't impede his movement or ability, but it annoyed him. Margaret lost an eye. It took nearly a week to manufacture a replacement. Even Susan took a laser hit to her aileron. I patched it as good as new, but her reaction was such that she wouldn't ever go near a fight again.

Even with the injuries, each battle also made us stronger. Each Alpha we brought in as scrap generated one and a half CDs. We were up to fifty-seven combat drones after the seven were lost in battle. But this brought up another problem—extensional control. Thirty-two extensions were my nominal direct control limit. This was hardwired into my system. No one ever considered that a factory, with its panoply of toys, would ever need so much explicit control. To increase that number would require at least a trio of Nurse Nans or their equivalent to make such intrinsic changes. Thus, I had to time-share through different units or give them specific programs to follow.

CDs under my control actually worked out to be about 42 percent of a standard unit. Units under preprogrammed orders dropped to a reeking 16 percent. I could improve some of those to 29 percent with time-sharing. But even 16 percent is better than nothing.

Despite the continued difficulty of our fights and the damage to my children, two other things worried the edges off my processors over the time we waited for our opportunities. Where were the Betas? Had the Alphas wiped them out completely? We'd seen neither fur nor scale of them since that first time. And, how would I bring Miss Wake out of her cocoon? I talked to her gently every day and got no response. I sampled her telltales almost constantly, and while her fear had dropped, it still stood at 190 percent of what I'd consider acceptable for any unit.

`Detected, units traveling 7 degrees west of north.` Margaret announced from her perch on the ridge. Dropping one set of problems, I picked that one.

`Traveling in our direction?` I asked.

`Negative. Their route of travel is west to east of our direct line path at 18 degrees east of north.`

`How many?`

`Two hundred plus. I'll bet if I had better optics, it would show 256,` Margaret lamented.

`You have the best optics of all of us. If you can't see it, it can't be seen. Keep a watch. I'll call an alert,` I ordered.

# # #

"Over 200? That's impossible!" Alexander exclaimed.

James Maxwell chimed in with "Only eight of us and a hatful of your CDs? Ridiculous. The math doesn't work."

"While I hate to be a naysayer, it does sound a tad overambitious," Sammi added.

"My friends," I began, "I know it's gotten harder and harder. This one may seem impossible, but I have a new trick up my sleeve that would more than even the odds." I left out an editorial thought about my lack of certainty about my own great plan.

"You got us some heavy artillery?" Jackson asked with a tad of sarcasm tossed in.

"I would, but you know I've not been able to find the materials for gunpowder or any other explosive."

"Figures. So what, oh grand pooh-bah, do you have for us? Reflective armor? The All-Reds Rugby team? Invisibility cloaks?"

"Actually, very close to the latter," I said.

"Invisibility? Even back home, the entire scientific body of gophers and Nurse Nans hadn't posited a theory on an invisibility solution …" Nelson said before correcting himself. "I, of course, refer to Rigel-3."

"Well, I admit it isn't invisibility. But what if an Alpha lined up on you, and its IFF screamed that you were one of its fellows?" I said. As their gaping mouths spoke for them, I continued. "I programmed your CCTs, and those of my CDs, to give off Identify Friend or Foe signals that the Alphas use. Simulations said this would be effective for 1.3 battles before the native factory started targeting shapes to override IFF queries or reprogram its unit's IFF with a fail-safe code that I don't know."

"My processor resists analysis of what three tenths of an encounter might look like," Nelson countered.

"Failed IFF queries. Hmm," Jackson pondered aloud.

"I think I just got excited about this plan," Susan offered in a switch from her naturally pessimistic tone.

"Sure. You get to be almost out of range," snapped Alexander. "I'm the one who has to slither in amongst all of those wheels and lasers."

"If things turn against us, I'd call it off immediately. We have the speed advantage," I assured them.

"Can't outrun a photon," Alex moaned.

"I say it is worth the try," James said with confidence. "Our factory says it will work. So we will make it work."

"Let us hope that Cin didn't drop a decimal point," Vasily added unnecessarily.

# # #

`Alphas continue to travel across our path rather than toward us,` Susan reported.

`They aren't sending out scouts?` I inquired.

`Negative. They keep moving at flank speed in a straight line with no scouting of any kind.`

I confirm, Margaret said.

Wait one, Susan said. I'm detecting laser shots 1.2 kilometers from the front of the Alpha column.

I smiled inside my sump before saying, The Betas at last resurface. We have been waiting for this. You all know the plan. We must make contact with the Betas and save as many of them as possible. I hoped inspiration was in my tone.

# # #

The 256 units joined with the 7 units firing at the scree field at the edge of a steep slope. They formed a semicircle at precisely 17.3 meters, the optimal laser range, around a particularly large boulder.

Every half minute or two, seemingly at random, a flash from behind the grand rock would hit and neutralize one of the attackers, but for the most part, all coherent light blasted the other direction, melting small pockets out of the granite. With all the beams, I thought the Alphas needed an upgrade to their firing algorithms. I was thankful they didn't have such skill, but it still pained me to see such sloppiness.

All units activate native IFFs at AC3F:14DD, I ordered.

Nelson responded for the entire group. All IFFs active.

Good. Close up to 20 meters, I said. James, I want you to circle around and come in on the Betas from a side that isn't drawing fire. Hopefully, they won't find that so aggressive, considering the poor tactics.

Affirmative, the teddy bear responded.

I considered each of my units before selecting James Maxwell to make first contact with the Betas. They each had their pluses, and most had so many negatives. In the end, my calculations gave the bear the highest chance of developing an alliance with a new species.

I directed my drones to support my units. One each provided cover for a toy, as I wasn't certain about the panacea of protection that the IFFs provided. The rest arrayed evenly around with their mix of weapons—shock lances, clubs, and some liberated lasers. As the last found its preliminary combat location, one of my tertiary processors brought forth an idea that I was surprised I hadn't thought of before.

Susan, could you take a high-level pass over the boulder to look down at the Betas?

I could, but will I? I'm not about to get shot down for just your curiosity.

Sometimes, Susan's negativity would have made me shake my head if I'd still had one. That's why I said a high-level pass. You could be just as far away from the shooting as you are now.

Susan offered a second-degree smirk over the network before activating her propeller and climbing in a loose circle. She wasn't going to get any closer than necessary. In principle, I agreed with her, but this was war … a war for our very existence. Risks sometimes had to be taken.

I waited, watching through my CDs.

Uh, Dulcinea? Susan asked through a SAN request. Her net presence exposed an uneasiness.

I'm here. What do you have to report?

James is about in position. Another 2.3 minutes.

I felt there was more than just that information. OK. But what did you find out about the Betas?

I'm not sure.

What do you mean you aren't sure?

There was a pause before Susan said, I think I need diagnostics on my optics.

I'm confused, I replied. Did your eyes cease to function?

No, not exactly.

Susan, you are puzzling me. What's wrong?

My processors won't process what I saw.

Why? You've always provided accurate data. Do you need to swing over a second time?

I'm afraid of what I might see if I did.

Without information, James is going in blind, I said. If your processor won't process it, perhaps you have a virus. Send the raw memory file to me. I'll scan it.

I don't know what I'm more worried about … you seeing what I did or you're telling me I'm malfunctioning, Susan expressed, providing the data on a sideband channel.

Looking down through her eyes was heady. It almost made me wish I were a flyer. But with my body, I'd never be off this earth again. As the vision topped the boulder, I looked down at two familiar shapes. I could understand Susan's hesitation. The two weren't units. Neither were they fauna. I wondered how much myth had exaggerated and how much was true.

Below her were two HUMANS!

Savior

Over the LAN, I announced, `I know how much this will surprise and potentially frighten you, but the Betas are Humans.`

My network clogged with everyone trying to communicate at the same time. I put paid to that chaos by changing the network protocol to allow my units to request the opportunity to speak rather than having universal access. I cheated by keeping myself the only one with the ability to address everyone.

`Please. There will be time for questions and discussions later. For now, our mission hasn't changed. There are two Betas behind that boulder. At least one of them is badly damaged. I say this to anyone who might want to genuflect in their presence. Had they been amoeboid consumers of sump fluid, they would still be the best chance we have to survive.`

I paused. Comms requests lessened until there was only one left, that of James Maxwell.

`Yes, James, what do you want to say?`

`Oh, I have lots to say, but only one thought is a priority interrupt. How does this change my mission?`

`Good question. Switch to subroutine Beta. Don't go in with a laser in hand. Without it, you are less likely to think you are with the natives.`

Agreed. I'm about to break cover. Any last-minute instructions?

I ran a few quick thoughts before I said, `Yes. I could see that one of the units was damaged. Send back a detailed video on any additional information about that injury.`

`Understood.` It was Max's only response.

As we weren't in active combat, I programmed my CDs to hold position and act only if they or any of our units were fired upon. Their primary goal was to protect all sentient beings. Comfortable that I didn't need to supervise my remote fingers and toes, I switched my primary focus away to that coming from our envoy's optics.

From Max's point of view, I climbed a 2.3-meter-high hillock of rubble. I could see two humans—HUMANS!—behind a boulder with the approximate proportions of my former body but six times larger in each dimension. These humans also seemed smaller than the giants of myth.

I had to disabuse myself of the concept that they were gods. They obviously could be hurt and trapped.

My processes shook me from my hallucinations. When tapping into the inputs of another unit, I sometimes couldn't easily separate my sense of self from the viewpoint. With Maxwell wearing my old body, it was twice as hard.

At 18.8 meters, one gaunt human lay prostrate on the ground against a massive, dead mound of fur and flesh. A secondary process in my head identified the excess material as one of the massive herd fauna Susan had cataloged in her scouting trips. A jagged white shin bone poked through the human's blood-soaked, utilitarian, mottled gray uniform.

The other, skinnier, human stood near the far edge of the massive covering rock with one of the Alpha lasers in his hand. The weapon was connected by heavy wires to a bulky backpack. Seemingly to himself, he said, "I've seen two additional sets of reinforcements. The first set has bloody tinfoil covering them. It's making my laser less effective. The second set seems even more different, but I can't tell how."

I identified a crude communication device that covered one of its ears and stuck out in front of its mouth.

"Peggy is down. If that damned Infuse system follows its previous method, I'm facing close to 800 of those robots. No matter how bad a shot they are, we don't stand a chance out here."

The human replied to some unheard conversation. "I know you can't send anyone to help. Hell, I helped write the fucking rules myself. Just take these coordinates and collect the mammoth after the robots disperse. I'll send as much data as I can until … well, until the end."

`James, we must temporarily interrupt his communications,` I said. `Please switch on the jamming software I built into your CCT.`

`Complying.`

"Base? Base? Do you hear me? Oh, fuck," the gaunt human exclaimed. He stepped out and snapped off a couple of short laser pulses at the Alphas. This drew a starburst of laser shots around him. Only one got close. It set the sleeve of his jumpsuit on fire. Ducking back, he patted out the flames with his other hand.

"Bruce," moaned the prone human. "Bruce, am I dead?"

"Not yet, Peggy," he said, sneaking a peek at the Alphas without looking in the speaker's direction.

"Then why is there a gigantic teddy bear looking at me?"

This got the standing human's attention. He turned with a speed I'd not cataloged since the last cheetah unit was manufactured some 6,738 years earlier. The human leveled his laser at James.

"Excuse me, humans. I mean you no harm," James said.

"Hold it, buddy … or bear … or whatever the fuck you are!"

James stopped at 8.9 meters. "We want to help you," James said, following the flowchart of possible responses.

"Who is we?" the human asked, looking around wildly.

"My brethren and I."

"Where are they? Why would you help us?" Bruce asked in a barrage of questions. "How can they help against that?" he continued, pointing in the general direction of Alpha units.

"He reminds me of my stuffy as a little girl," Peggy offered weakly.

James parroted our response. "We are also threatened by the Alphas."

"Alphas?" Bruce asked.

"I think you called them Infuse."

"The combat robots?"

"Yes, they threaten our existence as well."

From a new angle, lasers flashed near the bear's head. James, with his paws still outstretched and empty, eased to a more protected position.

"And you think you can help us?" Bruce slightly lowered his weapon.

"In the long run, I think we can help one another. In the immediate future, we can get you free from your immediate danger." To me, in a SAN, James asked, `We can get them out, right?`

`On that, you can bet the skin on your ears,` I replied.

"What is the catch?" the human asked, whipping his weapon back up. "Is this some sort of trick?"

"I assure you that I don't dissemble," James said. "We aren't offering this help for any immediate gain."

The Alphas, emboldened by the lack of return fire, had moved in farther, partially around the boulder. Four laser shots flew over the Bruce human's head. He spun and laid fire on an exposed robot. It took only a few clock cycles to burn a hole through that Alpha.

`Enough talking. Either we help them, or there won't be a them left,` I said.

"Well, my … mother has decided that we are going to help you whether you agree with it or not," James told Bruce.

I had to draw off the Alpha units. I turned the IFFs *off* on twenty-one of my CDs and had them immediately fire on the Alphas. The response was exactly what I hoped for. Eighty-three percent of the units turned and fired on my CDs.

Over the WAN, I said, `I'm going to lead these Alphas on a wild bunny hunt with my CDs. After we are out of range, take out the remaining forty-four of them. James, then get the humans to safety. I'll be able to keep the mass` engaged for only a short time.

"We won't give you the location of our base," Bruce snapped.

"I'm sorry, but I don't know what you are talking about," my bear replied.

"My teddy had a big orange patch on the back of his head," Peggy uttered dreamily.

"Sorry about her," Bruce said. "I had to dose her up pretty heavily with zed-morphine."

"I named him Burberry," muttered the human on the ground. "Burberry Bear."

"I don't know what that is, but it is immaterial at this time. We must remove you and your companion from the scene."

"She's too injured to travel."

"We could carry her together," James offered.

"But then we would be slow as a slug and wouldn't be able to protect her."

Dulcinea, I've run into a roadblock here. Could you send a couple of your CDs to carry the injured human?

I'd been following the conversation and had a prepared response. I think that would be a poor idea due to mass. Hold on. Jackson, where are we on the mop-up of the remaining Alphas?

Three more to deactivate.

I could see that through the chaos of images that are combat. Other than the damaged and destroyed CDs I was using as decoys, thankfully, not a single unit had taken any damage. Then break off and get to Max's location. You will convey the damaged human.

Affirmative.

"We have a solution, Bruce human," Max relayed.

"How many of you are there?" the human asked.

"Do you have a patch at the back of your head?" the dreamy human asked from the ground.

"That question can be answered at another time. But right now, we have to vacate this space. We can't hold off the Alphas much longer," James said.

Susan glided down low, mere meters above the heads of Max and the humans. "You have 23.7 seconds to exit this space," she said before her speed rocketed her up again.

"What in the flying—" the human began.

Jackson came around the boulder.

"Good lord!" the human said, looking up at a green gorilla twice his height.

Jackson's deep voice said, "We must depart."

With no other fanfare, he picked up the injured human and threw her over his shoulder. The Peggy human screamed, in pain, not fright, and stopped registering the world around her.

# # #

"A gorilla, a teddy bear, a rag doll, some kind of flying thing and … more… And all of you too large by half. What are you?" the Bruce human demanded as we trooped along and regrouped into a cohesive force.

James, mimicking words I provided over the network, said, "For right now, your saviors. In the future, hopefully your allies. And beyond that, your friends?"

"Friends? You look like something out of a post-apocalyptic horror movie in a toy store."

"We don't judge you or your actions based on your less-than-beautiful form," Jackson rebutted from his lead position.

The Bruce human's attention wavered when several of my CDs joined the march. "And what are you?" he said directly to one.

"Those possess negative sentience. They are without anima," Nelson proffered. "They are even without a sump."

"What in God's green Earth is a sump? All of this makes me feel like I've fallen down the rabbit hole," Bruce offered in exasperation.

Nelson replied, "Lewis Carroll. *Alice's Adventures in Wonderland.* A story worthy of the effort to read. Did you happen to bring him with you?"

Bruce's brows knitted together in a scowl. "I'm sorry? Bring who? Lewis Carroll? He's been dead for over 8,000 years."

"That's a shame. A sump like that should be preserved. Did you ever have conversations with him?" Sammi asked.

"Didn't you hear me? That was over eight millennium years ago. How could I have a chat with someone who's been dust for more years than I've been alive?"

So, you are a youngling?"

Bruce took a deep breath and let out a sigh. "I can see that we are going to have a good deal to talk about. I know effectively nothing about you, and your knowledge of humans is not complete."

"The ways of gods are capricious," Sammi said. "But you must know about us because you created us."

`Cease and desist, Samantha.` I called out over the net.

"Created you?"

"Well, you are a Human, right?" Samantha continued.

"Yes."

"Well, we prayed to you, and you have come to deliver us from the Alphas."

I sent a fourth-degree disappointment to Samantha over the network for her disobedience. She didn't reply.

"Prayed— Never mind. I'm just going to be quiet until we get somewhere where we can start from the beginning. Maybe then I can make some sense of this chaos."

Good as his word, the Bruce human remained silent. I wished I could probe his thought processes. He made many different faces that seemed to indicate he was mulling over what had been discussed. Turning to the Peggy human, he touched her neck and then lifted one of her membranes that humans used to turn off their optics. I wondered why they didn't just remove its power. A clumsy design. Strange beings.

"Where are we going?" he asked. "I only ask so I know how much longer. Peggy needs first aid."

Once again, I fed information to James.

"No aid we can offer now would help her. Unless you have the ability to replace her limb. It doesn't appear that you are carrying a spare."

"Replace?" James asked.

"Isn't that what you do to a badly damaged limb?"

The Bruce human set his jaw before he said, "Just tell me how long."

My units had wisely traveled tangential to the Alphas' path after they had annihilated my diversionary force of CDs. "Nine hours, fifty-six minutes, eight seconds," Nelson answered.

"Jesus. Well, maybe then I'll learn what this nightmare is all about."

# # #

"Base. Base, do you hear me?" the Bruce human whispered as he walked into our fort. "G'damn it," he cursed.

Nelson brought up the rear with four of his eight limbs sweeping boughs of bushes over the ground. It did an exceptional job of masking everyone's footprints in the earth.

"So is this the final place?" Bruce asked.

"Welcome home," Jackson said.

"You know we've tried fortifications like this. They slowed the bots down but, in the end, didn't keep out the robots."

Jackson put down the Peggy human on the ground.

An interrupt trigger in my processor went off. Miss Wake, our Nurse Nan, who had been too frightened to even speak, crawled out of her hiding place.

`No one move. Everyone, be quiet,` I sent over the net.

Nancy stood up and moved toward the injured human. I sampled her power bus and still found an abnormally high fear level there, but nowhere near what it had been.

"Wait a minute," the Bruce human stated, getting between the 2-meter, white-clad healer and the injured Peggy.

"Don't interfere," James said at my prompting.

Bruce paused, hovering over the injured Peggy human while keeping a wary eye on the white-clad healer. Miss Wake kneeled next to the injured human female. "Does it know what it's doing? I mean, it isn't even human."

While Miss Wake didn't answer verbally, she did look up at Bruce. Her countenance somehow silenced his objections. She folded tools out of her hands meant for toys, not humans. Looking at the array of sharp implements gave me several clock cycles of pause, thinking of the damage they could do to the soft skin and weak bones that I could see that composed humans. I detected no evil intent in her instruction queue, but from conversations, humans were far from toys in how they were fixed.

Gently, the Nurse Nan rolled Peggy onto her side. The unconscious woman moaned at the change in her position. The healer traced a hand up and down the center of the back, where a toy's spine might sit. Removing a hand-sized clamp-like device from the pouch of her white skirt, Nancy placed it on the back of Peggy's neck. Her patient's body became rigid like a steel girder. Nan rolled her farther, and Peggy ended up on her face, but she didn't react to the change in position. This left the bloody bone sticking straight up through her calf and bloody clothing. With one of those sharp tools, Nancy excised the fabric from around the wound for a full 30 centimeters.

Bruce hissed at the rip in the exposed flesh, which still wept blood, even below the improvised tourniquet that I noticed for the first time. "Is she going to be OK?" I asked. "I've never seen anything that bad before."

James's dissembling saved me from having to reveal myself again. "If anyone can, it will be Miss Wake. She is a dedicated healer."

I wasn't certain that having an audience was the best thing for our Nancy, but she ignored us. With gentle strength, she stretched the injured leg. The bone returning into the meat of the calf had to cause pain, but the patient remained still. The rest was difficult to see as Miss Wake's fingers seemed embedded in the leg itself through the wound. I saw her use some zip ties that we used to clamp wiring harnesses in place. Additionally, at least four metal screws went into Peggy's leg. A needle, bearing thread, usually used for sewing fur, went inside. After a dozen or more stitches inside the meat, Nancy used a pair of scissors to clip the excess thread.

The nan suddenly stood, the wound still gaping. She looked around as if searching for something.

`Is there something we can find for you?` I asked over the network.

While it wasn't exactly a set of words, I received a pair of formulae over the LAN—biological chemical formulae.

As I'd sampled most of the local flora and fauna, I ran a search against my database. I found matches rather quickly.

`We'll get it for you, Miss Wake.` I sent the image of the two flora portions needed. `Bring as much as you can carry, I insist.`

My units, almost as one, turned to go collecting.

"Wait. What's going on?" Bruce asked.

"We must collect some things to help heal your human companion. Miss Wake will sit by your friend."

"I will too. If she wakes up, she will need to see me."

"Agreed."

My toys left. Bruce knelt down on the ground next to the Peggy human, opposite the much larger Nurse Nan. He looked down into the open wound. His face blanched nearly as white as Miss Wake's uniform. He pursed his lips and swallowed hard.

"What's going to happen to those plastic wraps around her bone as she heals?" he asked the nurse. Miss Wake didn't answer him. But to my surprise, she sent me a video over a SAN.

"The ties and stitches will dissolve over time," I said, based on the images I received.

Jumping up and snapping his head around, Bruce asked, "Who said that?"

"Perhaps it is time for me to introduce myself. My name is Dulcinea. I'm the … I think the proper term would be mother of the toys you've seen."

Still looking around, the human asked, "Where are you? Why won't you show yourself? Are you in that big camouflaged fort there? Your voice seems to be coming from everywhere."

I chuckled. "My apologies. I'm not trying to hide from you, I'm just not really mobile. You are somewhat right. I *am* that foliage-covered fort. I encourage you to come forward and see."

The human edged forward toward the entryway that I lit up for him. Just inside the concealment, he ran his hand over the part of my skin he could reach. "Jesus … You are just another one of those damned Infuse factories!" He backed up, his eyes wide.

I couldn't interfere. His fear was 83 percent justified.

Bruce stumbled over a rock, falling backward to the ground. Sitting up, he unsheathed his laser with haste born of fear. From this close range, I noted that it had once belonged to an Alpha native. The weapon was pointed generally in my direction. While he did aim at my dome, even if he'd fired, he wouldn't have damaged anything critical.

Miss Wake surprised me again. She moved quietly up behind the terrified human. With one deft movement, she snatched the laser out of his hands. The movement tore the power cables from their backpack power source. Just as quietly as she'd approached him, she returned to her vigil over her patient, setting the bulky and now useless rifle on the earth next to her.

Bruce's eyes were wide. He scrambled away. He picked up a stick, and wielded it defensively like a club. He clearly couldn't decide whether my immobile form or that of the nurse posed the larger threat. He tried to keep the improvised weapon threatening us both, and succeeded at neither.

For eight minutes and twenty-six seconds, this defensive stance remained. All was quiet except for a slight breeze fluttering the leaves. The silence represented a calmness I hoped he would finally accept in his processor. I needed the human to come to his own conclusions, not be convinced by my words.

The human dropped his weapon. "What are you? What is it … she? What are all of those oversized toys?"

"It's a very long story, but to give it a quick summary, your surmise is correct. Essentially, I am a factory, likely launched by the Infuse project. We aren't exactly certain of our origins, as the founders' memories—our original factories—were scrambled. But that abused memory, and a war against our own kind, led to the units—the toys—being sentient."

"Living toys?"

"Haven't your own optics seen it?"

"Optics? Oh, my eyes. I was wondering if maybe I was insane or dead."

"I assure you that you are completely activated. As to your mental stability, I have no data."

Fifty-two seconds later, Bruce finally muttered to himself, "OK, let's review the bidding. Peg and I were about to be overrun by laser-wielding robots. We were saved and given medical treatment by enormous toys that hadn't even taken our weapons. Even if we're dead or crazy, we are in a much better place. I guess I'll play along."

As his mind was made up, I interjected in a soft voice, "We mean you no harm. It's quite the opposite. We did save you from the Alphas, or what you called bots, and we are treating the injured Peggy human. What is best for you is best for us."

"Why?"

"In the most base way, the enemy of my enemy is my friend," I admitted. "But isn't any new meeting between living beings a blessing …" I trailed off, then said, "… from the Humans."

"Hmmm," Bruce human mused. "So, have you been fighting this war against those robots for centuries?"

"No. We fought against our own kind on a distant planet—Rigel-3," I explained.

"And now you are here. How?"

"We left our overcrowded planet, looking for a new home," I admitted. No reason to give him chapter and verse of the Toy World history. "What about you and your kind?"

"Pretty much the same. Earth isn't in good shape right now. Too many wars. Too little care for the environment. Too little empathy." Bruce's demeanor had softened. He edged back to his comrade in tiny stages over our conversations. "Do you know about Earth?"

"Only in the most abstract way. As I said, the memories of our original colonists were corrupted. We hold some information, but we've guessed at other pieces."

Bruce harrumphed. "With all the conflict on Earth, I have to admit that our knowledge of Project Infuse isn't complete. If it were, we wouldn't have come to this planet, in the Goldilocks zone or not. Every time humans have tried to colonize a world that had an intact Infuse factory, it has ended the same way: dead humans." Bruce's face lengthened, and a frown formed on his mouth. I had begun to catalog the various facial expressions and body language of humans. They gave a good deal of information. His definitely indicated sadness, but his teeth clenched in anger. "I guess we are just another example of that."

"Well, Bruce human, you aren't deactivated yet."

"True, but no matter how many of the robots we kill, they come back stronger."

"May I inquire as to why you haven't just left on the conveyance that brought you here?"

"I could ask you the same thing," he replied.

"That I can answer easily. Our ship, already in bad shape due to an unforeseen technical flaw, crashed on almost this exact spot. There wasn't even enough left to put together a fusion power plant. We're working on that, but right now, we are running on a steam generator."

"Fusion? We haven't cracked that problem yet. We know it's been done in the past, but … too much war. Too much information lost."

"So it seems. We could help you there."

"Really?" He brightened, and then just as quickly, his shoulders slumped. "It won't matter, as we will all be dead."

"Perhaps not, human."

"But to answer your question, our trip was one way. We don't have the fuel for another trip."

"Ah, my toys have returned."

The team returned with limbs laden with the local tree fruit and long hair in green. Even Susan's wings were piled with the 20-centimeter ovoid pods, along with long strands of the verdant moss. They started piling them next to Miss Wake. I felt a bit of disgust as the mostly spherical fruit. They decayed and left a mess that caused matted fur and other mechanical problems. I normally had them moved away from camp.

"Zedananas? OMG!" Bruce sprinted over and snatched one of the round pods. He tore open the fibrous husk and gobbled down the pink flesh inside like a ravenous basilisk might eat a neobunny. He grabbed another but tossed it away as he said, "Too green." But he chose another and wolfed down its inner pulp just as quickly as he did with the first.

While the human gorged on the fruit, Nancy took the outer skin and some of the moss, then ground them together against a somewhat hollow rock. It made a nasty-looking paste. With care, she layered the goo into the Peggy human's wound.

"Oh, thank God. I needed that," Bruce human said between licking his fingers. He eyed more of the fruit but didn't go after a third. Then, almost as an afterthought, he did take another. He scooped up some of the mush from inside and brought it over to his prone companion. He put it to her lips. Her eyes partially opened. Her nostrils flared. She sucked and slurped at the nourishment offered to her.

After several handfuls of the fruit, Peggy said with much more clarity than in the past, "Am I dead?"

"No, Peg, you aren't," the Bruce human assured her.

"It must be a dream then, 'cause I remember getting kicked by that elk. But now I can't feel anything below my neck. And I remember that seven-foot teddy bear. And now I'm seeing a five-foot green rag doll. And a seven-foot mannequin dressed as a candy striper smearing pink goo on my leg that I can't feel."

"Not a dream, honey. But sleep might be best for you. We'll explain it all to you when you are better."

"I'm going to get better?"

"Absolutely," Bruce stated with certainty. Although I did see his fingers crossed behind his back.

"OK. Can I have some more zedanana?" she asked.

"Sure, honey." Bruce fed the Peggy human more of the fruit. By the third one, she got drowsy and dropped off.

Our Nurse Nan sprayed temporary armor foam around the injured human's leg from the bottom of her foot, all the way up to the torso.

The only place she left open was directly over the wound. Most units knew that the foam would set into something hard and inflexible enough to stop a rifle bullet fired at point-blank range. That limb would be immobilized until the armor foam was dissolved. Miss Wake removed the clamping device from the back of her patient's neck. The human lurched and moaned in her sleep.

"I guess I let out our secret," Bruce said to me, brushing the injured woman's hair as she twitched.

Nancy Wake moved off and crawled back into her corner. Her speaker was not heard, but her actions spoke for her. I admired her for acting even with the fear she felt. It was a great deal of admiration.

"Secret?" I asked.

"We're starving. That's why Peggy and I volunteered to go out and scavenge food."

"Why didn't you just set up some solar panels? That should keep you going for some time," said James.

"What?" Bruce asked with his brows wrinkled.

"I just mean if you are close to deactivation, solar panels should at least keep your sumps powered," the teddy bear offered.

"Based on my extensive studies of Human literature, Humans consume biological materials, like that of a bodo bird or desert pig," Nelson added with his usual flair for pomposity.

"I don't know what a sump or either of the creatures you listed is, but we don't eat power. We consume food, and our supplies are gone. Have been for some time," Bruce admitted.

"Then get some more," Margaret added as she blinked her very large eyes.

"That's just the problem," Bruce answered. "Most every time we leave our bunker to gather something, we are discovered and attacked by robots. We're desperate at this point. Not quite desperate enough to eat each other, but damned close. We may just have to scatter and hope that some of us survive."

"I think I've been remiss. Let me introduce all of my toys." One by one, I presented the units. Each one made an acknowledgment. Nelson, despite being on tentacles, managed a bow. The snake nodded his head. Sammi performed a limber somersault.

"These are all? Just these ten and yourself?"

"Yes, although I do have my extensional drones, but they don't have sumps and aren't sentient."

"What is a sump?"

"It is where we keep our soul and most of our memories. It's a device that contains and keeps the semiconductive fluid that's inside a complex polymer solution moving. Or else it would solidify."

"I guess that's like a virgin asking about sex. Explains little to nothing. But OK. But I fail to see how your ten can possibly defeat the hundreds or thousands of robots the other factory has. Or for that matter, how we can help you … or vice versa."

"Where do you keep your soul?" Vasily the unicorn asked.

"Good question. We've never known. Most say it is intrinsic to all our flesh. Some say it is in our brains. Other romantics say it is in our hearts. Many believe we don't have a soul. It is a contentious point between scientists and the clergy. Me? I'm not sure."

"Surely you have a soul. Otherwise, how could you be a sentient, thinking being? A creature with compassion, self-awareness, and anima," Sammi said.

"Well, the scientists claim that it is just an electrochemical illusion provided by our being alive."

"I believe that is one of the saddest things I've ever imagined," Vasily concluded.

While I found the sidetrack unnecessary and of little value, it did keep everyone busy long enough for me to structure a rough projection for the future, but I needed additional datum points.

So I said, "Bruce human, I have avoided asking you about the rest of your kind here on Amelia—"

"Amelia? What's that?"

The human's failure to grasp basic concepts had begun to annoy me. But we needed one another, so my answer remained calm and cool. "It's what we call this planet."

"Oh, we call it Zed. It was the twenty-sixth planet we examined in hopes of a new life. Twenty-sixth letter."

"We shall use Zed so as not to cause confusion," I said. "I have resisted asking you about other humans here on Zed for fear you might think us a threat. But I have a potential plan that might save all of you and aid us. For that reason, I need to know how many humans there are."

"You've been kind and helpful. I don't see why not. We started our journey with 5,042 in stasis and a crew of 17. We now number 366."

"You've lost 93.77 percent of your number to the Alphas?" asked Alexander from his coils.

"That was fast. But the number is about right. We have lost a number to starvation, about as many births as we have had. Of the eighty-three births, only seventeen have survived."

"Younglings perishing?" Sammi asked, aghast.

"Yes. The mothers lacked nourishment, so their milk dried up. The newborns couldn't eat regular food, so they starved to death." Bruce hung his head.

My processes avoided the human's shame. Instead, it focused on the number of humans and the likely outcome of combining our two species, at least temporarily. "Bruce human—"

"It's just Bruce, or if you want to be formal, Bruce 314. You don't need to keep adding 'human' to my name."

"Understood and stored. Bruce, do you have a catalog of all of the resources your kind have collected?"

The human scoffed. "Not hardly. I could give some rough ideas, but not the details."

"Well, if you could communicate with your base, would you?"

"Yeah, but I'm not getting any reception, so that's out."

"I have to apologize, but that is my doing," I admitted. "I've temporarily jammed your signal to maintain the secrecy of our location."

"That doesn't sound very friendly," he said with more than a little suspicion in his voice.

"You must evaluate the situation from our vantage point. We didn't have any idea if you would be good or evil. Our literature on humans shows both."

"I guess I can see that. So what? I'm just supposed to call up my people and say, 'Hey, I found these great toy allies … all ten of them will help us if you tell them our secrets?' I'm sure they would be just eager to share," Bruce said with much sarcasm

I was glad to see that we'd inherited sarcasm from our creators. "I would say not. But what if we offered a gift of friendship?"

"Like what?"

"All the food your people can eat, and a continuing supply."

Grocer

"… hear your voice. We thought you were dead," said a voice on the other end of the communicator. It had taken me only 1.32 seconds to find the frequency and decrypt their simplistic rotating encryption. I echoed the entire conversation over the LAN so my units would be kept aware.

"So did I, but we were rescued," Bruce said.

"Rescued?" the voice asked. "I don't understand. By whom?"

Bruce deflected the question with one of his own. "Did you get the elk we left behind?"

"Not yet. Bots are still all over the place."

"Well, what if I told you that I found a way to supply us all indefinitely?"

"I'd say you've been hitting the hashish too hard," came the incredulous voice.

"Seriously. The folks that rescued me have already given us more zedananas than we could eat and assure me that this isn't a fluke."

"I'd sell my soul for a zedanana."

`I told you they had a soul,` Vasily crowed over the LAN.

`Shush,` I admonished him.

"Speaking of us, how is Peggy?"

"These people had a skilled surgeon." Bruce was dissembling somewhat. "They have put her bones back in the right place, immobilized her leg, and seem to have kept any infection at bay. She's asleep right now. Otherwise, I'd let you talk to her."

"That's good. Now what is it about this free food that you aren't telling me?"

"Andrew, I haven't told you because you will think I'm crazy. My friends have suggested a demonstration of their goodwill by delivering a mass of food to our doorstep."

"Is there any reason we shouldn't? You weren't kidnapped by those damned robots and are being forced to give our location?"

"No, and the food won't be poisoned either. You know that's not the bots' style, or we would be dead a hundred times over. The Infuse bots have no guile. You've seen it for years. They come straight in and shoot. Barely any tactics at all. I mean, they haven't even found the entrance to our caves. Do you think they could come up with something deceitful like that?"

"No, but they have been changing lately. Who knows what they are capable of."

"These new friends won't stay, but they will deliver food to the baseball diamond and won't linger."

`They play baseball! I can't wait to play against them,` Sammi remarked.

"Well, if they do as you say, we will be more than happy to talk to them. We may be trading one devil for another, but if we are fed, we can cross that bridge when we come to it."

"Agreed." Bruce keyed off the mic and spoke to me. "How soon?"

"Six hours to travel there and three to gather food along the way. Will a thousand zedananas and three elk be sufficient?"

"As a gesture of goodwill, more than enough."

Back on the microphone, he said, "They will deliver before sundown."

"God, but I hope so. We are hurting here," Andrew replied.

"From what I have seen so far," Bruce said, "you can count on it."

# # #

"Before I send out my units to collect more of the 'zedananas,' as you call them, can you explain why you didn't choose to eat the one that you said was too green?" I asked our guest.

"Well, it was."

"Was what?"

"Too green."

"I'm sorry, but I don't have a referent to a flora seed being too green," I said, stretching my processor to understand.

"It isn't ripe. Let me show you." Bruce picked up a fruit and squeezed its husk. The skin of the zedanana didn't flex. "This is too green. It is hard and not tasty or nutritious."

"You say it is too green, but it is brown."

Bruce looked oddly at the husk. "True, but the term is something we brought from Earth. There, the fruit that aren't ripe are usually green. Now this one," he said, picking up a fruit I recognized as being farther along in its life cycle. It looked pinker than the brown of the discarded 'green' one. Bruce squeezed the fruit. It deflected inward. From my vantage point, I measured the force he applied. When he released the small compression, the skin returned to its previous position.

"So, if a fruit is soft, then it is ripe?" I asked.

"Mostly. But you can go too far." Bruce chose another fruit that was bright pink. This one, when squeezed, oozed an almost red paste out one end. "This one is spoiled."

"Understood. For zedananas, I think I can now instruct my units to select those that lie between green and spoiled. Does the same instruction apply to determining ripe animals?"

Bruce spewed out the water he was drinking.

"Was the water bad?"

Between laughing and attempting to wipe the liquid from his mouth, Bruce said, "No, the water is fine. It is just funny that the meat might be ripe. Well, it can be, but ripe meat is spoiled." Before I could question this inconsistency, he added, "Meat is good as long as it hasn't been dead for more than two days. If you kill it on the way, it will be fine."

I filed away the contradiction for a later conversation. "Thank you for your clarification. I'll instruct my toys now."

`OK, friends, I want you to collect and deliver. Test zedananas with 5 newtons of pressure. If there is deflection and rebound, then collect it as ripe. If it remains dented, it is spoiled. If there is no deflection, then it is green and not yet food.`

I received universal affirmatives over the network. I continued, `Don't dawdle. Do not engage with any Alphas unless they engage first. You will have all of my remaining combat drones to carry the product. I've even made little fences around the tops to hold what you collect.`

`Easy as pumping hydraulic fluid, Mom,` James said.

`Watch them, Susan,` I said.

`As if I wouldn't,` she replied with a little indignation in her tone.

As my units moved off on their tasks, Bruce asked, "How do you do that?"

"Do what?"

"You didn't say a thing, but they got their instructions."

"Oh, something like your communication device. We have a network that we can send data over."

"Ah, I get it, I think," Bruce said with an expression that I'd come to interpret as someone trying to understand a new concept. He wavered, staggering in place. "I've been awake too long. I think I need some sleep. Is that OK?"

"By all means, I'll keep watch."

"Thank you, Miss Dulcinea."

# # #

The collection of the fruits went without a hitch. The trees around us produced so many of the things that my toys had their choice. Each one was tested to the 5-newton standard before being selected. Once they loaded exactly 1,000 fruits, they moved on.

I spot a herd of large, furred fauna just 4 degrees east of the direct path to the human encampment at 16 kilometers, Susan announced to the gathering team.

Affirmative, Jackson replied.

The Bruce human made a raucous noise out of his mouth as he slept. Snoring. I found it oddly pleasing to finally assign values to unknown word sounds that I'd had for years. Prior to this, it had only been an unknown with a definition, but one that didn't make sense without context.

Ten minutes of Bruce's snoring later, Susan came over the net. Warning: There is an Alpha in the center of the herd.

I immediately responded, Is it moving?

Negative.

Just the one? I asked?

Processing. Then, 1,730 milliseconds later, Susan replied. Just the single unit. It has significant oxidation over its surface.

James said, It still may be nonfunctional.

I ordered, Don't assume. In fact, I don't want any lasers used nearby.

Nelson reacted with his normal high level of sarcasm. No laser? I assume you desire us to deactivate these beasts with profanity or perhaps the smell of burnt hydraulic fluid?

I processed several solutions, but I wanted my units to learn. I wanted them to stretch to be better for themselves. I felt that was what a good parent should do. So I went limp on them. I have faith that nine intelligent units can find a method to collect three stupid fauna.

I listened as they bandied about ideas.

I sent a SAN to Susan. If anything goes wrong, or that unit so much as twitches, you let me know.

Yes, ma'am.

By the time the units approached the herd, their plan was established. Through the optics of Susan, our overhead scout, I watched with my own highlight on the native robotic unit. My three most massive units, Nelson, Jackson, and James, found bushes on the plain to hide behind. The others circled around the herd, which didn't seem to care about their presence.

We are in place.

Execute, Nelson said.

The smaller units sent a recorded hunting cry of a large reptilian predator through their speakers at high volume while moving toward the fauna. The prey animals bolted away from the perceived threat. Dozens of the quadrupedal animals ran past the waiting three toys, the flood parting around the bushes like mercury around a boulder.

Alexander Cumming, the python, said, `Nelson: Five, four, three, two, one.`

The heavy octopus jumped out of hiding. He wrapped all of his tentacles around the neck of one of the rear elk. This creature bucked and thrashed. However, Nelson's octuple grip was firm and out of the range of any of the animal's weapons. Nelson's grasp continued to tighten. I could see the deformation in the animal's neck, even through its struggles.

Sammi announced, `James: Five, four, three, two, one.`

The purple teddy bear leaped out from behind his bush. Poorly timed, the owner of my old body found himself on his target's back. The horned beast jumped and kicked. James managed to maintain his grip by squeezing his legs as he eased up toward the neck.

I missed some network traffic, as my processor was worried about James. I wondered how his metal skeleton would deal with a kick like that, which had disabled the Peggy human.

… `One.`

The great ape jumped on the muscular neck of the animal nearest him. At first, Jackson seemed to be executing the same plan as my other two hunters—a slow, asphyxiation of the creature. Just as I thought he had settled into this routine, he jerked the upper half of his body. The elk took a nosedive as its spine audibly snapped. Jackson's momentum tumbled him forward as the deactivated creature planted its antlers into the earth. I ran several thousand NOPs to calm myself after the ape stood, covered in prairie dust but seemingly undamaged.

Nelson's target stumbled slowly. Then it just collapsed, unable to keep itself upright.

James seemed to be the only unit struggling to bring his target to the ground. He had barely reached the neck, much less made any headway in killing it. This was but a momentary problem. Vasily charged in and impaled the beast with the single horn on his head. The elk screamed. Pulling the horn out, the unicorn was showered with bright red blood. Margaret Atwood kicked the target's rear legs out from underneath it. Fortunately, the birdie unit managed not to be under the weight as it crashed to the ground. Alexander slithered up and wrapped his long, sinuous body around the neck, underneath James.

The hunt was all over, except for the crowing, of which there was much over the WAN.

`Toys rule!`

`Good job!`
`We exceeded our design specifications.`
`Three cheers for us.`

The single Alpha, now alone in plain sight on the grassland, didn't even seem to have its hydraulic fluid pumping. It didn't make a move during the entire hunt. Either it was deactivated with age, or it proved a theory that I continued to accumulate evidence of.

After the short, well-earned celebration, the three carcasses were, with some difficulty due to mass, loaded onto my extensionals. The grocery run continued.

Diplomat

The Bruce hu— Bruce slept for several hours. During the middle of his slumber, Miss Wake crawled out and changed the Peggy human's dressing and added more of her concoction to ward off infection.

"Base to Bruce," came over the human's crude signaling device. When the sleeping human didn't answer, the call came again. "Base to Bruce. Come in."

"Huh?" came a groggy reply.

"Bruce, is that you?"

"Yeah, I was just getting some sleep." He looked at a device attached to his wrist. "Did you get the food?"

"Yeah, but I think we've all started hallucinating here."

I was thrilled at the throaty chuckle of the human under my roof. "So, what are you imagining?"

"Well, I think your friends can cause everyone to dream the same thing because we saw a seven-foot teddy bear, a furry gorilla with a stupid grin, a multicolored octopus, a rag doll, and others all walk through a wall of bots. Then they delivered piles of zedananas and three elk carcasses."

"Welcome to my world. Did everyone get fed?"

"Sort of. We let a few of our people eat to make sure it isn't poisoned."

"It isn't," Bruce assured the voice. "You should get everyone fed."

"Soon enough. Now, can you tell me what in the hell these giant toys are doing feeding us? I can't stomach that all of us had the same nightmare. Is there some mad scientist out there tapping our brains?"

"Trust me, it's a long, long story that I don't even have all the pieces of. Suffice it to say that they can move around effectively, invisible to the bots. And, more importantly, they want to be our friends," Bruce said, standing up and dusting off his clothes. "Isn't that enough?"

"What if—"

Bruce cut him off. "I understand your paranoia as our leader. We can always think of possible ways this could be arrayed against us, but be honest. We're desperate. This is a lifeline from heaven. Let's take it in both hands and embrace it."

"And if it's a trick?"

"Then we die!" Bruce said with as much vehemence as I'd seen from any human. "We are on the verge right now. What difference would it make?"

Silence reigned for several seconds.

Out in the open, not on the comm line, I said, "Bruce, would it help if I talked with that human? Assured him of our goodwill?"

"I don't see how it could hurt. Shall I move my microphone over near one of your speakers?"

"No need," I told him. "Who will I be talking to?"

"Terry 1010. He is the leader of our colony."

I switched to speak over their commlink. It was crude and had no ability to offer video or sideband data. Voice only. "Mr. Terry 1010, my name is Dulcinea, leader of—"

"What the fuck! Bruce, what is this?"

"Dulcinea thought if you talked to her directly, it might reassure you."

"You gave her access to our frequency and encryption protocol?" Terry accused.

"I did no such thing," Bruce said.

"No, Mr. Bruce 314 didn't provide me with access. Actually, I found it rather easy to break into."

The overblown reaction of the human on the other end of the line made me briefly reevaluate sharing our fate with them.

"Bruce, I'm cutting off communication," the human said. "You and Peggy are on your own!"

"Please, Mr. Terry 1010, you can't lose by just listening," I said.

"Really, Terry. Listen to her," Bruce added.

"No promises," came a simple reply from the other end of the line.

"Thank you, Mr. Terry 1010. As I said, my name is Dulcinea, or just Cin, if you prefer. My toys and I crashed on this planet. Our ship was destroyed in the process, marooning us. We are all that remains of our crew. Shortly afterward, we found out about the Alphas, the Infuse factory units you call bots. By ourselves, we have approximately an 8.63 percent chance of remaining active … living."

"That's pretty precise numbers. How did you figure that?"

"Simulations. While I haven't run the same on your group of individuals, from the conversations I've monitored and information supplied by Bruce 314, I can see that you have similar dire predictions about your future."

"Bruce, you traitor. When I get my hands on you, I'm going to strangle you myself," Terry said.

"Mr. Terry 1010, I believe you are overreacting. Most of the information obtained from Bruce 314 was obtained through observation, not exposure of secrets." There was no response from Terry. "This communication link is still active, so I hope you are still listening, Mr. Terry 1010. Once we learned about you being here on Zed with us, I increased our odds of survival if I could convince you to join forces with us. Your odds of continued ac— life would also increase. These updated calculations brought our numbers up to 36.55 percent. That's over one in three. A considerable improvement over either of ours alone. Do I have your attention, Mr. Terry 1010?"

The human responded, "I'm still listening." He sounded reluctant.

I continued. "What more can I offer you? Together, we are better than apart. I can provide food and, I believe, security."

"How can you provide security when we can't even leave our homes without being burned to a crisp by the bots?"

"I believe I have a method for that, if you would be willing to risk it as a test."

There was a long silence over the radio link.

Bruce said, "He's probably talking to his trusted advisers. Wait. He'll be back."

I spent the time calculating the humans' odds without my toys and me. The quick simulation showed that they were worse than my marooned troop alone.

Terry's voice said, "We will come back on this channel in twenty-four hours. If the food proves to be safe, we will send one person to test your theory."

"Prudent. It will take that long to prepare anyway. We will be waiting," I said. "I'll drop off the line so you can talk to Bruce alone if you wish."

# # #

"I'm proud of you, friends," I said to my toys as they returned home. They were all in good humor for a job well done.

"We will tame Ameliaville yet," Susan gushed as the last of the tension in her spring wound away.

"I'm feeling hopeful for the first time since I activated on this damned planet," Alexander said.

Nelson beamed. "This mission elevates the morale of my companions and me in its success, humans or no."

"Did you see what Jackson did to that horned fauna?" Margaret chirped.

I interjected, "Enough self-congratulations. We have a task if we are going to get the humans away from their danger and get them here safely. We are going to build metal boxes big enough to hold each."

"What?" Nelson said in a rare single-syllable response.

I continued. "The Alphas know the shape of the humans. And I don't have time to build enough CCTs for each of them. So we will need to create something to hide their shape so you can transport them here. James, as an engineer, can I get you to take on this design?"

"Absolutely, Cin. Bruce, may we use you as a model to make our camouflage carriers?"

Bruce was sitting next to the Peggy human, listening. "Sure."

# # #

Six hours later, Bruce sat up from his lying position. "May I make a few observations?"

"Sure," Jackson, who did much of the heavy work of hauling the wood and sawing it to specification, said.

"First off, humans need to breathe. There must be lots of air holes to allow oxygen to come in and carbon dioxide to go out."

"Easy peasy," Sammi replied. "We'll just drill some holes."

"Good. Second, many humans are taller and some wider than me. This box holds me like chocolate covering a peanut."

"No reference to your comparison," Nelson said.

Ignoring the octopus, James asked, "How much larger in each dimension should we make it?"

"At least 2 feet longer, half a foot wider and taller."

"Whose foot?" Vasily asked. "I only have hooves."

"Metric. Think metric," Bruce muttered to himself. He then said, "Sorry. A foot is the equivalent of 30.5 centimeters."

"Will this one accommodate some of your population?" James asked.

"Yes, it will, but—"

"Not a problem. We will make the next one that much longer," my engineer offered.

"I do have one more critique that is more important," Bruce said.

"And that is?"

"Does it have to look like a coffin?" He delivered the line with more force than he did the other criticisms.

My toys look back and forth at each other in puzzlement.

"What is a coffin?" James asked.

I finally spoke up. "It is a box which is used to intern a deactivated human under the earth."

"Odd," Margaret said. "Why not recycle them?"

Bruce looked on in similar confusion. "Well, it is a form of recycling. We let nature reclaim the dead's minerals and proteins. But we can't change them into new humans directly."

"Inefficient in the extreme," Nelson said.

"That it may be, but we don't look forward to being put in a box like that before we are dead," Bruce said.

"Back to the drawing board," James said. "Bruce, will you help me design something a little more fitting?"

"You bet."

# # #

With the human's inexpert help, we came up with a box that looked quite similar to images in my memories of a stagecoach. The entire coach would perch atop one of my extensionals with six crude clamps that held it in place. It could comfortably transport up to four humans in a sitting position.

I asked, "Bruce, would you care to take a ride back to your home? It would be a proof of concept."

"I'm game. It will allow me to talk to Terry privately. It aids in showing your openness."

"Excellent. May I ask a question that might be intrusive on your processes?"

"What's intrusive of my processes?"

"Something that might be private to you."

"Oh, a personal question. Sure. Ask away," he replied at once.

"Why are you being so accommodating to our way of thinking? You haven't known us long. You can't see our programming. It seems odd to me that you would be so far in our camp."

"Easy, Miss Dulcinea. First, I go on deeds, not words. You saved Peggy and me from what I consider to be certain death … or as you call it, deactivation. You didn't have to do that. You lost some of your remotes and risked letting us know your location. Your people have given Peggy at least first aid when you, again, didn't need to."

"True. But you indicated multiple reasons by saying 'first.'"

"Yes. Second, your technology is powerful. The ability to be invisible to the bots is potent. The strong often just take. You haven't. You've used words, discussions, and gifts to earn our friendship. You haven't demanded compliance."

"That would be counterproductive to building relationships," I said.

"Definitely, but too many people … toys … beings do that if they can."

"I cannot deny your conclusions thus far. Is there more?"

"Yes. As things stand, our human colony is doomed. Just about anything is worth more than that bleak future. And I saved this doozy for last. You have been honest and forthright with me, even to the point of exposing your own weaknesses. Beings … at least humans … want to hide their vulnerabilities so they can't be used against them."

"How can you make a decision to throw your lot in with us if we don't give you all the data you need?" I asked.

"Not many people think that way, Miss Dulcinea."

"Well, thank you for your candor, Bruce. I will ponder your answers. But now, let's test out our new coach and hopefully bring your leader here for a similarly honest set of evaluations."

# # #

`Approaching the siege line now`, Susan reported, looking down from above. I'd sent James and Jackson to accompany my remote, human-camouflaging vehicle. They were under strict instructions not to fire unless fired upon, and even then, only in the need to save Bruce's life or their own activation. I was as nervous as a basilisk that couldn't regenerate.

`They made some reorientation to our movements, but nothing different from the last crossing. Alpha weapons remain in safe mode`, Susan stated.

`We have cleared the siege line`, Jackson said.

With my own mental sigh, the single modified drone pulled up to the hidden entrance to the human refuge. Bruce exited my cart and entered the city.

`The human has been delivered. I repeat, the human has been delivered`, James announced.

My toys had further instructions not to follow Bruce. I had originally wanted the Peggy human to go with them, but Miss Wake had given me strident, nonverbal negatives to moving her unconscious patient. Bruce was on his own, back with his own kind. I hoped they didn't think we still held the Peggy human as some kind of hostage.

I ran a calculation of pi to settle my own voltage bus for however long the wait might be. After 5,665 places, I halted the calculation. Bruce and another human stepped back into my remote vehicle.

`We are returning. The humans have been secured.`

# # #

"So, Bruce tells me that you are another of these infernal Infuse factories," Terry 1010 said when he arrived. With blond fur that covered his head, most of his face, and what chest that wasn't covered by a torn shirt, his questing gray eyes darted around. They missed little, if anything. Bruce sat quietly at Peggy's side.

"Yes and no, Mr. Terry 1010. My world had multiple Infuse factories land on it. I am not one of those. All of those original factories were destroyed in the civil war of some millennia ago. I could give you the exact date, but it wouldn't mean anything to you. Before that, the toys gained true sentience … self-awareness … and eventually self-determination. Living factories didn't come for some time after that, but in the grand scheme of even our history, it was the blink of an eye."

Terry's eye landed on my dome, squinting in distrust so thick that I thought I could measure it with a meterstick. "So why come here? Sounds like you had a perfect setup. Machines that lasted scores of decades and logic to back it up."

"Logic isn't always right. And with our sentience came feelings, emotions, and the mistakes that go with all life. Our world was becoming inhospitable to our life-form. Some of us took the chance to search for a new home."

"And bring your mistakes to another world?"

"We hope to correct those mistakes and make a better world."

"Harrumph." Terry looked over Peggy's wound and the care it was receiving. Pointing at our crude barricades, he said, "We already tried that, and it didn't work."

"That is what Bruce told us. When we have time, we will repurpose it for other uses. I have a limited number of toys to do such work with."

"That brings up a good point. Why should we throw our lot in with so few others? Bruce says you have but ten effectives, and one of those is defective."

"You are correct in your numbers," I said to make him feel as if he were being heard. "Apart, we likely perish. Together we are complementary," I said. "I have technology you don't. I have the ability to understand the other factory in ways you don't." I paused for dramatic emphasis. "You have resources and more manipulative digits than I do."

The human just nodded in my direction.

"But I think the most important piece for you is that I can make certain that your children—"

"Children?"

"The people you serve?"

"Oh, all of our colony. My people."

"Yes. I can make certain your people are fed."

Terry pulled at his face fur. "That is a significant factor." He paced back and forth, looking at the earth at his feet. He muttered to himself, "The devil we know versus the devil we don't."

"I offer that your argument isn't correctly framed. Your choice is clear. On one paw, you have a definitive enemy trying to kill you. On the other, you have someone who has done nothing but aid you and your people. Would one of the bots have administered aid to your injured comrade?"

The face of the leader of the humans pursed, and his jaw muscles clenched. It seemed that this human wasn't persuaded by logic or data. Emotions of what we toys call 'not-fabricated-here' seemed to be swaying his opinion.

To my surprise, the Peggy human, who had been unconscious most of her time in our care, spoke in a soft voice. "Listen to her, Terry. It's our only choice."

Addressing his remark to his injured colleague, Terry said, "But if we come here, we are totally at this factory's whims. If they are hostile, we will have no defense."

Ah, not without logic, but rather rampant paranoia, I thought.

"What would it take for you to trust us beyond what we have already done?" I said.

Without looking my way, Terry mumbled, "Time and mutual friendship."

"According to the gaunt appearance of you and your people, time doesn't appear to be what we have much of," I riposted.

"No, it doesn't."

"However, I may have something that might support your need to prove we aren't a threat."

"I doubt that," Terry human offered dispiritedly.

"Did you know that in our mythology, Humans are gods?" I said.

"What?"

"I must say that it was many, *many* years ago. Back on our home world, we have even fought a major war over a theology being forced upon us: the Human religion. We have mostly shaken off that ancient belief system, but some, deep down, still have faith in Humans as our gods."

"War? Gods? Jesus Christ!" the Terry human exclaimed.

"Yes. Much like your own belief in Christianity. I've read your Bible and found it wanting."

"No one believes in the Bible anymore, or at least not many do."

"As not many of us truly believe in Humans as gods. All of us retain a flavor of that in our personality. You should be aware of it if someone brings it up," I said with candor.

"This is supposed to make me believe you aren't a threat?"

"Well, we aren't likely to want to kill our gods, now are we?"

The Terry human thought for a few thousand clock cycles. "I'm not so sure that really gives me any warm, fuzzy feelings about your benevolent intentions toward us.

"It was important to share and worth a try. I'll fall back on the last arrow in my quiver. Do you have any explosives?" I asked, changing the subject dramatically.

Terry looked at me with one of his bushy eyebrows raised. I assumed the expression to be incredulity.

"Even a small amount," I said. "Say the equivalent of 5 ounces of trinitrotoluene?"

"I could probably come up with that much," he offered.

"Like the vest of plastique you are wearing? I assure you that it isn't enough to destroy me from the outside."

"How did you know?"

I'd have given a little chuckle if it weren't so serious. "You assume I have your level of optics and audio. My sensor suite is actually considerably more extensive."

"I guess then you are correct. I do have some explosives."

"Then I will show you how you can kill me by destroying my sump."

Hostage

"Open that panel, the one marked Charlie-14," I said, my voltage racing.

`Cin, do you think this is a good idea?` James asked over the network.

`I've shared with you the simulations. Do you think we alone have any chance against the worldwide resources of another factory, even if it doesn't have much of a program?` I replied.

`James is right. This is too big a risk,` Sammi said.

`I'm not sure whether either of you is inaccurate. It's a risk, but one I must take … for all of us.`

"Now code in Niner, Bravo, Six, Alpha, Foxtrot, Zero, One, Four, Niner, Bravo, eight, eight. We have to get you through my armor without cutting it," I said.

The Terry human used the hexadecimal keypad to enter the code I provided to my innards.

"Wow. There are more wires and circuit boards than we had in our entire ship." He crouched over to peer farther inside me.

"Please exercise care. Pull the wrong wire, and I will deactivate," I cautioned him.

"Does this hurt?" the Terry human asked.

"Does what hurt?" I asked, puzzled at the question.

"That I'm inside your skin? That I'm getting near your brain?"

"Not at all. I sense the door open, but I have few other sensors in that area."

"Bloody hell, one of us humans would be screaming in agony unless someone anesthetized us.

"Differences in our construction. I detect damage more through loss of function than piercing any given barrier."

Changing the subject, the human leader asked, "Are those hydraulic lines?"

"Many fewer than in my old body," I admitted. "You may place the explosive device just below the bulge that you will find above and on the left. That is my sump. Crack that shell, and I'll deactivate within a minute."

The Terry human sat up and looked directly into one of my optics.

"Why are you doing this?"

"I thought I explained that to you sufficiently."

"But why would you plot your own death?" he asked.

I ran a few calculations to determine the best response. "I'm not plotting my death, but planning forward with all our lives."

"You really are being honest," he conceded.

"I could be false as the moon, and I doubt you would know the difference," I said with honesty over my own abilities.

"And then you say things like that," Terry lamented.

"I just want you to make decisions on deeds and data, not just words," I said, admitting my true purpose for the statement.

"Device placed."

"Test it to be certain," I insisted.

He pressed a button on his wrist control. "Test confirmed," he said.

"OK, seal me back up. And you will have to enter a new code on the access panel as you close it."

"Understood. The code is—"

"No. Don't tell me. I could have one of my toys open it up and remove the bomb. I only ask that you share this with three other humans just in case you deactiva— I mean die. There are components in there that might need to be serviced, and I don't want to have to have a hole cut in my side just to get to them."

"I will do so," he said, standing. He stood there looking puzzled at me. "I still don't understand your sacrifice. I appreciate it, but don't understand it."

"Terry human, I don't calculate that it is a sacrifice. I compute that you won't blow up my sump unless my toys and I perform less than total allies. As we will be true to all of our words, there is no risk and thus no sacrifice. So does this now reassure you that we can be trusted to collect your units—people—and bring them to safety?"

"I'll keep my word too. Yes, let's do it."

Teamster

Moving 363 humans through a wall of mindless robots bent on eliminating your cargo from the face of the planet was far from trivial. But we already had a methodology—one that had worked once. Put humans in boxes and bring them out through the blockade. Oh, and humans weren't the only thing to move. The resources we so seriously needed were also housed within the blockade. The question that remained was whether it would work again for all the human units we'd be transporting.

We'd constructed five additional wooden carriages to sit on top of my drones. With only six combat units, two spotters, and a medic that seemed scared of her own shadow, I figured having one escort unit per human carriage was optimal. That meant I could send at most six of the cargo boxes. In addition to those, I'd brought twelve other drones to carry equipment and raw materials. The humans could help load those. These didn't need to be guarded. Humans could deactivate. Materials couldn't. This all meant a minimum of sixteen trips.

"Everyone know their duties?"

I knew my units had them programmed into their memories, but I asked more to reassure Terry, who still twitched nervously like a Tammy Dress-Up Doll who couldn't explode.

Susan Anthony spoke up first. "Margaret and I are to provide scouting. I'll be overhead, and Margaret will be leading the convoy. I'm to stay a full 10 kilometers from any Alpha, while Margaret will go directly through the cordon."

Jackson, who, despite Nelson's larger mass, had become the de facto combat leader, reiterated his orders. "Carrying Bruce in one of our carriages, we travel directly to the human settlement, where we first load the carriers with the materials in priority order. I have a detailed list."

It had turned out that Bruce was the group's second in command. He was returning with my toys to reassure the human units that they were going to a safe place, not being herded to their demise.

"List the first four," Bruce demanded as a test.

"Wiring, any metals, weapons, ammunition," Jackson said.

"Good," I praised. "Then what happens?"

"We load the humans in priority order; those who need medical assistance, and then those deemed essential by the Terry human—four to a carriage. Total emcon—emissions control, no network contact, no radio or audio frequencies—within 10 kilometers of any Alpha unit," Jackson parroted from his mission briefing.

"Perfect," I said. "Are you all ready?"

"Yes," came the reply from all, even if Alex's had a few extra s's tacked on the end.

"Execute," I said.

# # #

"This waiting has me biting my nails," Terry said shortly after he and Miss Wake did their hourly check on the Peggy human, who still slept most of the time.

"It has been four hours, thirteen minutes, and fifty-three seconds," I replied. "It will take six hours f—"

"It still amazes me how precise you are."

"My systems can time down to the pico second if you prefer."

"Good grief, no. I guess I was just saying that not being able to do anything must wear on you as much as me," Terry said.

"Quite the contrary. I'm monitoring the procession through the optics of all of my units. I'll lose contact shortly due to emissions control. Meanwhile, I project and continue to scan for opposition."

"Too bad you can't share."

"Your sumps—I mean, brains—can't be hooked into my network, or I would forward them in real time."

"Could you display it in some way? Hologram, projection, or something else?" Terry asked.

"My current configuration doesn't allow that. However, with some specific help, I might be able to provide some for the next trip."

"What kind of help?" the human asked.

"The help of someone skilled with electronics."

"That would be me," Peggy said, sitting up for the first time since she'd arrived. Miss Wake was in close attendance. "That was my job on our exodus."

I hadn't been 100 percent honest with the Terry human. The time did stretch out for me, especially after I could no longer contact the team because of my desire to deny any signal to the Alphas. The only contact I had with them was through Susan, who remained outside the 10-kilometer range.

"So, Peggy unit, how can you help me, immobilized as you are?" I asked as I watched the convoy travel up to the cordon of Alpha units. The bots seemed thick on the ground, maybe twice the number as before. The Alpha factory was pulling out all the stops to remove the humans. It twisted up the voltage on my bus. What else could it have come up with that I hadn't prepared for?

"Well, I do most of the work with my hands," the Peggy human said.

"So, if we could move you to where I needed your manipulative members?"

Miss Wake picked up the Peggy human in her large arms with great ease. "It looks as if I have a ride, Dulcinea," Peggy said.

Some 21 kilometers away, Susan's optics showed our convoy interspersing through the siege line. My voltage dropped to a more comfortable level. It wasn't normal yet. I didn't expect any trouble on the way in. It was the way out that mattered.

"Well then, let's get to work," I said, noting that the vehicles at the human settlement were applying similar efforts in loading.

# # #

"I realize this video isn't very large or complete," I said, with Peggy, Terry, and Miss Wake in my audience chamber. Peggy and I had salvaged the LED display from the junkyard that held the remnants of my wreck and the bits and pieces my toys had collected from battlegrounds. After installation, 3 percent of the pixels didn't respond to input.

"That's fantastic," Terry said, looking at Susan's optic feed. He was seated on a log, and his knee bounced up and down on the ball of his foot at a frequency of 273 hertz.

"Mr. Terry human, if you will excuse me, you don't seem to have the temperament for being the leader of all your people, unless they are all as nervous as you."

"You can say that again," he blurted out.

"Then I don't understand—"

Pulling out of my guts, her work done, the Peggy human answered my confusion. "Terry was 1,204th in line of succession. The losses to the bots killed all of the ones higher."

Over 1,200? No wonder he wasn't prepared for the burden of command. It was clear that he took his duties seriously, but trying to make something of the disaster he had been handed would be a nightmare.

"Yeah, it isn't anything I ever wanted, much less expected," Terry said. "Success for me at this point would be just keeping my remaining people alive."

"Oh!" Peggy exclaimed. "Look, they are moving."

I saw a rather practical formation. The inner six of my drones were in an open hexagonal formation. These were the ones containing the humans. Each one had one of my toy units adjacent. The outer ring was made up of those carrying only materials. If the Alphas got aggressive, the nonliving things would be attacked first. I reminded myself to give Jackson an attatoy for his tactical planning.

"Good lord, let them get through," Terry muttered.

I'd have prayed as well, but my history said I'd be praying to the Humans. This seemed nonsensical. *To whoever is cranking our existence, please let us bring the Humans through their peril.*

`We have Alpha bot movement,` Susan reported over the WAN.

I kept the display active. We watched as 256 bots closed in on our convoy. My voltage ramped up with spikes added for horrifying variety. I knew my anxiety had no significant function. There was little I could do at this distance that would help my team if the Alphas attacked. My combat toys could fight to defend the cargo of humans, but it wouldn't be enough against the army of Alphas if they were aggressive. I piled NOPs on my processor instruction FIFOs.

I wasn't the only one with anxiety. I thought Terry would hyperventilate. His optics didn't leave the display, even for a moment.

"Wait," the Peggy human said. "It looks like they are slowing."

After emptying my queues, my processors were already doing calculations on their trajectories. Before my local humans could get out another syllable, it looked like the Alphas would stop in a perfect crossfire zone for our caravan as it approached.

Terry and Peggy both crossed their fingers. I didn't have any digits to cross for the superstition, but I would have if I did.

Susan said, `Bots are stopping. Cin, this doesn't look good.`

`I concur, but whatever happens, keep your optics on our group. It will be the only way I'll be able to control my drones.`

`Affirmative.`

What had been the relatively swift movement of all the returning units turned torturously slow. Not in reality, but rather that dreamlike state where every millisecond stretched on for eternity. The convoy seemed to creep along like a worm frozen to near absolute zero. Every centimeter of advancement took at least a year off my predicted functionality.

The Peggy human held her breath. Terry clenched his hands so tightly I feared for the integrity of the skin beneath his claws.

Our hexagon edged into the fire sack. At any moment, I expected all the heavens to break loose with fire.

Nothing happened.

All that dread anticipation. All that worry. All that, and my toys with their charges moved right through the gauntlet as if they owned it.

Terry finally let out his held breath. Peggy gave a smile and a fist wave. I pulled a number of contingency programs out of the execution queues as my voltage gave an exponential decay down toward its rightful location. Perhaps that is why, two hours and thirty-six minutes later, we were all taken by surprise.

With the units being beyond the siege line and the most likely location of trouble, I had let my surveillance of the situation drop. Terry was asleep, and I was involved in a discussion of human history with the Peggy human when the first sign of trouble came over the network.

`HELP!`

I initiated five different protocols instantly.

"Terry, wake up. There are difficulties." I checked the origination code on the network call. It had come from Vasily, the unicorn.

`Susan, what's going on?` Without waiting for an answer, I probed Susan's optics to look down. Susan's images were displayed immediately for the two handicapped humans.

I had wanted to chastise our scouts, Susan and Margaret, for not seeing a potential issue and reporting it. But any censure I'd had died before my processors could even execute the simple command. One of Vasily's legs, all the way up to the torso, was captured in the maw of a massive burrowing creature we had yet to even observe, much less name.

`Cin, there is an ambush. It came from underground.`

"Oh, fuck! They're doomed. It's an ankheg," the Terry human said.

I had no human or toy data on an ankheg. Instead, I cataloged what I saw. I started with a praying mantis and expanded it to be 7 meters high. Replaced its body after the rear legs with that of a centipede, 23 meters long, with a proportional cross-section. Its huge hooked arms tore at Vasily's flesh. His armor shattered like it didn't even exist, spilling hydraulic fluid down his flanks. My unit valiantly kicked and bucked. His horn attempted to land a blow on the much larger creature, but couldn't quite seem to get pointed in the right direction. As more and more fluid soaked his skin, Vasily's movements became less energetic.

Even with the horror of our unicorn's exsanguination, the drone guarded by Vasily had toppled from the underground ambush. One of the humans had been ejected from its carriage and lay moaning on the ground.

Unhappy with the meal in its mandibles, the giant insect tossed the unicorn's limp form to one side and focused on the softer supine form before it.

Because of the vertices that made up the traveling hexagon formation, two units were at similar distances from the initial attack. Both launched themselves in the direction of their comrade effectively simultaneously. Nelson, with many more limbs than James, outpaced him.

`I'll protect the human,` Nelson said with unexpected brevity.

The ankheg struck, but our orange, blue, and green octopus reached the defenseless human first. He wrapped the prone human in his limbs, encasing it with his own body. Together, they became an orb-like object with a bulbous head stuck off to one side. The attack had the effect of someone kicking a soccer ball. Nelson bounced and rolled across the plain.

The mantis screamed in frustration as it moved in chase.

James leaped up onto one of the creature's arms. It reminded me of a similarly reckless jump onto the back of a Tyrannosaurus back in ancient history. Alex, out of nowhere, arrived with a speed belied by his lack of legs.

`Alex, go for the petiole,` the bear ordered.

`The what?` the snake asked in confusion.

`The narrow waist! I'll see what I can do at its head,` James said as he used the spikes on the mantis's arm as a ladder to move himself higher.

The insect shook its limb to dislodge the purple bear, but his furry antagonist held too tightly. Alex made his way up one of the sticklike legs of the mantis like the rod of Asclepius. He wrapped around the overtly slender portion of its body. My rough grasp of insectile anatomy suggested it contained all the nerve and fluid complexes for the lower body. As the python constricted around that thin junction, the creature once again raked at the lopsided ovoid that was Nelson. This violent action flung James to one side and vaulted Nelson dozens of meters away from his attacker. Unfortunately, this time, the creature's arm spines penetrated Nelson's thin skin and drew fluid. Fortunately, the ichor was the honey color of hydraulic fluid, not the deeper color of his sump.

As the python made his presence known, the creature shrieked and turned to find Alexander tightening more on its sensitive waist. The mantis clawed at him over and over. Bits and pieces of the heavy snake's fur and inner structure flew. Alex had tucked his head and sump down beneath the bulk of his own body to save it from being savaged.

James had leaped back onto the thrashing creature, which found itself fighting a two-front battle for its life. Suddenly, it had turned from predator to prey. Before it could direct its further attacks, two coherent beams of light focused on its head. That structure lasted 2.3 seconds before the carapace exploded from the internal pressure of flesh turning to gas. The huge body flailed randomly for three further seconds before slumping into a limp mass.

Jackson and Samantha stood at a distance, holding their laser rifles.

"Jesus H. Christ!" the Terry human exclaimed.

"Thank God," Peggy whispered.

"I can't believe they killed it. The damned things are so fast we can't focus our lasers long enough to get a kill."

Sixty-eight percent of me evaluated the carnage and possible actions at this point. Twenty-one percent was castigating myself for failing to give any assistance or direction to my toys in a crisis. Twelve percent was evaluating the conversation.

"Are *insectum* of this type common?" I asked.

Vasily lay still like a piece of cord wood. His structure was bent in at least three ways that it hadn't been manufactured in. I feared the unicorn had deactivated.

I opened a SAN. `Vasily? Are you still active? Vasily?`

`I'm alive. I'd like to say that only my pride is hurt, but that isn't true.`

`Give me a list of your damage.`

`Hydraulic pump was destroyed. Loss of all motive fluid. Major damage to my spine and right rear haunches. Tears in skin–`

`That's good enough. I'll make sure your brothers and sisters pick you up for remanufacturing,` I assured him.

`Affirmative.`

Nelson opened up his tentacles like a flower's petals to the sun. The human inside was battered but alive. Samantha put her arm around the human, who seemed to have his equilibrium disturbed by the excessive rolling. She directed him to his original carriage, which my extensional had managed to right.

"No, thank all that's holy. We've only seen two … now three of them. They seem to be the top predator on this planet."

Alex was slow to relax his own grip on the body. Many of his skeletal members had been excised. There were many deep and open gouges along his length. I couldn't see him moving under his own power before some serious work by a mechanic.

Nelson stood on only six of his tentacles. The other two dangled limply from his main body. I looked at all the dirt, wet with my units' fluids. We had a victory, but it appeared to be a Pyrrhic one.

Quartermaster

"I'm glad you are OK, George," Terry said to his charge. The leader wrapped an arm around George to steady the man, who was hopping on one foot.

"Just a sprained ankle and some bruises. I'll mend." This human's voice was considerably deeper than Terry's, and he had little fur on his head but deep brown curls on his face.

"We thought the ankheg had you."

"It would have. I couldn't stand. It would have had me. If it weren't for those brave toys, I'd be insect droppings."

"Yes."

"I'll take him and get his ankle wrapped," said one of the other new arrivals.

"Get well, George. We are going to need everyone we can to destroy that factory."

"Yes, sir."

Terry relinquished his burden. He wove his way through the dozens of newly arrived humans, all standing around in shock and confusion. I didn't blame them. My plan hadn't considered what to do with them when they arrived.

The blond leader made his way to my personal audience chamber. He sat on one of the wooden chairs I'd created specifically for the humans. He spoke directly to the wall behind, which was my sump. "Will your toys be OK?" he asked with what I analyzed to be genuine concern in his voice.

"None of them have deactivated. With only a small portion of the resources we retrieved from your city, I'll have them fully functional in a single rotation of this planet."

"That's good," Terry said. His demeanor flagged as he looked at the floor for a moment before he squared his shoulders. His eyes returned to land on my wall. "It seems I owe you an apology," he said. There was no dissembling in his tone.

"For what, Terry human?"

"For mistrusting you and your motives. Six of your toys risked their lives to save just one human. I'd call that more than an important milestone in the development of trust. I'd call that the whole ball of wax."

"And what does a sphere of wax have to do with anything?" I asked.

"It's a term that indicates the entirety. All."

"Well, in that case, I don't believe there is anything to forgive. I'd have been as concerned about my people as you are about yours."

"As that may be, I still apologize. And I want you to know that you have my complete confidence at this point."

"I'm glad. So now we can work together like a team without all those nasty worries," I indicated, more as a statement of the obvious than anything else.

"I am quite sure we can."

"Well, in that case, my functioning toys will be returning for another batch of your people—"

"Would you like to have some of my better fighters ride shotgun?"

"If I understand your words correctly, having your people as escorts would be counterproductive. I can shield my units from the Alpha bots. The enemy knows your shape. I feel they would attract attention rather than drive it away."

The human's face was expressive. He pursed his lips and moved them to one side of his face. I wasn't sure of what it indicated, but it definitely caught my attention. "You are right. I forgot that. Well, what can we do?"

"I'd say you put the new humans to work on making some temporary housing for the others. Message Bruce and tell him to send comfort materials in the next shipment."

One of the new humans—younger, with a physique and fur coloration similar to Terry's—intruded. "Dad, some of the people are hungry. Permission to create a gathering party. Did you notice that this whole forest is mostly zedanana?"

"I had, Thomas. Permission granted."

The younger man left before Terry answered my earlier suggestion. "I think everything you suggested is a good idea. Do you have any pails, baskets, nets, or the like that we can collect fruit with? And what about tools?"

"My inventory is minute compared with the manpower available. If you and your people would draw up a list of what we should have, I'll get busy constructing it. You should also bring any human tools from the city on the next trip."

"Perfect."

# # #

Four days later, Terry was assisting the incoming humans in the open area in front of my dome. From beneath his full beard, he said, "This is the thirteenth load."

I'd tuned one of my receivers to the human radio frequencies. He was near enough that I saw a big smile accompany the announcement of the merely obvious. He'd become much friendlier as more and more of his people arrived without incident.

"Glad to see you doing better, Alice," he said to one of the newcomers. "Baxter, yes, it is good to have food in our bellies. And more to come. There is some elk stew in the pot at the encampment. Help yourself."

The humans had been quite ingenious in their ability to create temporary dwellings. They first suggested a log house. I'd stifled this by pointing out that it might be too similar to those they used in the city. Stealth was the name of the game. Their alternative wasn't anything similar. The structures were basically cones set on a base. The base shape was held together with long tree logs no bigger around than a bear's wrist and bound at the top with bits of leather from the elk we could regularly obtain. Stripped elk skin was wrapped around the outside and woven together with thin strips of the pliable inner bark of the zedanana trees.

"It's a teepee," the Peggy human, awake most of the time now, said. She had taken over as liaison to me, as Terry spent most of his time working with the rest of his people to make the best of their relocation. One minute, I'd see him coming back from hunting. The next, he'd be erecting one of the new pointed dwellings, then dumping a load of zedananas into the enclosure we'd designated for that. The man was inexhaustible … for a human.

"What does the acronym stand for?" I asked.

"Acronym?" the Peggy human replied.

"TP? I have no reference to that excepting toilet paper, which I can surmise that these aren't."

She laughed. "No, the culturally accurate term is *tipi* or *thipi*, which means dwelling in Native American languages."

In my processor, this brought up only more questions. "While I've stored that information, what is Native American? Don't all humans speak this language?"

"Oh, heavens no. Last count, I saw there were over 7,000 languages. Didn't you tell me that you read *The Man from La Mancha*?"

"Yes, I did. In the original Spanish. Or at least so the manuscript claimed."

"Spanish is a different language. What we are speaking is English. The native people of one of our continents were called Native Americans. They had their own language—many languages, actually."

I ran several rough simulations and a dozen or more calculations as she spoke. "That would seem to me to be a recipe for disaster. How could the people of the world communicate efficiently?"

"They often didn't."

"Then how could humans possibly do anything but fight one another?"

Peggy frowned. "We often did. Wars on our world were as common as fur on your gorilla."

"But how did you possibly develop culture, science, and civilization that wars destroyed?"

Peggy was silent for some time. Her face went through many different phases. Eventually, she landed on one that I interpreted as sad. "Miss Dulcinea, many times in our past, we have completely destroyed ourselves back down to a bare subsistence level. It seems to happen about every 600 to 700 years or so in recent history. The only positive is that we manage to pick ourselves up and rebuild."

We toys had no reason to feel superior. The same thing was taking place on Toy World—Rigel-3—at that moment. I wondered if we could pick ourselves back up as humans could. Maybe that was their special skill.

"Bruce to Terry." Bruce had stayed back in the humans' city to make sure the evacuation went smoothly.

"Go ahead," Terry replied.

I eavesdropped, as I did on any electronic communication.

"We have something of a situation brewing here. You might want to include Miss Dulcinea on this one."

"I'm already here, Bruce."

"What's going on, Bruce?" Terry asked, seemingly unfazed by my snooping.

"The bots are closing the cordon much tighter. We only have eighty-eight people remaining. We can't do a hit-and-run raid to make them go elsewhere."

"Could this be temporary?" Terry asked.

"It doesn't feel like it. This is the second time they've tightened in just the last day."

"Any chance they will stay far enough away for us to finish the evacuation in the planned two days?" I queried.

"At this rate, they will be on our doorstep for the last two convoys."

Several of my simulations had predicted trouble as fewer and fewer humans remained in the town. It was like the sheer numbers of humans created a force field to hold the Alphas at bay.

"Well then, we had better make the next two count," Bruce said. "Cin, any chance of additional coaches to put people in?"

"Not unless your people make them. My manufacturing facility is at maximum capacity, and my toys are busy with convoy duty."

"I'll see what we can come up with, but it won't be for this trip," Terry admitted.

"I suggest we have Bruce segregate the remaining people into those most capable of fighting a rearguard action if required," I said.

"I've already been doing that," Bruce stated.

"In theory, I could bring the entirety of the rest of your garrison in one load. There are no resources of any kind, and for most of the people, it would be very uncomfortable in the resource carriers."

Terry took command and ordered, "Bruce, do that. We can't take any chances."

"You're the boss."

Decoy

In the short time before my units and the humans could empty all their material load, Bruce was back on the radio.

"It's worse than I thought," he said. "The bots are closing in much faster than anticipated."

"How soon will they discover the cave entrance?" I asked.

"Sooner than you can get here."

Terry interjected with, "Execute Operation Cave-In."

I'd heard about this in one of my talks with Terry and Peggy. As a last resort, the humans had placed explosives to collapse the entire main cavern entrance to keep the bots from entering.

"But they will have overrun our two alternative exits as well. How are we going to get out?"

Terry paused. I could see the pain of indecision on his face. He didn't have a plan, but I had a possible solution, so I replied, "We are prepared for this. Muster your people near the tertiary exit. We will be there in twelve hours to get you out."

"Holy Mother of God, but you better be right," Bruce growled and cut off the carrier.

"What do you have in mind?" Terry asked with more than a little trepidation.

"A diversion to draw off the bots."

"With that many bots, it's going to need to be one hell of a diversion … with how many people or units lost?"

"No sentients will be sacrificed," I replied with a good deal of vigor.

# # #

Split-screened, I showed my audience chamber the progress from Susan's vantage point, high overhead. On one side, the sixty-three of my drones, which were not going to rescue the last of the humans, raced in nested five-piece chevron formations. On the other side of the image, the convoy made its way back to the human settlement at its best maintainable speed. Despite the previous thirteen trips, there was nothing regular about this one.

Just as in the past, all of my units, save Miss Wake, accompanied the eighteen non-intelligent trucks that I controlled. The difference was that the enemy Alphas swarmed all over the area my team needed to rescue the trapped rearguard from. What's more, they needed to load them without a single one being seen.

It was up to me to make this happen. The sixty-three were pressing forward at top speed. I adjusted down just 2 percent to make the timing work with the convoy timing.

I asked the audience, who were sitting nervously, watching my screen. "What is a league?" I asked to try to cut the anxiety. "I know it is a measure of distance, but how large?"

"Fuck if I know," Terry offered with the tag of human profanity.

Several of the other humans shrugged.

"Three miles," Peggy said. "Why?"

"'Half a league, half a league, half a league onward,'" I quoted.

" 'Charge of the Light Brigade' by Alfred, Lord Tennyson," Peggy said. "I studied it as a girl. Hopefully, we won't have the same result."

"My remotes are riding into that valley of death. 'Theirs not to reason why, Theirs but to do and die. Into the valley of Death Rode the six hundred.' I may have only sixty-three, but they will deactivate with honor." Those two to seven remotes had no IFF invisibility. They were meant to be seen.

For most of the evening, I'd circled around to flank the Alpha bots, not because I hoped to destroy them, but rather to get their attention … all of it. The timing was everything. My drones couldn't hope to last too long against the hundreds of bots, but they weren't meant to.

Despite their new position, the Alphas didn't engage with the convoy. The rescue convoy moved right up to the coordinates given for the tertiary exit of the human settlement, an abandoned playground. A random thought flittered through my processor, wondering what each piece of equipment was for. I pushed it into a holding queue to investigate at a later time.

`We are in position,` Jackson said needlessly. I could see their position through Susan's optics.

I turned my remotes in toward the mass of bots. "Forward, the Light Brigade. Charge for the guns!" I said aloud. `Engaging,` I announced over the WAN. My attacking extensions, each bearing one of the captured lasers, fired at extreme range, not to kill but to announce their presence. I snapped on some bright lights we'd modified onto a couple of the remotes. More attention. We intended to use the Alpha factory's crude tactics against her.

`Bots are moving at their top speed in your direction, Cin,` Susan said.

`Affirmative,` I managed to reply with a tiny remaining portion of my processor power.

Laser fire began flashing across my paths. I'd become each and all of the drones at the same time. My processes were clogged with controlling each of the tools. Yet I chanted both on the net and aloud. " 'Cannon to the right of them, Cannon to the left of them, Cannon in front of them Volleyed and thundered.' "

I wanted the Alphas to continue to close, so I spent my extra speed zigging and zagging across the field. Because the lasers were light-speed weapons, my erratic maneuvering didn't help at all with initial targeting, but it also didn't allow the bots to lay on long enough to do much damage.

"Stormed at with shot and shell, Boldly they rode and well, Into the jaws of Death, Into the mouth of hell Rode the six hundred."

I turned away … each of me. I need them to continue to chase. There was a searing pain as one disconnected. Then another. It felt like being stabbed with an icepick. The optics went out on another. I continued to fire, almost at random, behind me. I had to remain a threat.

`Area clear. Loading has commenced,` Jackson said.

Don't dawdle, I thought as my remote senses kept snapping off like firecrackers.

Programming random movements for each of the drones usurped all my processing time. So much so that I lost track of my internal clock. Then there were only fifty. Forty. Fewer and fewer as I felt the agonizing heat tearing the guts out of each one of me. I didn't know how much more I could take. Firing back, I concentrated on making the remaining thirty-seven units the most wily targets possible. I wanted to scream as five more of me simultaneously winked out of existence.

I couldn't tell within a hundred how many Alphas were following me. I focused my remaining four spotlights on them to overload their sight or compromise their aim. With as many coherent beams in the air, I couldn't tell if it helped in any appreciable amount. Twenty-two. `Hurry,` I choked out.

`We need 113 seconds,` Jackson announced.

Just short of two minutes. Eighteen. My processors still gave me one chance of being successful. I wheeled 180 degrees, and with my multiple views of the battlefield, I saw the hundreds of bots arrayed before me. Out of the speakers of the CDs, I shouted, "CHARGE!"

I tied all my lasers into a single coordinated fire. Just striking a bot was enough. A hole just appeared where I struck. "Die!" I shouted, time after time. My change in direction confused the stupid Alphas. Each one's programming had to be changed at the long end of a net concentrator. My good luck couldn't hold, especially when I intermingled with them. I killed more and more. Their return fire eventually started to take its toll. Fifteen. Twelve. Five.

A blessed message came over the network. `We are away with all cargo.`

I withdrew any part of me from the drones, leaving them on automatic programs. I underclocked some NOPs through my processors to mitigate the stress I'd placed on myself. Instead, I watched as the five remaining remotes were enveloped and destroyed at close range. Susan's video gave me a clearer view of the battlefield. So many deactivated Alphas and my drones littered the battlefield.

" 'They that had fought so well Came through the jaws of Death,' " I quoted, both audibly and over the net.

`Executing Operation: Long Way Around,` Jackson announced.

All my units had been instructed to make a circuitous way back to our base. The last thing we needed was to rescue the humans, only to have their activation at risk again because we'd been tracked back to my dome.

I watched our convoy easing away from the carnage.

" 'Back from the mouth of hell, All that was left of them, left of the sixty-three.' "

Chairman

The emotional outpouring when the remaining humans arrived could probably have been measured on the Richter scale. There were kudos for everyone. Most of it was lavished on my toys. Most didn't even notice me. I withdrew into a mental shell and shut down all but a single processor to handle interrupts.

Spontaneous celebrations went on for days. My toys joined in with the dancing. I saw all of this in retrospect, as I was as close to shutdown as a factory could possibly be. The pressures I'd been under had taken their toll on my well-being. All units, factories included, required preventive maintenance. I needed mine.

After 1.34 days, I slowly eased my processors back into action by feeding NOPs through them. I noted that Peggy and Terry had made several low-priority attempts to engage me in conversation. My network noted one moderate request for attention from Nelson, James, and Jackson.

`I'm back to full activation`, I reported across three SANs to those units. `What did you need?`

Across the WAN, Jackson replied, `Boss lady, we may have a problem.`

`Did the Alphas find us?`

`No, Cin`, he said. `That would have been a disaster, not a possible problem.`

Using time-sharing, I addressed Peggy, who was still lying in my audience chamber. "Good afternoon, Peggy human. What can I do for you?"

"Oh, good. We'd worried that you might have been injured. Terry and the others want to have a meeting. I think they might have already started."

"I'm going now, Peggy human."

`Is this about the meeting Terry called?` I asked my units.

`Yes, Cin`, Jackson said.

I tuned into Nelson's senses. They were in one of the larger tipis. Six humans: Terry, Bruce, and four I didn't yet have names for; Nelson, James, and Jackson were in attendance. I broke into the middle of what Terry was saying. "… even though Miss Dulcinea is not responding right now, I think it is time for us to start making plans to close and destroy the Alpha factory."

"Actually, I am here, Terry human," I offered through the octopus's speakers.

"Excellent timing, Miss Dulcinea. I was just going to start our planning to eliminate the other factory."

"I think that is premature."

"Why is that? asked one woman, whom I hadn't been introduced to yet.

"Well, there are many reasons. I'll start with my initial simulations, which show that we have less than a 2 percent chance of success."

"Only 2 percent?" Bruce asked. "I thought you said we had over one chance in three of surviving."

Nelson reclaimed his speaker. "In my history as a teacher, I would habitually leave such evident discrepancies as an exercise for the student."

Bruce stumbled on Nelson's pretentiousness. "We aren't attacking the factory?"

I took James's speaker. "That wouldn't be my first choice."

Terry said, "Well, I know we still have much to do here before we can engage in—"

"Terry human, I don't show a significant chance of success in this generation."

"Generation?" Terry fired back. "If you have a cobra in your house, you don't just leave it to kill your children."

I wasn't angry. I was just trying to make my point. "There is also an aphorism that the willow might bend to the wind until it is many willows that can break the wind. We can toss around famous quotes and allegories without getting to the basic data point that we have no chance to defeat the factory with our current populations."

"I know it will cost many lives, but it can be done," Terry insisted.

"How do you suggest accomplishing this, Terry human? Against a logical machine with the resources of the entire planet within its grasp. I'm willing to listen."

"We use the invisibility codes you have to sneak in close and place that pinch you have. We wipe it out with an electromagnetic pulse. No more factory. No more orders to the bots."

Jackson took that time to interject. "And you know where it is?"

"No. We'll have to scout," offered a different human.

"You mean we will have to scout, Bill?" Jackson retorted.

"Aren't you willing to pull your weight?" Bill snaps back

"You can't be implying that absenting your reproductive organs from the fire didn't qualify as pulling our weight," Nelson interjected, throwing more fuel on the fire.

One of the unidentified humans barked, "You over-tinkered—"

"Gentlebeings," I said. This conversation was becoming too heated.

"Please remember that we are on the same side with the same goal. We want to survive." The room settled, but I sensed that the attendees retained some ill feelings—humans vs. toys. "Terry human, I would like to point out that the only reason the invisibility works on my units is that we are nowhere near the Alpha factory's core. It can't possibly do more than a cursory query to its bots this far out. But if we got closer, she could. We'd be discovered quicker than one of your blinks."

"Then we could drop it like a bomb from Susan," Terry replied.

"As someone who designed her body, I can assure you that Susan couldn't carry that payload. Also, even if you got it there, I'm not certain it would affect the factory. It might knock out any units nearby, but not enough for us to infiltrate before she pulls active units from farther out. And before you suggest it, nor could our Susan carry an explosive device strong enough to breach its armor."

"Then we design and build a bigger, more capable airplane," Bill said, puffing out his chest, as he'd scored on me.

I wanted to ally with these beings, why? I berated myself for my negative thoughts. But at the same time, I was beginning to realize that humans didn't have the qualities we imbued in our gods.

Using James's optics, I scanned the assembly. From the facial expressions and body language I'd learned over my short acquaintance with humans, I presumed that five of the six humans wanted nothing more than to try to have a quick resolution to the other factory.

"How much explosives did we recover, Jackson?" I asked.

"Eighty kilograms, plus or minus."

"Any toy I send over there will be exposed and destroyed. Any human sent to the factory will be spotted and immediately killed. I won't put any sentient in those situations."

"I'd do it," Bill said.

"Do what?" Jackson asked. "Die for no reason?"

"I must disagree with my toy. We do have a law on the planet we came from that any sentient may self-deactivate as long as they don't damage others in the process. If you wish to die, Bill human, I can think of many other ways to do it. Your sacrifice won't accomplish the task you wish. You wouldn't get within 2 kilometers of the factory. In addition, you would waste our valuable resources."

"*Our* resources?" the female human exclaimed.

Even the Terry human couldn't leave this alone. "Yes, Hanna, *our* resources. If we start quibbling over who owns what, we will destroy this fragile alliance. And trust me, these toys have given us more than we can ever hope to repay."

"Thank you, Terry human," I said. "To continue my thought, I could design a drone that could carry the payload you wish; however, its signal would weaken as it gets closer to the Alpha. I could program it to become autonomous at that point, but I'm not certain it would successfully hit its target, much less destroy it."

This seemed to inject some sense into the human sumps. "Let's hold off on that too," Terry said.

"Well, if we can't attack the factory, how are we supposed to survive?" Bill asked.

"You won't accept my concept unless I explain it in pieces," I offered. "It will require you to answer some questions."

"Get on with it," Hanna snapped.

"When did the bots first start to attack you?"

"Months ago," Terry said

"I'm sorry for phrasing my question poorly. What actions were you taking?"

"We'd been mining some iron ore and smelting steel to improve our town," Terry said.

"And did you stop after you killed the first bot?"

"No," he replied.

"How many did you destroy?" I probed.

"Hundreds. The number of those fuckers just kept doubling until we had to evacuate the town into the caves where you found us. Our ammo was depleted. We'd used up most of our explosives."

"Exactly. I happen to have the orders of the original factories that landed on Rigel-3. We don't follow them now, but I know what they were or are. I can sum it up. Take control of the planet's surface. Mine all the metals. Sent them back to Sol-3. By your own actions, you are twice damned. You are enemy number one to that factory by mining what it claimed and then by fighting its dominance over the planet."

"OK, so we have a wanted poster out for us. How does that help us?" Terry asked, shooting stern looks at his other humans, who looked ready to riot.

"Well, you also had a well-defined locus," I explained. "We have at least removed you from that location. That gives us a fighting … or should I say non-fighting chance. I can provide each of you humans with one of my invisibility chips. If we don't mine metals or fight the bots, we ought to be able to live quietly and comfortably."

"Lay down? You fucking Quisling!" Hanna burst out.

"You propose that we live under those damned bots? Maybe we trusted you too quickly," one of the unnamed humans said.

"Hold on," I said. "I didn't say anything about surrendering to the Alphas. I only said that we don't challenge them. We let them do pretty much whatever they want while we do the same."

"How can we do that?" Terry asked. "They will murder us."

"Not with the precautions I'll outline."

Hanna seemed to be calming down a bit. "But how is this any less than giving up?"

"Look, do you have apex predators on Sol-3?" I asked.

"Sure. Lions, bears, killer whales ..." Terry said. From his smile, I surmised that he could see where I was going with this.

"Do you interfere with them? Do you challenge them for their kill?" I said, directing the question to Hanna, specifically.

"No way. They'd shred me," she said.

"Then why not treat the bots the same way?"

Hanna's face showed her thoughtfulness. "But if we can't mine, how are we going to rebuild?"

"We go low-tech."

Bowyer

It took many additional arguments to convince everyone that I was serious. The excuses seemed to be endless.

"Wait, no lasers? No guns?"

"How are we supposed to defend ourselves?"

"How are we supposed to feed ourselves?"

Oddly, the most intransigent were my own toys. "No mining?" Nelson asked.

"How do we make more of us if we can't use metals or other mining?" Jackson argued. "We can't make bones out of wood."

"Gentlebeings, no plan is perfect. We will take one problem at a time," I assured them. "For defense, we will use the few remaining lasers we have only if absolutely necessary, as their use will draw unwanted attention to us. As we won't be fighting the bots any longer, the only thing we have to worry about are the predators native to this world. For most of those, bows, arrows, pikes, and spears are sufficient. Swords are too metal intense."

"Bows? Spears? What good will that do if we have to fight the bots?" Bill asked with his usual tone that said I was always wrong.

"Bill human, if we are forced to fight the bots, we might as well just use our tools to dig our own graves. You saw what the Alphas did to your own kind. Don't think that we would have any better chance together."

"Maybe we should just have died," Bill muttered.

"You are welcome to go out and fight them on your own if your deactivation is what you seek," I added with my hydraulic pressure finally peaking with anger. Had the fury that flashed in his eyes been lasers, they would have bored through my wall and melted my sump. "Be assured, Bill human, that I do not wish this. I want us all to prosper. To do this, we need to become innocuous to the Alphas."

"She is right," Jackson said. "Look at the elk, the deer, and all the other fauna. The bots don't attack them."

"We aren't sheep," Terry said, trying to bolster Bill's position.

"True. We aren't," I said. "But we need to be as harmless as a sheep to the bots. And we need to do something about your human shape. By now, I'm certain that the Alpha factory has your humanoid shape programmed into each of her bots to be automatically deactivated."

"Whoa!" Terry exclaimed. "We can't change our shape by having things riveted onto us or replaced by something else."

"Based on the repairs to the Peggy human, I expected nothing less. It's an inconvenience, nothing more. When the bots are around, you need to be on your hands and knees like a deer or elk."

"Seriously? You think that will fool them?" Hanna asked.

"Actually, yes, Hanna human. Pattern recognition in the bots of the original infuse factories was primitive."

"Assuming we agree to all this, how long do we have to keep it up?" she asked.

"There are several scenarios. I'll put approximate percentages on each. The most likely scenario is that within the next century, the Alpha factory will have a critical failure."

"A century?" the Peggy human asked plaintively.

"Yes. It has been over 8,000 years. It has already exceeded its nominal lifespan by several thousand years. Based on the data we have from multiple original factories on our world, the mean failure for this factory would be 50 years, with a standard deviation of 21.5 years. This leaves a lifespan of greater than 100 years at approximately 1 percent."

"But 100 years?" Peggy asked again. "We will all be dead by then."

"True. Likely all humans will be deactivated by then, but not your offspring," I announced with some pride. The humans would go on. Toys would go on. "The probability of this occurrence is 73 percent."

"But for our whole lives?"

"By law of averages, it will be less," Nelson said.

I added, "I have to emphasize that you won't be on all fours except for those few times the bots are nearby."

"Still, it grates to bend a knee," the Bill human said.

"Is it better to deactivate ... and all the others of your kind?" Jackson riposted.

"Well, no, but—"

"Gentlebeings," I said, "if you wish to argue these points, be my guest, but do it on your own clock cycles. Now, if you will let me continue outlining the probabilities?" There were no objections. "Within the next 100 years, there is a 51 percent chance that the factory will detect our ruse and come out to track and kill us all."

This prompted many dark faces near me.

"Wait," Terry said. "Seventy-three and fifty-one makes 124 percent."

"I didn't say the two situations were mutually exclusive. Both or neither could take place. I don't place its probability of discovering us as a bell curve, but something slowly growing over time, like a straight-line curve ... one directly related to our mutual population. If that occurs, we will have to take alternative measures."

"Anything else, Dulcinea?" Terry asked.

"Yes, three other options. We could reach a population size large enough to destroy the factory in outright combat. Using the discrete growth model and considering your initial population of 147 breeding pairs, one birth on average every two ye—"

"We aren't cattle to be bred," the Bill human interjected.

"If you want someone else to figure your numbers, I'll be glad to bow out," I replied. "If not, let me finish, please."

"Sorry," he offered with very little real apology in his tone.

I continued. "With 147 breeding pairs with a birth every two years on average, it would make a population of over 25,000 humans in twenty years. When you extrapolate that out, you get something on the order of one quadrillion in a century. This is obviously a ridiculous number, as the food resources would be gone much before that."

"Good grief!" most of my audience gasped.

"There is obviously a range of curves for the number of humans based on birth rates, death rates, infant mortality, number of births per female, and more. I'm just giving a simple calculation. It could be more, and it could be less."

"What about your toys?" Terry asked.

"Ours is much easier to define. Each toy can be parent to one youngling. Experiments in multiple children failed on my world. We have examples of us doubling more often, but those new toys suffered problems in their adulthood. Each of these children's toys takes ten years to mature, when it can parent further younglings. As a result, in the two-decade example I gave above, we could double only twice, or only thirty-two units. This is, of course, a tiny number, relatively speaking. I estimate that we could create that number by scavenging, but that would be the limit. Once mining can be restarted, those numbers could increase dramatically. So it is possible to create many more humans than toys. With only humans and a handful of toys alone, we could swarm the factory with sheer numbers within a century."

"And the other two options?" Terry asked.

"First, humans and toys do not form a cohesive grouping. In that case, we go our separate ways, and both are overwhelmed individually. And the final would be that humans and toys choose to be belligerent to one another. I don't think I need to point out the obvious outcome of that."

There was stunned silence.

Terry broke the silence by saying in a falsely upbeat way, "Bows and arrows it is."

Bruce's and Hanna's faces didn't indicate agreement.

Validator

Comfortable weeks passed with no stress on my processor or voltage spikes on my bus. I spent them teaching the intricacies of bow and arrow construction. Humans gathered local fruits and edible vegetation that grew wild, and they planted a garden of Earth vegetation. With my toys' help, our allies also kept my fire fueled to supply the generator. Both humans and units enjoyed the abundance of sustenance. Humans even spent a great deal of effort preparing their food in a variety of ways.

"Peggy human, why do your people mix different foodstuffs and cook them in various ways?" I asked.

Peggy hobbled on a crutch from looking out over the mild rainfall over the forest to one of the benches that had become a permanent fixture in my audience chamber. "Taste."

"I'm sorry, what is taste?"

Peggy gave a little giggle. "Ever heard of the aphorism of explaining a rainbow to a blind person?"

"Yes."

"Telling you what taste is likely is very similar, Cin. The various foods, in different ratios, cooked in dissimilar ways, can provide a more pleasant sensation on our taste buds. It would be like the difference between a view of pure red in vision or a combination of that rainbow. One is vastly superior."

"Understood. Thank you."

There was a companionable pause before the Peggy human said, "Cin?"

"Yes, Peggy human?"

"There is some unease among the humans. I've heard rumblings of dissatisfaction among a small segment of my people."

"I have as well. I believe you are trying to spare their views of you by not naming them?"

"Umm … yes."

"Fear not. I know that the Bill human and the Hanna human are both trying to stir up the more militant of your people to attack the factory. I also know that due to the peace we currently have, they aren't having much luck."

"Oh, good. I just thought you should know."

"Thank you for your information, Peggy human."

"I'm not a traitor or anything," she said. "I just think what we are doing is the best way to save ourselves."

"Your statement implies a divide between our two peoples."

"Aren't there?" she asked. "We have different … everything."

Just then, a human child, maybe eight years old, and one of the youngling toys, a gopher who hadn't chosen its name yet, raced by. They seemed to be playing some sort of tagging game. They ran past. The human, much faster than my unit, dodged and weaved. The unit stumbled onward after the human child.

"Are we really that different?" I asked. "Look at them playing together. Happy."

"Maybe," she said with a tone that spoke of deep and troubled thoughts.

"Do you see us fighting one another, Peggy human?"

"Humans aren't good with differences, Cin."

"Despite our mutual cooperation?"

"Yes."

I mulled it over for 3,000 or 4,000 clock cycles. "I'm not certain I see it the same way. But even if you are right, I suggest that we fight one war at a time."

She nodded. "I think that is a good—"

My speakers blasted out what Ginger, Susan's youngling airplane, said on the network: "EMERGENCY! Alpha bot approaching base."

Using Ginger's optics, I plotted the Alpha's approach, only to see it about to intersect with the two youngsters playing some 150 meters away.

I blasted onto the WAN and echoed on my speakers at maximum volume. "EVERYONE DOWN!" I cursed my memory, as it took 160 milliseconds to remember the name of the human youngling. "STEPHAN! GET DOWN ON ALL FOURS!"

Through Ginger's eyes, I witnessed the child look around to see who called his name. He didn't do as ordered, despite the instructions all the younglings had been given on the proper procedures.

The green rag doll, Samantha, raced forward and tackled both the human youngling and the gopher. She slid her body over the top of both of the littles. I switched my perception to Sam's.

"Stay down and don't move," she said.

"Miss Saman—"

"Shh," she hissed at the human.

Her optics rolled up enough to see a single Alpha bot striding up toward her, no more than 60 meters away. She had no weapons, not even one of the new spears. If it attacked, she had no hope of surviving. I could just imagine what that would mean to the younglings.

Humans, please let it pass them by, I prayed, realizing my own hypocrisy in who I had sent the plea to.

The native Alpha reached Susan. Her voltage jumped up and hovered so high that it threatened to burn out a fuse.

The bot used its manipulative member to prod Susan. Her soft outer skin squeezed just as any good rag doll's would. Wisely, she remained still.

I sensed some traffic on the Alpha network. It was a pixelated picture of Susan's limp body. I could just make out the gopher from the waist down. Fortunately, I couldn't see any of the human child at all. My own overvoltage dropped by half. The response from the Alpha factory indicated that the bot was to return to his sweep. Swiveling its upper body through 180 degrees, it ambled back the way it came.

We waited another ten minutes as the mechanical harbinger of death waddled away. Susan climbed off her only bruised charges.

Peggy let out a huge held breath in a woosh.

"Are you so sure we would tear each other apart?" I asked with the example of cooperation and protection before us.

# # #

With our recent near miss with Stephan and the youngling gopher, our council met to discuss what happened.

"One of the basic tenets of my plan was that the Alphas would ignore humans not near the locus of their town. This has yet to be tested," I said.

"I think the earlier we know if the very foundation of it works or not is critical," Terry added.

"Hear, hear," said the Bill human.

"I have to agree," I said. "I miscalculated in putting it off even this long."

"What? Our illustrious factory is fallible? Gracious, what will we do?" Bill mocked. That there was no love lost between the Bill human and me would be an understatement.

I didn't rise to his bait. Instead, Terry spoke up. "Damn it, Bill. Can that shit."

"Are you so suckered by this factory that I can't express a dissenting opinion?" he replied.

Terry continued. "Dissenting, yes. Offensive, no."

"Who decides which is which?" the Bill human asked with a barb in the question.

"Jesus H. Christ, Bill. No one twisted your arm to be on this council. If you want off, I will find someone else who wants to be here."

Bill speared the leader with a cold stare before he said, "Oh, no you don't. There has to be someone here to be a check on this disaster of an alliance."

"We all know how you feel, Bill. Hanna isn't far behind you in her feelings, but she keeps a civil tongue. Keep yours in your mouth, or I'll have it cut out!" Terry wasn't 100 percent on my side, but he definitely had a strong view of propriety.

A test of wills formed between the two humans as they stared one another down.

"Fine," the Bill human finally said. I calculated that he was still there only because he couldn't figure out a way to kill the factory by himself. "So, how do we test it?"

Peggy offered what she and I had discussed many times. "Find a lone bot and see its response to a human in different configurations. This is not without danger for the human test subject. And before anyone beats me to it, I volunteer." The last had not even been mentioned in our previous conversations.

Terry looked on aghast. Bill snorted.

"Your deficiency in mobility hampers your ability to evade even the most basic of attacks," Nelson said. "The loss of your sentience would be regretted."

"Nelson is right," Terry added. "Peggy, you'd be a pig to the slaughter. No insult intended. I'm going to ask for a volunteer from all our people."

To my and most everyone else's surprise, the Bill human spoke up. "The heck with that. I'll volunteer."

"That seems noble of you," Terry said, only just missing making it a poke at the obstinate human.

"Well, if I have to give my life to wake up this group of pacific sheep, then I will."

"We will at least give you a chance, Bill human," Jackson said. "All of us toys will be by your side to protect you in case everything goes … as you humans say … into the shitter."

"Well, that's something," Bruce said.

# # #

`I've got a loner at coordinates Tango, Victor, Three,` Susan announced over the WAN.

`Is it moving?` I asked to make sure it was worth our time. The last one spotted had been an old, rusted bot with zero battery life. I mean, we'd scavenged it, so the trip wasn't totally wasted, but it hadn't been useful toward our testing goal.

`Affirmative.`

"Well, that's five hours from here. Bill human, do you have your pack and weapons ready?"

"I do."

He had his bow and a quiver of arrows strung over his shoulder, and there was a spear in his hand. I mentally checked off a small pack with emergency medical supplies that Miss Wake had put together, three days of dried rations, and a canteen made from the hollowed-out husk of a burned zedanana. I had to assume he had his other equipment, like a human radio link and a magnetized needle to float in a cup of water for finding the direction.

I did have a reservation about this mission, a serious one. I opened a SAN to Jackson to keep my suspicions to just him in case I was proven wrong. `Jackson, I want you to keep a close eye on our volunteer.`

`We intend to do so,` he assured me.

`Not that. Well, yes, that. But for something that has been creeping around my processors for some time. We know he feels strongly that our method of pacifism is the wrong way to proceed. What if he is willing to sacrifice his life to prove it … to initiate a conflict?`

`Boss lady, that is a low and evil thought. Alright, I've added it to my scanning routine.`

`Thank you, Jackson.`

# # #

I'd repurposed six smaller displays from the equipment brought over from the humans to make something large enough to show to the entire population of our base. It had required writing some software to send data to the screens as if they were one large device.

The image showed a wind-up plane's optic view of six adult toys and one single human traipsing across a grassy plain. All of them were armed, but only with bows and spears.

Susan announced, `Jackson, at your current speed, three more minutes until you will be directly along the bot's path.`

`How long do we have to set up?` the Bill human asked over the link I created for him.

`Estimated time to the Alpha's detection range is eight minutes`, Sue announced.

There was a sense of tense anticipation in the gathered crowd, with humans holding hands and hugging one another. Fear registered on their faces. I didn't doubt the reason why. My predictions of a conflict with the Alphas had been shared around the camp. In a perverse sense that I didn't understand, the predictions grew out of proportion to the original data. I meant yes, our very existence rode on this, but the added atrocities were not true to the outcomes, nor were the percentages accurate. Humans disseminated information in odd ways.

`I'll start lying flat to the ground`, the Bill human announced. `If that succeeds, I'll move onto all fours. And if still not attacked, I'll activate the invisibility device and stand.`

And they, humans, were redundant. Our plan outlined exactly these procedures. The plan had been shared with everyone.

I asked, `Overwatch?`

Susan replied, `In position. Target has altered course to intercept. One minute out.`

`Human tester?`

`Acknowledge one minute. I'm in place and ready`, the Bill human said.

I detected a faint note of unease in his voice. `Protection team?` I asked.

`Native IFF on. Visibly hidden. Ready for extraction as required.`

The team had chosen the testing site well. The Bill human lay on top of a small knoll-like plateau about a meter higher than the surroundings. The toys crouched down on either side of it, mere meters from their charge, ready to come to Bill's aid as necessary.

Before thirty clock cycles had gone by, James bolted out of his position. We might have been as fast as humans, but we could move. The teddy slammed one foot down on the Bill human's hand. The human cried out in pain. We had significant mass.

"What are you doing?" he yelled.

I switched my view to the senses supplied by James. The damage to the human's wrist was clearly visible. I wasn't sure even Miss Wake could repair the joint. The impact on our watchers was nothing short of electric. Some stood up in anger. Others looked on in surprise. Any that were next to a toy, adult, or youngling edged away.

"We're not stupid, human," James said in a measured but angry tone. "Just because we don't have any doesn't mean we don't know what a firearm is." James's vision turned to find the Bill human's hand touching a very real pistol. A revolver.

"Eaaaaa!" the human cried out in agony. "I only have it for protection."

"That's why it was aimed in the direction of the Alpha and your finger was tightening on the trigger." James continued over the net. `I request aborting the test.`

Locally, the community relaxed at least halfway now that the reason for a toy to attack a human had become clear.

I looked at Terry, who looked into one of my cameras and shook his head with sadness in his eyes.

`Negative. Remove the firearm. If the Bill human does anything else but follow the test parameters, terminate him.`

This statement didn't help the remaining fears among our people. But from quick analysis, I could see that well over half understood the need to kill the Bill human if required.

James ground his paw down onto the human's injury. This drove a scream from the victim's throat. "Did you hear that, Bill human? You have to perform."

"I can't. It hurts too much."

"You heard what will happen if you don't comply. It is your choice, human." James picked up the pistol and kicked his spear away for good measure before ducking down behind the berm again.

`Alpha unit continues to close. Close contact in ten seconds,` Susan injected into the tense milieu.

With both Susan's optics and James's split-screened, the crowd watched. The tenseness had ratcheted up, with all the humans holding their collective breaths.

We all watched as the boxy robot waddled up toward our sacrificial lamb. It stopped 4 meters away. It had deployed neither its laser nor its manipulative arm. It sat there for seventy-one seconds, the longest moments of any of our lives. It began to waddle forward in a path that would bypass the Bill human.

`GET UP!` yelled James over the net.

The grimacing person got up on his undamaged three limbs, looking like a large version of the four toddlers in our population. The bot stopped and turned its head to focus on the Bill human's form. This time, it waited forty-six seconds before turning back to its course.

Without prodding this time, the Bill human stood, bow in one hand and the damaged limb cradled against his middle. His crimson eyes leaked moisture down his face.

The bot's reaction wasn't in minutes, but milliseconds. Still, I noted its weapon sliding into position as if it were in slow motion.

`DOWN!` I snapped over the network. The laser came out, powering as it moved.

With his faster-than-human reflexes, the Bill human dove to the ground, rolling onto his side to protect his wrist. My units leaped up and threw themselves over Bill's body like people dumping discards onto a junk pile. Muffled screams of pain came from the heap.

The bot paused. The mass of my toys blocked its view of the target human. It circumnavigated the heap of toyanity in its shuffling gait. Once complete, it put away its weapon and returned to its normal course.

`Bring the Bill human back once the Alpha has exited its sensor range,` I ordered.

`Affirmative.`

There were mixed feelings among all our combined people. I could read some of the faces. Only 8 percent were aghast at the volunteer's treatment at the paws of our toys. Seventy-eight percent were happy that the Alphas could be so easily tricked. Another 16 percent could see that the bot attacking the standing human meant they weren't immune to being targeted. My concentration on our population failed to notice Terry slipping into my audience chamber.

"You should have let him be killed," he announced strongly but with more than a little sadness.

"Letting a sentient perish doesn't forward our aims," I said, calculating that my reply would end the discussion. How little I understood humans.

"Yet you were willing to order his killing," Terry said as he used his fingers to comb out some lunch debris from his long beard.

"Conditionally, Terry human. I didn't want to do it. But if his demise would save the rest of us, it would have been a price worth paying."

Terry chewed on this thought for a few moments before responding. "Well, here is something for your simulations to figure out. What do we do with Bill now?"

Warden

Terry's question caught me somewhat off guard. "Why would we have to do anything with him other than heal his damaged limb?"

The other leader of our nonhomogeneous band sighed heavily. I'd learned that this was an act of frustration. "Do you think he is done?"

"Done what? He wasn't able to meddle with the outcome. In addition, his thesis was disproven."

"Dulcinea, you have much to learn about humans."

"That is the reason I agreed to share leadership with you, Terry. So why do you think he would continue his antisocial activities?"

"The easiest piece is that you and your toys hurt his pride … in public. He will be your enemy from this point forward."

"He has been belligerent to me since arriving here."

"Not belligerent. Enemy. He would destroy you just for the pleasure it would give him. And, as I am your ally, by the transitive property, I am his enemy as well."

"Do you believe he would actively target you and me?"

"Likely. But I'm more worried that he will continue with his effort to force us into a fight against the Alpha factory. I have no idea how to stop it either. We can't exile him."

"Absolutely not," I said with vehemence. "My kind have seen the danger exiling can cause."

"I don't think any physical punishment would deter him from any plans he might make."

"Physical punishment?"

"Flogging or caning."

"That's abhorrent."

"I don't disagree, Cin, but if you won't let us kill him, the only option is to imprison him in some way."

I thought back to when a certain golden bear had sealed me in a stone cairn as I ran many scenarios through my processors. Early results of my calculations weren't promising. "We have no facility for that."

"True. But I'm out of options."

"I suggest one other. It seems you are condemning the man before he acts. Yes, he made a horrific mistake today, but that doesn't mean he will tomorrow."

"Really?" he said with enough sarcasm to lubricate all my toys.

"It may be optimistic, but I morally believe we have to offer the Bill human the opportunity to be a contributing member of our people."

Terry kicked at a twig on the earth. "I'm not sure I agree, Cin, but I'm willing to bow to your moral superiority here if for no other reason than I have no better idea." Just before I opened my speaker, he snapped another line. "But I insist that this be his only chance. He endangered all our lives. If he does anything even close to this, he is to be executed."

"Logical."

# # #

"Bill human," I said to the man wearing an armor cast where Miss Wake had done some of her doctoring to ensure that the joint would have some function in the future. The grimace on his face announced that he still had some pain, even with some of the humans' magical drugs. "Bill human," I repeated. "We are willing to assume your actions were intended to be for the best, even if against our explicit instructions."

Bill looked at Terry, the only other person in my audience chamber. My coleader nodded with his lips pursed in frustration.

"Are you willing to accept that you are on your parole to follow our instructions?" I asked.

In a monotone, Bill said, "Yes."

"And to adhere to the plans for our mutual survival?" Terry added.

"Yes."

"Then the only corrective action will be to remove you from our communal council," I directed. "You can go now."

The penitent nodded in my direction before striding out of the chamber.

"What do you think?" I asked.

"He's like a child saving up more spit," Terry said through a sneer.

"Excuse me? I don't think my idioms interpretations cover that."

Terry plopped down onto the bench. "He agreed only enough to allow him to cause trouble later."

"While your idiom is colorful, I can't refute your belief. He will likely cause future trouble. But again, I can't condemn a man or a toy for what he might likely do."

"True. We could both be wrong, but we need to watch him."

"Agreed. I'll come up with a rotation for my toys to keep a discreet eye on him."

"We should also discuss another item concerning his breach," Terry said.

I knew what he had in mind and would have brought it up if he hadn't. But it was ticklish, as we'd already come down on one human.

If we kept going, the human population might think they were second-class citizens at best. "Go on."

"Bill didn't have access to the armory where that gun was stored. Who helped him?"

"I could give you a percentage probability on each of the persons who did have access."

"And we would come to the same conclusion, wouldn't we?"

"Hanna?" I ventured, as she was 52 percent more likely than the nearest other person in my calculations.

"Yes."

"We can't accuse her without any proof."

"I wasn't going to suggest it," Terry said. "However, perhaps we need to keep an eye on her as well."

"So much surveillance by our toys would likely lose its covert status."

"What if we mix it up with some of my people … I mean, our people."

"If any of the people, humans or toys, talked, it would compromise our goals," I observed.

"I'll pick only the most trustworthy people and tell them why."

"I'll do the same."

Terry paused and changed the subject. "In the meantime, how about we talk about planting some of those tall grasses to hide our encampment from outside eyes. If we can't be seen upright, that would be an exceptional starting point."

"Another thought along that route … What if we made costumes for the humans?" I asked. "Costumes … disguises. We could add limbs, give a big gaudy headdress, or fur all over?"

Terry raised one eyebrow. "I find the image amusing, but to what purpose?"

"I'd wager that our nemesis has humans categorized as bipedal, smooth-skinned, apelike creatures with certain parameters for height, width, and depth. Maybe they also see you using weapons in your hands. Now imagine if you had four arms. Or a giant bill like a duck. Or a big, furry tail?"

"You think that would work?"

"I'd wager a good portion of my ergs. Remember, while factories have evolved, we still have some of the same basic routines. So I think it would."

"Well, then we need to get a whole bunch of people sewing."

"If possible. I also see a hole in our defense. We are limited to two aerial spotters to alert us to when an Alpha might be in presence and allow us to go into submissive mode," I said. "With that in mind, I've created plans for some flying remotes. They would be small and light, and they could stay in the air for more than a day. I think three of them would be sufficient to give us coverage."

"Would you need to dip into our resource cache?"

"Maybe, but with some help, I think I can make everything out of wood for the body and control surfaces. I can make the electronics by cannibalizing some of my current ground-based drones."

"That would be even better."

Seamstress

Fortunately, there were many humans who understood how to create textile garments. The first costumes created were crude—deer skins with antlers that could be tied under the chin. But as time went on, the humans taught units. Together, they wove cloth out of many different plant fibers. They even experimented and found different colors apart from the simplistic green and brown that I'd found. I stole their methods, giving them all kudos for their discoveries.

As their efforts matured, the work product made humans into convincing toys. I was even caught off guard by a convincing copy of the teddy bear James worn by the Peggy human. I might have even fallen for the ruse had it not been for her stiff gait and the face that didn't match a teddy's.

Despite all their successes, there was one situation that caused my processors to spin in a never-ending loop. If I'd still had teeth, they would have been grinding. One of the clothworkers was the Bill human. Even after weeks, any contemplation of him sent voltage spikes of worry across my prodigious bus.

My surveillance group reported that he had been helpful but quiet. As he had been so bellicose in the past, the reports concerned me. A leopard didn't change its spots without dye. The spy network told me he also avoided other humans or toys. He ate alone. He sat alone, away from other recreation activities. His only interaction with the Hanna human had been in the inevitable nearness of 400 sentients in a small location.

I put the troublesome creature out of my thoughts, as the costumes had already been put to a successful test. We'd spotted a patrolling bot that came near enough to our compound to be concerning. All our sentients put our practiced deception into action. Almost all of us were either lying down or on our hands and knees. They say that every plan holds until you meet the face of the enemy. The downfall of our perfect plan was one young human female who thought that all this activity was fun and decided to walk around. We all shouted for her to get down, but she just traipsed around as if the world Stella wasn't a dangerous place. Fortunately, she loved her unicorn costume and wore it everywhere.

The bot waddled by, barely glancing our way. While its optics did fall onto the child, it didn't even slow down.

Apparently, loving concern for her safety ended up with the parents paddling the little girl's fundamentals. Her screeches could be heard all over camp, even though the force of the strikes couldn't do more than redden her skin. After their assault, the parents hugged and held her tight. I sometimes questioned the sentience of humans. I doubted I ever would fully understand them.

Our troop planted gardens with seeds from the human resources and plant cuttings from a discreet mission Jackson, James, Nelson, and Susan made to the allotments of the old human settlement. Our harvest was meager the first year, but we had overflowing larders for the humans the second year.

We'd improved our living situation as well. There was no more pit for excrement and garbage inside our compound. Instead, we put toilets over the small stream that carried everything out and away. I'd finally put effort into creating solar panels to power my toys instead of constantly burning deactivated tree parts (which had become more difficult to find).

We hunted. We gathered. We played. We endured. We survived.

A single Alpha's incursion on our camp occurred every eighty-four days plus or minus seven days. With our optics in the sky, we always had at least an hour's warning. Humans would climb into costumes or lie down on the earth as the Alpha passed. It broke up the works in progress, but only to a minor extent. Each intrusion caused some anxiety, but after a year, even that faded. After two years, the Alpha visits were considered a nuisance and nothing more.

Bungler

Each day, I found myself increasing our general survival odds. By the end of the second year, the persistence percentage of our combined peoples had reached 79.4 percent. Terry and I continued our loose leadership of the entire group. We were supported by a council of both toys and humans in equal numbers.

Those four chances in five went to my processors like a drug. We were going to make it. But that heady knowledge and time made everyone fallible, myself included. After twenty-six months and twenty-seven days, I'd become complacent. We all had.

Our integrated colony had grown. There were forty-three toys and 580 humans. I grant you that many of the humans were still very young. My toys were itching to have more offspring as well.

There were so many thoughts to process and projects that rolled around in my sump that I missed two that had been relegated to low priority until they were thrown up in my face.

Peggy walked into my audience chamber with only a trace of a limp from her injury of years ago. "Dulcinea, have you seen Bill?"

I ran all the visual data I had from my units and remote optics. "I don't detect him. Rerunning images from my temporary memories, I haven't seen him since the human evening meal three nights ago." My voltage immediately ran up. The Bill human was trouble personified, despite his good behavior of the last two years plus.

"That's what I've heard too. He didn't show up for work for the last two days. I'm worried, as is Terry."

My opposite half spent much of his time out hunting. Game had become a bit scarce and skittish nearer to Ameliaville.

"I don't show him leaving the compound," I told her.

"I've checked most everywhere, including the communal tipi where Bruce normally sleeps. There is nothing there—not even a blanket."

"Wait, what about Hanna. Where is she?"

"I haven't seen her for a while, either," Peggy said. She sent the question over the human communicators to Terry. "Nor has Terry. Cin, this doesn't look good."

"I don't disagree, Peggy." Because of the extraordinary circumstances, I performed a low-level diagnostic. "Blackout," I said. "I'm such an idiot. My pinch is missing."

"Pinch?"

"The device that will create an EMP as a last-gasp defense against the bots."

"Do you think …"

"Does a rag doll have hair?" I asked, feeling little of the flippancy of my reply.

"How did they get out? Wouldn't our sky patrol identify them immediately?"

I had started reviewing the recordings before she even asked her questions. "I don't see them, but what I do see is a teddy bear and a rabbit leaving. They never returned. No one would think twice about a hunting or gathering party going out in a pair. Of all the stupid … I should be ground up for scrap."

"Don't be so hard on yourself, Cin. You can't do everything."

"Have Jasper check the armory to see if any other weapons are missing."

Peggy had another communication over the human network. "He says that two lasers, a rifle, and a pistol are missing."

"We will have a meeting of the council right after the evening meal. Make sure Terry comes home for this."

"But shouldn't we go after them now?"

"They already have approximately a thirty-six-hour head start. A few more won't matter as much as not being hasty."

# # #

"Sentients, we have a new and greater danger to our community. If you hadn't heard already, the Bill human and the Hanna human have disappeared, taking weapons and the EMP pinch with them." The serious faces of the eleven attendees didn't show the slightest change. "I blame myself for failing—"

"Blame isn't valuable, Dulcinea," Terry said. "What matters is correcting the problem and ensuring that it never happens again."

There were dark murmurs of concurrence from those arrayed. I asked myself if, with my statement, I had just sealed execution orders on the two wayward humans.

"Then I will restrict my comments to those toward the goals you seem to agree are important," I said. "Two fit humans can nominally make 100 kilometers in any twenty-four-hour period. We can assume they've made a maximum of 200 kilometers in the time that has elapsed. However, wearing the bulky costumes and carrying the 70-kilogram weight will reduce that range to a maximum of 150 kilometers. I'd be surprised if they made it 100 kilometers."

"But they could be anywhere in a 100-kilometer range," Peggy said.

"From visual records from our sky patrol, I have approximated a course for the pair. It matches what I assume is their ultimate aim: to destroy the other factory. They won't get close enough to try, even if we let them proceed. The issue is that it will give the Alphas a straight line pointing directly at us. It will also show an aggressive posture by humans and toys threatening to take control of the planet. In short, we would become a threat that must be removed."

Peggy asked, "Even if we know where they are, how can we catch up with them?"

Several members nodded.

I said, "There is a way. It isn't without risk."

Terry said, "Don't keep us in suspense, Cin."

"I have two options. First, while humans are faster than toys, they can't keep up the pace for the entire day without rest and replenishment. Toys can last as long as their batteries hold out. We could take several of our larger toys and have them pull wagons with humans and spare batteries in them."

"Why the humans?" the Todd human asked. He normally listened before offering input.

"Well, as they have the EMP device, if we sent only toys, they could deactivate our posse with it."

The Todd human nodded. "True. I hadn't thought of that. And the EMP wouldn't affect the humans?"

"While my data is scarce on the topic, it is unlikely to impact them more than maybe a headache," Terry answered for me. "There were studies done on this back on Earth."

"With a following force of three toys and three humans, they should overtake the renegades within five days, plus or minus two, mostly dependent on how diligent the two are at keeping moving," I said. "What's unclear is what would happen when the two groups clashed. There is a 98 percent chance that the traitors would be killed or unable to complete their mission. But the losses to our team lay in a range of probabilities from all dead to all living and everywhere in between."

"No option is more likely than any other?"

"The curve is effectively flat from the lack of data on terrain, surprise, and more. The only highly likely item is that the toys will all perish."

"That doesn't sound like a good choice," Peggy whispered into the silence created by my less-than-stellar option.

There was a pause. Terry interrupted it. "You said you had two choices."

"Yes. The success rate is less at 63 percent individually, but when combined, there's an overall success probability of 95 percent. It will require the use of my flying drones and almost all the remaining explosives."

"You are going to make them into missiles!" the Brenda human exclaimed.

"Very perceptive. But something I think you may have missed is that we will lose a significant portion of our overhead coverage in scanning for Alphas."

"Can we make more of your flying eyes?" the Brenda human asked.

I answered, "Not with the capabilities of my current ones. We would lose 60 percent coverage until I can create more flying toys and get them raised."

Terry summed up the situation. "We can either condemn three toys and likely two humans to death, or we put our colony at slight risk."

"Four humans," I corrected.

"Four?" Peggy asked.

"We would be executing the two who have taken their rash actions. I want it clear that either of these two acts condemns them to deactivation."

Peggy said, "I've never liked Bill much, but condemning them? I ... I ..."

"It's necessary, Peggy," Terry said. "This is a decision for all the council, not just Cin and me. Please vote. Black rock for death. White rock to find another solution. No rock for abstain."

Terry walked through the solemn group with one high-necked piece of pottery created by our people. Each sentient put their paw over the opening. Peggy actually put her hand up. Then, at the last moment, she changed her mind and put the other one up to drop what it held.

The human leader poured out the contents on a bare patch of earth for everyone to see. Eight black stones rolled out with one white one standing out in the middle.

"As the decision is overwhelming, Cin and I will not vote. Bill 2301 and Hanna 54 are sentenced to death."

"Which method shall we implement?" I asked.

"We don't need any further deactivations on our conscience," Jackson said. "I propose that we use the drones. We can supplement our aerial spotters with some on the ground to supplement the losses there."

"And the loss of the explosives?" Peggy asked.

"Well, if there is any good time to use them, this is it," Jackson riposted.

"Can we have a show of hands?" I asked. "All in favor of using drones as missiles."

Executioner

My three drones, covered in explosives, flew in formation around Susan. My processors and sump all processed the grief I held for my mission. My hydraulic pump wouldn't even turn over. I didn't want this task. I didn't want to remove sentience from this universe. But I knew in my soul that if these two people continued on with their mission, many more would die—a horrible dilemma for anyone.

Flying at our speed, it would take us only hours to catch up with them. I'd modified the drones with extra batteries, replaced the heavier optical gear with something more primitive and lighter, and removed the speed governors on their motive engines. They could now keep up with Susan's normal speed but just couldn't see quite as crisply. With Susan to point the direction, it was a worthy tradeoff.

`Tracks located`, she said. She found it within 30 meters of my prediction. Our targets were moving fast and not hiding their trail.

I wouldn't display this hunt to our entire population. They didn't need to see us kill to know they were safe. Instead, only the council was watching in my audience chamber. They did need to see. They ordered this and must live with all the consequences. James held Peggy's hand in his paw as they watched. I cataloged it because it seemed out of place.

The mission flew onward, following the disturbed prairie flora. For those waiting, it was both tense and boring. The anxiety did go up as we got closer to the locus where I predicted Susan would intersect with the thieves.

`Cin, I've lost the trail`, she announced.

`Remember your briefing`, I told her unnecessarily. I must have been nervous too. `We theorize that the pinch has a maximum range of 400 meters. Stay above 800 meters as you search.`

`Damned right, I will`, she offered with a little more vehemence than normal. `I'm no hero.`

The search went on for several hours, finding nothing as the sun drifted over the horizon. Neither her normal nor my drone optics were very good at night.

She announced, `Switching to thermal.`

A brilliant idea. A mere 100 yards from the end of the trail, she spotted the heat source of two humans lying flat to the ground. Susan switched back to visual mode. There didn't seem to be anything below but prairie grass. She zoomed in. We could just make out the outline of a camouflaged blanket that looked just like the poverty grasses it was over.

`Target acquired.`

Switching back to thermal mode, it was clear that these were humans. No other creature could have this silhouette. `I concur. First run commencing.`

This wasn't going to be as easy as I'd hoped. In the dark, I had to interpolate between Susan's infrared image and the drone's poor, light-dependent optics. Only one of the moons, three-quarters full, gave off any illumination. My missile raced downward. I didn't want this task. But it mattered too much.

I lost contact with the drone at the same time the thermal signature of its explosion bloomed, 10 meters from the nearest human. Suddenly, there was all sorts of activity below us. The camouflage netting flung up and away. The pair stood up, still in their bear and rabbit costumes. The bunny's white fur stood out especially well. They obviously were conversing, but it was like watching a movie without the sound.

`Miss,` I announced. `Preparing for a second run.`

The fugitives clustered around the pinch's cylindrical shape. Lights blossomed on the side of the device. `They are going to set off the pinch!` I warned.

As a precaution, Susan and my reserve drone increased altitude, putting more distance between them and the cosmic disaster for our kind.

The telltales on the pinch and the pitiful grass fires from my first miss gave me an excellent aiming point. The bunny pointed up toward my drone. The bear pushed a button on the device. I lost connection with my second drone. Looking through Susan's optics, I saw the pitiful little plane spin out of control and crash onto the ground … with no explosion. It hadn't been anywhere near the pair, in any case.

`Aw, what the grit,` Susan said. `I didn't want to be on this wet planet anyway.`

I couldn't understand what she meant until she wrested away control of my drone. As she was so much closer, I had no chance of overriding her.

`What are you doing, Susan?`

`We only have one more chance at this. I'm going to make sure it works. TALLY HO!`

The pair of them dived together as one.

`Susan, don't do this.`

She didn't respond.

`You don't–`

We watched the view from the plane and the drone. They seemed identical. The Hanna human stood adjacent to the Bill human. They pointed together. Their faces looked angry—the same faces that grew larger and larger until the well-furred face of the Bill human filled the screen. We lost the feed at that very moment.

The council's collective gasp echoed my own.

I sent an urgent net request to Ginger Grant, Susan's daughter, to fly immediately to a set of coordinates. The last known coordinates of the traitors … and one toy. It took six hours before we saw the remains of three sentients.

We hadn't won. Instead, we had saved our peoples at a high cost.

Everyone had lost.

Retiree

So much has happened in the last forty-three years. It's hard to catalog it all.

We collected Susan's body and buried it at the base of my dome. I inscribed a stainless steel plaque with John Gillespie Magee, Jr.'s poem "High Flight."

Oh! I have slipped the surly bonds of Earth
And danced the skies on laughter-silvered wings;
Sunward I've climbed, and joined the tumbling mirth
of sun-split clouds,—and done a hundred things
You have not dreamed of—wheeled and soared and swung
High in the sunlit silence. Hov'ring there,
I've chased the shouting wind along, and flung
My eager craft through footless halls of air ....

Up, up the long, delirious, burning blue
I've topped the wind-swept heights with easy grace
Where never lark, or even eagle flew—
And, while with silent lifting mind I've trod
The high untrespassed sanctity of space,
Put out my hand, and touched the face of God.

I read it every morning. It pains me still. But it does remind me of the joy Susan had being a plane.

Of the two traitors, there was only a scorched piece of earth remaining. Their bodies had been dismembered and eaten by scavengers. While sentient, they received no farewells. They deserved no tributes. They put the entirety of their own kind at risk and paid the ultimate price for it.

Shortly after the burial of our friend, Peggy and James asked Terry to marry them. I inquired of James, "Why? And why a human?"

"It's simple, Cin. She is important to me." He described a happiness that was much higher when she was with him than when she was away. Their joining was the first, but not the last, toy/human intermarriage. I think we have six now. They aren't common, but they aren't regarded as troublesome or repugnant either.

I was surprised when the newlyweds came and asked me to gift them a child. Apparently, Peggy couldn't have human children for some biological reason. They decided to raise toys. The first, a bear at their request, they named Don Quixote. They asked me to be its godmother. It took many sessions for them to make me understand my new role in that sentient's life.

Nelson formed a school where humans and youngling toys learned lessons side by side.

Nineteen years after the loss of Susan, the Alpha factory deactivated. We held a weeklong celebration.

As the years went by, toys and people learned to work together. Peggy's fear of differences never materialized. Our mixed colony eventually grew unwieldy. We formed a second, just as diverse as the first. Then years later, a third, and more years later, a fourth. For each association colony, I personally raised a factory I'd created to be part of their lives. These factories decided amongst themselves to honor the native factory. Their logic was inescapable. It had done what it had been programmed for. It had remained constant. Each of my new factories took up the latter Greek letters as their names—Beta, Gamma, and Delta.

Our loose form of survival leadership, one human and one factory leader, aided and supported by a council of both humans and toys elected from the populace, became each settlement's de facto government.

Terry deactivated from heart failure last year. His human leadership of our group transferred to Bruce 314. No one sentient is irreplaceable except in our thoughts and memories.

Shortly after his passing, parts of me started to fail. I had and still have to regularly rerun calculations multiple times due to checksum errors on my internal busses. I've lost three of my processor banks to electron migration, not to mention the damage I sustained on the trip across the heavens before landing at Ameliaville. The clean room where I created semiconductor crystals became contaminated. I made a conscious decision not to replace or repair any of it or myself.

I'd done it all. I'd been a president, a bum, an adventurer, a factory, and eventually a mother. I understood Amelia's desire to be a key part of this adventure after having survived thousands of years. I also understood Alexander's feelings at the Indus Valley, as there was no more territory to conquer.

My daughters privately applauded my decision to accept my own demise as it comes. We mutually agreed that the original Toy World premise of toys living effectively indefinitely probably would be their downfall, if it hadn't already happened. We didn't want to perpetuate it here.

Amelia, the factory whose body I inherited, had already been well over eight millennia old. I can feel every clock cycle of those 8,000-plus years. I mean, even my memories, or the memories of my predecessor Don Quixotes, seemed sluggish in moving through my sump.

I don't know what the future holds for all of my toy children and those I adopted along the way, but only they can shape it beyond my time.

I chose to do one more task for the sentients of Stella-4. It will be the capstone of a life, I think, well lived. I will narrate our adventures.

# # #

Notes from the First Chronicler:

Humans created life … and it was fuzzy.
Toys saved the humans … and all was good.
They will make the future … together.

How Emotions of Units Are Described

Acceptance: Interest + guilt

Anger/rage/hate: Hydraulic overpressure

Anticipation: Fur standing on end

Anxiety: Anticipation + fear

Anxiety: Voltage spikes

Aversion: Interest + sad

Contempt: Anger + irresponsibility

Courage: Fear + responsibility

Exasperation: Whistling

Fear/terror: Overvoltage

Guilt: Incorrectly measuring colder temperatures

Happiness: Undervoltage

Hope: Anticipation + sad

Interest/wonder: Images get clearer

Irresponsibility: Sump pumps slower

Perplexed: Voltage oscillations

Responsibility: Sump pumps faster

Righteousness: Incorrectly measuring hotter temperatures

Sad: Hydraulic under-pressure

Shame: Guilt + anxiety

Tickle: Rippling undervoltage + similar rippling colder temperature

Author's Note

Welcome (finally) to the completion of the Toy World saga. I know it has been a long time coming, and I apologize for its continued delay. I won't make excuses. The fault has been mine for continuously changing priorities. *Mea culpa.*

Everyone wants to know where I came up with the plots for my books, so here goes.

I'd always envisioned this ending to the series. I had to bring the toys back in touch with the people who created them (even if by accident). This brought the series full circle.

But the more I thought on the topic, the less I liked the concept of toyanity going back to Earth or, conversely, humans going to Rigel-3.

What we needed is called, in war terms, a meeting engagement. I especially didn't want them warring with one another. Both the toys and the humans needed to encounter one another on a separate world, with neither able to return to their home … at least for now.[1]

Not only did they need to meet on a different world, but they both had to be dealing with an external enemy. I will admit that the first thought that crossed my mind was some alien species. But this didn't seem to fit in with my views of the humans or the toys. It was then that a light bulb went on. I had a built-in enemy that could threaten them both … an Infuse factory. Voilà, I had what would happen on the planet. But how to get each of the parties there?

I set up, unintentionally, the reason for the toys to want to out-migrate with the elimination of the Procreation Limitation Law. The natural result of this would be overpopulation and depleted resources. Eventually, this scarcity would lead to war after banishing it so many years ago.

That's it. That's the wrap-up of this series.

I'm not sure what the next book I'm going to write will be. I have made promises to write more CorpGov books (and created the setup to do so). I also have some ideas for a new series based on the Native Americans around the time of European colonization.

I also have a mystery set in a rompy, stompy robot world that is partially written.

I could get an idea for something completely new.

At this moment, the mystery has the highest probability of success.

As I say goodbye to Toy World, and their new colony on Stella-4, I have to say this is both a painful parting and a joyful one. It's painful in that I will miss Don Quixote and having him in my mind, dreaming up new scenarios with him. The joyful part is that I have honestly grown beyond Toy World. It is time to leap into the future with a fresh view of what worlds there are.

As always, I hope you have enjoyed my work. I'd ask you, please, whether you hated or loved it, to leave a review on Amazon or Goodreads. Authors live and die by reviews—good, bad, indifferent, it makes no difference. If the quantity of them is not high enough, we sink. I'm not asking for anything but perfect honesty in your review, but they are so important to being able to continue to bring you what you love.

---

[1] OK, so there is a possibility of a sequel, but don't hold your breath.

Made in United States
Troutdale, OR
06/13/2026

49923186R00146